Jasper's Diamond

Frances Parker-Smith

First published 2021
by Rowanvale Books Ltd
The Gate
Keppoch Street
Roath
Cardiff
CF24 3JW
www.rowanvalebooks.com

A CIP catalogue record for this book is available from the British Library.

Paperback ISBN: 978-1-913662-36-3

Life has so many strands.

Never look back.

It's never too late to follow your dreams.

Contents

Prologue

The light aircraft bounced along the grassy runway, lurching to a halt next to the only completed hangar. A young Englishman wrenched the door of the aircraft open. He cast a wary eye around the field before slipping a well-worn satchel over his shoulder and jumping down. The woman stood precariously on the lip of the open door. He opened his arms and gave her a reassuring smile.

"Jump!" he quietly said.

He caught her and held her for a long moment. She had been sobbing ever since they had watched the German officer shoot her only child.

Her son had stood alone against the wall, silently waiting to be searched. A crowd had anxiously looked on, waiting and hoping.

The sound of the gunshot had pierced the silence. A loud gasp echoed from the crowd as they watched her son slide to the cobbled street. The bullet had hit him in his head. His only crime was being a Jew.

His mother had screamed; her husband had tried in vain to stifle her sobs. The young Englishman who was stood by them had put his arms around them and slowly guided them away from the crowd and the angry German officer.

"You can't stay here," he'd whispered. "Come with me."

"We can't. We have our home," Jacob Isaacs had answered, still comforting his distraught wife.

"If you go back there, you'll be tortured and shot or sent to a camp."

The young man's worried tone had done nothing to change the couple's minds. They had insisted on returning to their apartment one last time.

"There's more diamonds in the apartment," Jacob had said, hoping to tempt the Englishman.

"Many?" The Englishman's uninterested tone had masked his addiction to the glittering gems. But the Dutchman knew he couldn't resist them.

They'd quickened their pace, weaving through the back streets until they'd reached the Englishman's car, an open-top MG. His heart always missed a beat when he gazed upon the car. He didn't know how it had come to be in Amsterdam, but he was thankful.

After his velvet tongue had persuaded the Isaacs to stay in the car, he quickly walked to the apartment block. The Isaacs' home was on the second floor. He'd rattled their apartment's locked double doors. A forceful kick, and they had swung open. Mr Isaacs had given him detailed instructions on where to find the diamonds.

The young man's eyes settled upon what he considered to be the ugliest desk he had ever seen. Each drawer had a carved head instead of a handle. He'd twisted the head of the main drawer, and a secret compartment opened. He'd snatched the velvet pouches from inside and stuffed them into his jacket pocket.

With the Germans snapping at their heels, he'd felt sorry for the couple, and that was unusual. He never felt sorry for anyone.

Hastily, he had pulled a battered suitcase from the top of a wardrobe and stuffed it full of clothes, along with Mrs Isaacs' jewellery box.

The MG had skidded to a halt next to the aircraft, where the pilot and a teenager were waiting.

"You're late!" the disgruntled pilot had said, throwing a cigarette onto the grassy runway and snubbing it with his shoe. He'd raised his eyebrows when the Isaacs had struggled out of the car, Mr Isaacs still comforting his wife, Hannah.

"A few problems," the young man had said, pushing first Hannah and then Mr Isaacs into the plane. He threw the car keys to the teenager. "Hide it well."

The accomplice had nodded and leapt into the MG.

"Colin! Did you get them?" the pilot had asked, glancing at Colin Carmichael, who sat next to him staring at the uninviting English Channel. He was referring to the diamonds, but Colin's thoughts had been on the Isaacs.

Jacob and Hannah Isaacs had been Colin Carmichael's main diamond contacts in Amsterdam. They were part of a group of men—bankers, jewellers and the like—that were smuggling diamonds to England before the Germans could get their hands on them.

However, there was one problem with the Isaacs— their only son. They'd ignored his overconfident manner and his anti-German behaviour, which hadn't gone unnoticed. Colin had asked him to take a low profile, but the young fool wouldn't listen. It was just a matter of time before he was picked up and the Isaacs' apartment raided.

Colin had turned in his seat so he could get a good view of the Isaacs. Hannah's head was tucked into Jacob's shoulder; they were both crying. Colin's eyes had momently filled, but his mind was already turning to life after the war and how he could tap into Jacob's expert diamond knowledge.

He had already decided that they could live in his Wellsbury house, which he had bought when the ministry started to develop the airfield. Wellsbury wasn't much of a place. Not many people lived there, and it wasn't marked on any map. An ideal place for a secret airfield and diamond dealing.

"What you going to do with them?" the pilot had asked, nodding towards the Isaacs.

"The bloody Germans shot their son, right before their eyes. What could I do? I couldn't just leave them."

"Getting soft, Carmichael?" The pilot had grinned.

"You know me; I have a plan for everything," Colin Carmichael replied, tapping his pocket where the Isaacs' stash of diamonds lay.

The moon had peeped from behind the clouds as the aircraft circled the airfield.

"You're a lucky bastard, Carmichael," the pilot had said as he gazed down at the moonlit runway. "The moon would only make an appearance for you."

Colin had grinned. He knew he was lucky.

Chapter One

Present Day

Rupert Manning stood staring at the empty chairs in the boardroom of the Carmichael trust fund. The fund had been run from its conception by Meredith Spencer, the Carmichael family's trusted and influential lawyer. Old Jasper Carmichael Senior hadn't paid much attention to the fund; consequently, Meredith had ruled with an iron rod. The board members were weak and had treated him as some kind of god.

Manning had always disliked Meredith and considered himself to be just as competent—if not more so—and after Meredith's unexpected death, Manning had stepped into his shoes.

That was until the missing Colin Carmichael was pronounced dead and his bastard son, Jasper Carmichael, decided to honour his birthright, becoming Lord Carmichael and head of the Carmichael trust fund.

Manning was furious. He hated all of the Carmichaels—Jasper Carmichael Senior; Colin Carmichael, the renowned diamond thief; and the current Jasper Carmichael, the last of the rich and powerful Carmichael clan.

The boardroom's door creaked; a cough echoed through the empty room.

"Come in, Higgins," Manning said in his characteristic deadpan tone.

Higgins, Meredith's old butler-cum-Man Friday, shivered as nerves welled in his empty stomach.

Manning slowly lowered himself into the soft leather desk chair. He pointed his long index finger at Higgins.

"What do you know about Kate Carmichael?"

The question wrong-footed Higgins.

"Nothing. I didn't even know she existed until Meredith went to Wellsbury," he lied, for he had read Meredith's journal before giving it to Jasper along with the other documents that had been in Meredith's safe.

Manning reached inside his jacket pocket and dropped a brown envelope onto the large mahogany table that filled the room.

"This is a copy of Meredith's last will." He paused. "Kate is a very rich woman. Meredith changed his will when he returned from Wellsbury, leaving her his estate. No wonder his sons are contesting it." He picked up the will, glanced over it pointedly, and dropped it back onto the table. "Did you know?"

"To be fair," Higgins nervously stuttered, "she has refused the money."

Manning raised his eyebrows; he couldn't understand how anyone could refuse a fortune.

"What's she like?"

"I don't know her well enough."

"Get to know her—and that no good husband, Carmichael." Manning's voice rose. "How did he meet her?"

"She worked for him."

"He fucked her, you mean. He has a reputation. Women fall at his feet. God knows why."

Manning paused, jealously reflecting on Carmichael's charisma. Carmichael was a known womaniser, and Manning had tried to pay women to get into his bed. But for some reason, Carmichael wasn't interested, only having eyes for Kate. Why?

Manning's fingers drummed on a folder resting beside him.

"I've had a private investigator look into Kate Carmichael." A photo of Kate skimmed across the table to Higgins. "Not a great beauty, is she?"

Higgins stared at the photo of Kate getting out of her Evoque. "It's not a true likeness."

"But she dresses like a hippy. Not like Lady Carmichael," Manning scoffed.

"I wouldn't say a hippy. Kate likes her jeans and white blouses. Her trademark, if you like."

"I'm told Carmichael had a court order for the boys," Manning continued in the same derisive tone. "And now she has them back."

"Kate hasn't the resources that Jasper has. The boys were very unhappy living in the castle. Harry, the eldest, isn't the same boy as he was before."

"What do you mean?" snarled Manning.

"He cried a lot. Wouldn't eat. Oliver, the youngest, fought the school bullies for him. Harry was covered in cuts and bruises."

"See? You do know stuff." An awkward silence lingered between the two men before Manning said, "They now live with her in Wellsbury. Carmichael has moved his office there. She's in charge when he's not there."

"I believe that's correct," Higgins nervously replied, wondering where this was going.

"She's opened a bookshop and gallery."

"Y-yes," Higgins stuttered.

"Very popular, I believe. Making money."

"Kate works very hard." Higgins' tone had become defensive.

"'Carmichael Books' hangs above the shop."

"That's correct."

"You haven't mentioned the first editions."

"Not a lot to say. I believe Kate came across some first editions left by Mrs Isaacs," Higgins explained.

"She's buying these fucking books, and you failed to tell me." Manning was growing impatient.

Higgins' face reddened.

"There's an advert in the paper: Carmichael Books. First Editions." Manning pulled a folded paper from the desk drawer and threw it towards Higgins. "How's she funding this? Fucking Carmichael, I suppose." Manning paused, gathering his thoughts. "Have you any idea what these books sell for?"

Higgins nervously shook his head.

"How is Carmichael financing his growing empire?" Manning glared at Higgins. "It's only a matter of time before he develops that airfield."

A tense silence hovered between the two men. Higgins didn't want to annoy Manning, so he kept quiet.

"I've paid for top people to look into Carmichael's finances. Nothing! Fucking nothing! His only records are public and legit. The trail of his shell companies and bank accounts ends at the Caymans."

Higgins watched as Manning's expression stiffened and his face reddened. He took a step back, readying himself for a quick exit.

"What do you know about Carmichael's diamonds?" Manning calmly asked.

Bile filled Higgins' mouth, making him cough. Manning glared as Higgins struggled to answer.

"Meredith mentioned them just before he went to Wellsbury," Higgins managed to say.

"I'll tell you about those diamonds." Manning's bitter tone returned. "The authorities knew Colin Carmichael organised that robbery. The thing is, how did he know that the shipment was coming in from Amsterdam? No one will say how much it was worth. He was finally put in prison, so we are led to believe. But he resurfaced as Lord Carmichael."

Manning paused to regain his composure. Talking about Colin Carmichael always stirred his temper. "Who did he pay off? There were some powerful men in cahoots with Carmichael. His son set up a new business in Wellsbury."

Higgins went to speak, but Manning silenced him with a wave of his hand. "Jasper Carmichael is a murderer and money launderer, to name just two, but he has never been investigated. And now he struts around as Lord Carmichael." The air thickened as Manning's temper rose. "Colin Carmichael left those diamonds with his son. I'm convinced. I'm also convinced that Jasper is in cahoots with Zak Cohen. Do you know, my investigators can't find any link between the two? No emails, text messages, phone calls. Yet Cohen and Carmichael prosper. I'm also convinced that Mrs Carmichael is involved."

"This is all conjecture," Higgins finally interrupted. "You have no proof."

"You will get that proof. You will wheedle your way into Carmichael's confidence, and you'll report to me. Me alone. I want gossip about his private life, who he's fucking, whether she's seeing another man, and diamonds. Cos you believe me, Jasper's empire is built on diamonds."

Chapter Two

Lord Jasper Carmichael gently inserted the key into the lock of his ancestral London home, a four-million pound Georgian terrace.

His meeting at the Freemason Lodge had been uncomfortable. Although he had been made welcome, there had been periods of silence where some of the members glanced furtively at each other as if they knew something that Jasper didn't. The strong handshakes and tapping of his shoulders cut no ice with Jasper. He had been greeted like that before, and that was by a group of criminals.

He wondered what this group of well-heeled men wanted. Whatever it was, their silence put Jasper on his guard.

However, it wasn't the Freemason meeting that was prominent in his mind but his wife, Kate, and Sebastian Manning, Rupert Manning's son. He had watched them earlier, through the camera installed in the gallery. It was obvious Sebastian was making a play for his wife. Jasper was familiar with foreplay; he was a master at it.

Kate had looked tired. He wondered if the burden of his diamond arrangement with Zak was too much for her. But she wanted her sons, and he needed her. *There's a price on everything*, he thought.

While Jasper was watching the camera, the gallery's glass doors had suddenly bounced open and in marched Oliver, who'd looked as if he'd spent a couple of rounds with Mike Tyson.

Jasper had to fiddle with the sound controls of the live feed to pick up Oliver's voice.

"I told 'em!" Oliver had bellowed, his little chest bulging. "If they touched 'im again, what would 'appen."

Kate had turned away from Oliver. Jasper couldn't see what she was looking at, but he knew it was Harry.

"School phoned just as we were loading the car with groceries." Jasper recognised Malcolm's abrupt voice. Malcolm and his wife, Clare, were more like family than housekeeping staff. "They insisted I brought 'em here. I told 'em you were busy with clients."

Kate knelt and Harry had raced into her arms. Oliver's face fell until Kate held her arm out so she could cuddle both.

Where had that precocious five-year-old gone? Jasper had thought as he gazed at the unrecognisable Harry, who was withdrawn and cried a lot.

"What do you want me to do? Take 'em back to the house?" Malcolm had asked.

"No. They can stay here," Kate had said.

Sebastian moved assertively next to Kate. Oliver gave him the evil eye, and Jasper couldn't help but smile.

"I'd thought we could have lunch, and you'd show me around the hotel?"

Jasper had watched Kate turn and stare disbelievingly at him.

"I'd like to see the penthouse suite," Sebastian continued. "I'm told it's out of this world."

"I don't do that sort of thing. You should know that." Kate's voice was a little curt.

11

"I thought I'd be the exception, considering how well we get on."

"You two go into the bathroom and clean up," Kate had said to the boys. Oliver wasn't happy; he obviously didn't like Sebastian.

"Do they always come first?" Sebastian tried to sound hurt as he watched the boys dragging their feet towards the bathroom.

"Yes!"

"No wonder Jasper spends time away."

"What does that mean?" snapped Kate.

"You won't keep him if you don't pay him any attention. There's already gossip."

Kate had lifted a first aid kit from the corner cupboard.

"What do you want from me?"

"I thought I'd try my hand at fucking Lady Carmichael. But you're nothing like a lady. I mean, look at the way you dress. Like some hippy," he'd said bitterly, his tone changing abruptly as he realised he'd failed. Jasper hoped Manning's father would be angry.

Jasper had stood and punched the antique desk. Sebastian Manning wanted what was his.

Jasper was content with his marriage and their sex life. Kate loved him and he loved her in his own way; they trusted each other. But Manning was right: there was talk about Jasper and other women. Beth and Joanne had both wheedled their way back into his life.

"Malcolm!" Kate had shouted. "Show Mr Manning out."

"You'll regret this. I have friends in high places. They'll ruin this pathetic effort of a gallery." He'd begun to walk towards the door. "And if you think you're going to inherit Meredith's fortune, think on."

Jasper's musing abruptly ended when he heard his name.

"Lord Carmichael!" whispered a voice.

Jasper's hackles rose. It was late, and his immediate thought was *mugging*.

"It's Willis. Our fathers were friends. They had a mutual interest."

Who the bloody hell is Willis?

Jasper slowly turned, preparing himself for an attack, but he met the gaze of a small man dressed in a long black overcoat that had seen better days and a black homburg hat.

Who the fuck wears homburg hats?

"Can we walk?" whispered Willis.

Not bloody likely.

"What do you want?" asked Jasper, trying to hide his churning stomach.

"My father knew yours, back in the day. He taught me everything I know. He was fifty when I was born." Willis paused and nervously chuckled. "A late starter. I can remember your father, Colin."

Jasper's initial thought was *Colin's inside man*.

"Colin delivered diamonds to my father. They'd meet at the Isaacs'—I believe you know the house. The diamonds would then go to various locations to be cut. Even after the war they kept in touch. Colin was addicted to diamonds and the thrill of robbery. I know everyone thought he had an insider in Hatton Gardens. He was a good liar."

Jasper couldn't believe his ears. Was he talking to Colin's insider?

"I could go on about Colin, but that's the past and I want to talk about the present and make you an offer you can't refuse." Willis paused, making sure he had Jasper's attention. "I know a little about you. How you fence diamonds. I imagine you still have some. I know you had Colin's diamonds. Zak

Cohen must be cutting them." He paused again, giving Jasper a few moments to digest what he was telling him. "There was a lot of guessing in the diamond community who this mystery dealer was, but I knew it was you. You'd waited and waited until it was safe to sell." Another pause as he stared at Jasper, hoping for a reaction. But there wasn't one. "I want someone to sell some diamonds for me. Some may need re-cutting. No questions. No paperwork. No calls except on burners and definitely no texts or emails. Interested? Yes or no?"

Jasper's gut was nervously churning as he stared at the man. *Trap, trap*, shouted through his mind.

He took a deep breath. "You've got the wrong man." His firm tone had such weight that Willis took a step back into the poorly lit street.

"I don't think so," Willis retorted. "Think about it. Talk to Zak. I know where to find you." His words faded into the night air.

Jasper turned the key in the lock and the door clicked open.

"Lord Carmichael, is that you?" shouted Chester, the butler of the London house.

In the absence of a Carmichael, for the last several years Meredith Spencer had taken it upon himself to maintain the London house and employ its butler. Jasper considered this to be unnecessary as the house was rarely used.

"I phoned the lodge. They said you'd left ages ago. You didn't go to the club!" said Chester.

"No. I needed to walk and think."

"It will take some adjusting being Lord Carmichael," continued Chester, not noticing Jasper's preoccupied mood as he helped him remove his all-wool overcoat. "Probably you should wear a hat. All members of the lodge do."

"Hat!" exclaimed Jasper in disbelief.

"I'll accompany you to Saville Row. All gentlemen go there."

Jasper stared at Chester. He had no intention of wearing the Saville Row uniform, as he termed it. For a brief moment, he appreciated Kate's reluctance to wear the Carmichael and Swain uniform. She was the only member of staff that referred to the dress code that way.

He turned and pushed open the oak doors of Lord Carmichael's study, a depressing, musty room clad in dark wood panelling. Thick velvet curtains covered the floor-to-ceiling windows that overlooked the manicured garden.

"I hope you're not going to start work. It's very late and I've got an early start." Chester had followed him.

Jasper clenched his fists.

"Don't forget Higgins and Mr Manning are coming, and you're taking your seat in the Lords."

"Go to bed, Chester. I just want to relax for a minute," Jasper calmly replied.

Chester hovered by the door. After a long moment, he uttered, "Very well."

Jasper carefully lowered himself onto the Chesterfield leather couch. He speed-dialled the first number on his phone. She answered after one ring.

"Miss me?" His words were soft and loving. "Did I wake you?"

"I'm going over accounts. Would you mind if I sack your accountant?"

Jasper laughed. "How are the boys?"

"Harry still is withdrawn and being bullied, and Oliver is fighting his way through the school."

"And you?"

"Well, I'm not withdrawn or fighting."

"Tell me you love me."

"You know that."

"I need to hear you say it."

"What's wrong?"

"I need to be inside you, Kate. I need to feel your love." There was a hint of despair in Jasper's voice.

"Come home."

"I've been to the lodge."

"It's not for you."

"It's a different world here."

"Come home. I'll be at the office tomorrow. The penthouse is waiting."

"Tell me you love me."

"I'll tell you tomorrow."

"I'm not sure the Bentley will make it."

"That wouldn't stop my Jasper."

A warm glow passed through his body when she referred to him that way.

"What are you wearing?"

"Just a robe."

He sighed at the thought, and could almost see her teasing smile in response.

"I couldn't sleep. I was waiting for you to call."

Jasper briefly closed his eyes as images of his wife naked flashed into his mind. Her soft skin. Full, heavy breasts. He fidgeted and adjusted his trousers when he recalled her delightful sigh and soft whisper—'*Don't make me wait*'—as he slipped into her magical place that quelled the demons that stirred inside him.

"Come home. I'll work my magic." Her voice had taken a soft tone. "I love you."

"Kate!"

The phone was dead. She'd ended the call.

Chapter Three

"Where the fuck is he?" bellowed an angry Rupert Manning.

"I'm not sure," Chester mumbled, red faced.

"Sure! Sure!" shouted Manning, thumping Lord Carmichael's desk.

"He wasn't in bed when I took his morning coffee."

"Had his bed been slept in?"

Chester hung his head. "No."

"He's gone to her!" yelled Manning, his fist beating the desk. Thump. Thump. Thump.

"The Bentley's still here," mumbled Chester.

Manning turned his wrath onto Higgins. "Find him. Try her first."

***

A contented Jasper Carmichael lay with his wife nestled against his shoulder, their legs entwined.

He had left the London house just after midnight. He had slipped out of the kitchen door dressed in black and carrying a messenger bag bulging with paperwork and his laptop. He'd briskly walked towards his old London apartment, occasionally stopping and listening to see if he was being followed. He'd deftly dodged the security cameras installed in the underground carpark, where his old Focus was still parked at the back, and lifted the key fob hidden under the rear wheel arch. The Focus had fired first time and he'd slowly exited the carpark, turning into the one-way system and then towards the motorway and Wellsbury.

There were tinges of grey in the night sky when he'd stopped at the back of Isaacs' House, out of sight of prying eyes.

Catlike, he'd walked through the house to their bedroom. She'd been asleep. His clothes fell onto the carpet; naked, he'd slipped beside her and trailed his lips slowly down her neck and to her breasts. The familiar moan escaped her mouth, and he'd smiled.

"Jasper."

"Yes, my love."

"Tell me," she'd mumbled.

"I need you," he'd said into her hair.

**

"You're late!" shouted Oliver, glaring at the ruffled bed.

"Oh!" exclaimed Harry, turning, not wanting to look.

"Make-up sex!" said Oliver as he slammed the bedroom door.

Kate jumped out of bed and ran into the bathroom. Jasper inwardly debated if he should join her, but he thought she might be sore. He could wait till later.

"I thought he'd stopped saying that." Jasper's voice was soft and calm as Kate returned into the bedroom. He was silent as he admired his wife dressing.

Kate lifted her head and flicked her hair off her face. She gazed into his blue eyes and smiled.

"Where are you going?" he asked.

"School run!" She leaned into him, planting a soft kiss on his cheek, and before he could react, she ran to the bedroom door.

***

There was a black Mondeo parked in the Isaacs' driveway when Kate returned from the school run. A small thin man dressed in black was leaning against the passenger door.

Clare rushed out of the kitchen, wiping her hands down her pastry apron. "It's Inspector Watts. He arrived not long after you left."

"What's he want? And who's that man?" Kate nodded towards the Mondeo. "And why are Bruce and his team milling around?"

"Dunno," Clare lied. "But Zak must've been waiting for you to leave. Jasper was still in his boxers when he arrived."

Zak, Kate thought, her mind whirling around diamonds.

"You're back!" said a surprised Malcolm, taking a step back so Kate could walk into the kitchen. "He wants you inside."

Kate was more than a little surprised by his 'where the hell have you been' tone.

"Kate!" shouted Jasper. He stood at the kitchen door with a concerned expression on his face.

What the hell is going on? thought Kate. She smiled and planted a soft kiss upon his red cheek.

"What's that for?" he murmured so only Kate could hear, his arm snaking around her waist.

"You look as if you needed it," she teased, hiding her concern. "Who's that man leaning on the Mondeo?"

"Willis," said Jasper in an abrupt, dismissive tone.

Kate was surprised at Jasper's tone, so much so she stopped to look into his eyes. He looked away so she wouldn't see the concern.

"He's with Watts," said Jasper, taking her hand and leading her to the living room.

Watts sat in the living room, drumming his fingers on the arm of one of the white leather chairs. He jumped up when Kate entered the room.

His impatience softened. "Mrs Carmichael! Always a pleasure."

Kate nodded and lowered herself onto the overstuffed couch.

"I called in on the off chance of killing two birds with one stone. Two things. Have you noticed a man hanging around the gallery and the coffee shop?"

"Can't say I have. But that doesn't mean there hasn't been one. I'm very unobservant."

"That's what Jasper said."

The inspector hadn't expected Jasper to be there. His informant had told him Jasper was in London and had a full day of engagements, including the House of Lords. The inspector preferred to speak to Kate alone, and had hoped he'd get lucky and Clare and Malcolm would leave him in the library, where he could snoop around. But luck hadn't been with him; his inspection of the first edition book collection would have to wait. His informant wouldn't be pleased.

The inspector looked at Kate. She was smiling at Jasper.

"The other thing." The inspector coughed. "Is a more delicate matter. Do you know a Sebastian Manning?" He waited for Kate's nod. "He claims that you behaved..." Watts coughed, and his cheeks went a shade of pink. "...inappropriately towards him."

And so it begins, thought Jasper.

"Did he?" said Kate, more than a little puzzled.

"I've sent for Carl," interrupted Jasper. He had already exchanged a few heated words with the inspector.

"Why do I need a solicitor? I've never behaved inappropriately towards him."

"Can you give us your version of the last time you were in his company?" asked the inspector tentatively.

Kate's stomach began to churn. "I'll wait for Carl."

Jasper smiled and nodded.

The inspector reached into his inside pocket and pulled out a brown envelope. He emptied the contents onto the coffee table.

"We could do this at the station," he said, as Kate looked at the photographs. "Is that you in these photographs?"

Kate uncharacteristically jumped up. "You honestly think I would do that?! To him?" She looked at Jasper.

"He handed them around the George. Eric pinned them up by the door," said the inspector, who was suddenly feeling sorry for Kate as her cheeks reddened and her eyes filled. Kate didn't deserve to be ridiculed in this manner, but she had refused Manning's son, and no one did that. Rupert Manning wanted Kate to suffer, and Watts was Manning's errand boy since he had accepted his money.

Kate slumped back onto the couch and wrapped her arms around herself, trying to control waves of fear.

Why is this happening to me? she thought, as tears fell from her eyes.

The inspector turned to Jasper, but he stood staring into space, unaware of the emotional turmoil his wife was going through.

Jasper's thoughts were elsewhere. Zak had waited for Kate to leave before rushing to show him the photographs. He was cocky, too cocky, using the photographs to make veiled threats about their diamond arrangement.

Jasper had waited till he was alone to vent his anger. Clare had rushed into the living room to find Jasper standing in his boxers, glaring at the upturned coffee table and photographs lying on the floor. She had gasped when she picked them up.

Kate's soft, emotional voice suddenly registered with Jasper.

"I said no!" It was barely a whisper.

A tear dripped onto her white blouse.

"He wanted to take me to lunch followed by a private viewing of the hotel penthouse."

Another tear fell.

"Harry and Oliver were sent home for fighting. He asked if they always came first. When I said yes, he said I wouldn't keep Jasper if I didn't attend to him. You can ask Malcolm—he showed him out."

The tears were flowing. Jasper's gaze turned towards the inspector, who was staring at Kate.

Jasper suddenly realised that his wife was upset and she needed him. He wrapped his arms around her and rested her head on his shoulder.

"I'm sorry, Mrs Carmichael—sorry, Lady Carmichael—but he's already contacted a solicitor."

"Anyone can see these photos are the result of photo manipulation. It's not Kate. The wedding ring is on the right hand. The hair is too light," Jasper angrily declared.

They all gazed at Kate's left hand, where her wedding ring snugly sat at the base of her ring finger.

Jasper's phone rang. He stood, leaving Kate alone.

"Ah! Carl. We have a problem."

An expectant silence filled the room as they listened to Jasper's telephone conversation.

"Yes! They have!"

Jasper ended the call and smiled at Kate.

"Carl is already on it. Manning's solicitor has been in contact. Carl's already contacted a photographic expert. We should have a report tomorrow. You should take Manning to court."

The inspector thought that Jasper's tone and words were not of a loving husband. But Kate's reaction shocked him even more. She stood abruptly and walked into her studio without so much as looking at Jasper, closing the door firmly behind her.

'*Take Manning to court,*' repeated in her mind.

How could Jasper even think that? Surely he knew her well enough to know the thought of her private life being dragged through the courts and picked over by the tabloid press would destroy her.

Chapter Four

Jasper turned a shade of red when the boys cornered him, asking questions about their mother. He tried to reassure them that she was fine, but observant Harry marched off in a huff, mumbling that his dad didn't care.

Jasper had been too involved with his own problems to notice that Kate was unusually quiet and withdrawn. The only time he noticed other people was when he wanted them. Unfortunately, he hadn't wanted Kate until now. She wasn't in his bed, and he needed her, desperate to fuck her.

The thought of sex in her studio pleased him; he knew she would be there.

She was hugging an empty mug and staring into the clear night sky. He slipped his arms around her waist.

"I missed you," he said seductively.

He felt her body stiffen. She would need seducing, and sex with Kate was always good after seduction.

"As long as Eric lives, it will never stop," Kate said. "He hates me. He lies. I refused him."

Jasper eased her round so he could look into her eyes. They were brimming with tears, waiting for the dam to break.

"I don't know what you saw in him," he said in his best caring voice.

"I was drunk. My evil father had shattered my dreams." She hesitated as she recalled the night Eric had pinned her against a wall and fucked her until she wept. "They finished me. Jasper. They left me at the bottom of the stairs. Bleeding. Life was seeping out of me. I could hear them talking and laughing. I didn't want to live."

Jasper guided her head onto his shoulder.

"Let it out, Kate. Cry." His hand rested on the back of her head as the floodgates opened.

Jasper guided her to the chaise longue and nestled her into his body. Sex would have to wait.

They lay there all night, Kate sleeping and Jasper lying awake, feeling uncomfortable. His conscience was bothering him. He had done many unforgiveable things, and his conscience had never plagued him before. But he had ignored Kate. He should have paid closer attention to her emotional state. She was always there when he needed her; the least he could do was to be there for her. She had proved her love and loyalty over and over, even accepting his arrangement with Zak. But he wanted more. He needed the adrenaline rush a bigger diamond network would give him, but Kate wouldn't understand.

The least he could do was pay Eric a visit.

The next day, Kate put on a brave face as she took the boys to school. He should have done the school run instead of wandering into his new office nursing his morning coffee.

It had been Kate's idea to convert the unused breakfast room into his new office. He had initially objected, wanting to keep family and business separate, but he had rapidly warmed to the idea when he realised that he could work from home in complete secrecy. To hide the true reason for his sudden change of heart, he had lied to Kate, saying he would see more of her and the boys.

Amanda, his long-standing PA, would be in charge of the Carmichael House office, which would now only be used for meetings. Against Kate's wishes, Jasper had decided to keep the London office, but he hadn't told her about his plans for it.

Bruce and two of his team caught his attention. They were standing outside the open French doors, balancing his desk on a trolley.

"Where do you want this, boss?" Bruce shouted.

Kate had stored Jacob Isaacs' furniture in one of the outer buildings. The desk had caught Jasper's eye—it was good quality, carved from solid oak, of unusual design, no inlay. The drawers had heads carved where the handles should have been.

"Here! Facing the French doors."

Bruce smiled; Jasper had chosen the only place in the room where he could see Kate's studio. *Jasper still has the hots for his wife. Like most of his men,* he thought. Including him.

While the men went back to the storage building, Jasper took the opportunity to admire Kate's tasteful remodelling of his office.

The old Victorian wood panelling had been removed, walls re-plastered and painted off-white. The old wooden windows had been replaced by one-way, triple glazed units. He had insisted on French doors that led out onto the patio and to Kate's studio. He needed to see her, touch her, be inside her when his demons stirred. He often wondered if she realised the power she had over him.

She had left the choice of artistic decoration to him, but there was only one painting he wanted and that was one of her that a London artist had painted from a poster-size photo. She'd had her hair down, she was happy, a smile filled her face and her green eyes were on fire. He had been nervous of her reaction, but she had dispelled his nerves when she flicked her hair and smiled that 'I love you' smile. He could still feel her lingering kiss.

In no time, the men had placed a large oak table, another Jacob Isaacs creation, exactly where Jasper instructed, along with a new glass coffee table, a white overstuffed couch and chairs. While Jasper debated where he was going to hang Kate's painting, Bruce and Malcolm busied themselves fixing wooden filing cabinets along the windowless wall.

It was early afternoon by the time Jasper was finally alone. He settled into the high-backed leather desk chair; his fingers glided over the desktop, still in as-new condition.

He glanced admiringly at the detail of the heads carved into each drawer of his new desk. He pulled on the head of the middle drawer. It didn't move. He pulled again with more force. He tried to move the drawer up and down, but it remained firmly shut. Jasper stretched his open palms under the drawer, searching for anything that would open it. Nothing.

He pushed the seat away from the desk, his eyes and mind working to fathom where the secret catch could possibly be. Kate had mentioned that Mr Isaacs was a skilful carpenter, and Jasper suspected that he had made this ornate desk with a very secret compartment.

After a long moment, he slowly and carefully ran his fingertips over and around each head. When he pulled, the other drawers easily opened. In desperation, he continued his search along the lip of the desktop. His finger caught on a tiny protrusion. He pressed, heard a click and the middle drawer opened. But this was no secret compartment, just an empty drawer. In frustration, he walked to the French doors and gazed at Kate's studio.

"What's wrong?" Kate's soft, caring tone took him by surprise. He hadn't heard her walk into his office.

"No school run?"

"Malcolm and Clare are doing it."

Their eyes met.

"Don't you like your office?" she said, wandering around the room. "I see you've taken advantage of the Isaacs' furniture."

"Kate! As much as I love being with you, why are you here?"

"I want to talk."

"About?" Jasper moved close to her.

"Everything. Clear the air."

Jasper waited for her to continue. Her serious expression concerned him.

"I don't know where to start." She slumped into the sofa.

"We could christen the new couch," he said, trying to lighten the mood.

Her green eyes lit up, and she smiled. "Later."

"I'll hold you to it."

"Good." Her smile had a fragile quality. "But I'm not Lady Carmichael material."

"I'll be the judge of that."

"I'm far too trusting. I should've realised that Sebastian Manning had an ulterior motive. I dismissed his attention."

Jasper joined her and took her hand.

She looked into his caring eyes and smiled. "I would never cheat on you."

His arm slipped around her, and he pulled her into his chest.

"If the boys see those photos, I'll die."

"If the boys see those photos, I'll explain," he said, somewhat sternly. His fingers stretched to the band that held her hair. His lips caressed her ear as her hair fell onto her shoulders. "Kate, you must trust me. Let me deal with these people. I'll protect you and the boys."

"You can't deal with these people the same as you've always done. I don't trust Watts. I think he's…" Her words faded as Jasper interrupted her.

"Watts is fishing. I've taken my eye off the ball. But I'm here to stay." He paused, savouring the comforting warmth from her. "This is my main office. My office at Carmichael House is secondary. Amanda can run it."

She lifted her head. "But your meetings?"

"Some will be here, but most will be at Carmichael House."

A mutual silence settled between them as they each thought through Jasper's words. Uppermost in Kate's mind was the possibility that the house would be the hub for Jasper and Zak's diamond business, while Jasper's thoughts rotated between diamonds and his new business ventures that hopefully only he and Kate would know about. He glanced over to the large oak table and envisaged a model of Wellsbury's airport, which would become the hub for his various businesses.

After what seemed like an age, Kate broke the silence. "You're expanding the diamond trade?"

Jasper lifted her from his chest. "What makes you think that?"

"The desk. I noticed the middle drawer was open."

"So?"

"You've found the secret compartment."

He watched as Kate walked to the desk and twisted the head of the open middle drawer. Jasper's eyes widened when the whole of the left-hand side panel opened.

"I thought that was just the side of the drawers," he said.

"It is." Kate slipped her hand inside and pulled out a box. "I thought you'd found these."

She flipped the box open. A sparkling white light greeted him. Diamonds, all cut. Jasper was mesmerised.

"There're all the same," Kate said matter-of-factly, handing Jasper the box.

"You knew?"

"I found them not long after we moved the desk into storage. The side panel was slightly open. I was curious. The men must have accidently opened it. It's a heavy brute."

Jasper wasn't listening; the diamonds had his complete attention. His fingers slowly and carefully moved between the glittering gems.

"You do know what this means." Jasper turned to face her. He was surprised to see watery eyes.

"Well, I suppose they belong to you! You bought the house with all its contents." She collected her thoughts. "You're rich."

"No! *We're* rich."

"I don't want anything to do with them."

"Kate!"

"Well, they're probably stolen," she said. "And I'll lose you to the Carmichael curse."

"And that is?"

"Diamonds!"

Jasper slipped the box back into the secret compartment.

"How did you open it?" he asked.

"You can't twist the head unless the middle drawer is open, and that won't open until the button is depressed."

"Were you going to tell me?"

"Probably!" She hesitated. "Later. When you were free from diamond fever."

"We're home!" echoed two happy voices outside the office.

"This conversation isn't over," said Jasper.

"I know."

Chapter Five

Jasper stood wearing only his boxers, gazing out into the night sky from Kate's studio. He felt at ease there, surrounded by her paintings. He needed her. He couldn't lose her again, not over diamonds. The last time they'd separated had been disastrous for them both.

Jasper had slipped out of bed. He didn't want to wake Kate. He needed to think.

They had been wrapped in each other's arms when their conversation continued. They had just made love, but somehow it seemed tainted by diamonds that hung over them like the Sword of Damocles.

He'd thought she was asleep when he whispered, "I love you, Kate Carmichael. But I'm not worthy. You're right—I do have the Carmichael diamond curse. But I'm holding my most valuable diamond in my arms."

His heart missed a beat as she rolled on top of him.

"I love you, Jasper Carmichael. I'll never leave you."

Time stood still as they had reaffirmed their love.

"We'll compromise," he had whispered just before she slept.

But he couldn't envisage how they could. The diamonds in the desk had changed everything. They would keep Zak busy making his designer diamond jewellery; his upmarket designs were in demand, and that had caught the attention of the authorities. Zak had an endless supply of quality diamonds, and the finger had been pointed at Jasper as the supplier and mystery buyer of black-market diamonds.

His thoughts leapt to Willis, the man who had approached him about buying diamonds. Willis had played the Colin card, claiming he had met him. And not only that but Willis had claimed his father had done deals with Colin. This had put Jasper on his guard. Colin rarely did deals; Colin worked alone. He was a master thief.

Suddenly, a masked face was pressed against the bi-fold doors, arms outstretched, gloved palms flat against the glass.

Jasper stumbled back. He knew the figure couldn't see him, but that was little comfort against the shock of a Halloween-masked face.

"Carmichael." The evil voice made Jasper take another step back.

The figure's gloved hand snatched a crowbar from inside the black cloak that was wrapped around him. He forced the crowbar between the doors and frame.

Jasper quickly scanned Kate's workbench, looking for a knife. The figure grunted and cursed when the door refused to budge.

"I'll fucking kill you. You and that fucking woman of yours. You'll pay."

Fists thumped the glass, making the doors move.

"I shouldn't have seen that." Kate's nervous voice surprised Jasper. He strode towards her, wrapping her in his arms.

Kate moved her head towards the doors, but the figure was gone.

"You should be in bed." His voice was low and calm.

"I was cold."

"Come," he said, quickly guiding her out of the studio.

Instead of joining Kate in bed, Jasper was throwing on his black clothes.

"What are you doing?" Their eyes briefly met. "Jasper, no!"

"These people think I've gone soft being Lord Carmichael. They're in for one hell of a surprise. This will end once and for all."

"Jasper! Stop!"

Kate's words faded as Jasper turned and ran out of the bedroom, still jamming his foot into a trainer while opening the house security app on his phone. The front of the house was lit up like a Christmas tree. The figure was climbing out over the locked front gates.

Jasper was now on autopilot. He opened the electric double garage doors and leapt into his Ford Focus while pressing the front gate fob. The Focus skidded out onto the road just as red taillights were disappearing into the distance.

He floored the Focus as he followed the car out of Wellsbury, taking the road that led to Don's old house. Don had been one of his trusted men, until he'd betrayed him and disappeared. Jasper assumed he was dead.

He switched off the headlights and engine, coasting to a halt not far from Don's old house. Catlike, he slipped out of the driver's door, careful not to fully close it. He didn't want to wake any neighbours.

He jogged towards the house, keeping close to the walls that surrounded the houses opposite. He caught a glimpse of the wafting cloak disappearing into the open front door. Jasper stopped and pressed himself against a six-foot wall. He was out of breath, and his heart was pounding.

Suddenly, Don's old driveway was awash with light. A tall, well-dressed man exited the front door and hurried towards a Range Rover parked at the side of the house. Jasper's mind raced; this wasn't the same man that he'd followed. The Range Rover left the house at some speed. The figure behind the wheel reminded Jasper of Sebastian Manning.

Jasper stood perfectly still, waiting for the security lights to go out. But they stayed bright as two men left the house, one tall and well-built and the other small and thin. Jasper could hear raised voices as if they were arguing. They got into a dark Ford Mondeo and slowly exited the drive. The taller of the two was driving while the other slumped in the passenger seat.

The image of Inspector Watts flashed into Jasper's mind, but he didn't want to believe what his gut was telling him: *Watts is somehow involved with the criminal world.*

Ten minutes later, Jasper was driving past Kate's youth centre, his mind mulling over the possibility that it had been Watts driving the Mondeo. He stopped and pulled over onto the demolition site opposite the youth centre; Kate had finally agreed that some of the old Victorian building couldn't be saved. He sat for a long moment, debating if he should get rid of the Focus. If it *was* Watts driving, he would have clocked the parked Focus.

Jasper picked up an old newspaper he had meant to throw away from the passenger foot-well. From the boot, he retrieved a small petrol can he kept just in case he ran out of fuel. He soaked the dry, old newspaper in petrol and stuffed it into the tank. The remainder of the petrol was sprinkled over the interior of the car.

The car was well alight when Jasper jogged away. He momentarily stopped and gazed over his shoulder at the blazing car, only to be surprised by the sight of teenagers gathered around the inferno.

He went into a run, zigzagging between the old buildings, just in case they followed him.

Chapter Six

The smell of coffee woke Jasper from an uneasy sleep. He was alone. He hadn't thought of Kate; he hadn't thought of anything but Watts leaving Don's old house.

Breakfast was an irritable affair. Jasper was like a bear with a sore back, but he had promised himself he would join Kate on the school run.

They had just pulled out of the driveway when Oliver's nervous voice filled the car. "There's that man. Again."

The Range Rover came to an abrupt halt. "Again?" questioned Jasper.

"We'll be late," said Harry.

"Fuck being late! What man?"

"Jasper, language!" cried Kate.

At some speed, Jasper reversed back to the house.

"Malcolm!" he bellowed, parking the car and jumping out of the driver's seat.

"What's up?"

"I want to go to school," shouted Harry.

"Kate, phone the school. Make an excuse." Jasper then turned to Malcolm. "We need more men around the house."

"On it," answered Malcolm, returning to the garage.

"Tell me about this man," asked Jasper, trying to keep a calm voice as Kate and the boys got out of the car.

"I told you what would happen. And now we're not going to school!" Harry screamed at Oliver.

"He's been outside the gallery. He wears different clothes, but it's the same man," stuttered Oliver. "He was outside. Just."

"What man?" exclaimed Kate.

"Do you know who bought Don's old house?" Jasper turned to Kate.

"Does it matter?"

"Yes!"

"Are you two going to have a domestic?" asked Harry, trying to hide his nervousness.

"No!" answered Kate and Jasper together.

Oliver grinned. "A lot of make-up sex then."

"Oliver!" shouted Kate and Jasper.

"Kate, who bought the fucking house?"

"You won't like it."

Jasper forced his voice to be calm. "Just tell me."

"Beth."

"Fucking Beth!"

"I told you. You wouldn't like it."

Beth had been Jasper's long-time girlfriend, who'd betrayed him. He had to be wary of her; she had her own agenda. He preferred to keep his enemies close.

"Where did she...?" Jasper trailed off as he tried to remember the sale of Don's old house.

"Ask your property company," snapped Kate.

"Why didn't you tell me?"

"You were away being Lord Carmichael." Their eyes met, blue on green. "I didn't think it was important. She leaves me alone. We move in different circles."

Jasper placed his hands on Kate's shoulders, his eyes never leaving hers. "Have you any idea how important you are to me?"

Before she could answer, his mouth devoured hers.

"Make-up sex!" shouted Oliver's small voice as he strolled towards the kitchen.

"He must stop saying that," said Jasper. "Does he have any idea what it means?"

"I'm trying, but the school isn't helping with their new ideas."

"That policeman's here," said Oliver, shouting through the open kitchen door with a mouth full of Clare's biscuits.

"Did you put my clothes in the wash?" whispered a worried Jasper.

"Of course. Smelt of petrol though."

Oliver joined them with a mouthful of biscuit. "He's been in the garage."

"Oliver, how many times must I tell you?" Kate said. "Don't speak with your mouth full. And how many of those have you eaten?"

Oliver grinned. "Not as many as Harry."

Kate turned towards the kitchen, but Jasper caught her arm. "Hide my trainers. Watts mustn't see them."

By the time Jasper joined his sons in the kitchen, Inspector Watts was trying one of Clare's biscuits.

"Didn't know you could enter the garage from the kitchen," mentioned Watts, his eyes studying the kitchen floor. "Early risers in this house. Freshly baked biscuits, sparkling kitchen floor, washing machine finishing its cycle."

"Nothing unusual about that," snapped Clare. "It's a school day. Breakfast, biscuits and cleaning while they're in the oven."

"Who put the washer on?"

"I did, Inspector," answered Kate.

"She always does. Wakes us up with a kiss and collects yesterday's clothes," offered Harry.

"And my trainers. I get very dirty," grinned Oliver, reaching for another biscuit.

"At this rate I'll 'ave to bake another batch." Clare smiled, ruffling Oliver's hair.

"The thing is," said a business-like Watts, "a car was set on fire. Not far from your youth centre, Mrs Carmichael."

"You suggesting it's the boys from the centre?"

"Not suggesting anything. A man dressed in black with a hoody, was seen jogging away from the car just before it caught fire. They tried to follow him, but he knew the area and disappeared around those old Victorian buildings you're renovating. Had a few men poking around, but they found no trace of our man in black."

A tense silence filled the kitchen as the inspector waited for a response.

"You know the area, Mr Carmichael."

"I bought the whole block with the intention of knocking the lot down. But Kate persuaded me to renovate."

"Yes, I'm aware of that," retorted the inspector. "You know Beth? She complained of a prowler last night. I'm putting two and two together. The prowler and the car fire are linked."

Another tense silence.

"Malcolm was cleaning the garage when I arrived," the inspector added, changing the subject.

"So?" answered Malcolm, who was standing in the internal garage door.

"My gut tells me something's going on here. You're involved, Carmichael. I suppose I'll 'ave to get a warrant to search this place and your office."

Jasper smiled. "You're dead right."

"If you've nothing to 'ide."

Jasper's temper was starting to rise. "Stop this, Inspector. If you have evidence, let's have it."

Jasper waited for the inspector to mention the car parked near Don's old house, but the inspector was too clever for that.

"Well, at the very least I'd like to see your shoe closet. Interested in trainers; found a footprint or two."

"He doesn't wear trainers," said Oliver smugly.

***

Before the inspector was out of the gate, Jasper was walking towards the orchard.

"Where's he going?" asked Oliver.

"He needs to be alone."

"He's acting a bit strange," said Harry, joining his mother and brother.

"It's tough being at the top," said a downcast Kate.

"Can we paint with you?" Oliver said cheerfully.

"I don't see why not."

Harry and Oliver raced towards her studio, pushing and laughing.

"Trouble's coming." Malcolm's gruff words made Kate's stomach churn.

"I hope not."

"Watts is after 'im. Just like Lawson."

Kate stared at Jasper's back as he turned into the orchard. Trouble would put their marriage under more strain than it already was. Sometimes she felt as if it was the boys and sex that kept them together instead of love.

***

Jasper entered the orchard and started to pace, his mind bursting with impending conflict. He knew his enemies: Beth, Joanne, the Mannings,

Eric, Inspector Watts and the mysterious Willis. He couldn't make his mind up about Higgins, but knew he was working for a new master, Rupert Manning.

He pondered on what could be their endgame. Put him in prison? Take over his company? Diamonds?

Who could he trust? Kate, and probably Zak, Malcolm, Clare and Bruce?

Malcolm's loud cough brought him out of his reverie. "Bruce is 'ere, and Rupert Manning and Higgins."

Jasper had sent for Bruce and his team to erect a fence around the house, but he had no idea why Manning and Higgins had taken it upon themselves to visit.

"Bruce can unload and start. I want this fence finished today."

"Should 'ave done it years ago."

Jasper stared at Malcolm. "Tell Manning I'll be with him shortly." He turned and continued his pacing.

"Clare's put 'em in the living room. Kate's with 'em. Cut the atmosphere with a knife," said Malcolm, leaving the orchard.

Jasper had to be one step ahead of his adversaries. He had mistakenly thought he could have everything—a lucrative diamond trade and a happy marriage with Kate—but forces were working against him. His priority was to protect Kate. At the top of the list was the one that had hurt her all those years ago.

The atmosphere in the living room was electric when Jasper walked in. Kate was sat on the edge of a chair opposite Manning and Higgins.

"I don't like to be kept waiting, Carmichael," barked Rupert Manning, sipping coffee from a china cup. "What the fuck are you doing in this godforsaken place? Lord Carmichael should take his place in society, not play silly games here." He leaned towards the biscuit plate and placed one on his china saucer. "Those boys should be away at school."

"We'll decide that." Kate's curt voice was slightly louder than she intended.

Manning abruptly whirled to face Kate. "No woman has ever told me what to do," he growled, his red face showing annoyance. "I make the decisions and only me. Carmichael, you've gone soft," he said, turning to Jasper. "We've come to take you back to where you belong. Where you can have as many women as you like." His eyes settled on Kate, and with an evil grin, he said, "From what I'm told, she's lacking in that department."

Jasper grabbed Kate's arm.

"Fight the battles you can win," he whispered so only she could hear. "Don't fall into his trap."

"Look what Olly's done." Harry's worried voice sidetracked Kate's attention from Manning. He was covered in paint.

Clare appeared, carrying a towel. "He's done a runner."

"That's it," Manning said. "Little wife, go and…"

"Enough!" shouted Jasper. "Go back to London and take Higgins with you."

The china cup and saucer fell on the thick-pile carpet. Clare cussed.

"You'll regret speaking to me like that, Carmichael," snarled Manning. "You have no idea what we're capable of." He stood, glaring at Jasper. "You could ask your father, if he was alive. He was taught a lesson that he never forgot."

Manning stopped in his tracks; he shouldn't have said that. He looked at Jasper to see if he had picked up on his mistake, but to his relief, Jasper was too occupied with his son.

Manning reached into his jacket pocket, and threw the car fob to Higgins. "You drive."

He stared at Jasper's back as he strode towards the kitchen.

"Now! Where's Oliver?" Jasper shouted to no one in particular.

It was much later, when Jasper recalled Manning's visit, that he realised Manning had said too much. Manning had used *we* instead of *I*. Who were his friends that had bettered Colin?

Jasper hadn't thought about Colin for some time. He'd assumed he was dead, but his gut was sowing the seeds of doubt in his mind.

Chapter Seven

Jasper stood in the shadows of the new garden gate, his eyes focused on the police that Watts had scattered around his property.

He took a moment to reflect on his disagreement with Kate. He understood her concern; he was playing a dangerous game visiting The George late at night. But she had ignored Eric for years, hoping he would stop humiliating her. Jasper was determined to make tonight the night he finally would. However, he had promised that he wouldn't use violence.

Instead, Jasper was going to look for hard evidence of Eric's illicit beer and drug activities. Then he would use the law to ruin Eric's business. Jasper wasn't going to settle for anything less than a jail sentence.

Jasper briskly walked towards the shopping centre, taking care to mingle with Wellsbury's night revellers until he could see The George. Instead of heading towards the front doors of the pub, he walked up the side alley. He stopped by the metal doors that covered the beer chute. If gossip was to be believed, it was only used for beer deliveries that were off the books. Without hesitation, he opened the metal doors and slid down into the cellar. He opened the torch app on his iPhone and scanned the neat rows of barrels. Some clearly displayed the brewery's marking whereas others were blank.

Jasper's torch light picked out a shelf that was hidden behind the barrels. He carefully squeezed through the narrow gaps between the barrels. He stopped dead when the light from his phone shone on the recognisable packaging used for drugs.

Eric's too confident, he thought. *He doesn't bother to hide the stuff.*

A raucous noise drifted towards him from the bar. The pub was still in full swing. Licensing laws meant nothing to Eric.

Jasper froze when the cellar door opened and light flooded in. Eric stood in the doorway, swaying, holding onto the door handle. He finally steadied himself and stumbled onto the stairs, missing the first two steps. He righted himself and cursed, gripping the rickety stair rail.

Jasper carefully retraced his steps between the beer barrels so he could get a better view of Eric as he fumbled for the light cord. He swayed and stretched until he pulled the cord. The bulb popped. Eric loudly cursed, calling the lightbulb all the fucking names he could think of.

He gingerly walked down the steps, holding onto the rail and cursing with each step. He paused, looking towards the open chute as a cold breeze ruffled his hair. His eyes narrowed.

He stopped.

"Eric, hurry the fuck up!" A loud voice drifted from the bar.

"Shut the fuck up!" Eric hollered back.

Jasper stepped out so Eric could see him.

"What the fuck?"

Eric missed the next step.

"You!" he shouted at the top of his voice.

He reached for the handrail and missed.

His overweight body lurched forward. Unable to steady himself, he fell headfirst onto the flagstone floor.

Jasper didn't flinch when he heard the cracking of bone as Eric's head met the cold stone. He stood over Eric's crumbled form, watching the blood ooze from the gaping wound in his head.

Justice, he thought. He didn't care that he had played a part in Eric's fall. If he hadn't shown himself, Eric may not have fallen to his death. But Eric had pushed Kate down the stairs in the flower shop, hoping she would die in a pool of blood. *You won't humiliate her again. You piece of shit.*

Without a second thought, Jasper quickly walked towards the chute. He stumbled. Eric's mobile phone skidded in front of him.

"Eric!" bellowed a loud voice behind him.

Jasper pocketed Eric's phone before scrambling up the chute and closing the metal doors.

"Where the fuck are you, you old bugger?" a voice boomed from the top of the cellar stairs. There was a pause, and then, "Bloody hell. We need help down here!" as Jasper vanished into the night.

Chapter Eight

It was mid-morning when Jasper heard Inspector Watts' dull voice booming through the house. He was alone; Bruce had taken Kate to the school prize-giving rehearsal. Jasper was beginning to regret making Bruce Kate's bodyguard. He had jealously watched them exchange glances when Bruce opened the Evoque passenger door for her. Bruce had a soft spot for Kate, and he didn't care who knew it. But did Kate have a soft spot for Bruce?

"What can I do for you, Inspector?" Jasper said in a helpful tone, walking out of his new office and closing the door.

The inspector pushed a warrant into Jasper's chest. Jasper made a show of opening it as he continued into the living room.

"It's not signed, Carmichael," the inspector angrily bellowed. "Just how many people do you have in your pocket?" His eyes were firmly fixed on Jasper. "Eric! You know Eric from The George, don't you?"

"You mean that slob that got Kate pregnant and pushed her down the stairs? Nearly killed her? Sure, I know of him."

"Hate 'im, do you?"

"I wouldn't say hate," Jasper retorted in an aggressive tone that matched the inspector's.

"He fell down the cellar stairs. Broke his neck and cracked his skull."

"I'm not going to say I'm sorry. I'd be lying."

The inspector slumped onto an overstuffed couch, sitting opposite Jasper. "I've just come from The George. They want your blood."

Jasper raised his eyebrows. "What for?"

"Pushing Eric down the stairs."

"You don't believe them."

"It smacks of you. But no proof. Had forensics go over the cellar. Nothing. The one place you could have got in is the old barrel chute, and it was being used. The deliverymen said Eric liked their barrels rolled as close to the pumps as possible. Apparently he had phoned for an urgent delivery."

"That's all very well, Inspector, but what does it have to do with me?"

"There's no record of Eric making that call from the pub's landline." The inspector paused, watching Jasper's expression. "His mobile is missing."

"And you wanted a warrant to search for the mobile."

"Not sufficient evidence. Plus, your fancy lawyer would get you off." The inspector stood. "I thought you'd got a new office?"

Jasper nodded. "I'm very particular who goes in there."

The inspector looked daggers at Jasper. He might as well have said, '*That doesn't include you.*'

"Why aren't you in London like a good little boy and doing as you're told?" Sarcasm oozed from the inspector's voice.

"Fuck off," Jasper snapped back.

"Manning and his son were at The George last night with Beth and Joanne." The inspector walked to the side window, hiding his annoyance at his failure to rile Jasper. "Eric would keep us entertained with his stories about the young, couldn't-get-enough Kate." He turned and laughed into Jasper's stern face. "She loved being fucked against a wall."

Jasper clenched his fists, knuckles turning white.

"Dare say you know all about that." The inspector grinned to himself, satisfied that, although this time he hadn't managed to arrest Jasper, he had succeeded in riling him.

***

Jasper put Watts out of mind and tried to concentrate on organising the files he had brought over from Carmichael House.

He needed a break and to relax. He needed Kate.

He opened his new French doors and stood on the newly laid patio between his office and Kate's studio. His gut began to churn like it did in the old days when trouble was brewing. He'd have to be ready if things got messy, have getaway cars stashed and safe houses prepared. But Kate mustn't know, just like the old days.

His thoughts meandered to Zak and their diamond arrangement. Zak had been disappointed when Jasper told him that he wasn't going to supply any more diamonds until he found out what Beth and the Mannings were up to, and if Inspector Watts was involved. It was too risky.

"How do I look?"

He turned at the sound of Kate's voice. His heart skipped a beat. She stood before him in the cerise dress she had worn when he'd first met her at the mayor's ball. His eyes were drawn to the long vee that emphasised her beautiful breasts.

Her legs were shown to their best effect by cerise heels.

"Jasper!"

"Where are you going?" he stuttered.

"Prize-giving."

"Dressed like that?"

"Lady Carmichael has been asked to present the prizes."

"My god, Kate. You're stunning." He walked over to his desk and pulled the top drawer open, taking out Zak's latest pendant.

"Zak made this for you."

He clipped the three-carat teardrop pendant around Kate's neck. He stood admiring how the pendant nestled just above her cleavage, as if Zak had made it to measure.

"Jasper! I can't."

"Wow!" Harry's voice echoed.

"It's too much."

"Nothing is too much for you, my darling." Jasper planted a soft kiss on her pink-painted lips. "I think I'll join you."

"Is Dad coming?" asked a bewildered Oliver.

Chapter Nine

It was two o'clock in the morning when Kate tiptoed to the kitchen and made herself a mug of tea. Her mind was in turmoil; Jasper had suddenly decided he had to go to London.

She wandered into the place that gave her solace, her studio. She didn't switch on the lights, preferring to stare at the night sky, gripping her tea between her hands.

She closed her eyes and Jasper's smiling face danced before her, his eyes wandering admiringly over her dress and diamond pendant.

He had been happy and proud as he'd gazed upon his family at the school prize-giving. His sons were miniature Jaspers dressed in grey designer suits, with grey waistcoats and white shirts. He'd laughed along with the rest of the audience when Kate presented Oliver with a book token for the pupil that had made the greatest progress during the academic year. Instead of leaving the stage, Oliver had stopped and turned to Kate.

"Will you loosen my collar? You promised… if I was good."

Kate had blushed a delightful pink, knelt and loosened Oliver's collar. Oliver threw his arms around her neck before hurrying off the stage grinning and waving his book token.

She had tried to talk to Jasper about the diamonds in the desk, but he was an expert at avoiding whatever she wanted to talk about. This normally involved giving her three orgasms, but this time he'd made slow, passionate love as if he was saying goodbye.

Her heart missed a beat. It was just a matter of time before he returned to his criminal ways and the Carmichael curse took hold. Her love couldn't compete with the lure of diamonds. To keep him, she would have to compromise—but could she?

The sun slowly rose over the horizon. It was Saturday, and Kate had promised to take the boys to the beach. She wasn't going to disappoint them just because Jasper wasn't there. Luckily, the ever-reliable Bruce offered to drive.

Clare made a picnic. Harry helped pack the back of the Evoque while Oliver dressed in his pirate outfit—patch over one eye, bandana around his head, white T-shirt, shorts, bare feet and a cutlass—and practised his moves.

The car was filled with happy, excited voices as Bruce drove to the beach. Kate didn't offer any conversation, just the occasional smile when Oliver tried to stab her with his cutlass.

When Bruce parked on the firm sand, Oliver chased Harry out of the car, waving his cutlass and shouting. They were happy as they raced along the beach, giggling and shouting.

Bruce gazed over to Kate's expressionless face.

"Where do you want your easel?" he asked.

"Just leave it there for now."

Bruce could hardly believe his ears. Kate always sketched or painted when they came to the beach. He watched with hopelessness as Kate walked along the beach past the boys without so much as a second glance.

The boys looked at Kate. Harry shouted her name. But she kept walking.

"I'm hungry," said a slightly out of breath Oliver when he and Harry had returned to the car.

Bruce arranged Clare's picnic on the small folding table. Oliver smiled as he tucked into cheese and ham sandwiches, Clare's homemade biscuits and orange juice. But thoughtful Harry never touched his food.

"What's wrong?" asked Harry, whose eyes were trained upon his mother. Harry was a sensitive boy and could read his mother's moods like a book.

"I don't know." Bruce tried to hide the concern in his voice.

"They didn't argue. But he still left," said Harry while Oliver looked on with his mouthful of biscuit.

"Probably urgent Lord Carmichael business in London."

But Bruce's explanation cut no ice with Harry.

"He's going to leave her—I can feel it—and take us to that castle." Harry's voice had taken on a frightened tone. "She's no match for him, and she has no money."

Bruce had no experience of talking to twelve-year-olds, but he was astute enough to realise he had to tread carefully.

"Kate—your mother will never leave you. You know that. Anyway, she has her own money."

Harry's and Bruce's eyes met.

"Money?"

"Inherited her grandfather's fortune."

"No one told me," said Harry, somewhat indignantly.

"Now help me tidy up. Your mother's heading back."

Harry raced towards Kate and flung his arms around her. She ruffled his blond hair.

"Love you," he said as they walked hand-in-hand to the car.

***

Jasper sat in his old London apartment, relaxing after a day of reacquainting with old associates and visiting a car auction to replace his Ford Focus that he had set fire to. He had organised for the new Focus to be collected, serviced and parked at the back of the underground car park below his apartment block, when his burner phone rang.

"What the fuck have you done?" his investigator, John, sounded somewhat annoyed.

"What do you mean?"

"I told you what would happen if you hurt Kate."

"I haven't—"

But Jasper didn't finish.

"She's been walking along the beach. Ignored the kids. No food. No painting."

Jasper stood, his concern piqued. "Alone?"

"No. Bruce was with them. What the fuck have you done?"

"Was! Where is she now?"

"What do you care if she's at the gallery?"

The word 'care' repeated in Jasper's mind. Of course he cared, but did he care enough?

"You and that Cohen bastard are up to summot. I'm guessing diamonds. The streets are buzzing with a new diamond dealer—or should I say fence."

Jasper was clenching his fists, his temper was rising, but he daren't alienate John—he was too useful.

"Sold all Colin's diamonds, have you? But you have a new source—or is it sources? And Kate doesn't approve. Or haven't you told her?"

Jasper remained tight-lipped, fearing he would give the game away if he spoke.

"Your silence tells me everything. You've gone behind her back. My threat still stands: if you hurt her or drag her into the Carmichael dark side, I'll come for you."

The burner phone went dead.

"Fuck! Fuck! Fuck!" Jasper yelled, throwing the phone across the room.

He slumped into his leather chair. He should have told Kate, but then he would have had to tell her about his plans for a diamond network and that would have led to another argument.

Chapter Ten

"Where you going?" asked an anxious Harry, who hadn't left his mother's side since returning from the beach.

"Check on the gallery and bookshop."

"But it's late and Bruce's gone home." Harry's voice was full of concern.

"Where we going?" interrupted Oliver, still dressed in his pirate clothes.

"Gallery," said Harry.

"I'm coming."

***

Oliver was first out of the car, eager to keep practising his pirate moves.

"Oliver! Give it a rest," Kate shouted, but her words fell on deaf ears.

Harry didn't join Oliver, preferring to follow his mother into the gallery. He switched on the gallery lights and unlocked the glass front doors while his mother went to the counter and opened the gallery diary.

"Why don't you go into the bookshop, Harry? You'll be bored standing around here."

"It's okay—I'll wait for you."

The phone rang. Kate momentarily stared at it in disbelief. Harry walked over to the counter, eager for her to answer. Deep down he was hoping it was his dad.

"Kate Carmichael." There was a degree of nervousness in her voice as she picked up.

"This is Jason. You don't know me. I look after Jasper's properties. Well, one in particular. He seemed very keen for me to look after this." He paused, waiting for a response, but none came. "I've been trying to get hold of Jasper, but his phone is switched off."

"Yes," said Kate.

"It's about his property in Wellsbury."

What property in Wellsbury?

"Jasper helped the lady. He bought the house so she could move back to London."

"You mean Milly."

A sigh of relief echoed into Kate's ear. "I'm so pleased you know about it."

"Beth James bought the house."

"Yes. That's right."

"Is there a problem?" Kate asked.

"Well, yes! Jasper asked me to collect all the paperwork together, and I can't find it."

Kate's mind was putting two and two together. Jasper had bought Beth a house, and he didn't want Kate to find out.

"Jasper's not here, but I'll certainly tell him."

"I'll leave it with you then."

"Yes, that's fine."

Kate put the phone back in its cradle.

"Who was that?" asked Harry.

"There's a problem with one of your dad's properties."

"So?"

"It's complicated."

Their heads snapped up at a commotion at the front of the gallery.

"Where the fuck is he?" bellowed Joanne as she pushed open the front door.

A sly-looking Beth slipped in behind Joanne and stood at her shoulder.

Scared, Harry joined his mother behind the counter.

"That's right, run to Mummy," snipped Beth. "Mummy's little boy. Well, she isn't going to help you this time."

The atmosphere thickened.

"He's not answering his fucking phone," Beth said in a belligerent tone. Her footsteps echoed on the gallery's marble floor as she moved from Joanne and stepped towards the counter.

"What're you doing here?" yelled Oliver, walking into the gallery from the rear entrance. He lifted his cutlass as if to hit Beth with it.

Joanne and Beth burst into fits of uncontrollable laughter.

"What're you going to do, squirt?" said Joanne between bursts of laughter.

"I'll show you!" yelled Oliver, lifting the cutlass.

Kate moved from behind the counter to stand between Oliver and Beth. A worried expression covered Harry's face as he noticed that his mother's features had stiffened into an angry scowl.

"Get the fuck out!" she yelled in a voice that no one recognised.

Both Harry and Oliver froze in surprise as they watched their mother aggressively grab first Joanne's arm then Beth's. She pulled them towards the glass doors.

It took Joanne and Beth several seconds to react to Kate's uncharacteristic aggression, sparked by this threat to her family. They pushed on the closed doors, trying to unbalance Kate so she would loosen her grip.

All three women were taken aback to see a tall, casually dressed man standing the other side of the glass door. He slowly inched the door open and moved inside. His steely eyes moved between them before settling on Kate.

"I was wondering if I could be of assistance," he said in a calm, firm voice.

Beth and Joanne stamped their feet and shrugged Kate's hands away. They both momentarily glared hatefully at her before storming out of the gallery.

"See you in court, bitch!" shouted Beth.

An eerie stillness drifted through the gallery as Kate struggled to regain her composure.

"Thank you. We're fine." Kate's voice was barely above a whisper.

The stranger looked at Harry and Oliver, who had joined their mother, standing either side of her. An uneasy silence lingered.

"This is my first visit," he said smoothly. "Is it alright if I stroll around?"

"Please do," Kate hesitantly said.

The stranger stood perfectly still, pretending to study a painting while he watched Kate's reflection in the glass doors. She had stooped down to comfort her sons.

"We're too small now. But if she had touched you…" Harry's voice quivered. Suddenly, he flung his arms around Kate's neck. "If anything happens to you, he'd sent us back to that awful place and her." Harry sobbed on Kate's shoulder.

Oliver placed his hand on Harry's shoulder and, in his mature tone, said. "I'll look after you, Harry."

Kate held her arm out so Oliver could join Harry.

"Listen to me. Nothing is going to happen to me or the pair of you… Now let's dry those tears. I'll close the gallery, and we'll go and have ice cream."

Kate could have sworn a relieved smile crossed the stranger's lips at that, as if his attention wasn't truly on the painting he was standing before.

"Chocolate?" asked Oliver, giving Harry a sly grin.

"What else for my knights?" Kate said, planting kisses on their heads.

"You should phone Dad," said Harry, wiping his watery eyes.

"Joanne was right—he's not answering." At that moment, Kate noticed the stranger intently watching. "I'm sorry. We're having a… er…"

"A family moment," the stranger interjected. "Can I help you with anything?"

"It's kind of you to offer, but we're fine."

Kate nodded and smiled, her business smile.

She walked over to the counter and handed him a business card. He smiled. Written in an Old English script was '*Kate Carmichael Gallery and Bookshop*'.

"We sell new and old books, plus paintings," she said.

The stranger was staring at the card.

"May I call you Kate?"

Kate smiled, but this time the smile was friendly and reached her eyes.

"Of course! And what do I call you?"

"John. Just John."

He moved towards the door with a satisfied grin on his face.

***

Jasper's first thought when the gallery security app pinged on his iPhone was that it must be a break in. He was surprised to see Kate and Harry walk into the gallery on the video feed.

What the fuck? he thought.

He cursed when Beth and Joanne came into view.

His temper flared when Kate moved between Oliver and Beth.

He stood and gasped when Kate grabbed Beth's and Joanne's arms and marched them towards the door.

His stomach churned when his investigator, John, appeared.

Jasper kicked a small wastepaper bin as he realised John intended to take Kate from him.

He cursed when Kate's smile reached her eyes.

John was making a play for his wife, and she'd liked it.

Jasper hurriedly packed his bags; plans would have to wait. He couldn't allow John to wheedle his way into Kate's life.

Chapter Eleven

It was the early hours when Jasper crept through the kitchen door of Isaacs' House. He turned on the coffeemaker before he settled into his office.

He couldn't bear to see Kate after the smile she had given John. Nursing his coffee, he slumped in his desk chair.

He'd seen her smile that way at Bruce and he was her bodyguard—but in Jasper's opinion, Bruce wasn't her type. But she would be attracted to John, with his gentlemanly ways.

Jasper took Kate for granted. She was always in the background supporting him. She didn't like being the centre of attention. Only the people close to him knew how much he relied on her.

He had promised to take her to dinner, to the cinema or theatre. But he hadn't. Part of their arrangement had been that she would accompany him on Lord Carmichael socials, but he had preferred the likes of Joanne for that.

Joanne who, with the help of Beth, had persuaded him to introduce her to his Lord Carmichael friends so she could expand her escort business.

Jasper wondered if Kate knew.

A gentle knock on his office door broke his concentration.

"Come in," he growled, thinking it was Malcolm. Kate wouldn't knock.

Harry and Oliver took a step into the office. Jasper was taken totally by surprise, so much so he spilled his coffee onto his desk. He stared at his sons.

If he didn't know better, he would take Oliver as his elder son. He stood confidently, holding Jasper's gaze, whereas Harry stared at the carpet. Where had that precocious boy gone? Harry looked ill.

"Boys!" Jasper said in a forced calm voice.

Oliver pulled on Harry's arm. "Tell 'im," he whispered.

Harry lifted his eyes to meet Jasper's. His eyes filled, then his shoulders slumped and his chin rested on his chest.

"Why don't you start at the beginning?" said Jasper, voice still calm and soft, as he walked towards the white couches arranged around the coffee table.

"Tell 'im," Oliver impatiently repeated. "It's man's talk."

"Come. Sit." Jasper gestured towards the couches.

"We'll stand," Oliver answered, taking the lead.

Jasper was becoming increasingly concerned and wished Kate was there. She would instinctively know what to do.

He didn't know that Kate had been standing in her dark studio, just staring into space, until she'd heard his light footsteps. Her ears had pricked when whispers from the stairs had drifted towards the studio. She was curious; she'd followed the whispers to Jasper's office and stood listening behind the slightly open door.

"It's that woman," said Oliver, tugging on Harry's sleeve.

"What woman?" said Jasper, who was racking his brains as to who they might be referring to.

"Are you 'aving sex with 'er?"

Jasper was taken aback; he hadn't expected Oliver to blurt anything about sex. He was becoming increasingly concerned with Oliver talking about sex. *He's too young for such words.* Jasper made a mental note to talk to Kate.

"I'm not following you, Oliver."

The two boys looked at one another, unsure what to do.

"Harry won't talk about it."

"Harry," said Jasper. "We have always had man's talk."

Harry nodded, and Oliver tugged on Harry's shirt sleeve.

"You have to promise not to tell Mum," uttered Harry. "Promise."

"I promise." Jasper knelt in front of the boys. "Now tell me." He made eye contact with Harry, brushing his hair aside.

"She started when you were away. It got worse when both of them were there."

"Who are you talking about?" Jasper said, worried.

"Joanne and Beth," blurted Oliver. "Said stuff about you and Mum. Show 'im." He tugged on Harry's sleeve.

Harry's hand hesitantly moved between his legs.

"It was the same as that nasty man."

"Nasty man?" Jasper said. "What nasty man?"

Kate covered her mouth as visions of Matt Wilson flashed into her mind. For a brief moment, she was back in the penthouse trying to shield Harry from Matt. He had broken into the penthouse, along with his brother Charlie, intending to rape her as revenge for the death of their brother, Max. They blamed Jasper for Max's death.

"Let Harry go back to his room."

"No chance. The Carmichael bastard is going to watch," snarled Matt, grinning and stroking his crotch in such a manner that his intentions were obvious.

Harry had never mentioned that evening. Even when Kate had tried to talk about it, he acted as if he didn't remember. And all this time, the memory of Matt Wilson had festered in his subconscious. Her heart cracked. Poor Harry.

Harry's loud sobs brought her back to the present.

"They broke into the penthouse and you saved us," blurted Harry.

"Kids at school bullied him. But I soon stopped that," said Oliver, proudly sticking his chest out and talking in an adult manner.

Jasper vaguely remembered the boys being suspended from the private school for fighting. Joanne had bent his ear complaining that Kate hadn't been strict enough and the lads were out of control.

"It's started here," continued Oliver.

Jasper was becoming confused. What were the boys talking about?

"Let's start at the beginning," he said, concerned. "Who touched you, Harry?"

"Joanne," Oliver piped up.

"While we were at the castle?" Jasper asked.

"She didn't touch me. Just moved her hand. Like that nasty man."

Nasty man again, thought Jasper.

"They were at the school, and the next day the kids got on to me," murmured Harry.

"Joanne and Beth?"

Harry nodded.

"I soon sorted 'em tho," interrupted Oliver.

"Expelled..." said Jasper thoughtfully.

"Suspended," said Harry. "She laughed in my face. Said you wanted her." Tears were now uncontrollably trickling down his face.

Jasper's temper was rising.

"She was lying. Right? Cos you love Mum. Right?" said Oliver.

Jasper reddened. Now was not the time to discuss adult behaviour.

"She said you were wanted by the police for murder," continued Harry, as if he hadn't heard Oliver. "She said if I told you, she would send a man after me."

Kate had heard enough. She burst into the office. As soon as the boys saw her, they ran into her open arms.

"You still love us. Right?" asked Oliver.

"Of course I do," she said between planting kisses in their hair. "That will never change."

"Dad loves you. Do you love 'im?"

"I'll never stop loving you, Oliver." Kate stroked his dark hair. She lifted her head and caught Jasper's stare. "And I'll always love your father."

Jasper mouthed 'I love you', and Kate nodded and smiled.

Chapter Twelve

Jasper stayed in his office all day trying to concentrate on work, only nipping out for a shower and change of clothes when Kate was in the kitchen with the boys. He was on tenterhooks waiting to talk to Kate. They had to clear the air before this minor spat turned into a major problem.

It was dark when she pushed open his office door. Her hair was wet and she wore a silk nightie and matching robe.

Kate took Jasper's breath away.

She is really aging well. Joanne and Beth don't hold a candle to her. And she's sexy as hell.

She slumped into the chair across his desk and crossed her legs. The robe fell open, revealing the curves of her body.

Jasper thought, *She's teasing*, but her stern expression told him otherwise.

"I didn't know you owned property in Wellsbury," she said curtly.

Jasper hadn't expected that. He'd thought the conversation would be centred on the boys.

"Don't give me that surprised look. Jason phoned. Paperwork had disappeared. I pretended I knew all about it." Kate's voice rose when she emphasised 'disappeared'.

Jasper reddened. He hadn't told Kate about asking Jason to look into Beth moving into Don's old house. He had to be careful what he said. He didn't know how much Kate knew about him owning the house.

"Milly wanted a quick sale. She came to me for help." His words were rushed.

"So you bought the house."

"It was to help Milly. I didn't know Beth had moved in. You told me, remember?"

"Where's the paperwork, Jasper?"

Jasper reddened.

"I'm guessing that Jason collected all the documents. And you made them disappear."

Jasper remained silent and waited for Kate to finish.

"You own Don's old house, and Beth lives there scot free."

The tension between the two flared.

"And now!" She took a deep breath. "Joanne and Beth made lewd gestures to Harry."

"I had no idea about that."

"No! You were too busy fucking her!"

"Kate! Stop this! I didn't fuck Joanne. You have to believe me."

***

Two worried boys had tiptoed to their dad's office and pushed the door slightly open. They looked at one another when Kate said, 'fucking her'. Both were fighting back tears. Both had heard stories from their school friends about the argument parents had before they divorced. It was always about fucking.

***

"I'll deal with it," Jasper mumbled into his laptop.

"No! You won't! I'll deal with it."

"Don't defy me over this, Kate!"

Their eyes briefly met. Kate stood and walked to the French doors, gazing out into the night sky.

"You expect me to stand by while my sons are subjected to disgusting sexual behaviour." She briefly paused to gather her words. "They're children, for Christ's sake. And that woman—that woman!—made comments and gestures to Harry." She gulped, trying to hide her anger. "They stormed into the gallery with…" She paused again, trying to control her temper. "At the very least, humiliating intentions. And you! Calmly sit there and expect me to do nothing!"

"Don't push me, Kate! I'm as concerned about Joanne's behaviour as you are."

A heavy, angry tension drifted through the office as they both stared at one another.

"I'm not sitting by, Jasper."

"Don't fight me! You know I'll win… I fight dirty."

"I have money this time. Even if it takes every penny, I'll fight until the bitter end."

Jasper had forgotten about Grandfather Meredith's fortune, which Meredith's sons were contesting. His angry expression morphed as he realised she was going to fight back.

"You won the case?" he said in disbelief.

"There was no case to fight. Meredith's sons hadn't a leg to stand on. It was airtight; Meredith made sure of that. He was a far better lawyer that his two sons put together."

Jasper stood and walked towards his drinks table and poured a very generous malt.

Kate watched every flicker in his emotions: the lip quiver, his tight grip on the decanter, furrows on his brow.

Jasper's nervous, she thought. *He's frightened that he might lose.*

"If Meredith was alive, he would run rings around your hot-shot lawyer," she snipped, pushing her advantage.

Jasper moved away from his drinks table.

"I think we should both calm down and take a deep breath." He paused to sip his malt. "And look at this problem calmly and logically."

Kate didn't answer but continued to stare at him.

"You're angry. Rightly so. I should have told you about Beth and the house." He hesitated, staring at Kate's stern face and her fiery green eyes.

"The solution is easy. Ask yourself what you want," Kate snapped.

Jasper raised his eyebrows.

Kate was surprised to see a puzzled expression cross his face.

"I thought you knew what I want? She stands before me." He drained his glass and slowly placed it upon his desk. His features relaxed with a half-smile.

Kate's eyes never left him; her stomach flipped.

"I'm not Colin or my powerful grandfather. I'm me. Jasper Carmichael, my own man."

"I disagree. You're not your own man. All the Carmichael traits are surfacing. You want power… Power is just a diamond away. Beth and Joanne can see it. And Beth wants to be part of it."

"That's not true!"

But he knew it was. He wanted the power that belonged to Lord Carmichael, he longed to be head of a worldwide diamond syndicate, and he wanted Kate. She was his rock, she calmed his demons, she was very loyal, and as such, he had relied on her to run his business while he was away. Kate didn't realise the power she held; she knew the ins and outs of his business. Somehow, he would have to make her reliant on him. Her weakness was sex.

He smiled and moved towards her. His intention was obvious.

Her eyes flared and her cheeks reddened.

Oh, Kate! he thought. *You have no idea what awaits you.*

"Explain the house," she snapped, trying to concentrate.

"Nigel's house was unsuitable for her and her baby." He hoped that was the right answer.

"Is that what she told you? Lies! She wanted a big house to run her business from. Open your eyes, Jasper!"

"She needed more space for the baby."

"Where're you living?! Michelle looks after Beth's baby."

Jasper wanted another large malt, but he needed his wits about him. Kate was getting the upper hand.

"I know about their account with NRJ."

Kate's change of tact derailed Jasper's intentions. Their eyes met.

"I have nothing to do with NRJ," he lied. "How do you know these things?"

"Not important."

Somehow, Kate had managed to move past Jasper. She had to leave before they both said things that they didn't mean or she gave in to his seduction.

"What about that man?" Jasper yelled.

Kate stopped and stared at him.

"What man?"

"The one you smiled at in the gallery."

"I smile at a lot of men."

"Not like that you don't."

Kate's complexion turned a lovely beetroot colour as visions of John flashed across her mind.

Chapter Thirteen

Jasper's heavy footsteps echoed through the house. Doors banged.

"Kate!" he shouted.

Clare, Malcolm, Harry and Oliver silently waited for him to burst into the kitchen.

"Where's Kate!?" His eyes speared Clare and then Malcolm, but they didn't reply.

"It's your fault," sobbed Harry.

Reluctantly, Jasper turned and looked at his sons. He was shocked to see them red eyed, tears running down their faces.

"She's gone," Harry whimpered.

"What does he mean, gone?" Jasper impatiently looked to Clare and Malcolm, ignoring his sons.

"She left before dawn," Malcolm said bitterly.

"I don't understand," said Jasper, running his hand through his hair.

"She said she needed to be alone. Needed to think," answered Clare, fighting back tears.

"You made her go… And now she doesn't want us," cried Harry, putting his arm around Oliver.

Clare moved to the boys, wrapping her arms around them.

Jasper gripped the work surface and leaned onto a breakfast stool. "Think!" he repeated. "Alone."

Jasper's mind was whirling. What was she thinking about? *Divorce!* sprang to the forefront of his thoughts. He should have followed her to bed, but he'd preferred malt. His foggy brain tried to recall their argument. She'd been incensed with how Joanne and Beth had behaved towards Harry. She knew about Don's old house. He wondered if she knew about him preferring Joanne's and Beth's company to hers during his trips to London.

Jasper started to pace, running his hand through his hair. His mind was working overtime. How much did Clare and Malcolm know? Had Kate confided in Bruce?

An uncomfortable tension descended, the only sound being sobs from his sons.

Oliver looked up into Clare's eyes. "Does she still love us?" he gulped. "I'll tell her everythin'."

"She'll never stop loving you."

The heavy silence was broken by the familiar sound of Kate's aging Evoque pulling up outside. The boys lifted their heads, jumped from their stools and raced out of the kitchen. Kate was walking towards them, smiling, and the boys ran into her arms. She knelt and rubbed her thumbs over their puffy cheeks.

"Thought you'd left us," Harry sobbed into her shoulder.

She squeezed Oliver's waist and kissed his hair while her watery eyes met Harry's. "Never," she mouthed, giving him a smile.

"I'll tell you everythin'," cried Oliver. "Only don't leave us."

Tell me everything? Kate wondered what Oliver meant, but her eyes suddenly settled on a dishevelled Jasper, his blue eyes a mixture of concern and relief. He offered her a half smile but she didn't respond.

Last night, she had left Jasper refilling his glass with a more-than-generous portion of malt. This morning the decanter was empty beside him as he slept.

The boys pushed past Jasper and leapt onto their stools, giving Clare beaming smiles.

"Glad you're back," said Malcolm, closing the door behind Kate, while Clare busied herself making breakfast.

Kate flicked on the kettle, beginning the morning tea ritual. She scanned the kitchen, looking for Jasper, but he'd left.

The boys couldn't contain their smiles as they eagerly tucked into their favourite Coco Pops.

"He's beside himself," said Clare in an uncaring manner. "Thought you'd left him. But I knew you wouldn't leave the boys."

Kate didn't answer, just smiled as she waited for her tea to finish brewing.

"Here!" said Clare, handing Kate a tray. "I'll bring the teacakes in when they're done."

Jasper was sitting at his desk with his head in his hands. Kate placed the tray on the central coffee table and poured a coffee for Jasper and a tea for her.

"Why didn't you wake me?" he said. "I'd have come with you. It's dangerous for you to be out alone."

Kate walked to the French doors, holding the piping tea between her hands.

"You were asleep. The malt decanter was empty. Anyway, I needed to be alone and think things through."

An uncomfortable silence settled between them while Jasper sipped his coffee, waiting for Kate to say something.

"Tell me—what happened at the castle?"

Jasper's eyes widened; he hadn't expected that. "With who?"

"I'm missing something. I now know how Joanne treated Harry."

"Kate! I swear I didn't know."

"I believe you. You were too busy being Lord Carmichael... But there's something else. What happened between you and Joanne?"

"Nothing!"

Kate raised her eyebrows.

"Joanne and Beth think they have rights... Rights with you. You know, those rights between two people who have had sex."

"I didn't fuck Joanne!"

"What about Beth? After all, I'm told she's good between the sheets." Kate's venomous tone surprised Jasper.

He hesitated as his mind flicked back to that drunken night when a naked Beth and Joanne had tried to seduce him. He didn't want to talk about how they'd flaunted their naked bodies over him. How they'd derided him when his dick remained soft. They had offered him cocaine, but the thought of his drug-ridden half-brother had flashed before him. And then they'd threatened to tell Kate if he didn't introduce Joanne to his Lord Carmichael friends.

"Your silence tells me everything I wanted to know."

Jasper jumped up and hurried towards her.

"Don't touch me!" she exclaimed.

"You have to listen to me... Then you can judge for yourself... There was a night. I was drunk. Beth and Joanne were there. They were high on drugs. Prancing around naked. Beth flaunting her large breasts that I'd paid to be enlarged." Jasper still begrudged paying for that.

"Were you naked?"

"Yes!"

Kate took a deep breath, trying to control the rage that was swirling deep inside her.

"For once, my dick wouldn't react... They laughed in my face. Called me names. And then Beth showed her evil side. Threatened to tell you... Joanne wanted to do just that—she wants to become Lady Carmichael... Beth wanted me to introduce Joanne to my new so-called friends. They wanted to expand the boutique and escort business. I swear, Kate, that's all."

"So you've not been financing her business."

"Not exactly. I set them up with an NRJ bank account. The London branch closed temporarily after the accounts were hacked." Jasper stared at Kate, waiting for her reply, but none came. "I stood guarantor. That's all."

"Who stood guarantor? Jasper Carmichael or Lord Carmichael?"

A perplexed Jasper was silent.

"What are you not telling me?!" Kate took a deep breath. "I know that they're bragging about having Carmichael Law at their beck and call." Jasper reddened. "The thing is, they have my husband at their beck and call."

A tense, awkward silence filled the room as Jasper began to pace, running his hand through his hair.

"Just tell me if you've fucked them, cos they're very cocky." She paused, recalling their attitude in the gallery. "Like they have the upper hand."

"I haven't fucked them." He stared at her pair of angry green eyes.

The silence deepened as Kate mulled over Jasper's words.

"What happened with Harry and Oliver?" Her angry voice broke the silence.

"You know most of it. Harry cried the moment he left you. Oliver, being younger, didn't really understand what was going on. Harry cried, didn't eat. He was bullied at school. That's when Oliver started to defend him."

"Oliver's a child."

"The kids taunted him about his cry-baby brother, and Oliver lashed out."

"And you did nothing!"

"I was with the Freemasons when the school rang."

"And that was more important than your sons?" Kate's anger was boiling over.

"Kate! I'm just not you… You have to understand, I was with men who have different values. Looking after children is women's work."

"So you sacrificed your sons to save face." Their eyes met. She was surprised to see tears waiting to fall from his puffy eyes. "Joanne called Harry 'Mummy's boy' and Oliver 'squirt'. I tried to stop her, but she just laughed in my face."

A tense, uncomfortable silence returned as their eyes locked. Jasper wanted to kiss her and bed her, but he read her body language. He'd have to wait.

"That day you collected them. I watched you chasing a giggling Oliver, and Harry skipping on the spot. I knew they needed you, and so did I… I've never stopped needing you, and neither have the boys."

Her mind was so full of guilt that she hadn't been there to protect her sons that she didn't notice Jasper move next to her. He stretched out his hand and cupped her cheek. Without thinking, she leaned into him.

"We belong together," he said in a calm, soft voice.

"What was in that envelope that the guard insisted I sign?"

Jasper's thoughts flicked back to the day Kate had arrived at the castle to collect the boys for a visit.

"Divorce papers."

Kate could hardly hear Jasper. She took a long moment to savour the comfort from his hand cupping her cheek.

"You want a divorce?" Kate hesitantly asked.

"No! That's why I snatched the envelope. It was Beth and Joanne's doing."

"I can't do with Joanne and Beth interfering," she said. "And I can't do with us fucking arguing."

Kate's guard momentarily dropped, and Jasper seized the moment. He pulled her into him so her head rested on his shoulder.

"I can't stand arguing with you. All I know is that I want to be with you… I love you, Kate, and that will never change… I learnt that the hard way."

"I was so angry when Joanne and Beth came into the gallery as if they owned the place. Demanding to know where you were, as if you were at their beck and call."

Jasper wasn't listening; he had Kate in his arms and that was what mattered. But there was something he had to know.

"What about that stranger you smiled at?"

"I've told you—I'd never seen him before. He sort of came to my rescue."

"But you smiled at him."

She pulled away so she could see Jasper's concerned features. "I sell paintings. I smile at a lot of people."

"Not like that."

"You're jealous because I smiled?"

"His name is John. He's my private investigator."

"What?!"

"He's been watching you for years… I think he may be a little in love with you. But that's out of character. He told me if I mistreated you, he would step in. And that's just what he did."

"And you think I'd leave you for him. Really, Jasper!"

She walked towards the coffee table and picked up the teapot.

"Kate, you've got to tell me. Were you attracted to him?!"

"I thought he had nice eyes. The sort of eyes you could trust... The sort of eyes that you would accept a dinner date with." Kate's voice had taken on a lighter tone. But Jasper didn't notice. He loudly cursed.

"However, he didn't ask me to dinner, and if he had, I wouldn't have accepted. I don't know him. I've only been spontaneous with a man once. And look where that got me." She planted a kiss on his cheek and walked towards the door, carrying the teapot.

A puzzled look replaced Jasper's worried features.

She opened the office door carefully, gripping the teapot in her hand.

"Think about it, Jasper!" She turned, giving him a wicked grin.

Chapter Fourteen

A familiar jingle disturbed Kate's sleep. She opened her eyes as her hand reached for her phone.

"Yes," she murmured sleepily.

"Kate! Security here. The bookshop alarm has gone off. We need to get inside."

"What?"

Security? Bookshop? Her sleepy brain was confused.

"There's been a break in." The security guard raised his voice.

"Phone the police," she said as the sleepy fog started to clear.

"On the way. But we need to get into the shop."

Before she could answer, the guard hung up.

She staggered into the bathroom and splashed cold water on her face.

She looked for Jasper, but he wasn't in bed. Her mind flashed back to their argument. They hadn't made up like they normally did. She had spent time with the boys; they needed her. And Jasper had stayed in his office, working.

She found him sprawled on the office couch with an empty decanter on the carpet.

She didn't see two pairs of eyes watch her lift the Evoque keys off the key rack.

The cool night air was a shock to the system, but it cleared her head.

She cursed when her Evoque was blocked in by Jasper's Range Rover. She returned to the kitchen, swapped keys, and then went back to the Range Rover.

***

Jasper woke with a start. His neck ached, his head throbbed, he felt sick and his mouth felt like sandpaper. He eased himself up, accidentally kicking over an empty decanter. He cursed. These arguments with Kate were taking their toll. He stumbled out of his office, in need of the bathroom.

Moments later, he opened the kitchen door. Whispers floated towards him. The light from the large American-style fridge shone on Harry and Oliver. Two shocked faces glared at Jasper. Bottles of water were arranged on the work surface, along with bread, cheese and ham.

For a long moment, no one spoke. The boys had been caught preparing for a getaway, and Jasper was utterly embarrassed that he had been caught with the mother of all hangovers.

He strolled to the Belfast sink, turned on the cold tap and plunged his head beneath the running water.

Harry appeared at his side and handed him a towel. "She's gone. It's all your fault," he said in a resentful manner.

"Who's gone?"

"Mum! Of course!" Harry followed Jasper to the coffeemaker. "We're not going back to that place, or her."

Jasper's stomach violently somersaulted. He was unsure if it was the effects of the hangover or that Kate had gone for a second time. *What the fuck is happening?*

He daren't make eye contact with either Harry or Oliver; he was too frightened they would see fear in his eyes. So he pretended that he wasn't listening, preferring to concentrate on making coffee.

"You're not listening!" yelled Harry.

Oliver raced to his brother's side and gripped his hand.

"Come on. We don't need food."

"Where's she gone?" asked Jasper, sipping a very hot cup of coffee.

"She left about an hour ago. Woke us up." Malcolm's rough morning voice made Jasper jump. His head began to spin, and he momentarily lost his balance.

"You're a mess!" declared Clare, picking up the boys' rucksacks so Jasper could see that they were serious about running away.

Jasper took a moment, letting her harsh words sink in. He *was* a mess. He had the mother of all hangovers, he needed a shower, a change of clothes—but above all, Kate.

Jasper poured a second cup of coffee and dropped two slices of bread in the toaster.

"Is that your answer? Coffee and toast?" yelled Clare, putting a jug of milk in the microwave. "Don't you care?! Kate's not here, and the boys are leaving."

"He's not fit for anything," said Malcolm, turning his attention to the kettle and teapot.

"Will she come back?" asked a worried Oliver, staring at Clare.

At that moment, headlights lit the back of the house.

To everyone's surprise, Jasper burst out of the kitchen at a speed any sprinter would be proud of. Kate hadn't switched off the engine before he'd wrenched open the driver's door of his Range Rover and pulled her into his arms.

Harry climbed onto the Belfast sink and Oliver pushed beside him.

"Wow!" They both grinned, their mouths wide open.

"That's some kiss," mumbled Harry.

"Does that mean we're not leaving?" asked a confused Oliver.

Outside, Kate struggled in Jasper's grip. "Jasper, too tight," she said.

"I thought you'd left me," he stuttered, releasing her. "Where have you been?"

"The shopping centre. Security rang. Someone tried to break into the bookshop."

"What? And you went alone!"

She was taken aback. She couldn't believe he had just said that.

"Who could I take with me? Not you."

Kate's words didn't register with Jasper.

"The boys have packed a bag and were preparing to leave."

"What?!"

"I suspect they think we're divorcing."

"Why should they think that?"

"I think two days of arguing may have something to do with it."

"I must go to them. Reassure them."

She moved towards the kitchen, but he caught her arm. "Before I lose you to the boys…"

He didn't finish. Kate consumed his mouth.

"No need to be jealous," she muttered.

"Of course I'm jealous. You spend so much time with them. And now there's John."

"How can you be jealous of John? All I did was smile. Did I do this?" Her mouth covered his and their tongues danced. A sigh escaped from deep inside Jasper.

"Or this?" Her lips trailed soft kisses along his neck while her hand slipped under his crumbled shirt.

"You'd better not," mumbled Jasper as he pinned her against the car, deepening their kiss.

Several kisses later, they walked into the kitchen. Harry and Oliver ran to Kate while Jasper turned his attention to Malcolm.

"She had a call. Someone broke into the bookshop," he said, accepting a fresh coffee from Clare.

"And?" asked Malcolm.

"That's as far as I got... Kate!" shouted Jasper. She looked at him, smiling. "Was security at the bookshop?"

She kissed the boys' hair before joining Jasper and Malcolm.

"That's what I can't understand. The place was in darkness. No sign of a break in, or security."

Jasper and Malcolm exchanged worried glances.

"Where did you park?" asked Malcolm. He was well aware Kate was a stickler for parking at the back of the shop.

"I didn't. I drove through the centre and stopped outside the shop."

"Bear with me," asked Jasper. "Why did you take my car?"

Kate gave him a 'that's a stupid question' look.

"You'd blocked me in."

"Did you get out of the car?"

"No."

"Why?"

"No point. The alarm hadn't been activated. I drove right up to the shop."

"Did you see anyone?"

"No!"

"I'm curious why you drove through the centre rather than park round the back."

"I thought the bookshop had been broken into. Quickest way is through the centre and not the back of the shop."

"Toast!" shouted Clare.

Kate returned to the boys, who grinned at each other while they tucked into lightly browned, soft toast.

Chapter Fifteen

Kate was thankful for the peace and quiet of her studio, even if the boys had joined her. In moments of quiet, Jasper filled her thoughts. He wouldn't talk about the diamonds in the desk. He was hiding something.

Clare tiptoed into the still studio. She didn't want to disturb them, particularly Kate who was deep in thought, staring at one of her beach paintings. Harry was sketching Kate, and Oliver had more paint on him than on the paper.

Clare coughed. Kate looked up, and Harry and Oliver gave her the 'how dare you disturb us' glare.

"Michelle's here," Clare said in a low voice. "She'd like a word."

It took a long moment for Clare's words to register with Kate.

Michelle. This is unusual.

Michelle had been Kate's best friend at school. She had fallen love with Nigel, and even though she had married Dan, Nigel had fathered her boys.

What does she want?

***

Jasper stood at the French windows of his office and watched Michelle walk into Kate's studio.

"She wants a word," said Harry, standing in the doorway to Jasper's office.

"We can 'ave biscuits," added a grinning Oliver.

Jasper followed the boys into the kitchen. Clare was waiting for him. "Before you ask, I don't know. Appeared at the gate asking to see Kate."

After a long, awkward moment, Clare continued, "It might be something to do with her leaving."

Jasper raised his eyebrows in disbelief.

Harry took Jasper's hand and silently led him to the place where the boys would secretly listen to the goings-on in Kate's studio. Harry put his finger over his mouth and left Jasper listening.

***

"I was surprised you agreed to see me," said Michelle.

"Why wouldn't I?" Kate replied, somewhat surprised.

"I often think back to that happy time. You know, when we thought we were invincible." Michelle looked at a bewildered Kate. "You know, the last year at school. You had got into uni. And I lost my virginity to Nigel."

Where's this going? thought Kate.

"I only ever wanted Nigel. You could never imagine the depth of our passion."

Oh yes I can.

"He wouldn't marry me, you know. Even when he got me pregnant. I tricked Dan into marrying me. Silly, gullible Dan, who has suddenly grown some balls." Michelle paused, walking to the bi-fold doors to stare into the garden. "He's refused to let me have Beth's little girl. Beth doesn't know who's the father. My money was on Jasper, but apparently he hasn't touched Beth for years." Michelle turned to face Kate. "She hates your guts. Blames you for taking Jasper away from her."

"She did that herself," Kate interjected.

"Beth thinks she can win him back. But any fool can see Jasper's in love with you. He has eyes for no one else. Things may have been different if I'd let Nigel go after you. He wanted his hands on the shop money… But I was jealous. Why should you wear my Nigel's ring and sleep in his bed? Nigel was mine." Michelle's voice had become a little bitter.

An uncomfortable silence developed between the once-best friends.

"Look at you now!" Michelle continued, trying to control her jealous anger. "Married to rich Carmichael, inherited Meredith Spencer's fortune, two intelligent boys, living in the Isaacs' old house. Who'd have thought it? Boring, virginal Kate." Michelle paused again to gather her thoughts. "You were always different. Even at school, you were different. Nigel and I used to talk about you and how different you were. You're nothing like that evil bastard Reynolds—more like your mother, a Spencer." Michelle's bitter tone lingered on 'Spencer'.

Kate didn't know how to handle Michelle. There was every possibility that if she said the wrong thing, Michelle would flip into an uncontrollable angry tirade. Or she might collapse in a chair in a fit of tears.

"I'm leaving," Michelle blurted. "Dan's already taken the boys to their London school. I'm closing the house and joining them."

"I'm sorry," Kate said in a low voice.

"I didn't come here for your sympathy but to tell you Beth's after revenge. She wants everything you have: Jasper, the boys, this house—even Meredith's money if she can persuade the lawyers. She's tried twice." Michelle stared at Kate, who was having difficulty processing her words. "Don't look so surprised. Beth and Joanne followed you to the gallery when you were alone with the boys, and then the other night they lured you to the bookshop on the pretence of a burglary. Beth never expected you to drive up to the front of the bookshop in Jasper's Range Rover. She won't make the same mistake twice." Michelle smirked as Kate slumped onto the wooden chair. "She's behind the boys' suspension from school and Harry's bullying. Oliver's in her sights. She recognises the wild young Jasper in him," she added, relishing in Kate's discomfort.

"He's a child," said Kate.

"Makes no difference to Beth if they both go the same way as Uncle Richard and my poor Nigel."

Michelle paused and stared at Kate, waiting for her to make some comment. But none came. Kate was in shock; she couldn't believe what she had just heard. Beth had betrayed Jasper—what did she expect? Jasper had moved on and found his true self along the way, not the one controlled by his past. And now Beth had the boys in her sights.

"You don't understand, do you?" Michelle asked.

"No!"

"Not everyone is like you, Kate."

"I know that."

"In the end you'll have to fight for what you love. I guess that's Jasper and the boys."

Kate nodded.

"I tried to fight for Nigel, but she'd got her evil hooks into him. First step was tapes of him in a comprising situation. In Nigel's case he was fucking Joanne, although he couldn't remember it. I suspect he was drugged. She threatened blackmail but Nigel stood his ground. But it was too late; he was hooked on drugs. She tried it on with Dan, but he's in love with two men. One in London and another in Wellsbury. He'll have to choose one day."

Kate's eyes widened.

"You're such an innocent, Kate. Why do you think he stayed in London?"

"He didn't mind you and Nigel?"

"Of course he did. He went in search of love and loyalty and found men."

Another uncomfortable silence developed.

"I came to say goodbye for old time's sake and that deep friendship we once had. You never grassed on me and Nigel. So I owe you."

Michelle waited for Kate to say something but Kate remained silent.

"Beth's trying to get her hooks into Jasper. She already has Watts, and the St Martin's headteacher. Even Willis. But Jasper's the one she wants."

Michelle had inadvertently piqued Kate's curiosity. "Where does Willis fit into this?" she hesitantly asked.

Michelle's look said it all: she had said too much. "You mean that little weasel that follows Watts about? Don't know anything about him. Don't trust him though. Why the interest?"

"No particular interest," Kate lied. "I thought he may have replaced Lockwood."

"Who said he's replaced Lockwood? Take some advice: keep away from him. He has his own agenda." After a long, thoughtful moment, Michelle added, "Lockwood was transferred."

Kate was sure Michelle knew more but wasn't going to tell.

"Oh!" said Kate. "But tell me, what's happening to Beth's daughter?"

"Gone! Been put up for adoption."

Kate was speechless. How could a mother just simply give her daughter away?

"You don't get it. Beth's not the mothering type. A child would get in her way."

"Why didn't she have an abortion?"

"My opinion—and it's only my opinion, mind—she had plans to blackmail Jasper into having her back, but first he'd 'ave to sleep with her. He'd already won custody of the boys, so he could do it again." Michelle stared at Kate's shocked expression and shook her head. "You've no idea, 'ave you? She thinks Jasper is hers. She compares every man to him. She'll go to any length to get him back."

Kate went deadly white as the implications of Michelle's words were sinking in.

"Look, I've got to go. I've stayed longer than I was going to and probably said far too much."

"You're welcome to eat with us in the kitchen," Kate automatically offered.

"No thanks! I only came to say goodbye, for old time's sake."

Kate stood and gave Michelle a hug.

"For old time's sake," she whispered.

Chapter Sixteen

Kate found the boys in the kitchen. She put her arms around them and whispered, "I need to go out."

"You coming back?" asked a concerned Oliver.

"I'll tell you everything. Promise."

"Mummy needs to think and clear her head."

"It's Michelle," said Harry, looking at Kate.

"Sort of. I just need to get a few things straight in my head."

She kissed each boy's head in turn and left.

At the sound of Kate's Evoque starting up, Jasper ran into the kitchen.

"What's happened?" he shouted.

"She's coming back," said Harry. "It's Michelle."

"Mum needs to sort her head out," said Oliver.

"I'll follow her," said Malcolm.

"No need. She'll be by the river. I know where."

The boys looked at one another and smiled, relieved that Jasper was going after Kate.

***

Kate had stopped at her favourite thinking spot, the confluence of the Wells and Bury. She sat on her thinking bench, trying to understand the week's events.

The confrontation with Joanne and Beth in the gallery, meeting Jasper's private investigator, two arguments with Jasper, the fake bookshop break in, Harry and Oliver planning to run away, Oliver promising to tell her everything—whatever *'everything'* was—and Michelle leaving.

She stared at the constant flow of the two rivers as they greeted one another, like two old friends.

Her mind drifted to her meeting with Michelle. She couldn't decide if she liked the Michelle she'd met today. There was a degree of bitterness in Michelle that perturbed Kate.

Kate tried to make excuses for it. Michelle's life was in turmoil; she had lost the love of her life, Nigel; Dan was forcing her to go and live in London; he wouldn't let her adopt Beth's baby—but Michelle hadn't been able to hide that there was some malicious intent behind her visit. Kate didn't dwell on the motives that were driving her school best friend, but on the deep hatred Beth had for her. Kate had married the love of Beth's life, had his children and was living the life Beth thought was hers.

A cold shiver suddenly trailed down Kate's spine, and the hairs on the back of her neck quivered.

"You shouldn't be on your own," a menacing voice whispered. "There're people that wish you harm. But I'm not one. You have Meredith to thank for that."

She turned just as Willis moved closer.

"Anyone can see you're a Spencer."

The contents of Kate's stomach rose into her throat as fear stirred.

"I didn't agree with Meredith leaving you his fortune, though. But I shouldn't be envious. I've had my share over the years."

"What do you want?" Kate asked, forcing her voice to stay calm.

Willis walked in front of Kate, his back facing her. She watched his body stiffen as he fought to control his emotions. He hated her.

"I thought Jasper would be like Colin, but he's not. You've done a good job. But he's still a Carmichael."

"What do you want?" Kate snapped, trying to regain some of her confidence.

"What do you know about diamonds?"

"Nothing!"

"How about Jasper?"

"Colin was the diamond man."

"Diamonds run through Carmichael veins. I suspect Jasper's no different. Even your son is drawn to them."

"What do you mean?"

"He goes and helps Zak."

"So?"

"Like I said, diamonds are in Carmichael DNA."

A tense silence drifted between them.

"He's in love with you. I say *in love* not *loves you*. There's a difference."

"I'll ask again. What do you want?"

"I wanted to meet you, Kate. Michelle said you were different. I believe she's right."

"What do you mean, different?"

"Your Spencer DNA shows. Meredith told me you were like his Laura. Kind, thoughtful, gentle. You have qualities that Beth and Joanne are jealous of."

"You should go. Jasper will be here soon," Kate said.

Willis turned and faced her.

"You're the power behind Carmichael's success. Jasper leaves you in charge when he goes away. He trusts you. I'll go as far to say that you could run the business without Jasper." Willis was on a roll. "You saved him once. Jasper was a mess, couldn't live without you." He scoffed in disgust. "Then you appeared with Jasper's child. In one innocent, simple move, you saved him and Jasper found his love." He paused. "Manning and that useless son think they're going to fill Meredith's shoes and run the Carmichael trust fund. Hah! Over my dead body. That fund owes me, and me alone."

Fear returned in Kate as Willis's tirade became increasingly venomous.

"Well, you're wrong," she retorted, trying to hide her unease. "Jasper runs the business. And I certainly have nothing to do with Manning."

"Don't put yourself down. I'm an exceptional judge of character. Kate, you have the power that Manning never will. Who would've thought Jasper would convert the castle into luxury apartments… I wonder where he got that idea from." Willis grinned as he watched Kate redden. "But do you really know your husband, I wonder! Do you trust him? He spends a lot of time in London."

Kate's stomach flipped. She blinked. Willis's words had struck a chord.

He couldn't hide his delight. "Jasper's like a chameleon. He changes his persona to suit whoever he wants to impress. He's a master at it. At the moment, he wants to impress you. And that will change. But you! Mrs Carmichael is 'what you see is what you get.' I look forward to our crossing of swords. Figuratively speaking. You'll be a worthy opponent, Mrs Carmichael."

Willis grinned and hummed as he walked away. He was more than pleased with himself. He had planted seeds of doubt in Kate's mind. He now was looking forward to helping Beth bury everything Carmichael.

There was a noticeable spring in his step as he strode along the river path.

A preoccupied Kate slowly walked back to her Evoque, her eyes fixed on the gravel path. Willis's words added to her uneasiness. '*At the moment, he wants to impress you. And that will change.*'

She was surprised to see Jasper waiting by the Evoque, with Harry and Oliver holding his hands.

Oliver released his dad's hand and ran towards her. "I'm sorry," he mumbled.

Kate knelt beside him, pulling him into her arms. "Why are you sorry?"

"They threatened me." Tears spilled down Oliver's cheeks.

"Tell me," she whispered, her hand cradling the back of his head.

"They were going to beat up Harry if I didn't tell."

Jasper appeared, holding Harry's hand.

"You argued. Then you left," Oliver choked.

"Oliver, look at me. You had nothing to do with me leaving. I will never leave you and Harry." Kate pulled a tissue from her pocket and gently wiped his face. "Sometimes adults need to be alone to think."

"You needed to think?" His green eyes grew wide.

"Now tell me who threatened Harry."

Oliver lifted his gaze to Harry.

"Those women," Harry said. "They want to know things about you and Dad."

Kate and Jasper shared a knowing glance.

"Do you know what? I need a cup of tea, and I bet my little heroes could manage a chocolate ice cream."

Oliver rubbed his eyes and flung his arms around Kate's neck. "I didn't tell them anything."

Kate's worried eyes settled on Jasper.

The walk to the café was in silence. The boys walked either side of Kate, holding her hands, and Jasper held Oliver's. They sat outside the café, Oliver and Harry exchanging grins while Kate sipped tea and Jasper coffee.

When the boys ran to the river's edge to do their customary stone skimming, Jasper said, "Was that Willis leaving you?"

Kate nodded.

"Were you going to tell me?"

"I don't know where to start."

"The beginning is a good place."

"He just appeared. My mind was on Michelle leaving and Dan finally putting his foot down. She said Dan's gay but I find that difficult to believe. I didn't know Nigel refused to marry her." After a long, thoughtful moment, Kate blurted, "Beth's put her daughter up for adoption." She lifted her head so their eyes met. "Can you believe that?"

"Beth's capable of anything that suits Beth."

"Willis knew Meredith. Or so he says."

Jasper raised his eyebrows.

"He said he didn't agree with Meredith leaving me his money."

"What's it to do with him?"

"You tell me. He compared you to Colin, but then he asked about diamonds."

"Fucking diamonds! Again!" Jasper cursed.

"He then declared diamonds were in Carmichael DNA. He said Meredith told him I'm like Laura, my mother. He reckons I'm the power behind you."

"He's right." *You're the power I daren't let go.* His mind flashed to his business. Kate knew it all. He had to make sure he was the power over her.

"Jasper, that's not true and you know it."

He held her hands and their eyes met.

"There would be no me if it wasn't for you." He lifted her hands to his lips and kissed them.

"He doesn't think much of Manning. He commented that the trust fund owes him. I'm not sure what he meant." Kate paused, reflecting on

Willis's claim that he knew Meredith. "Meredith seems to be the centre of everything." She voiced her thoughts. "He finished by telling me I'd be a worthy opponent. I didn't understand that."

Jasper's eyes settled upon his wife. She was gazing at their sons giggling as they threw stones into the river.

Kate is such an innocent, he thought. *She has no idea how much power she has over me or that she's more than a worthy opponent for Willis. She has that inner strength that so many envy.*

Chapter Seventeen

It was late when Jasper finally closed his laptop. He casually poured himself a malt and sauntered to the French doors of his office, intending to gaze at the night sky. But the light from Kate's studio caught his eye. He thought she had gone to bed.

Kate couldn't sleep; her mind was in turmoil. She had stood under the shower until her skin had wrinkled. She had slipped into one of Jasper's white shirts and, barefoot, tiptoed into the kitchen to make herself a mug of tea.

She had more to tell Jasper; she should have told him before now. In the past, the beach had been her go-to place when she had Jasper on her mind. But since they had moved to Isaacs' House, her visits to the beach had become less and less frequent. Her studio and the river were becoming poor substitutes.

How to broach the subject of the NRJ bank with Jasper plagued her. He had lost money, and he never talked about it except in anger.

Jasper stood in the doorway of Kate's studio, gazing admiringly at his wife. She had just showered, wet hair resting on her shoulders, cheeks flushed, and if he wasn't mistaken, her green eyes sparkled. She held a cup of steaming tea between her hands as she studied one of her unfinished paintings of the beach.

"It's been a while since I've seen you in one of my dress shirts," he said, smiling as he recalled the last time.

His calm, husky voice made her jump. She turned and smiled over the steaming tea.

"What's wrong?" he asked, taking a step towards her.

"I can't settle. My mind's swirling with everything," she mumbled. "I thought painting would help. But I've so many unfinished… I miss the beach. I miss the rhythmic sound of the waves." Her voice began to quiver. Jasper moved to her side and pulled her into his shoulder.

"It's been a bad week," she murmured. "I should stop being so maudlin. We have a lot to discuss. But Michelle's bombshell knocked me for six. Then the mysterious appearance of Willis, and then there's Oliver."

"We'll stop Oliver being threatened. I'll talk to the head. If he does nothing, we'll move the boys." Jasper's voice had taken a stern tone. "It's probably for the best, Michelle moving." He paused. "Willis is going to have my full attention."

"Agreed. I'll see the head when the boys return after their suspension."

"*We'll* see the head! I'm prepared to move the boys and stop my contributions." Kate gazed up, studying Jasper's stern features. "We haven't decided what to do with the Isaacs' diamonds," she tentatively said.

"I think we should leave them alone. Watts is poking around. It's not a good time for me to be dealing in diamonds."

Kate nodded and placed her empty cup onto the workbench. She leaned against a high stool.

Jasper silently waited for Kate to continue. He knew his wife's moods. When to interrupt her thoughts, and when to silently wait.

"To my amazement, I've sold many paintings," she said.

"Why are you amazed? You're talented, Kate."

"The thing is, I'm running out of paintings to display at the gallery. The sixth-form students are going to show their paintings, but that's just a stop gap."

"Haven't you got photos you could refer to?"

"That's just it. Photos from my early paintings were on my old laptop."

Where's this going? Jasper thought.

Kate leaned across her workbench and picked up a pile of photos. She seemed unaware that the shirt had ridden up, giving Jasper a view of her naked backside.

"They are no substitute for the real thing," she said.

Jasper grinned—he couldn't agree more. His eyes fixed on her thighs.

"I'm not following you," he said, stepping towards her. He was no longer interested in photos or paintings; desire had filled his mind.

"You know my old laptop that your IT man sorted?"

Jasper nodded.

"Well, I… er… I was… It has the NRJ app on it," Kate continued, trying to ignore Jasper's obvious sexual intentions. What she was about to tell him couldn't wait any longer.

Jasper was a little perplexed. Kate never ignored his advances.

"I opened it."

"Opened what?" Jasper's voice was somewhat short.

"I knew you weren't paying attention," Kate snapped. "The app."

"It doesn't work. The bank was hacked. Client's names, passwords, addresses. They closed the branch," Jasper bitterly replied. He didn't like Kate's lack of interest in him.

"Well that may be, but the app opened. A list of its current customer accounts—"

"Impossible!"

Kate slipped her hand into the top pocket of the shirt and threw a USB stick at Jasper.

She had piqued Jasper's interest. They hurried back to his office and Jasper inserted the stick into his laptop port. A heavy silence filled the room as Jasper read the files.

"This is dynamite. Where's the laptop?"

"In a safe place."

"Is it connected to the internet?"

"No."

"Fuck! Kate, I haven't got an account with NRJ."

"Lord Carmichael has."

Their eyes met over his laptop.

"Not me!" Jasper's temper started to bubble. "There's a B James—Beth to me and you. I didn't realise she married Nigel," he commented.

"She didn't," said Kate.

"R Manning is investing a lot. I wonder where the money's coming from?" Jasper mumbled to himself as he scrolled down the list of names.

"My guess is the Carmichael trust fund." Kate paused. "You haven't mentioned W Carmichael. I was curious. He has regular payments from the same bank number as Manning."

"Willis Carmichael! He's a bloody Carmichael. But where from?"

"When he speaks, there's traces of an accent. American or Canadian is my guess," Kate reflected.

"The only Carmichael to go to America was Alice, my mother. I'm her only Carmichael son. She married an American."

"There's someone else we have never considered. Colin's wife. What happened to her?" asked Kate.

"She just disappeared. I suppose she could have gone to America. Probably joined Alice." Jasper spoke his thoughts aloud.

"Willis did say the Carmichael fund owed him. He didn't like Meredith leaving me his fortune."

A thoughtful silence filled Jasper's office.

Kate left him deep in thought, returning to her studio and her unfinished painting. She was flicking through the pile of photos when Jasper joined her.

He gazed at her longingly. His beloved wife had no idea how sexy she was.

"Come to bed."

Kate turned to looked at him. She smiled at his hungry expression.

"You can look at these tomorrow," he whispered, taking the photos from her hand and dropping them on the workbench.

She looped her arms around his neck, pulling him into a sensual kiss. Jasper gripped her naked buttocks. His hands wandered up her back as their tongues danced. A loud sigh escaped his mouth as he lifted her into his arms and walked towards the stairs.

Chapter Eighteen

Alice Thorpe stepped into Jasper Carmichael's luxury hotel as if she owned it. She was an attractive woman and she knew it. Even at her age she turned heads as she strode towards the reception desk. She didn't consider herself old—just like her half-brother Meredith Spencer hadn't. She resembled him in many ways: straight, tall form, high cheekbones. Her once long blonde hair was now a shining grey bob. She gazed around the foyer; her son had an obvious eye for luxury—marble floor, glass chandelier, overstuffed white leather couches and chairs. But what was *Jasper* like? Meredith hadn't liked him, so she suspected he was like his father, Colin.

'Your son,' Meredith had bitterly said, *'has impregnated my granddaughter with his Carmichael seed. Not once but twice.'*

That was how she'd found out that she had grandchildren.

So when she received a letter informing her of Meredith's unexpected departing and that her signature was required on some legal documents relating to her inheritance, she had set sail for England. She hadn't been invited to Meredith's funeral, but he had included Alice Spencer of Boston USA in his will. She was always Alice Spencer to Meredith; he had never recognised any of her husbands.

It was her first visit back to the country she still called home. Her husband Jasper Carmichael Senior had disowned her when he'd found out she had a child with his son Colin. It was Meredith who had organised her new life in America, on the condition that she never returned to England. It was Meredith who introduced her into the American trophy wife circuit, her name for it. She'd had three American husbands, all rich. All had left her considerable sums of money as reward for being an excellent trophy wife.

However, her aristocratic first husband, Jasper Carmichael Senior, hadn't given her a penny. Something she'd never forgiven him for.

The hotel bellboy adjusted his collar as he waited for Alice to complete her registration. He was more than a little nervous being in charge of four matching Louis Vuitton suitcases. Alice didn't believe in travelling light.

***

Later that evening, Alice relaxed in one of the many plush couches that littered the bar area. She was sipping a complimentary Macallan after enjoying dinner in the hotel restaurant. She was pleased when the waiter suggested steak but she declined the house red, preferring Pinot Noir. She may not be a food expert but she knew her wine and malt. All her American husbands had had excellent wine cellars.

In her relaxed state she recalled the events of the past three weeks. Meredith had changed his will just before he'd died, leaving the majority of his fortune to his granddaughter, Kate. That hadn't gone down well with his two sons, but Meredith Spencer was a superior lawyer and their legal challenge had fallen at the first hurdle.

She had taken a day to wander down memory lane, visiting Carmichael Castle, and was surprised that Jasper, her son, had converted it into luxury apartments. As far as she was concerned, that dark, cold place should have been demolished, but converting it seemed a sound investment.

She had visited Aunt Connie, living in a luxury dementia home. Connie hadn't recognised her, and it saddened Alice to see such a vibrant woman being ravaged by such a devastating disease.

She had met Rupert Manning at her nephews' law offices. She instantly disliked the man. He obviously thought he should be the one running the Carmichael trust fund, the position Meredith had held and now Jasper. It was Manning who, during one of his rants, jealously told her about Jasper's business based at Wellsbury. She suspected he wouldn't have mentioned Jasper if he'd known she was his birth mother.

Many journalists had questioned her about her relationship with Colin and the rumour that she'd had his son, but no one alive knew the truth about her love for Colin Carmichael.

***

The following morning, Alice left the hotel for the coffee shop opposite Kate's gallery.

She felt a little uncomfortable as she gazed at Kate's bookshop and gallery. She wanted to see the woman Meredith had left his fortune to, after she had overheard the barman in Jasper's luxury hotel enthusiastically complimenting Kate to a group of men who appeared to have more than a passing interest in her. Apparently he had gone to school with her. He had boasted that, while at school, she had had a number of admirers, but she was destined for better things. When asked how she met Jasper, the barman boasted that he had witnessed their first meeting; the sexual attraction was palpable.

The barman had laughed. *'Kate must be good between the sheets. She has Jasper wrapped around her little finger.'*

That was how Alice found herself staring at the gallery, hoping to get a glimpse of the woman her son loved.

Her heart missed a beat when a black Range Rover stopped outside the bookshop and gallery. She immediately knew it was Jasper, her son; only he would drive through the centre, as private cars were banned.

He stepped from the driving seat and gazed about him. He was taller than she'd imagined. Meredith had bitterly told her he was the spit of Colin. After all these years, butterflies still sped through her when she thought of Colin.

Her mind flashed back to the first time she'd approached her half-brother Meredith Spencer. Alice was the Spencer family's dirty secret. She shared the same mother with Meredith but not the same father. She was destitute and had needed help. Initially, Meredith had disowned her, empathy not being part of his character. She'd been surprised when he invited her to dinner, gave her money for clothes and an expensive salon treatment. Then she was introduced to Jasper Carmichael Senior. A week later she was in his bed. She'd heard stories similar to Carmichael's many times: a rich, powerful man locked into an unhappy marriage.

Apparently, Meredith and Jasper Senior had had a falling out, resulting in Jasper not sharing his business with Meredith. Meredith was furious and wanted an insider to spy on Jasper. So, Alice became Meredith's spy.

Jasper considered all women, and that included Alice, to be inferior and uneducated. He couldn't have been more wrong. She understood perfectly his dubious business deals. Consequently, he talked freely about them and was careless with confidential documents, leaving them where she could read them.

At her high society engagement party, she had met Colin. The whole of the Carmichael clan had been there with their respective families. Alice couldn't take her eyes off Colin—his dark hair, shining blue eyes and that irresistible smile. He was clever, charismatic, a true Carmichael. He'd asked her to dance—it was a slow dance; the electricity that had sparked between them was unbelievable. She didn't care that Colin was a renowned womaniser, she didn't care that he was married, she'd wanted him. The first time was in a dark passage in Carmichael Castle.

Alice briefly closed her eyes as she recalled the pleasure from Colin's hands wandering over her body, squeezing her breasts, their exploring tongues, and his fullness. No man had satisfied her like Colin.

The unmistakable sound of children brought her out of her reverie. They were walking towards the Range Rover. Jasper had his arm around a woman's waist; Alice noticed his fingers squeezing her side. He was whispering into her ear, and a smile slowly crept across her face. *Kate*, Alice thought.

Kate looked into her husband's eyes and planted a kiss upon his cheek. His swift reaction surprised Alice as he pulled his wife into a deep kiss. They didn't care who was watching or taking a photograph.

A tinge of jealousy spread through Alice as she recalled Colin being that passionate with her.

It was then she decided to meet her son's family. She had something to tell them.

Chapter Nineteen

The nonstop shrill of the doorbell at Isaacs' House echoed.

Clare cursed as she raced to the front door. She wrenched it open, and a tall elderly lady pushed past her, leaving her luggage outside for Clare to deal with.

Alice's strident voice replaced the shrill of the doorbell.

"Alice Thorpe to see Mr Carmichael."

Her eyes wandered admiringly at the open hallway, the wide staircase that led to the bedrooms off a wide landing.

"They're in Kate's studio," Clare said sharply.

Alice followed Clare towards the kitchen and the glass corridor that linked the studio to the house.

The boys sat at a table. One was drawing and the other was covered in paint from head to toe. Alice's nose turned up as '*out of control*' flashed through her mind.

Kate was washing her hands in the small sink at the far end of the studio. Jasper, who had been outside, hurried in.

For a long moment he stared at this stiff, elderly lady dressed in the best designer clothes and jewellery. He knew who she was; the last time he'd spoken to Manning, all he could talk about was Meredith's sister from America. But Jasper knew she was more than Meredith's sister.

"Kate Carmichael!" she said. "Mrs Thorpe."

"You were at the coffee shop yesterday," piped up Oliver.

"Forgive him," said Kate. "This is Oliver and Harry."

Harry politely nodded and Oliver grinned.

"I don't think Alice has come to visit the boys, Kate," Jasper said bitterly, staring at the woman who had never felt the joy of holding him in her arms.

Alice began to feel uncomfortable. Jasper's stare unnerved her, just as Colin's had.

"Please sit," said Kate, glaring at Jasper.

"I hadn't intended this," Alice blurted, her confidence waning under Jasper's stare. "I wouldn't have come to England if it hadn't been for Meredith's will." She took a deep breath as she met Jasper's eyes. She continued in a garbled manner as if they knew who she was. "I've been on a tour of England. I like what you've done to that mausoleum. Hated it. I'd have pulled it down, but making money from it is a better idea." Her voice began to quiver.

She paused while Clare brought tea and cakes and set them down on Kate's workbench. "I've been to see Connie. Poor soul. Dementia is a terrible disease. She remembered meeting you all at the castle. I still have the Carmichael London house to visit," she added.

"I'm sure it hasn't changed since you were last there," Jasper commented in an uninterested manner. "I'll tell Chester to expect you. It reeks of grandfather. Meredith didn't change anything, according to Chester."

Alice was a little perplexed. "Chester!" she repeated.

"The butler," Jasper answered. "His father was butler to grandfather."

Alice remembered a Chester, but he had never married, and to her knowledge, he'd never had a son.

"Did you ever visit the London house?"

Jasper was a little miffed. "Never visited anything Carmichael until I inherited the title."

Alice waited while Kate poured the tea and the boys washed their hands. Her thoughts filled with the mysterious butler, Chester.

"I'm sorry," Kate said in an apologetic manner. "I should have asked—do you take tea? We just assume everyone does because we do."

"All the years I've been in America, never lost the habit."

"We should go into the living room," offered Kate.

"No, I like it here. There's something about this studio," replied Alice.

"It's the Kate effect," said Jasper, smiling. He stepped towards his wife, planting a soft kiss on her cheek.

Harry and Oliver raised their eyebrows in disgust of their parents' show of affection.

"I wasn't going to meet you," continued Alice. "It was the barman at your hotel who lyrically praised your wife that encouraged me to have coffee and watch the gallery." Alice took a sip of tea, trying to put her thoughts in order so they would understand. "I like to think that Colin loved me, and you're the result of our love. But you never knew with Colin; he always had his own agenda. We had an arrangement. As soon as you were born, Colin would take you to an orphanage run by some nuns. But he took you to that godawful criminal world and that whore. How could he! I knew I couldn't keep you. Jasper would have killed me. Meredith had organised everything; he had no idea what Colin intended." Alice sipped her tea. "When Jasper found out that I'd given birth, he kicked me out. Thanks to Meredith, I ended up as some rich American's trophy wife—not once, but four times. They all left me well off. Except Jasper. It was Meredith who made sure I didn't starve, but he wanted a return on his investment."

"Bastard," mumbled Jasper.

"Yes! He wasn't a nice man except to Helen and Laura. But I digress. What I must tell you is that Willis is your half-brother, according to Meredith, who apparently looked after Colin's family. I don't know why Colin behaved in such a heartless manner to his wife and children. All I know is he cut all ties with them. It was Meredith who set them up in America."

"Where are they?" Jasper impassively inquired.

"Dead, except Willis who wants his inheritance."

"Why doesn't he come to me? I have enough. He could join the company."

"He doesn't want to share with you. He wants it all, including"—she looked at Kate—"Meredith's fortune."

"We've met," said Kate.

"Then you know the type of man he is." Alice paused. "Meredith thought that Willis had a legitimate claim to the Carmichael fortune. All he had to prove was that he was Colin's legal heir." She looked at Jasper. "You are Colin's bastard. If you and Willis had a DNA match, Meredith could have proved Willis's case. He anticipated he would make a lot of money from a court case."

"He wouldn't have made a penny. There wouldn't have been a court case. Willis could have had the lot. I've made my own money." Jasper's voice took on a cold tone.

A long, awkward silence ensued, no one wanting to say the wrong thing. It was Alice who broke the tension.

"I often wondered what type of man you'd become. My fear was that you'd be like Colin. Meredith painted a picture of an ill-tempered aggressive criminal wanted by the police. It doesn't matter what you may or may not have done in the past. I find a son to be proud of, one that loves his wife and family." Alice smiled at Kate. "I think you're the one to thank for making my son the man he is today."

Then her gaze turned to Jasper, but his expression was like his tone, cold. It reminded her of Colin's dark moods. She knew it was time for her to leave.

"I must go. The taxi's waiting."

"Taxi? I'll take you," Jasper suddenly blurted.

"No! My luggage is inside. I have a train to catch. Heathrow then Boston. It's been a pleasure," she said, gripping Jasper's hand and planting a card inside before giving Kate a hug.

The name on the card was Alice Carmichael Thorpe, and there was a phone number.

A small hand tugged Alice's sleeve. Alice looked down into Oliver's green eyes.

"Who are you?"

Kate put her arm around him.

"This is your grandmother, Alice."

"I didn't know I had a grandmother."

Alice averted her gaze, looking back to Jasper.

"Tell me, Jasper. Did you see much of Colin?"

Jasper turned his head while putting the last of Alice's luggage in the taxi boot. "Truth be told, can't remember much about him. I suppose I look like him."

"Oh, you do look like him! Piercing blue eyes, black hair, and you have his smile." Alice eased herself into the back of the taxi. "Where's he buried? In the vault?"

"I don't think so. He should be, but I don't think they had a body. He just disappeared."

Alice smiled at him as she pulled the rear door shut.

"That's a lot of luggage for flying," said Kate as the taxi turned onto the road.

"She's not going to Heathrow. More like Southampton and a ship," Jasper suggested.

"Tell me about Grandmother." Oliver hadn't left Kate's side.

Kate smiled and ruffled his hair.

Chapter Twenty

Jasper shut himself away in his office. He didn't want Kate to see the anger that surged deep inside him. He'd known Alice would appear one day, but he'd never anticipated the dark emotions she would stir. He had put on an impassive persona, but the darkness was rearing its head. Kate would want to be with him when he faced the demons of the past that he had never admitted to.

He was the love child of Colin and Colin's stepmother. He had been given away as soon as he'd left her body. Meredith Spencer had arranged a place for him in an orphanage, but Colin had given him to a whore to bring up.

He stood from his desk and started to pace the length of the room as he recalled his early life with criminals—because that's what they were. How he was bullied as soon as Colin disappeared. How he'd locked himself in his bedroom while his whore of a mother entertained men behind Colin's back.

He slumped onto a couch and rested his head in his hands while memories tormented his mind and body. His temper craved the relief of a physical fight or a rough fuck. He pulled at his hair until Kate pulled his hands away. She stood before him dressed in one of his white shirts. He pulled her into him, his head nestled in her stomach and his hands gripped her buttocks.

Instead of throwing Kate onto the couch and fucking her, to his surprise, he mumbled, "Why did she come?"

"She wanted to see the love of her life for the last time. You could see how proud she was of the man you've become." Kate gently stroked his hair.

But no words, not even Kate's, could stop the angry turmoil surging inside him.

"Do you think she loved me?"

"She loved you deeply and has never stopped loving you. She'll always love you." Kate held out her hand and said, "Come."

He took her hand and followed her like a lamb to their bedroom. He stood before her while she slowly undid the buttons on his shirt. She took her time peppering his chest with kisses.

Jasper sighed and began to relax.

"Kate," he uttered as she slowly pushed his trousers and boxers onto the carpet. He was naked before her.

She took a step back to admire her husband's muscular form.

With slow movements, she eased her dress shirt onto the carpet. She was naked before him.

She smiled and held out her hand. He was mesmerised by her glowing face and sparkling green eyes. Electricity sparked between them.

She lay atop of him, planting soft kisses upon his face. His large hands nestled on her buttocks, stroking and squeezing.

Words were not needed as their bodies moved together, passionately. When he slowly entered her, she reached for him so they could kiss.

A delightful sigh drifted from her.

"Don't make me wait."

They moved as one, climaxing together.

He didn't remember when the darkness had left him. All he remembered was that Kate had made him whole again.

He daren't think what type of human he would be without her.

***

Jasper was still sleeping when Kate slipped out of bed and into their bathroom. He was still asleep when she tiptoed along the landing and down the stairs.

It was Harry and Oliver's morning argument that finally woke him. Kate was no match for them that morning; she was tired and the boys were taking advantage. Jasper threw on a T-shirt and trousers and joined them in the kitchen.

The boys shut up when they saw him with that 'don't mess with me' look.

"I was going to suggest that you joined me visiting the airfield. But this noise!"

"I'll be good," interrupted Oliver loudly, thinking, *What noise*? "When are we going?"

"That's the point, young man! You're not going if you don't eat your breakfast in silence. And say sorry to your mother."

"But we're only jesting," mumbled Harry.

"I expect better from you, Harry."

Jasper turned towards his office.

***

"They haven't said a word," said a relieved Kate as she placed a tray of toast, tea and coffee onto the coffee table in Jasper's office.

Jasper closed the door before pulling her into his arms.

"Did I tell you how much I love you?" His lips trailed along neck. "I want to say thank you."

A delightful sigh escaped as he consumed her mouth. His hands deftly unclipped her bra. In one swift movement, her top fell to the floor followed by her jeans and panties while his mouth gently appreciated her soft, full breasts. He lifted her legs around his waist and walked her to his desk.

Her face was flushed, eyes on fire. Electricity sparked.

"I'm going to thank you for last night."

***

"The tea and coffee are cold," murmured Kate as she calmed.

"What do you prefer? Hot tea, or me inside you?"

Kate smiled and kissed him. "There's no contest. You every time."

"They take advantage of you. If I join you, breakfasts will probably become easier," Jasper thoughtfully mumbled.

A surprised look passed over Kate's face. Jasper didn't appear to notice.

"Do you really have to go to the airfield?" said Kate as she pulled on her jeans.

"Yes. It's time I checked the security measures. And, er… see for myself what's going on."

***

The boys sat in the back of Jasper's Range Rover, neither wanting to upset their dad any more than they already had.

The security man opened the gates, and Jasper drove through to park outside the first hangar. The boys jumped out and waited for Jasper and Kate.

"Harry's coming with me, and you, Oliver, can practise your running. Mum will time you." Jasper's tone was still stern.

The security guard watched as Kate and Oliver walked to the runway. Oliver gave Kate his jacket, and before she could say a word, he sprinted along the runway.

***

The security guard continued to watch the family and it was clear that it was Jasper that he was most interested in.

Jasper was talking to Harry, who was writing on his iPad and occasionally taking photos. The guard walked out of sight and made his call.

"Jasper's at the airfield with Kate and the kids," he said. "He's parked by the hangar."

"Has he tried to get in?" Beth nervously asked.

Jasper's sudden appearance at the airfield had taken her by surprise. Her stomach had flipped; did Jasper know about her using the airfield?

Willis had convinced her that Jasper wasn't interested in her or the goings on at the airfield. He was preoccupied with Kate; he was in love, impossible as that may seem to Beth.

She was now regretting listening to Willis.

The security guard's voice brought Beth's thoughts back to the present.

"Not yet. But he must have noticed the padlock. He's with Harry, walking round the perimeter."

"Is he inspecting the new security fence?"

"The kid's taking photos."

"What about the section we've removed?"

"Jasper's there now."

Beth knew Jasper wouldn't miss the alterations to the fence. She just had to hope that it would be a day or two before he reacted. Cancelling the night's drug drop was not an option. Her business depended on a successful drop; it would convince her new partner that she ran a well-organised operation.

***

But Jasper had already noted that the section of fence by the disused gateway had new, shiny bolts and there were tyre tracks leading up to the gate. He walked a short distance from the fence and picked up traces of tracks leading towards the hangars.

Jasper took a long moment staring at the fence, his mind mulling around Beth. He had refused to give her money. He had been a fool to give her any help, whether it was being a guarantor for a bank account or helping with the house. She'd needed money to fund her drug smuggling business. The airfield was an ideal way to get drugs into Wellsbury.

Oliver came bounding towards Jasper and Harry.

"Mum says I'm the fastest runner in school," he proudly announced.

"No you're not!" shouted Harry, slightly jealous.

"I am too!"

Jasper's hackles began to rise when the boys started their tit-for-tat bickering.

"The two of you, shut the fuck up."

"You're not supposed to use that word. I'll tell Mum."

Harry's reply fuelled Jasper's simmering temper. "Don't you backchat me!" His anger surprised the boys. "I'll say this once and once only. I will ground the pair of you. Believe me, Mum's had enough. And if you dare go running to her…" His gaze rested on Harry. "I'll stop your visits to Zak's."

"You wouldn't dare," Harry said defiantly. "I don't believe you. Mum wouldn't allow it." He flung the iPad onto the grass and stormed towards the Range Rover.

Oliver stood, mouth open. He had never seen his dad and Harry so angry.

Kate was leaning on the bonnet of the Range Rover, watching the argument. She knew it was trouble.

Harry stomped passed her, not giving her second glance. He flung open the rear door, but Kate stopped him before he slammed it shut.

"No you don't, young man!" Their eyes clashed. "What's going on?"

"You'd only take his side." Harry shrugged.

Kate took his arm. "Look at me!"

Harry tucked his head into his chest. Kate held his shoulders.

"He's going to stop me going to Zak's," Harry blurted.

"Why?" Kate's impatient tone made Harry look at her.

He took a deep breath. "Oliver said you said he was the fastest runner." Another deep breath.

"I said he wasn't."

Gulp.

"We began to argue," Harry said. "And Dad flipped."

Gulp.

"He said you were fed up with us."

"Now tell me the rest," Kate prompted in her calm voice.

Jasper watched Kate open the Range Rover tailgate and sit just inside so her legs trailed over the lip. Harry joined her.

An uncomfortable silence hung between mother and son. Kate took Harry's hand in hers, but Harry remained silent.

"You know, Harry." Her fingers circled his knuckles as her calm voice continued, "The pair of you do argue a lot." She paused for a long moment. "Like at breakfast time."

"He's always showing off."

"Oliver's different to you. He can't do the things you're good at, and you can't do the things he's good at. Like running."

Harry turned his head to look at his mother.

"Do you still love me?" Harry's voice quivered and a lone tear trickled down his cheek.

Kate put her arm around his shoulders and pulled him into her side. Her head rested against his hair.

"Of course I love you, and I love Oliver. I'll always love you."

Oliver came bounding up to Harry, taking both his hands.

"Don't cry, Harry. I'll always look after you."

Somehow, Oliver had managed to ease Kate out of the way. Her smiling eyes met Jasper's. He shrugged his shoulders and raised his arms in disbelief.

"I don't believe it," he whispered into her ear as she tucked her arms around his waist. "One minute they're fighting. The next they are holding each other."

"There're kids. And that's what kids do. They don't mean anything by it."

***

When they arrived at the house, the boys raced from the car. Kate opened the passenger door, and Jasper caught her arm.

"I'll be going out tonight."

Kate's stomach flipped. "It's too dangerous."

"Maybe. You must have seen the padlock on the hangar."

Kate nodded.

"The airfield is being used. And I want to know who's using it."

"You could involve the police."

"Oh, Kate. You know that's not an option."

Her watery eyes met his.

"Kate, my love! Don't be concerned. But if I don't return…"

"Jasper! No."

"Tell Bruce. He'll look after you. The business is yours." His hand cupped her cheek, and she moved into it. "The boys have trust funds."

Their lips met.

"Who's doing this?" she said.

"I have a feeling Beth's involved."

"Drugs?"

"I'm not sure."

"I think a lot about how Nigel died," Kate said.

"That's how drugs are, Kate. You smoke a joint or two and before you know it you're injecting heroin. Look at Richard."

"But in Nigel's case, it was so quick."

"Have you thought he may have had encouragement?"

They sat for a long moment with Kate resting her head on his shoulder.

"I've got to find out what's going on," Jasper said eventually.

"I know."

Chapter Twenty-One

Under the cover of darkness and dressed all in black, Jasper slipped out of the Isaacs' garden, avoiding the watchful eye of the police. He jogged towards his lockup to his recently acquired black Ford Focus, which had replaced the one he'd set fire to. He headed to the wood above the airfield.

He slowly and carefully brought the Focus to a stop behind a mass of brambles. His senses were on full alert as he slowly made his way to the edge of the wood that overlooked the airfield.

He lay on his stomach and lifted his night-vision goggles from around his neck and scanned the airfield. He didn't know what to expect. Would the airfield be used tonight? Who would be waiting? Jasper's stomach churned.

Two men appeared from the padlocked hangar and jogged towards the fence by the disused gateway. They lifted a section of fence, leaving a gap wide enough for a vehicle. Headlights lit the lane, and a pickup suddenly drove through the gap at speed. As the pickup skidded to a halt, the hangar door opened and a woman confidently strode out.

A lump appeared in Jasper's throat. He immediately recognised the familiar gait of Beth.

A giant of a man jumped from the pickup and hugged her. His large hands rested on her buttocks, lifting her. His loud, roaring laughter echoed through the still night air. Fear rested in the pit of Jasper's stomach. All his instincts were telling him to leave, but he was transfixed by the image of Beth and this giant strolling into the hangar. One man followed the giant and three other men stayed by the pickup.

Jasper had begun to move from his observation point when his ears pricked to the sound of an aircraft engine. The dim runway lights switched on as the aircraft circled above. It bumped along the runway before coming to a halt. The men by the pickup jumped into action, and the truck sped towards the aircraft. Packages were thrown from the aircraft into the pickup. Jasper could only guess as to what they contained. By the time the pickup reached the hangar where Beth and the giant were waiting, the plane was taxiing towards the hangar at the far end of the airfield. Doors were opened, and red lighting guided the aircraft inside.

Beth and the giant were already at the pickup when Jasper trained his night-vision goggles back towards them. One of the men jumped into the back, lifted a brick-like package and threw it at the giant. He slipped a knife into the package and scooped out a white powder.

He grinned at Beth before licking the powder. He roared with laughter again before marching inside the hangar, followed by one of his men carrying a suitcase.

Jasper had seen enough. He belly-crawled from his observation post, and when he was confident he couldn't be seen, he briskly walked back to the Focus.

***

It took all of Jasper's strength to secure the doors of the lockup. He felt unusually hot and weak, and his stomach violently churned. He placed a hand on the Focus for support as he coughed and retched.

From the shadows, a figure moved quickly towards him. He stood, ready to defend himself. Relief sped through him as he recognised a jeans-clad Kate holding a plastic bag.

"Kate…" he stuttered.

"What's wrong?" Her voice full of concern, she put her arms around him. "Jasper," she murmured as he nestled into her. "What happened?" She stroked his damp hair.

"Oh Kate… Why are you here?" he stammered, relishing the warmth and comfort of his wife.

"You need me. And I brought you fresh clothes and a bottle of water. We have to get home while it's still dark," she said, shaking his clothes out of the bag. "Here, put these on."

Jasper started to gather his thoughts as he slowly changed his clothes while Kate collected his night-vision goggles and camera from the car.

"Where's your car?"

"In a dark alley."

"Were you followed?"

"Jasper, really. Wellsbury is my backyard. I know every hiding place."

He cupped her cheeks, planting a soft kiss on her lips. "Take me home."

Kate opened the lockup's side door and checked no one was hanging around. After locking the side door, he willingly followed her along a Victorian passageway. It didn't smell very nice, and a rat ran across their path. They turned right and left into other passageways before they reached the Evoque.

"You'll have to scramble over the driving seat," whispered Kate.

"What's this?" said Jasper, lifting a chemist bag off the passenger seat.

"Harry's tablets."

"For?"

It was a long moment before Kate answered. She was concentrating on manoeuvring the Evoque along the narrow alleyway. "I've had them a while. I don't like giving him tablets." She paused. "If we're stopped, we went to collect Harry's tablets from the night chemist."

"Do Clare and Malcolm know?"

"About Harry? Yes. They're also watching the fort, so to speak."

A comfortable silence filled the car as Kate negotiated the side streets of Wellsbury.

"You'd better hide in the footwell," said Kate as they approached Isaacs' House.

She pressed a button on the dash and the security gates opened. She parked around the back, well out of the way of prying eyes.

Malcom and Clare appeared from the darkened living room nursing cups of tea.

"Christ, what happened to you?" exclaimed Malcolm, staring at a very dishevelled Jasper. Jasper slumped into the overstuffed couch and rested his head in his hands. Kate appeared by his side, handing him a coffee. After a long moment he took a sip.

"I've seen the devil."

Kate's hands gently wandered up and down his back.

"What the hell were you doing going out alone?" said an exasperated Malcolm. "Anything could have happened to you."

"I knew something was going on. Sections of the fence at the airfield were loosened. Padlocks on the hangars. A very worried-looking security guard." Jasper paused, sipping his coffee. "I was lucky. They were overconfident. A fault of Beth."

"Beth!" Malcolm and Kate said together.

"I watched it all from the wood. The section of fence blocking the disused gateway was removed and a pickup drove through to the hangar. Not long afterwards, a light aircraft appeared. Its cargo dropped into the pickup. The aircraft taxied into a hangar. I'm not a hundred percent certain, but it looked like a drug drop. The devil was more than a little friendly with Beth."

"Where did the pickup come from?" asked Malcolm.

"I'm not sure. But Bruce is going to repair and reinforce the fence in the morning."

"It *is* morning," commented Clare, collecting the empty cups.

Chapter Twenty-Two

It was mid-morning when Jasper arrived at the airfield. He was stunned by the amount of activity. A honking horn caught his attention. It was Bruce, bouncing the old Defender towards him from the far end of the field.

"Expected you earlier!" shouted Bruce.

Jasper thought it was prudent not to enlighten Bruce of last night's activities.

"I said this job was urgent. Not to bring the whole of Carmichael Construction here."

Jasper's voice was a little sharp, but Bruce just grinned. He was used to his boss's moods.

"We'll be finished by this after. Fence strengthened and the disused gateway section replaced."

Jasper nodded his approval.

"Did you bring the bolt cutters?" he asked.

"In the back." Bruce nodded towards the car. "You didn't mention Inspector Watts would be poking around."

"I wasn't expecting him," said a puzzled Jasper. "Come on—let's see what's in these bloody hangars," said Jasper.

One snap of the bolt cutters, and the padlock fell from its hasp. Jasper and Bruce walked inside an empty hangar. Discarded paper and packaging were strewn about.

"Some fucker's been using this," said Bruce.

Jasper nodded and continued walking towards the partitioned office. He opened the door to find a small desk and two wooden chairs.

"Is that Beth's perfume?" Bruce had joined him. "What's going on?"

"Come on," said Jasper, striding out of the hangar.

The only other hangar with a padlock was the one at the far end. Bruce snapped the chain attached to the padlock while Jasper pulled open the heavy hangar doors.

"Bloody hell," exclaimed a shocked Bruce.

Jasper left Bruce staring open-mouthed at the aircraft while he busied himself taking photos.

By the time Bruce had joined him, Jasper was repeating the aircraft number that was on the tail of the plane into his phone. Jasper had already looked up the number for plane registrations.

An unmistakeable voice rang out behind them. "What's going on 'ere?" bellowed Inspector Watts.

"You have no right being in here," snapped an annoyed Willis, who was standing behind the inspector.

What the fuck is this to do with him? thought Jasper.

"You've overstepped the mark," said Watts.

Jasper's temper flared. "I'll say this fucking once. And once only." He turned to Willis. "I own this fucking airfield, I fenced it off, I had the hangars repaired, I pay for the security guards. But I didn't pay for two hangars to be padlocked. I have every fucking right to see what's in these fucking hangars and find out who's fucking using them." Jasper took a step closer to Willis. "Do I make myself clear?"

"Calm down, Mr Carmichael," retorted Watts. "We'll sort this. But you should take some of the blame. You 'ave showed no signs of using it."

Jasper whipped round and glared at Watts.

"Blame!" he shouted. "This is private fucking property. The pair of you are trespassing, unless you have some official business."

"There's a small matter of planning permission," Watts sheepishly replied.

"What the fuck is that to do with you?"

"I like to assist the council wherever I can."

"I've been trying to get fucking planning permission. But the council turns down every fucking plan. But you know that, don't you, Watts?" Jasper took a step closer to him. "The Flying Club and the Drone Club have approached me about using the airfield. The council is sitting on my application. I now see why."

His loud, angry voice made both Watts and Willis take a step back towards the open doors.

"What the fuck's going on here?" bellowed a loud, unfamiliar voice.

"This is Jasper Carmichael." Willis's silky voice made Jasper cringe.

"Lord fucking Carmichael!" The voice belonged to a very large man, at least six foot four and twenty stone. His weather-beaten face, long hair and scruffy clothes made it hard to judge his age.

Is this what the devil looks like? thought Jasper.

The devil stepped closer to Jasper, his dark, menacing eyes slowly meandering over the man who could scupper his drug business. Beth had told him how Jasper abhorred drugs after the death of his half-brother, Richard. Jasper Carmichael, the man the police had failed to convict for murder. He looked harmless in his Armani suit and handmade leather loafers. But he had been warned: Carmichael was a wolf in sheep's clothing.

A heavy, hostile tension settled in the hangar, with neither man wanting to give ground.

After what seemed to be an age, one of the devil's men burst through the doors, shattering the tense atmosphere.

"Helicopter, boss!"

The devil turned and walked to the open doors, watching the helicopter land. Without a second glance at Jasper, he jogged towards his truck.

Jasper and Bruce exchanged a 'what the fuck' glance as a man leapt from the helicopter, holding onto to his cap.

"You must be Carmichael," he said, slightly out of breath. He took a moment to study Jasper and readjust his cap.

"Who are you?" said a puzzled Jasper. He had phoned what he'd thought to be the FAA. Now he wasn't so sure, as this man had arrived as if Jasper had called him.

"Duncan! Just Duncan. Now, tell me the story."

Duncan was of medium height. Cap, cord trousers and tweed jacket. His grey eyes never left Jasper.

"Not much to tell. Came to check on the place. Fence needed repairing and two hangars had been padlocked. Not by me."

"So you came to investigate," Duncan said thoughtfully as he looked to Watts and Willis, who had been trapped in the hangar by his men standing in the open doorway. "And you are?" Duncan's tone had suddenly become demanding.

"Inspector Watts and my assistant Willis," Watts stuttered, somewhat embarrassed.

Duncan's eyes moved from one to the other waiting for Watts to continue.

"I 'eard there may be a problem," Watts explained.

"The problem, as you put it, is not a police matter." Duncan's dismissive tone made it perfectly clear Watts and Willis should leave.

Watts turned and stepped out of the hangar, and Willis followed.

"You have quite a reputation, Carmichael," said Duncan, walking towards the aircraft. "I'm waiting for your file."

Jasper didn't answer. His gut churned, putting him on his guard. Lord Carmichael had met men who had the same superior attitude as this Duncan, and they were British Intelligence.

Duncan opened the aircraft door. He leaned inside and pulled out a holdall. He didn't seem surprised to find bricks of drugs.

"Inherited the Carmichael title." Duncan turned to face Jasper. "We'll have a talk when I've read your file."

Jasper remained silent.

"My colleague mentioned you married a Spencer. Now there's a thought. Carmichael and Spencer mix. No file though."

Jasper remained silent.

"A little bird whispered that a Carmichael has bought that run-down garage. You'll soon own the whole of Wellsbury between you."

Jasper's stoic expression dropped. He knew nothing of this. Who would buy a rundown garage? Kate flashed into his mind.

Duncan grinned; the unflappable Carmichael was rattled.

Chapter Twenty-Three

A shriek of brakes was followed by heavy footsteps and the kitchen door bouncing open.

"Kate!" bellowed a red-faced Jasper.

The boys stopped eating. Clare closed the oven door with a thud. Malcolm stopped washing his hands, and Bruce snuck in behind Jasper.

"Kate!"

"What's up?" Kate gazed at Jasper in her casual way, reading glasses on the end of her nose, blonde hair resting on her shoulders, white shirt open to her cleavage, jeans resting on her hips, her feet bare.

Jasper stopped in his tracks, his eyes suddenly brimming with desire. If they'd been alone, he would have had her on the kitchen work-surface. He turned his back to her.

He took a deep breath. "Why are you dressed like that?"

"Like what? I always dress like this."

"You know what you do to me."

Bruce looked at Malcolm, and they both sniggered. Kate was pretending ignorance of how she affected her husband when dressed in a provocative manner.

"Jasper! What is it?" she said, swallowing a grin.

Jasper gulped and faced his wife.

"A total stranger has just casually mentioned—"

"What stranger?" she cut in.

"Immaterial. Were you going to tell me about Hill's garage?"

"How can I tell you anything when your head's stuck in Lord Carmichael business?"

"Tell me about the garage."

"I will, but first things first."

Kate raced into the library and picked up a tray of notebooks and photos. With a thud, she placed it on the kitchen surface.

Jasper went to speak but she held up her hand, in that 'be quiet' manner. The boys' mouths were open, and Clare, Malcolm and Bruce looked on in amazement as Jasper gave way to his wife.

Kate was a little angry. Her cheeks were flushed, her green eyes glowed. When Kate was like this, there was only one way Jasper could get his own way, and he couldn't do that in front of a kitchen full of people.

She ran her hand through her blonde hair and pushed her reading glasses up her nose. She handed Jasper a photo from the tray.

"It's a drone photo of Hill's Garage and the airfield. I didn't realise how close they were. I went to show Mr Hill. He was in a state. Needed a wash, fresh clothes, tears running down his face. The council and Carmichael Property were putting pressure on him to sell." She paused and met Jasper's eyes. "Don't you people understand? Hill's Garage is part of Wellsbury's soul."

"Kate! You can't save every little piece of Wellsbury," Jasper angrily retorted.

"But I can stop Carmichael Properties destroying some of it."

Clare gulped, putting her hand to her mouth. None of them had seen Kate openly defy Jasper. But none of them knew what went on behind closed doors. He always appeared to be the one in charge and Kate followed. But was this the case?

An awkward silence bounced between Kate and Jasper.

Jasper broke it. "You've bought Hill's Garage with Meredith's inheritance."

"I'm a silent partner in Hill's Garage."

"Don't play semantics with me, Kate."

Kate ignored Jasper's comment. "With some reorganisation—"

This time, it was Jasper who interrupted Kate. "It wants knocking down and the whole area redeveloped."

Kate ignored him. "I've already—"

"Don't ignore me, Kate."

"Don't tell me how to spend my money."

You could have heard a pin drop.

"My team told me someone else was interested. They didn't know it was you."

"Ha! Your team? You mean that overpaid, lazy, overconfident, complacent bunch that you employ at Carmichael Properties."

Jasper took a moment. "You had a good legal team?"

"The best."

Jasper glared at Kate's smug face.

"You fucking used my legal team."

"What's good enough for Beth and Joanne is good enough for me."

Jasper's temper flared; his hand thumped the work surface. He abruptly turned and stormed out of the kitchen. Oliver opened his mouth to speak, but Clare shook her head.

Jasper's loud, angry cries could be heard in the kitchen, but they didn't seem to have any effect on Kate as she casually brewed a pot of tea.

Jasper strode back in. "Let's start again." His tight voice hid his anger.

"Tea or coffee?" Kate asked, in her matter-of-fact manner.

"Coffee." Jasper's voice was louder than he had intended.

"I had no idea Hill owned the land right up to the airfield and the land opposite."

"Christ! She's going to tell me she owns the whole fucking lot," an exasperated Jasper said to no one in particular.

Kate nodded. "Let me try and explain how it all unfolded." She placed her pot of tea on the work surface and perched on a stool. "I've been reading Hannah Isaacs' diaries and journals. They were in no order, no dates or days."

"I don't believe this. You bought Hill's because of some fucking journals of a dead woman."

"Jasper! Shut up and listen."

A heavy tension filled the kitchen. No one told Jasper Carmichael to shut up.

Their cold, angry eyes met. After a long moment, Jasper reluctantly pulled up a stool. Kate stoically watched.

"Hannah couldn't have known how important these journals would become." Kate picked a journal from the tray with the photos and opened it at a marked page.

"It was Colin." She turned to the boys. "That's your grandfather. He brought them to this house. Hannah had watched her only son shot dead by German soldiers." She looked lovingly at Harry and Oliver. "If I lost you two, my life wouldn't be worth living. That must have been how she felt."

Kate's eyes filled. Harry, followed by Oliver, rushed to her, each planting a kiss on her cheek. The tension in the kitchen suddenly became emotionally charged. No one could imagine life without mischievous Oliver and studious Harry.

Kate cleared her throat and began to read from the journal.

"*I can't forget my boy. I know Colin thought he acted for the best. But I should have died along with my son. One minute, my boy was standing, putting on a brave face, the next he was lying in a pool of blood. Colin dragged me away. I was in a daze as we ran back to our apartment. Colin was in control. The Germans were close behind. He found the diamonds and flung some clothes into our old, battered suitcase. Without thinking, we followed him to the plane and Wellsbury.*

I've never seen such an unwelcoming place. It was cold, dark and damp. Colin made a fire in the grate, and we slept on the damp wooden floorboards with only a damp blanket for cover. The next morning, Colin was gone, but somehow he'd managed a few pieces of food: mainly bread, a scraping of butter, milk, two eggs and coffee.

I felt ill, I hadn't slept. I cried all night into Jacob's shoulder. The image of my poor boy lying in a pool of blood danced before my eyes.

I thought Jacob didn't care. He didn't speak. He went outside in search of wood. He had to occupy his mind, he told me later.

It was only when we sat eating very soft boiled eggs next to the fire I saw his red cheeks and sore eyes. Jacob was struggling to get heat into the kitchen. He was covered in coal dust from shovelling coal in one of the outer buildings. His black fingers left marks on the ration book Colin had left.

'Go to the shops,' he told me.

I had no idea where the shops were, but it turned out to be easy. I just followed the flow of people.

The meagre rations from Colin's book had to feed three. I cried all the way to the shops.

A woman took pity on me. She held my hand and we walked to a small roadside garage. The shop. In the distance, I could see the airfield.

Behind the garage I could see pigs and vegetable stalls. An oaf of a man greeted us. He wore a round-necked shirt and trousers that were held up with a tie. He smiled and dropped a newspaper parcel into my basket. He gave the woman that had befriended me the same.

The oaf's grimy hands dropped potatoes and carrots into my basket. A pig's trotter was wrapped in newspaper.

'That pig's trotter will keep you going for a bit. Me and the boys will be up tomorrow to turn over that garden.' He dropped small brown paper bags next to the vegetables. 'These are seeds.'

My brain was fuddled. What did I need seeds for? I knew nothing about seeds. I remember he told me to keep a few behind, just in case. In case of what, I thought?

'You can eat most of the veg, but let some go to seed, for the next year.' He picked up a potato. 'You can cut this into four. Each piece will grow, providing there's an eye.' His thick finger pointed to a little blemish in the potato skin.

I didn't understand what he was on about. We had no idea how to grow veg. I was a seamstress; I could cook but couldn't grow, and Jacob was a carpenter."

Kate closed the journal and poured another cup of tea. She searched inside the tray and pulled out another journal.

"This is a passage from a later journal."

"*Jacob and I have settled. His woodworking skills are in demand, but no one knows he's an expert in diamonds. Colin comes and stays, and they shut themselves away for hours talking diamonds.*

I don't mind. I have dresses to repair, food to cook and vegetables to grow. We have chickens roaming, but not in my vegetable garden."

Kate turned to another page.

"Colin has taken the place of my son. He was the youngest of four. He was unloved after his mother died. He has a bit of a reputation with the ladies, but to us he's a much-loved son."

Kate closed the journal, returning it to the tray. The kitchen was deadly silent.

"You all feel it. Don't you? You all feel love. Hannah gave Colin the love he so badly needed, and he gave her hope. Jasper, don't you see? That 'oaf' was probably Hill's father or grandfather. He gave Hannah and Jacob food and help when he hadn't much to give. Colin gave people he knew hope. He shared his wealth, even if the means he came by it were questionable. A wartime Robin Hood.

"All I want to do is to give something back. The airfield and Hill's Garage, along with the Victorian buildings, are part of Wellsbury's heritage. It shouldn't be lost to steel and concrete."

Jasper stood, lifted Kate off the stool and kissed her. "I've never loved you more."

"Who's Robin Hood?" asked a puzzled Oliver.

Chapter Twenty-Four

Kate tiptoed into their bedroom and carefully closed the door. She leaned against it, slowly opening her blouse. Her eyes meandered over her husband's muscular back. His shirt lay at his bare feet, and his designer trousers hung on his hips. She sighed as sexual desire spread through her. Jasper knew how to stir her.

She had injured his pride when she defied him in front of the staff. He would be seeking sexual retribution.

Jasper whipped round. He momently gazed at his smiling wife, her eyes glowing with desire, her blouse undone, giving him a tantalising glimpse of her white lace bra. He rushed towards her and pinned her to the closed door, crashing their lips together. Tongues danced as his hands caressed her body while her fingers threaded through his soft hair.

"I don't like you defying me," he murmured as he deftly unclipped her bra.

He sighed as he admired her full breasts, which he knew very well.

"I know," she breathlessly uttered as his tongue circled her nipples.

"You're mine."

Her head tipped back and a delightful sigh escaped her mouth when his kisses trailed to the top of her jeans. He glanced up at her; their eyes met as her jeans and panties fell onto the carpet.

"You're mine," he whispered as he lifted her into his arms, his mouth buried into her neck.

He gently laid her onto the bed and gazed at her flushed cheeks and glowing eyes.

"Don't make me wait."

Their eyes locked and they both smiled as his trousers drifted onto the carpet. In an instant he was a top of her, nestled between her legs. His kisses slowly trailed over her body. Her hands rested on his shoulders.

"Jasper!"

"Yes, my love?"

He slipped inside. A delightful sigh escaped her mouth as a satisfied expression filled her face.

***

The night was slowly turning to dawn. Jasper stroked his wife's hair. She was still sleeping, stretched across his chest, skin to skin.

This was as it had always been, since the first time. He no longer craved other women, like so many of the London set he had become involved with. No other woman had given him so much pleasure as Kate. He had never considered there to be such a thing as soulmates until he met her. And this frightened him.

The Carmichael curse was slowly rearing its head. Jasper craved the power that diamonds would give him. He was torn between diamonds and desire for Kate. He needed her by his side to support him, be in his bed, but that gave her power over him. He had to leave.

She stirred. "What time is it?" she mumbled, still half asleep.

"I'm going to London."

Her eyes shot open as his words registered. "But you've only just got back."

"I want you to come to the airfield with me."

"Today?!"

"Now!"

She eased herself from his chest, their eyes locked.

"I've got the school run."

"No! My needs come first. I don't like playing second fiddle. Not even for the boys."

"That's unfair."

"You'll be in charge while I'm away. You need to be up to speed with the airfield."

"Will you be away a long time?"

"I'm not sure. You'll have to watch the airfield. You need to know about Duncan, and Beth's new partner. They might make a move."

"Who? What? I'm not up to this. Why don't you stay?"

"Duncan's probably MI5. Tweed jacket, cord trousers, cap. Beth's new partner, black evil eyes, big man, scruffy."

"Stay!"

"I can't."

She jumped out of bed.

"I don't like playing second fiddle," said Kate.

With lightning speed, Jasper caught her arm. For the briefest of moments, their eyes met, before he consumed her mouth. But not even his kiss could prevent a little voice in the back of Kate's mind repeating, *You've lost him.*

***

Two confused boys stared at their mother.

"Why are you going with Dad?" asked Oliver between mouthfuls of scrambled egg. "It's a school day."

"Why are you dressed like that?" asked Harry, staring at her wellingtons.

"We have to go to the airfield," answered Jasper, opening the kitchen door for Kate. He turned to Malcolm. "I'll be going to London. We'll be back around ten. I'm catching the eleven o'clock to London."

***

Jasper briefly stopped at the airfield gates before the new security guards waved them through. He made a left towards the repaired fence at the disused gate.

"I've sacked the old security, replaced it with some of Bruce's team."

Kate was barely listening as the Range Rover bounced across the field. "I don't understand why we're here. You could have just told me if Bruce is in charge."

An uneasy silence drifted between them.

They got out of the Range Rover. Jasper leaned on the car bonnet, kicking the dead earth, while Kate stared at the fence.

"You could get Luke Jones to test this field. Nothing has grown since the fire," he commented as he watched the dust settle.

"Jasper, you didn't bring me here to look at dirt and a fence."

"It's important we're alone and no one can hear."

"Go on. I'm listening."

"I reckon drugs were smuggled in by plane. Beth's new partner and his men came in through here. I'm guessing, but I reckon Beth arranged the drug drop, probably using his money. The drugs were divided between Beth and him. The aircraft was hidden in the hangar until it was needed."

"And you think they will continue, even with MI5 sniffing around?"

"I think Beth won't let go. It's not in her nature. She needs money… She will probably make a move on Duncan. When Beth makes her move, men find her irresistible."

Kate whipped round to face him.

"Don't look at me like that. I know Beth very well."

"Why do you have to keep rubbing it in?" Kate retorted.

Jasper pushed himself away from the car. "You have no need to be jealous." She went to move, but he caught her arm. "I love you. I want you, not Beth!"

"Then stay."

"I can't. Manning's making his move to take over the Carmichael trust fund."

"For fuck's sake, Jasper! Dissolve the trust. You don't need it. Manning only wants a Meredith lifestyle."

Jasper placed his hands on her shoulders. "It's not that easy."

Her cheeks were flushed, her eyes on fire. "You're not telling me that Meredith didn't have a get-out clause."

Jasper stared at her, the words *'get-out clause'* repeating in his mind.

She tried to push his hands off her shoulders. "You haven't bothered to see if there's a get-out clause." Their eyes met. "Will Beth be there to keep your bed warm, or is it Joanne?"

"God, Kate, what you do to me when you're angry…" He leaned into her, crashing their mouths together. She tried to push him away, but it was futile; she knew where this was going.

"Hangar or here?" he whispered.

"Here."

He opened the rear door of the Range Rover and lifted her onto the seat.

"There's not much room. We could go to the hangar."

"Don't make me wait."

***

In the woods, two men had their binoculars trained on the Range Rover.

"Bloody hell, he's going to fuck her."

"Lucky man," replied a gruff voice.

"Thought you said she was frigid?"

"My source was wrong," said Beth's new partner, Gypsy. "Kate is his Achilles' heel."

"What the fuck are you on about?" said his right-hand man.

Gypsy grinned, but his attention was on Kate, who was unfastening her blouse. Her jeans were open.

"She wears white lace."

"So?"

"Haven't you ever peeled off a woman's clothes so she's naked before you?"

"No time for that."

"It appears Jasper is very skilled in the art of lovemaking."

Chapter Twenty-Five

Kate sat at Jasper's desk in Carmichael House, loading files from the backup hard drive onto her laptop. She wasn't concentrating; butterflies filled her stomach and Jasper occupied her thoughts. She felt that she was losing him to the lure of diamonds and the Lord Carmichael lifestyle, including the attentions of other women. She couldn't bear the thought of him fucking other women.

Her back ached and she was sore. She hadn't felt this sore for some time. The back seat of the Range Rover wasn't exactly comfortable. But their intense lovemaking had been worth the physical discomfort.

She tried to think of happier times, when she had settled into a day's painting on the beach with Harry. Or the days she had spent with Jasper on his yacht. He loved sailing along the coastline. She often recalled how happy he had been and how he longed for her to be with him.

Her musing came to an abrupt end when the office door burst open.

"So! He's left you in charge," said Carl, head of the Carmichael legal team.

His slightly aggressive attitude riled Kate, particularly when he slammed a pile of papers onto the desk.

"I've done all the legwork. All you've got to do is write a cheque for this amount." He picked the top sheet from the pile and placed it in front of Kate.

"Cheque?" She was more than a little surprised. She thought Jasper had stopped using cheques, and she felt sure that he would have warned her that she might have to write one.

"Jasper signs a cheque. The book's in the top drawer. I suppose you might have to use another account that has joint signatures... I suppose you can do that."

Kate tried to ignore his condescending manner. "This is for a lot of money," she commented, glancing at the paper.

"Jasper never bats an eyelid. He just signs. He must be good for a few mill."

"I don't understand. What do you need the money for?"

"Work I've done," he said, tapping the pile of papers. "It's all here. All legit."

"I didn't say it wasn't legit. But I'll have to make sure the account has sufficient funds."

"Just sign the fucking cheque."

Angry eyes met.

Kate stood, resting her hands on the desk, cheeks flushed.

"There's the door. Use it. No one fucking speaks to me like that."

"Who the fuck do you think you are?"

"Lady Carmichael. Now get the fuck out."

"You're not my boss. I'll see what Jasper says." He turned and opened the door. "And she said you would be a pushover," he snipped as he left the room.

"She?!"

Carl hurried through the office, cursing. Staff lifted their gaze towards him. In his haste, he pushed Harry and Oliver to one side as they opened the main door.

Kate's expression softened when she saw the boys walking through the main office.

Oliver smiled and broke into a run.

"We've been good." His happy voice brought a smile to her face.

"He's upset you," said Harry, glaring at Carl's back.

"To what do I owe this pleasure?" said Kate, ruffling Oliver's hair.

"You didn't do the school run this morning, and Clare and Malcolm have food shopping. So I asked them to drop us off here," Harry said in his 'organising' tone.

Pangs of guilt sped through Kate. Instead of doing the school run, she'd had Jasper inside her.

She stopped what she was doing and slipped the laptop into her bag. As if Harry was reading her mind, he collected Carl's papers and put them in a folder. He looked at his mother and smiled.

"Riverside Café?"

***

Kate parked in the café carpark. Harry and Oliver raced towards the café with Harry shouting, "Tea!" By the time she reached the picnic tables, they were tucking into chocolate ice cream, and a mug of steaming tea waited for her.

Oliver, as usual, had chocolate around his mouth, and Kate was wiping it clean with a tissue when an unfamiliar voice said, "Lady Carmichael."

Kate lifted her eyes to a tweed jacket and cord trousers. *Duncan.*

"I hope your husband mentioned me. I'm—"

"Duncan," she said matter-of-factly.

"And this must be Harry and Oliver. I wonder if we might have a chat," he said, glaring at the boys with that 'go and play' look, but they refused, preferring to take their time over their ice cream.

"I don't suppose Jasper mentioned why he had to dash to London?" Duncan said in his soft, calm voice.

"Believe it or not, Jasper has always operated on a need-to-know basis. I don't get involved with his London business."

"But he's left you in charge here."

"That's different. It's Wellsbury business."

"So you know about the incident at the airfield."

"More or less. Not specifics."

"But enough for a visit."

Kate looked at Duncan over her mug of tea.

"It was important to him that I saw for myself the fence repairs. Also he wants the soil tested."

"Soil?"

"It's nothing really. Since the fire, the grass hasn't regrown."

"He thinks there's a problem."

"He wants to check."

Duncan took a long moment to study Kate. He suspected the soil testing was a ruse to hinder his investigation.

He stood. "I'll be in touch."

Kate nodded.

She didn't notice that Gypsy and his right hand had taken a window seat in the café.

"He doesn't look very happy," said the right-hand man.

"I'll put money on it our Duncan didn't get the answers he wanted."

Chapter Twenty-Six

Jasper sat in the study at the Carmichael London home, nursing a generous portion of malt. He should have been going over the Carmichael Trust documents, but he couldn't get Kate out of his mind. He shouldn't have left her to deal with Duncan and Beth.

She answered on the first ring.

"How's your day been?" he tentatively asked.

"Well, I was ravaged by this sexy man."

He grinned. "Did you enjoy it?"

"What do you think?"

"I think I'm a lucky guy. Now tell me about the rest of the day."

"Carl wants me to sign a cheque for a few mill. Went to the café and Duncan joined us. A bit boring really."

"Don't sign any cheques. What did Duncan want?"

"Why you had gone to London. I told him I didn't need to know."

"What are you doing?"

"Looking into the night sky. Thinking."

"About?"

"How little time we spend alone."

"I know."

"I was pondering on the possibility of a beach property," she said in her matter-of-fact tone.

"You want a beach house?"

"I miss painting, and I'm sure you miss sailing."

"I miss you."

She giggled. "I know."

"Any beach property?" asked Jasper, interested.

"Hadn't thought that far ahead."

"Big, small, old, modern?"

"Painting studio with views of the sea. Strict rule… no work."

"Strict rule: you'll come sailing."

After a long moment, she agreed.

"I love you."

"I love you too."

"I'll phone tomorrow."

***

Duncan sat in a large white van with his IT technician. He ripped off his headphones and threw them onto the floor.

"This is married couple talk!" he shouted at his associate.

"You said to bug his phone."

"They're hiding something."

"He's left her in charge. He was just checking in."

"No! My gut's never wrong."

"Carmichael's not into drugs. We're monitoring his activities in London. What more do you want?"

"It's diamonds. Carmichael's involved with diamonds. His old man was a master thief. His son is a master at fencing diamonds."

His technician shook his head.

"You're wrong."

***

Gypsy was unrecognisable as he sat at the bar of Jasper's luxury hotel. The scruffy clothes had been replaced by an Armani suit and leather loafers. He was clean-shaven, his hair neatly trimmed. He slowly swished his brandy bowl, his mind mulling over the mess Beth had got him in. She owed him money. Money he needed to pay for drugs. She had messed up; Carmichael had exposed their operation to the authorities.

Beth had told him Carmichael knew about them using the airfield, but Carmichael had known nothing. And when he'd found the aircraft, Carmichael rang the authorities.

Gypsy would have to go into hiding. Duncan never gave up; he had a reputation for getting his man. But first, Gypsy had a reckoning with Beth.

Chapter Twenty-Seven

Kate stopped outside the school gates and waited while the boys organised their school bags.

"When's Dad coming home? He promised to play football." Oliver's small voice was full of disappointment.

"Hurry up, you two. I haven't got all day."

"You didn't answer," said Harry as he opened the rear door.

"That's because I don't know."

The boys left her and hurried through the school gates without giving her a second glance.

"Enjoy your day!" she shouted, but her words were lost in the happy voices of children. Kate had a lot on her mind. She needed some me time, so she drove to her favourite spot by the Wells and Bury.

As she settled on her thinking seat, her phone buzzed. She knew it was Jasper. He hadn't phoned last night.

"Why haven't you picked up?" he said in a commanding tone.

"I was driving."

"You mean you didn't want to." His tone suddenly became accusing, as if he was looking for an argument.

His sudden change in tone took Kate by surprise. *What's he hiding?* she thought. *Who's he been with?* Beth came into her mind. She knew Beth and Willis had been seen on a London-bound train.

"What do you want?"

"Are you alright?"

"Yes," was Kate's curt reply.

Silence

"Are you still being followed?"

"Yes."

Silence.

"I'm worried."

"No, you're not! If you were worried, you'd have phoned last night. I've got to go." Kate switched off her phone.

***

Jasper stared at his silent phone. He redialled, but she had switched hers off. Chester, the butler, hovered over him, refilling his morning coffee.

Jasper had returned from the club in the early hours. Manning had insisted on buying him dinner to celebrate a new era for the Carmichael trust fund. He had outmanoeuvred Jasper. The trust fund board had voted, by one vote, for Manning to become chairman.

Jasper picked up his phone and dialled Malcolm.

"What's Kate doing today?"

Malcolm was more than a little puzzled. He had already texted Jasper Kate's day.

"She's at the bookshop and gallery. Zak wants to see her, as well as the market stall holders. She has a full day."

"She was a bit off when I phoned."

"She's very busy."

"Give me that." Clare snatched the phone from Malcolm. "She's losing weight. Her jeans are starting to hang. Missed breakfast again. I've phoned Zak to take her to lunch. She insists on spending time with the boys. And you can't be bothered to phone. I suppose you were with Beth."

Jasper tried to cut in, but Clare continued her rant. "She knows that Beth and Willis are in London. Did you 'ave a good dinner and drinks?"

Malcolm snatched the phone off Clare. "You'll 'ave to forgive her. You know how worked up she gets when Kate misses meals."

Jasper abruptly ended the call. He stood and walked to the cold inglenook fireplace, leaning on the uninviting stonework. He'd thought he could cope with being Lord Carmichael, spending time with Kate and developing a diamond network. But he had lost control of the trust fund, and Kate was off with him due to the pressure of work. So for the time being, his diamond dealing had been put on the back burner.

He would have to decide soon between living with Kate in Wellsbury, or diamonds in London.

He wasn't unduly concerned about Wellsbury. Kate could handle Zak, probably better than he could. The market stall holders would gang up against her, but he was confident that she would negotiate a compromise.

He slowly walked back to his desk and flicked through the diary. A lunchtime meeting with Manning was pencilled in. He cursed at his overconfident behaviour with Manning. He should have acted sooner to prevent Manning getting a foothold with the board.

Jasper looked, expecting to see Chester hovering by the door.

"Chester!" he shouted.

Chester scurried into the study.

"Sir!"

Chester watched Jasper's finger moving over his diary.

"Who's this?" said Jasper.

Chester moved so he could read the name Jasper was pointing to. "A Mrs James phoned for a luncheon appointment, but you were already booked with Mr Manning. She suggested dinner as she's an old friend. I agreed. I hope that's alright. She assured me that it was business."

Jasper was inwardly fuming. He dismissed Chester and waited until he was sure he had gone into the kitchen. He reached into his laptop satchel and searched for a burner phone he had never thought he would use again.

"Well, this is a surprise. Never thought I'd hear from you again, after I made that pass at your delightful wife." John, his investigator, sniggered.

"This isn't easy for me, John."

"I bet it isn't. You selfish bastard. If I thought I'd stand a chance with her—"

Jasper interrupted. "I've lost control of the Carmichael trust fund."

"I know. Manning broadcasted it. Having dinner with Beth?"

"How do you... No! I'm going home," Jasper blurted as he realised he should go back to Wellsbury and concentrate on a new plan.

"What do you want?"

"Kate wants me home all the time. She wants me to dissolve the fund. It was Carmichael money that set up the fund for the family. Meredith had a good life off it. But to be fair, he did all the work."

"Too late, old man. Manning's in control."

"Kate thinks Meredith would have protected himself against such a takeover."

"Wouldn't Manning have worked that out?"

"I want you to dig into the fund. Find the initial papers between Carmichael and Spencer."

"It'll take time. And it'll cost. It'll involve people who understand these things."

"That's not a problem. Just don't say who you're working for."

"Is she worth it?"

"What do you mean?"

"Kate! Is she worth it?"

Jasper ignored him.

"Look, I'll give you the heads up," said John. "Rumour has it that there's a new diamond dealer in town. The finger points at you. You have a reputation, and you're very friendly with Zak. Frequent trips between Wellsbury and London... I hate to bring this up, but Colin's diamonds have never been found. And there's a new investigator that's very interested."

"Duncan," Jasper mumbled.

"Ah! You've met."

"I found a plane in one of my hangars."

"Yeah, I know! Beth and Gypsy were using the airfield. Drugs."

Is there anything this guy doesn't know? thought Jasper.

"Is that his name?"

"You mean you didn't know?"

"Why should I know?"

"He's well known in the drugs world. Don't mess with him."

"Drugs are not my thing. What do you know about Duncan?"

John hesitated, before saying, "He has a rep too. He always gets his man. You're in his sights, old man, but Gypsy is who he really wants. My advice is leave diamonds alone and enjoy your family. I'll be in touch."

That wasn't the answer Jasper was expecting. Not for the first time, Jasper doubted John's loyalty.

Jasper slipped the phone back into his satchel and slumped into the old leather desk chair that his grandfather and Colin had sat in. He logged on to his laptop and stared at the wallpaper. Kate was playfully laughing at him. Her hair was down, her eyes on fire and her cheeks flushed. A smile crept across his face as he recalled slowly removing her fitted white blouse. He had worshipped her breasts, first through her white lace bra and again when she was naked. Her fingers had gently massaged his head while delightful sounds escaped her mouth.

Suddenly, a life with Kate painting and him sailing seemed very appealing. He knew, though, that he would be content for a while but he would become restless with the shopping centre. He needed more than Wellsbury. He needed diamonds.

"Sir!" Chester's loud voice shook him out of his reverie. "Mr Manning's office has just called to cancel luncheon. Should I call Mrs James?"

It was a long moment before Jasper understood what Chester was saying.

"Cancel all my appointments. Something has come up."

"All, sir? You have Freemasons, and meetings with their Lordships."

"All, Chester."

***

Jasper called his property manager, instructing him to sell Carmichael Castle and his London home. It was time to resign his grandfather Carmichael, Colin and Meredith Spencer to history.

The final call was to his investment manager. Jasper intended to disassociate himself from the Carmichael trust fund. The shocked investment manager explained it would take some time for all his investments to be sold. The fund would find it difficult to attract new investments without Carmichael involvement—it might well collapse.

Jasper had already accepted that he would take a financial hit for freedom from the clutches of his powerful ancestors.

He closed his laptop and went in search of Chester. He wanted to explain to him that he should have no worries about a place to live. Jasper would find him a house or apartment, and his monthly salary would continue.

Jasper thought something was a little odd when Chester took the sale of the London house in his stride and his only request was for a waterfront apartment. However, Chester did express concern about the future of the Carmichael historical papers and the Carmichael library. Jasper hadn't considered the Carmichael library, but he reassured Chester that a place at the Isaacs' House would be found for them.

Hours later, sitting in the first-class compartment of the last train to Wellsbury, he mulled over how, over the last twenty-four hours, his life had put him on a new path. He couldn't wait to tell Kate—but he wouldn't mention Beth trying to wheedle her way back into his life.

Chapter Twenty-Eight

It was turned midnight when Jasper's train finally stopped at Wellsbury. A signal malfunction had delayed it for two hours. However, Jasper had used the time productively, searching for beach houses. In desperation, he had phoned John and asked for his help.

Wellsbury Station was in darkness. Both the station management and Wellsbury Council switched off the lights on the stroke of midnight. Jasper cursed at this money-saving measure. He hoped Kate would be waiting.

He stepped out of the station concourse onto the pavement when he felt something stab into his back. Jasper stumbled.

"Harder, you bloody fool! Come out of the way," said a familiar silky voice.

The second stab was much harder, piercing Jasper's suit and jacket. Jasper crumpled and his head hit the pavement.

The last thing he heard was a car horn.

***

Kate had been waiting and started the Evoque as soon as she heard the train. To her horror, the headlights shone onto two attackers stabbing Jasper.

Kate floored the accelerator.

"Get his bag. Not that one—his computer bag," yelled the female attacker breathlessly.

"Give me a hand—it's over his neck."

"Move, you fucking piece of shit!" she yelled, kicking Jasper in the kidneys. Jasper groaned.

"It's no good. Come on," said the man, whose attention was on the speeding Evoque.

"That fucking bitch saved you," the female attacker spat before kicking Jasper in the head.

The man lifted his eyes just as Kate hit the brakes, veering away from Jasper but clipping the assailant, knocking him to the ground. A painful cry echoed through the night air.

"Don't leave me! You fucking bitch," the fallen man screamed after the fleeing woman.

Kate leapt from the Evoque, ignoring the man's pained yells. Her attention was solely on a groaning Jasper. She opened the rear door and pushed, pulled, slid Jasper into the footwell.

"Satchel!" he mumbled.

Kate lifted her eyes just as the attackers disappeared into the dark shadows of the station.

With headlights flashing and horn blasting, she sped to Carmichael's Health Centre. Using speed dial, she gasped a message to Malcolm.

"They've stabbed Jasper! Health centre!"

The staff were waiting as she skidded to a halt in front of the health centre doors. Jasper was semiconscious; Kate couldn't understand his mumbling. A lump appeared in her throat when she saw two knives sticking out of his coat.

When Malcolm, Clare and two fretting boys joined her, Kate sat with her head in her hands.

"They insisted," blurted Clare before Kate could tell her off for bring the boys.

"They've just taken him to x-ray. The doctor wouldn't give me any idea…" Kate paused to wipe her eyes as the two boys stood by her side.

Clare gulped, a tear trickling down her face. Malcolm found it difficult to swallow. A tense, worried silence developed.

After what seemed like an age, Malcolm choked out, "Did you see 'em?"

"There were two. Dressed in black. Probably a man and a woman. I clipped the man with the car." Kate paused to regain her thoughts. She didn't want to let on that she'd recognised the voices of Beth and Willis. "I couldn't see him. I just felt something was wrong. I switched on the headlights. Jasper was stumbling to the floor."

She made no effort to stop the flow of tears. Harry and Oliver moved towards Clare. They didn't know what to do. They had never seen their mother so distraught.

Malcolm walked into a corridor, speaking quietly into his phone. "Bruce! There's two. Man and a woman. The man's injured. She hit him with the car. Check the hospital."

"How is he?" asked Bruce.

"We don't know yet. Be careful. We might be dealing with Gypsy."

"If it was 'im, Jasper would be dead."

When Malcolm returned to the waiting area, Clare had her arms around the boys.

"It's serious, isn't it?" said Harry.

"Is he going to die?" Oliver blurted between sobs.

The swing doors opened, giving Kate a glimpse of Jasper lying on a bed with his eyes closed. She stood and rushed through the doors. The boys went to follow, but Clare caught hold of them.

"You can't come in here, Mrs Carmichael," snapped an authoritative-looking nurse. Kate brushed her aside and held Jasper's hand. He opened his good eye and tried to smile.

"Home," he mouthed.

Kate leaned into him, stroking his forehead. The authoritative nurse stood at the other side of the bed. "You've lost a lot of blood, Mr Carmichael," said the nurse. "You need a transfusion."

He closed his eyes, and after a long moment, Kate rested his hand on the bed.

"No!" Jasper's broken voice was unexpectedly loud.

"He'll be groggy for some time. Got a nasty cut on his head."

Kate turned towards a calm voice. A doctor.

"You did well leaving the knives in his back," he said softly, looking at Jasper's hand gripping Kate's. "The knife missed his lung. You saved his life, Mrs Carmichael," continued the doctor. "He'll need time to heal. Rest. Bedrest… Jasper won't like that." The doctor's gaze moved from Jasper to Kate.

"What do I need to know?"

"Nothing really. He's been stitched up. He'll have blood and fluids, here, and then bedrest at home." The doctor's eyes returned to Jasper's hand gripping Kate's. "The nurse will find you a chair so you can spend the night… He was mumbling your name while I was working on him."

Kate caught the doctor's eye.

"Don't be alarmed. He didn't feel a thing. We just don't like giving too much anaesthetic."

The doctor turned towards the door and was greeted by two pairs of worried eyes.

"You two can say goodnight and then return home."

Oliver was quick off the mark. He took his dad's hand from Kate. "Love you," he whispered.

"We'll look after her," whispered Harry in his mature tone.

Chapter Twenty-Nine

After five days in hospital, Jasper was becoming more and more irritable. As far as he was concerned, he should be at home helping Kate, but she had insisted he stay in hospital until the doctors gave him the all-clear.

But Kate was worrying Jasper. She looked tired. Ignoring the cost to herself, she had selflessly given herself to him and his business while finding time and energy to comfort the boys. Kate didn't grumble; she just did what was needed.

His memories of the attack were patchy. He wanted Kate to fill in the blanks, but she skilfully avoided the subject. Bruce had had his ear to the ground, and two names had come up: Beth and Willis. Bruce had waited till he was alone with Jasper before telling him.

Inspector Watts had made a duty visit, but he made it clear that the chances of finding those responsible for the stabbing were slim. There were no leads, and Kate couldn't identify the attackers.

Inwardly, Jasper vowed revenge.

The door to his private room slowly opened. At first, he didn't recognise the figure standing at the end of his bed. The alarm on the blood pressure reader shrieked as he tried to lift himself.

"Get the fuck out of here!" Jasper yelled as he pressed the emergency buzzer on the side of the bed.

"I don't like being stood up," Beth sharply retorted.

"Stood up?!" Jasper's face reddened as his temper flared.

"You came running back to her," Beth snipped. "And you'll pay for that."

Jasper stared into Beth's evil, scowling eyes, stiff face and tight lips.

"She put Willis in hospital. That bitch will pay."

Willis in hospital, Jasper thought. He didn't hide a grin.

Beth's anger bubbled over. "We watched you working on the train. Didn't even see us. Too busy staring at the fucking screen."

"What do you want?"

"Money!"

A tense silence hovered.

Blackmail flashed into Jasper's mind.

"*Sex with Jasper Carmichael.* I thought that would be an apt title."

Jasper still remained silent.

"I've written a journal about our sex life." Beth grinned as she reached into her shoulder bag. "Knew this would come in useful someday," she sniggered while waving a dog-eared hardcover notebook. "I bought this after a particularly brutal night of sex. You made me bleed. I crawled to the fucking bathroom. And you fucking left me." Angry hatred spilled from her mouth.

Jasper's face showed no emotion as he fought to control his temper.

He recalled that night. She had taunted him; her words flashed back into his mind. *'Is that the best you can do?'* She had laughed in his face. He had snapped. And she'd never taunted him again.

As calmly as he could, Jasper reminded her of her own sexual behaviour with Jack and Richard. She brushed that aside as insignificant and took advantage of Jasper's present vulnerability, threatening to give her story to the tabloids if he didn't pay up.

"Look at you. You don't care. You only care about her. Well, she's not so perfect. Eric told us all about her."

Jasper's temper was bubbling over. With his hands flat against the mattress, he pushed himself up.

"Get the fuck out!" he yelled.

Loud, running footsteps echoed along the corridor.

Beth stepped back, fumbling for the door handle. She had seen that contorted, angry face many times before.

"You'll be hearing from me."

Jasper reared out of bed. As she ran, Beth glimpsed Jasper falling and sending the bedside table crashing to the floor. She raced along the hospital corridor, dodging the hospital staff that were running towards Jasper's room.

In her haste, she didn't notice that she pushed past Bruce. He turned and watched her run towards her BMW, where Willis sat in the passenger seat.

Bruce turned back to the hospital and ran towards Jasper's room.

"Malcolm!" Bruce whispered into his phone. "Summat's up. Just seen Beth leaving the hospital. Jasper's raging. Where's Kate?"

"She's at the office. I'm on my way."

Bruce joined the hospital staff gently lifting Jasper back into bed.

"Where's Kate?" Jasper said, looking into Bruce's eyes.

"Office."

"Go to her."

Bruce nodded and left his boss in the capable hands of the doctors and nurses.

***

While Bruce was dealing with Jasper, Beth was marching through the general office of Carmichael House towards Jasper's office, where Kate sat staring at her laptop screen.

Amanda jumped up from her desk and tried to stop Beth. But with her temper raging, Beth pushed her with such force that Amanda stumbled, knocking over some chairs.

Beth stormed through the office door, glaring at Kate.

"Who the fuck do you think you are?" Beth snarled.

Kate was a little dazed as she looked up into Beth's angry eyes.

"Don't give me that innocent look. I know all about you and Eric."

Beth now had Kate's attention. The laptop closed.

Beth sniggered. "Couldn't get enough of him. *'Harder, harder.'* He had to cover your mouth so your screams wouldn't be heard. And then you refused him. You had a lot of headaches back then."

Kate stood, her temper rising. "What do you want?"

"Granddaddy's left you rich. As if you fucking need it. You have Jasper eating out of your fucking hand."

"What do you want?" Kate walked from behind the desk.

"A share."

"Of?"

"Your millions."

Kate stepped towards Beth. Her body had stiffened, her face hardened. Her green eyes bulged and her cheeks reddened.

Beth took a step back towards the open door. Memories of Kate's temper flashed into her mind. She suddenly realised that she had made a big mistake.

"Get the fuck out! Take your fucking threats with you!" Kate yelled.

Beth stumbled backwards into Amanda. She quickly righted herself and ran from the office.

"You alright, Kate?" Amanda tentatively asked.

Kate nodded and slumped into Jasper's very comfortable desk chair. Beth had destroyed her last reserve of patience.

The day had begun badly. She had missed breakfast; the boys had argued on the way to school. When she'd arrived at Carmichael House, there was no tea. She had sent an office junior to the local shop, something she hated doing.

Her first meeting with Jasper's newly appointed accountant didn't go well. She had refused to sign off invoices without first checking them. He had questioned her authority, and Kate had reacted uncharacteristically angrily. Another layer of her patience peeled away.

When Beth appeared, the last remnants of her resolve had melted away. Kate had a horrible feeling she might be heading for a nervous breakdown.

She needed to calm; she couldn't let Jasper see her like this. She wanted him to recover.

Kate placed her laptop along with the accountant's invoices into her messenger bag. She left Carmichael House deep in thought.

***

Kate sat staring at the rivers Wells and Bury, mingling together as they made their way to the sea. The tightness in her neck slowly weakened as she lost herself in the gentle movements of the water.

Her peace of mind was disturbed when a very large man squeezed beside her. Their shoulders rubbed, making Kate move to the edge of the bench.

"I've been wanting to meet Carmichael's woman for some time. Saw you pull up and thought, 'This is my chance to meet Kate Carmichael.' I've 'eard a lot about you," he said in a low, gruff, menacing voice.

Kate shivered and made to move, but a large, hairy hand gripped her knee.

"I mean you no 'arm, Mrs Carmichael. Just information," he continued, in the same menacing manner.

Kate's stomach began to rise into her throat.

"You saved his life. A bit of skilful driving to clip that bastard Willis." He grinned. "You should've hit him harder. But it's his boss I want."

Kate remained silent.

"She's double crossed me. I suspect she's in cahoots with your lawyer or accountant. Probably swindling money from Jasper." He paused, gathering his thoughts. "At first I thought Jasper was in on it, but when the police arrived at the airfield, I knew that wasn't the case. What do you know, Mrs Carmichael?"

After a long, thoughtful moment, Kate carefully answered. "I know Jasper doesn't do drugs. I know Beth and Willis have some sort of vendetta against him."

"And you, Mrs Carmichael. But do not concern yourself. They're my problem now."

Kate tensed. She was unsure what he meant or what he wanted.

"They went to the hospital. Upset Jasper. He's discharged himself."

"What!?" Kate went to move, but his hand held firm.

"That bitch owes me. That episode at the airfield has the law breathing down my neck. Fuckin' Duncan is closing in."

"I really know nothing about it." Kate went to move again but he kept her pinned.

"Tell me about Beth and Jasper."

"Look, I must go. Jasper will be—"

His grip tightened on her knee.

"They were lovers," Kate blurted.

"Why did it end?"

"What do I call you?" she said, trying to avoid answering the question.

"Gypsy."

After a long moment, Kate finally murmured, "Jasper caught her in bed with Jack and Richard."

Gypsy was silent as he mulled over Kate's words. His initial thought was *So what?* He shared his women, but obviously Jasper didn't.

"And what did you do for Jasper?" he said.

"I worked for Jasper."

"Don't put yourself down. You did more than work for him. You had his kid." A sly grin slowly crept across his face. "Not so frigid, eh? Like the other day in back of the Range Rover."

Gypsy didn't hide his delight when Kate blushed.

"Where would she hide in Wellsbury?" he asked.

"Hide? She doesn't hide; she has a house."

"She's not there. So where would she go?"

Kate hesitated. "I suppose she might go to Joanne's."

"Joanne? Sells clothes?"

"She also runs an escort business."

"Brothel, you mean."

Kate didn't respond. A moment passed, each of them deep in thought.

"I shall pay it a visit," Gypsy said eventually.

"You haven't asked where it is?"

"No need. I saw Willis waiting for a shining black front door to open. I remember thinking, 'Where's he going?' Now I know." He grinned. "To get laid."

Gypsy squeezed Kate's knee.

"It's been a pleasure, Kate. If I had more time, I would've taken you to dinner. I'm not the animal you think I am. I would surprise you. I'm much like Jasper. A sexual man. Knows what he wants and goes after it. Has the best clothes, food, wine. Can be ruthless. Protects what's his. I know Beth's good between the sheets, but you must be *more* than good between the sheets. You must 'ave that special something. I look forward to experiencing it."

He stood and lifted her hand. Their eyes met as his warm lips slowly kissed the back of her hand. A smile crept across his face, reaching his eyes.

"Till next time."

Kate's stomach nervously churned. The sensual hand kiss and the glint in his eye were full of desire. His intentions were clear. She sat still for a long moment, calming herself and putting Gypsy out of her mind, before driving home.

***

"Kate!"

Jasper's loud voice bellowed through Isaacs' House. Against medical advice, he had discharged himself from hospital.

The unexpected visit from Beth at her evil best had disturbed him. She had Kate in her sights, and he considered his beloved no match for Beth. She was intent on blackmailing him, threating to publish a book on his particular cruel brand of rough sex. That angered Jasper; he wasn't proud of what he'd done to Beth, even if in his opinion she'd deserved it.

"Kate!"

"She's not here," answered Clare defiantly.

"Where the fuck is she?" Jasper glared at Clare. He didn't like her tone.

"Running your business." Clare had moved closer, eyes bulging, hands resting on her hips.

"She should be here!"

"Here! At your beck and call. No sleep, no food. Dealing with people she has—"

Jasper spoke across Clare. "What do you mean, no sleep, no food?"

"Jasper Carmichael, can't you see what's happening to her?"

"Where's Mum?" asked Harry, pushing his head around the kitchen door. He took one look at Jasper and closed the door.

Jasper stared at Harry's back.

"Who did the school run?"

"I don't know. Bruce or Malcolm," answered a perplexed Clare.

"Kate's alone?!"

Jasper suddenly felt faint. He staggered into the living room and slumped onto one of the overstuffed couches. Beads of sweat covered his forehead.

"Malcolm!" shouted Clare.

Malcolm raced into the living room, followed by two very concerned boys.

"Find Kate," Jasper murmured, just before he passed out.

Chapter Thirty

The black of the night was turning into the grey of the dawn when Jasper stirred. He was naked, lying on his side. His beloved was naked, nestled into his body like two peas in a pod. She was asleep, her breathing slow and relaxed. He gently lifted her hair to plant kisses on her neck. He had taken to thinking of her as his beloved; all other words failed to describe his deep feeling for her.

He lifted his lips from her neck and she wiggled her bottom into him. Even in sleep she responded to him. He smiled and planted another kiss.

The bedroom door creaked open. Soft whispers drifted through. Slow, careful footsteps moved towards the bed. Jasper felt warm breath upon his naked shoulder.

Light footsteps scurried back towards the door.

"There're still asleep," said a small voice. "They've no clothes on. You know what that means."

"Mum's too tired and Dad's hurting too much for that."

The door clicked shut.

Jasper felt Kate smile.

"You won't be hurting so much tomorrow, and I won't be so tired."

Jasper smiled and Kate turned and rolled into his body. Their lips met.

"No more, Kate."

She pulled away and gazed into his concerned face.

"No more what?"

"Us being apart."

She smiled and he pulled her atop of him. Even though it hurt, the need to feel skin against skin was greater than any pain.

***

It was mid-afternoon when they had finished retelling the previous day's events. Kate made to move for the school run.

Clare appeared in the open doorway of Kate's studio, staring disbelievingly at the pair. They sat on the chaise longue, Jasper with cushions supporting his back. Kate's legs dangled at the sides. He had his arms wrapped around her waist, resting his head upon her chest.

"Malcolm's gone to fetch the boys. I'll bring tea," Clare said in a disapproving tone.

"That'll be lovely," said Kate, trying to move, but Jasper's grip tightened.

A slightly embarrassed Clare quickly turned away, leaving them alone.

"I don't care a shit what she—or anybody—thinks. You're mine. And I don't play second fiddle to anyone. That includes the boys." His hands cupped her breasts. "And if Gypsy or anyone else thinks they are going to touch what's mine..." His words drifted away as her nipples hardened and his trousers suddenly became uncomfortable. "I don't share you."

"I don't want to be shared."

Their lips met. Her hands moved to his hair as their kiss deepened. Mutual desire was stirring when an aristocratic voice echoed through the studio.

"You're in no fit condition to fuck a woman, even if she's your wife."

Kate's head was tucked into Jasper's neck, his fingers were toying with her bra strap, his arousal pressing into her. Another minute and she would have been naked atop him.

"What do you want?" Jasper snapped.

Kate carefully lifted herself off Jasper, straightening her blouse, and walked to the bi-fold doors, keeping her back to Duncan.

Duncan's eyes settled on Jasper's bulging crotch. "Christ! Carmichael, can't you control yourself?"

Two happy voices burst into the studio.

"She's awake!" cried Harry, running past Duncan and towards his mother.

"Who are you?" Oliver's bitter tone echoed.

"Oliver!" admonished Kate, while stroking Harry's hair. "Apologise. That's not how you greet guests."

"I don't care. This place is ours."

"Oliver!" Jasper tried to shout, but a pain shot through his back when he tried to move.

"Tea's in the living room," announced Clare.

Malcolm appeared and helped Jasper off the chaise longue. Jasper leaned against him as they walked into the living room.

Oliver refused to move, preferring to stand with his hands on his hips, glaring at Duncan.

"If you were mine…" said Duncan, returning Oliver's glare.

"But he's not," said Kate, taking Oliver's arm as she walked from the studio.

"It's you I want to talk to." Duncan's voice was raised. Kate carried on walking.

Duncan reluctantly walked into the living room. He was surprised to find Jasper already propped up in one of the overstuffed chairs.

"Help yourself to tea or wait for Kate. She may be some time."

"What do you mean?"

"Oliver's for it."

"I should think so," Duncan replied impatiently, pouring a cup of tea.

"You don't understand. Kate's studio is special."

"I don't give a fuck!" Duncan said between gulps of tea. "Where's Beth?"

"How the hell should I know?"

"She visited you in the hospital and then you discharged yourself. What did she want?"

"Blackmail."

Jasper's abrupt one-word reply made Duncan sputter. "She then visited your wife. I suppose you talk between fucking?"

"Blackmail."

"That's convenient. Blackmailing you both, and now she's disappeared."

Jasper tried to stand but quickly slumped back into the chair. "I don't give a fuck what you think. What I do with my wife is none of your fucking business. Now get out!"

"My gut tells me you're up to your neck with drugs and diamonds. Beth was in cahoots with Gypsy. He'll run rings around you."

"Get the fuck out!" boomed an angry Jasper.

"Duncan!" Malcolm's angry, 'don't mess with me' tone took Duncan by surprise. He'd thought he was alone with Jasper.

Duncan was annoyed—no one told him to 'get the fuck out'. But as soon as he was on his feet, Malcolm was by his side, escorting him out of Isaacs' House.

Chapter Thirty-One

With Jasper starting to take control of the business, Kate had time to concentrate on the bookshop. To capitalise on the success of Carmichael Books, she had organised a special release day event from the up-and-coming author, Frances Parker-Smith.

She was at the bookshop worktable slipping pre-ordered books into envelopes when Harry slipped on to the stool next to her.

"Thought you were with Zak?" she said matter-of-factly while packaging another book.

"That man's there," he said, handing her another book.

"What man?"

"You know. That giant."

Kate stopped and stared at Harry. "Is he a regular visitor?"

"Yeah! Comes in through the back."

Kate took the book from Harry's hand and placed it on the table. "Harry, tell me."

"It doesn't matter."

"Yes! It does."

"Zak made it clear that I wasn't wanted. Not for the first time either. I earwigged. I know I shouldn't, but I'm fed up with Zak pushing me out. I look forward to spending time in the back with Zak. He knows his stuff and he's a good teacher." Harry paused and looked at his mother. "It's something to do with the shopping centre and… and diamonds.

I think the giant said he wanted in. He said, 'Jasper's gone soft; he's pussy whipped.' Is that you?"

Kate closed her eyes and put her arm around her son.

"Dad loves you. He wants to be with you." Harry's voice quivered. "Why can't they leave us alone?"

"The past has a habit of rearing its ugly head. But as a family we'll rise above it."

"What's up with Harry?" said a concerned Oliver, pulling up a stool next to Kate.

"Thought you were playing football."

"Nah! That man came with Zak. Don't like it." Oliver flicked through the stack of addressed envelopes. "What you doing?"

"It's for the book launch. Mum used her Carmichael name to get them on release day." Harry grinned proudly at his mother.

"Does Dad know?" asked Oliver, already losing interest.

"Help me fill the envelopes, and we'll go for ice cream."

The boys looked at each other and grinned, each taking a book and slipping it into an envelope.

When they had finished, Oliver jumped off the stool. "Ice cream!" he shouted. "Race you," he said to Harry.

Kate had parked at the rear of the bookshop. The boys were waiting; Oliver was doing his dance when she pressed the key fob.

"Did you see that car?" asked Harry as Kate started the engine.

"Been here a lot," said the observant Oliver.

"Malcom!" she said into the car phone, not bothering to answer the boys. "We're going to the café. Ask Bruce to join me."

***

"She's on the move, boss," said Gypsy's driver, who was watching Kate's car from a black Mercedes G-Class.

"Where's she going?" Gypsy responded down the phone, turning to Zak.

"Riverside Café, I'm guessing. She has the boys."

"Pick me up," Gypsy commanded. He turned to Zak. "Go on."

Zak reddened; he was about to slag Kate off. "Her fuckin' benevolent behaviour is preventing me from expanding my jewellery business. If she carries on at this rate, she'll own Wellsbury."

"Go on."

"The indoor market is barely covering its costs. I wanted to expand into it but Kate has become the silent partner. Does their books for free."

"And the café?"

"The same."

"Hill's Garage?"

"The same."

"Jasper owns the airfield and she owns the adjacent land…" Gypsy said, thinking.

A car horn blasted.

"We'll finish this conversation later."

***

Kate parked in her usual space at the Riverside Café carpark. She smiled as Harry and Oliver leapt out of the car and raced into the café. The smile disappeared when, through her rear-view mirror, she noticed a black Mercedes G-Class had pulled into the car park. She was certain it was the same Mercedes that had been parked behind the shop.

The boys were already sitting in the picnic seats when Kate joined them. Oliver was grinning, chocolate ice cream covering his mouth. Before Kate sat down, she held his head and wiped his face. Oliver shook his head, laughing.

Kate didn't notice two men slip into the café, taking a window seat.

"Look!" said Harry, with a mouthful of ice cream.

Jasper was slowly walking towards them. He was using a walking stick; he still hadn't fully recovered from the stabbing. Smiling, Kate stood and went to meet him. She looped her arm through his and planted a soft kiss on his cheek.

"This is a lovely surprise," she whispered so only he could hear.

The boys looked at one another and grinned.

"Couldn't stop 'im, Kate," boomed Bruce, carrying two coffees. Following close behind was four of Bruce's team.

"Work party?" said Kate, smiling.

"No! Going to the airfield," answered Bruce, eyeing the two men from the G-Class. "Two of 'em are in the café."

"Is he one?" Jasper asked.

"Think so. Don't like to stare."

"Who?" asked Kate.

"Don't worry about it," said Jasper.

Kate tried to catch Bruce's eye, but he looked away from her. She felt uneasy; she didn't like Jasper not telling her.

She forced a smile while the boys laughed and finished their ice cream. Oliver stood up to go stone skimming, but Kate caught his eye. She stood, shivering as if someone was watching her.

"Not today, Oliver. I have to finish up at the bookshop."

Chapter Thirty-Two

"Will you two stop it?" Kate's voice shrieked from the kitchen.

Harry and Oliver continued tip-tapping while running into Jasper's office. They abruptly stopped; Zak and Gypsy sat facing Jasper, who was propped up in one of his overstuffed office chairs. The boys turned and ran back to Kate, who was listening to Clare and tasting hot fruitcake.

"You'll 'ave indigestion. How many times 'ave I told you not to eat hot cake?"

Kate was waving her hand in front of her open mouth. The boys grinned.

"And you two! Go and change while your mother recovers from a burnt mouth."

Kate eased out of her light grey jacket as she walked towards Jasper's office, leaving Clare in the kitchen, still ranting on. Kate ignored the visitors, her green eyes sparkling at a smiling Jasper. She leaned into him, kissing his hair as he wrapped his arm around her waist, pulling her into him.

A loud cough echoed from the open doorway.

"You'll be taking tea then," said a miffed Clare as she abruptly turned and stormed back to the kitchen.

"You're a difficult woman to see, Mrs Carmichael." Gypsy's voice had a touch of impatience.

Kate slipped between Jasper and the arm of the chair. He didn't hide his pleasure as their bodies touched.

"What do you want? I haven't the patience to play games." She pulled her ponytail free so her blonde hair could fall onto her shoulders.

"This is not a game, Kate," said Zak.

"I'm guessing you want the farmers' market closed."

"I could make better use of the space. Make more money."

"Zak's diamond centre. Or Cohen's gems. Or—"

"Enough!" Gypsy's angry voice cut across her. "You've pussy-whipped Jasper, but you won't do that to me."

An angry, deep silence filled the office. Clare appeared at the open doorway, holding a tray of tea and cake. She abruptly turned back to the kitchen.

Kate's soft, calm voice sliced the tension.

"The outdoor farmers' market and the indoor market are staying."

Gypsy clenched his fists; Kate was going to defy him.

"I'll 'ave your fucking business, Carmichael."

Kate continued as if Gypsy hadn't spoken. "The Carmichael Centre is for the people of the town. The markets are the soul of Wellsbury. People travel to experience the vibrant atmosphere. The market square is the place for musicians to entertain. Small theatre groups practise performing. Coffee shops. Foodies can enjoy delights from around the world. The market is slowly building a reputation. And you want to replace it with jewellery? Really!"

"Kate and I have discussed this," Jasper said. "I want the bookshop and gallery to separate. The bookshop is taking off, particularly now Kate's negotiated a deal with various publishing houses."

"You mean she's cashed in on the Carmichael name," snarled Zak.

"And? I suppose you don't use the Cohen name." Jasper eyed Zak. "The bookshop will move near the market area. There're a number of units coming up for renewal. Some owners have already approached me about moving into the vacant units. Some are moving on. I intend the bookshop to take over that block. I've managed to persuade Kate that we should expand the gallery into the present bookshop. I'm offering the designer labels a chance to move nearer the hotel, and probably a boutique in the hotel." Jasper paused. "The centre is evolving; I have to get the mix right. Entrepreneurs must see opportunities."

"You're experimenting, Carmichael. You're taking your eyes from where the money is," snarled Gypsy.

"And where's that?"

"Beth knew where the money lies," Gypsy evil-eyed Jasper.

"If you mean drugs—over my dead body. Drug dealers will be kicked out. It's going to be a safe place for children." Jasper's voice took on an angry tone. "And if you doubt me, ask that London cocaine dealer that tried to sell in the hotel."

Kate turned and stared at Jasper; she had no knowledge of this. Jasper's hand slowly trailed along her shoulder.

"You had a reputation for fencing diamonds. But your pussy has made you soft." Gypsy's bitter words were directed at Kate.

Jasper gripped her shoulder. "Gossip! Stories are made up when there's no information." He purposely focused his eye contact on Gypsy.

Zak went pink as he recalled the deal he had with Jasper. No paper trail, no text messages, only phone in an emergency, use a burner once only.

"Don't fucking give me that, Carmichael. The word on the street is about an anonymous dealer. It's common knowledge you're dealing again."

"Old news. If the police had any evidence, they would be knocking at my door."

"You're a person of interest. Journalists are investigating the Carmichaels. Your grandfather was a piece of work, and your old man a master thief. And you!" Gypsy's voice rose. "A money launderer. Murderer!"

Jasper nervously fidgeted. Kate gripped his arm.

"I don't think we'll be surprised at anything the journalists find." Kate stared at Gypsy. "We've been there. Got the T-shirt."

Gypsy ignored her. "You're no loving husband. Beth told me about how you treated her. Rough fuck is gentle compared to you."

Kate's grip tightened on Jasper's arm. "Careful what you repeat, Gypsy. Beth has her own axe to grind. She has a habit of using men then dropping them when they are no use to her."

Kate's words hit a chord with Gypsy. He turned his evil glare towards her.

Kate wasn't deterred.

"If you want to know about the wartime Carmichael"—she lifted her eyes towards Gypsy—"his activities are extensively documented, except for his secret missions. There are so many myths and legends surrounding Colin Carmichael that make good reading. And, I suggest, if a journalist wants true facts about Carmichael and Swain, I might be a good source." Kate paused as Jack, Richard, Don, Anton, Beth, the Wilsons, the Cohens and Mr Smith, everyone from Carmichael and Swain, flashed into her mind.

"Who'd believe you? You're in love with the guy!" Gypsy snarled.

"Yes, I am! But that wasn't always the case."

Zak smirked. Kate had skilfully manoeuvred Gypsy's thoughts off Jasper.

"We seem to have digressed. What exactly was the purpose of your visit?" Kate said casually. "Don't underestimate me." She held Gypsy's gaze. "If you intend to take over the centre—game on."

Gypsy stood. His giant frame towered over Kate and Jasper.

"You think you're so fucking clever. But you've met your fucking match, Mrs Carmichael. I'll 'ave the fucking centre and you with it."

Zak stood and sauntered towards the door. He turned and smirked at Kate, touching his forehead with his forefinger.

***

Duncan slipped into the white van parked half on the footpath close to Isaacs' House garden. His focus had changed; Jasper Carmichael was in his sights. He had taken the step of bugging Carmichael's house.

"What's up?" he asked his surveillance man.

The man dropped his headphones around his neck.

"Gypsy and Zak are making a move on Carmichael's empire. Got a bit ugly. It's all on here." He handed Duncan a small card. "If you want my opinion, Gypsy will go after Mrs C."

"That's when Jasper will show his true colours," Duncan gloated. "He'll make a mistake. Kate's his weakness."

"I thought you wanted Gypsy! He's not a patient man. He's angry. He's more likely to make a mistake than Carmichael."

Duncan wasn't listening. He hopped out of the van smiling, relishing the fact that a Carmichael was in his grasp. He was so occupied with his own thoughts he didn't notice Bruce slowly driving towards Isaacs' House. But Bruce noticed him.

***

Kate's anger was overflowing. She was pacing through the orchard, up and down, up and down, when Jasper caught up with her.

He held her shoulders and pulled her into him.

"I'll deal with them," he whispered into her hair.

"*We'll* deal with them," Kate corrected.

"He'll be targeting you, my love. You're not like any woman he's met."

"Why can't they leave us alone?"

"I'm a Carmichael, and they want revenge."

"Revenge for what?"

Jasper kissed her forehead.

"I have what Gypsy wants. Airfield to bring in drugs. An established network to sell to. Hill's Garage to expand into whatever he wants. He wants to be kingpin. But to be kingpin, he must control the diamond and drug trade." After a thoughtful moment, Jasper added, "He appears to have Zak on board."

"You're not dealing in diamonds."

"No. Not at the moment."

"Jasper!"

Jasper felt Kate's body stiffen. She wiggled, trying to free herself, but his hand held her face to his chest.

"We still have the diamonds in the desk to deal with," he commented.

"Leave them there."

"You know I will never do that."

Kate's stomach churned; she felt hopeless. She was losing him to diamonds.

Jasper held her close, waiting for the words that would tell him that she was with him or against him.

"Do you need Zak?" asked Kate.

"No!"

Jasper couldn't hide his relief. He cupped her face and claimed her mouth.

Chapter Thirty-Three

Duncan had waited all afternoon for Jasper to join Kate at the book launch. He had spent some time admiring Jasper's wife. Her blonde hair rested on her shoulders, her high cheekbones had a light covering of makeup, her purple dress was simple in design. It flowed over her hips, resting just above her knee to show her shapely legs to best effect. Her ample cleavage nestled in the long V-neck, and her heels were just the right height—not too high or low. He had never seen Mrs Carmichael attractively dressed, and he liked what he saw.

His attention shifted when a black Range Rover stopped in Kate's parking space. Jasper eased out of the driving seat. He gazed about, and Duncan had no doubt that he'd been spotted. For a long moment, he studied Jasper. Something was different about him. Although he was immaculately dressed, he hadn't a jacket, preferring a waistcoat, and he walked with a stiff back, apparently still feeling the effects of the stabbing.

Duncan waited till Jasper entered the rear of the bookshop before following. He was just in time to watch Jasper slip his arm around his wife's waist and plant a kiss on her cheek. She blushed when his lips caressed her ear.

Duncan scanned the room, looking for signs of Gypsy. One of his men was leaning against the front door sipping wine. Zak walked over to him and nodded towards Jasper. Duncan had some comfort that Jasper had not only given his men the slip but also Gypsy's men.

The question uppermost in his mind was where had Jasper been?

People were leaving, most holding copies of the book in Carmichael Books paper carriers.

The book launch had been a success, with Kate's entire stock sold. Duncan had dismissed the book; he didn't read what he considered trash, but apparently a lot of people did. However, the finger food and wine compensated for the poor reading material.

Duncan's phone buzzed; he lifted it from his pocket. It was the news he hadn't expected to hear. He was annoyed. He needed to know what Jasper was up to. He needed to search the place, but Jasper's IT people were already there, installing what looked like new equipment.

Duncan's stomach flipped. Jasper had not only given his men the slip, but he was planning something Duncan knew nothing about. He had underestimated Carmichael; he had taken all warnings about him with a pinch of salt.

He always got his man. He would have to up his game.

***

Jasper had left Isaacs' House as soon as Kate left for the book launch. He'd anticipated being followed. A quick manoeuvre into the multi-storey carpark was all it had taken to lose his tail. He'd then switched cars, leaving his Range Rover in his old lockup.

He drove to the cottage that had been Kate and Harry's home, parking the black Ford Focus out of sight. Kate would be surprised to discover that the property was still in her name and he had not sold it, but how could he sell it when it meant so much to her?

Am I becoming soft or am I pussy whipped? he mused.

Jasper took a long moment settling himself before the meeting with John, his private investigator. He focused his mind on Gypsy and Duncan, the adversaries that would give him the most trouble. He prepared himself for the bad news about the Carmichael trust fund or the sale of Carmichael property.

However, he regretted telling John about the beach house. He would have guessed it was for Kate, and as far as Jasper was concerned, the less John knew about Kate the better.

John sat in the living room with an over-confident expression.

"Lost interest in the trust fund?" John jibed as Jasper sat opposite him. He dropped two files onto the coffee table. "Can't find out much about Gypsy. He just appeared. Member of a travelling community. Duncan's been after him for some time. Now, Duncan I *can* spill the dirt on. It's all in there." He pointed towards the file.

What John had omitted from the file was that Duncan had offered him large sums of money for information on Jasper. John's greed had got the better of him. He had fed Duncan titbits about Jasper, but he'd been very careful not to implicate Kate. He wanted her for himself.

Jasper was about to play a dangerous game with two men far more ruthless than himself. John would wait on the sidelines as Duncan and Gypsy outmanoeuvred Jasper. While Jasper was consumed with the fight to save his business,

John would step in and seduce Kate. He would wait until she was at a low point and in need of a shoulder to cry on. Her seduction would finish Jasper Carmichael.

John stared intensely at Jasper, hoping for a flicker of emotion, but Jasper was at the top of his game. His impassive expression gave nothing away.

"How good is Duncan?" he asked, flicking through the file.

"Very. But relies too much on his surveillance team. Whereas Gypsy relies on nobody."

"There has to be something."

"I suggest you set them up against each other. A good dose of Carmichael deceit, and Duncan can kill Gypsy—or the other way round." John sarcastically said.

Jasper didn't bite. "Any luck finding a beach house?"

"Kate wants a beach house." John grinned. "Is it true Gypsy said you're pussy whipped?"

"Shut the fuck up and answer the question."

John roared with laughter. "There's an old house. Empty, just along the coast. Needs some work. Path leads to the beach. Some artist had it built in the twenties. A short drive and there's a modern marina, just waiting for a Carmichael yacht."

Jasper ignored another John-jibe.

"Diamonds?"

"You'll have no problems opening up the old network. Does Kate know?"

"Leave Kate out of it."

"You do realise that the money from the Lord Carmichael investment and property sale won't cover the opening of a diamond network, a beach house and the demise of Duncan and Gypsy?"

Jasper gave John a curious look.

"A professional hitman won't come cheap."

"Who said anything about a hitman?"

***

The beach house was situated at the end of a car-width lane a short drive along the coast from Kate's old cottage. The hedgerow scraped along the sides of the Focus. Jasper was thankful he was in the Ford and not the Range Rover. He'd changed his expensive Italian loafers for a well-worn pair of trainers. His crisp white shirt and waistcoat were hidden under a black fleece.

The path that led to the small bungalow was completely overgrown. Jasper took one look at the bungalow and thought '*demolish*', but Kate would see an ideal artist's retreat.

She's such a romantic, he thought.

"If yo thinking of buying, better be quick."

Jasper turned. The voice belonged to a small, round, elderly man—wellingtons, parka, cap and walking stick. An old Labrador walked behind him.

"Public footpath, this." He stopped next to Jasper, giving him the once over. "Goes through the trees to the beach." He lifted his stick and pointed. "It belonged to a painter back in the day. Been for sale for some time."

"Needs more work than I thought," said Jasper, casting his eye over the bungalow.

"A month ago you'd've bought it cheap, but some fancy property company's after it. Plans 'ave gone in to the council."

Jasper frowned. Something about the man's tone seemed off, a little too practised. As if he were reading from a script.

"My pockets won't be deep enough, then."

The old man nodded. "Not many can compete with this company. Carmichael something or other. Buying up empty property all along the coast."

"Ah! Well. I'll keep on looking," Jasper said, turning back towards the car.

The old man and Labrador followed. "Yo sound disappointed."

"I am," Jasper lied.

"For yourself, is it?" The man eyed Jasper's old Focus.

"Wife. She likes to paint."

"Pity! She must be summat special."

Jasper opened the driving door. "Oh, she is."

He watched the elderly man and dog slowly continue along the lane. His gut churned in that 'be careful' way. Where had the elderly man come from? He'd appeared just as Jasper had arrived, as if he'd been waiting.

His property company wasn't buying housing in the area. They hadn't submitted planning to the council.

Who was spinning a web of lies?

Only John had known he'd be there.

Chapter Thirty-Four

The constant pounding of rain on the bedroom window had kept Kate awake. She was cold and alone.

She slipped on her robe and tiptoed downstairs barefoot in search of Jasper. She found him in her studio, staring out of the bi-fold doors. For a long moment, she admired her husband's muscular form. Her eyes filled as they gazed on the scars that marred his once flawless back. She slid up to him and opened her robe. A slow smile crept across his face when her naked body touched his back. She planted soft kisses on each of his scars.

"Kate, no!" Jasper's voice was sharp. Too sharp. He pulled her round so their chests touched.

"Why won't you let me heal you?" Her voice quivered.

"You do heal me, my love," he murmured into her hair, pulling her into his chest.

"Tell me."

The silence was so tense you could have heard a pin drop as Kate waited.

"I looked at a beach house yesterday."

"You did!" she said hopefully. She tried to slacken his grip so she could see his face, but he held her tight.

"An old nineteen-twenties build." He could feel the embers of excitement stirring in his wife. "Needed a lot doing to it."

"When can we see it?"

"I was too late. A company called Carmichael something-or-other has already submitted plans to the council."

"What?!" She pushed at his chest, but his grip held firm.

"According to an old codger I met, this company is buying up properties along the coast."

"But you're not."

"No, I'm not."

"Then who?"

"A good question, my love. A good question."

***

Bruce sat in the Evoque, waiting for Kate. She stood at the school gates, watching Harry and Oliver walk up the school drive.

When she got back into the car, Bruce could see she had been crying.

"I have to watch, just in case they turn and wave. They'll think I don't care if I'm not watching."

They never do, he thought.

"Bookshop?" Bruce asked, starting the engine.

"No. I'm feeling hungry."

Bruce turned and stared at Kate. The only time he could remember her feeling hungry before was when she was pregnant.

"Home, then?"

"No, the café. I need to think."

"You can't be alone."

"I need your company."

"Kate!"

"I feel…" She paused and looked at his face. "Since the stabbing. I feel… I feel as if I'm drowning."

"You did too much. Jasper should never have expected you to run the business. You need to rest."

"I can't. Jasper expects me to be by his side, and the boys need me more and more."

An uncomfortable silence hovered between them.

Bruce had had a soft spot for Kate since that day he'd emptied her flower shop. She was an innocent who had fallen for the criminal Jasper Carmichael. She was still the same Kate, but a little more streetwise. As far as Bruce was concerned, leopards didn't change their spots.

Jasper Carmichael was hiding something. At the moment, he needed Kate, but when he no longer needed her, he would drop her like a stone. And Bruce intended to be there to pick up the pieces.

He parked outside the café and turned to face Kate.

"I'm sorry. I shouldn't have said that," she blurted. Kate had been feeling emotional last night when Jasper had hurt her feelings. She had wanted to caress his scars, but he didn't want her to.

"Kate, you can tell me anything. I'll always be there for you."

"I know." Her hand stretched and touched his knee. "I could use your long arms wrapped around me."

Their eyes met.

"If circumstances were different..." There was no mistaking the meaning of his words.

"I know."

***

"One bacon sarnie, tea, and coffee for me," said Bruce.

Kate looked up at him, smiled and walked to the outside seats.

With his eyes fixed on Kate, Bruce dialled Jasper. "Jasper! We're at the café."

"What?"

"Kate just needs a minute. She seems quite emotional."

Bruce heard a sound as if Jasper had thrown his phone against a wall.

"Have you told him?" Kate asked as she tucked into the bacon sarnie.

"He's my boss. Can't repeat what he said. But you know Jasper."

"You like putting yourself in danger, Mrs Carmichael," said a gravelly voice.

Gypsy manoeuvred his big frame onto the picnic seats.

"Relax!" His command was directed at Bruce. "I mean her no 'arm."

"What do you want?"

"Let's say it's getting too hot for me, Mrs Carmichael. I wanted to say goodbye. You made me angry the other day. That superior casual manner of yours got under my skin. You are superior, Mrs Carmichael, and I would 'ave enjoyed taking the centre from you and your husband." He took a long moment to study Kate's impassive expression. "If I'd 'ad more time, you'd 'ave found me irresistible."

Kate raised her eyebrows with that 'in your dreams' expression.

Gypsy roared with laughter.

"I'm very skilled at the art of seduction." His confident smiled reached his eyes. "If I 'adn't believed Beth, I wouldn't 'ave bothered with Wellsbury. I was greedy, and I've no need to be. I make more than my share."

"Just out of curiosity, where did you meet?" Kate asked.

"Beth? London! Her drug business was failing. She needed a partner." Gypsy paused. "She was very persuasive, particularly between the sheets. Don't looked so shocked, Kate. She led me to believe that the Carmichael empire was up for grabs. *'Get rid of Jasper Carmichael, and his envied diamond network will be yours.'* Pound signs flashed before my eyes." Gypsy paused. "She crossed me, Mrs Carmichael. Drugs and money. People don't cross me and get away with it."

Kate wanted to ask what had happened to Beth. But truth be known, she didn't care and wouldn't shed a tear at her demise.

"Zak waved the diamond carrot in front of me. Got big ideas, 'as our Zak. But he's nothing without Jasper. He spun me some tale about Jasper 'aving Colin Carmichael's diamonds." Gypsy stared at Kate for a long moment, waiting for her impassive expression to slip, but he was wasting his time.

"You're very loyal, Mrs Carmichael. But you're in love. Lucky bastard. A bit of advice: keep away from diamonds. People in high places are after Jasper. He needs to keep his head down."

The sound of an outboard engine drifted up the river.

"Boss!" Gypsy's right-hand man had suddenly appeared.

Gypsy nodded. "Your husband has just arrived, and my ride is here."

He stood, taking Kate's hand. Butterflies filled Kate's stomach when his warm lips caressed her hand in a most sensual way. His desire-filled eyes gazed into hers. He smiled.

"Boss!"

"Until next time, Mrs Carmichael."

Gypsy turned and jogged towards the river's edge. He leapt into the boat and sped away downriver.

Somehow, this giant of a man had captured Kate's vulnerable emotions.

"Kate!"

Jasper's loud voice pushed all thoughts of Gypsy from her mind. She turned and smiled.

Jasper wasn't smiling.

"What the hell?!"

She stood and stared into Jasper's empty eyes, looking for the love she had seen in Bruce's.

"I was hungry, and we had a visitor. He meant me no harm. He's left and wanted to say goodbye."

Jasper looked puzzled.

"Wellsbury is getting too hot for him," Kate explained. "I have a feeling Beth might be dead or imprisoned somewhere. She pulled a fast one over him. And no one does that."

She waited, hoping for Jasper to kiss her, but he turned away. She looked at Bruce.

"Bookshop?" Bruce asked.

Kate nodded as tears trickled down her cheeks.

Jasper was driving away.

Bastard, thought Bruce. *You don't deserve her.*

Chapter Thirty-Five

Duncan sat in his Range Rover, impatiently drumming his fingers on the steering wheel, waiting for ten o'clock.

Rupert Manning had summoned him to London. Duncan didn't jump for anyone, let alone a man like Rupert Manning. A man he wouldn't have given the time of day until he'd flashed a small attaché case full of fifty-pound notes in front of him.

Duncan had been spellbound, and Manning had grinned.

"There's more. Much more," Manning had said.

Duncan had been all ears. A group of rich, powerful men would pay him handsomely to get rid of Jasper Carmichael. Hatred for the Carmichael family was deep-rooted, and Jasper was about to pay the price for their deception and dishonesty.

Rupert Manning, with the help of his associates, had outmanoeuvred Jasper for control of the Carmichael trust fund. Manning wasn't capable of running such a trust fund, but his associates were. Jasper had retaliated by trying to offload his investments. Manning and his associates hadn't expected that, but Jasper was renowned for doing the unexpected. Consequently, they had resorted to other means for revenge. Hence employing Duncan's services.

Manning had counted ten thousand pounds from the case and handed it to Duncan. The rest would be his when the job was done. Duncan had shaken his head and taken the attaché case.

"This is a down payment. Another caseful when the job is done."

Manning had stuttered but reluctantly agreed.

Duncan didn't let on that he hadn't read the Jasper Carmichael file or that he was going to rely on Jasper's private investigator, John, to fill in the blanks. John wasn't alone in his dislike for Jasper or the envy of his wealth—and that included Kate.

On the dot of ten, an irritable Duncan briskly walked into Meredith Spencer's old office. It had a strange, cold, musty smell, as if Meredith was still watching over things. Manning sat at Meredith's desk. He appeared nervous, fidgeting and touching his face. He pulled a white handkerchief from his pocket to wipe his sweaty brow while his eyes concentrated on the laptop screen.

Duncan lowered himself into the chair opposite and waited.

Manning suddenly coughed. "What happened at the airfield? We expected Carmichael to be in police custody."

"Carmichael had no idea that his airfield was being used."

"I find that difficult to believe," Manning retorted.

Before Duncan could answer, Manning asked about Gypsy.

"I shall get both of them," Duncan confidently replied.

"Then why haven't you?" Manning's voice was a little curt.

Duncan had to divert Manning's attention from Gypsy, who had left the country and was out of Duncan's reach.

"I had the house bugged, but Jasper's IT team found them and increased his security."

"Carmichael was one step ahead!"

"I think it was luck. We had hacked into his WiFi."

"What IT company does he use?"

"His own. Some young start-up kid." Manning was silent as his eyes went back and forth over the laptop screen. "I'm not clear about his IT people."

"It's not people. It's a kid. He's a computer wizard. Jasper gave him a job. The kid's brilliant."

"Make this kid an offer."

"Waste of time. He feels he owes Jasper. He was unemployed. Jasper recognised the kid's ability and potential. Jasper pays well, gives him a free hand as long as Carmichael has the best IT and security on offer. The kid never dreamed that such a job existed. He *is* Carmichael's IT. He designs the system and updates. He's his own boss. Jasper turns a blind eye to his own development work. Jasper knows how to treat his employees."

Duncan felt increasingly uneasy as Manning continually wiped beads of sweat from his forehead.

"Have you another plan?" Manning suddenly asked.

"As we speak, my men are setting up surveillance at Isaacs' House. We'll have all the inside information on Carmichael to put him away."

Thanks to greedy John, Duncan thought.

"Are you convinced Carmichael is dealing in diamonds?"

"Where else is he getting his money from? He's going to take a big hit selling Carmichael assets and property. He's looking for a beach house for Christ's sake. And he's the son of a master diamond thief. He hasn't blood in his fucking veins, but diamonds."

"You better not fail this time. That would displease my associates."

Duncan's temper was overflowing when he left the office. Manning's veiled threat repeated in his mind. No one threatened him.

Duncan floored his Range Rover as he drove back to Wellsbury. He cursed when a blue flashing light appeared in his rear-view mirror. His temper was already bubbling, and he could do without a jumped-up copper adding to his rage.

The policeman took a long moment reading Duncan's security ID.

"In a hurry are we, sir?"

"I'm on an urgent call," Duncan meekly replied, not rising to the officer's remark.

The officer walked back to the patrol car, still holding Duncan's ID, and spoke to his colleague. Duncan smiled as he watched the officer's cocky expression morph.

"Seems you're a very important man," the officer sneered as he returned Duncan's ID.

Duncan slipped his ID back into his inside pocket and slowly returned to the dual carriageway.

Two hours later, the Range Rover was parked at the empty Riverside Café carpark. The rear doors of the car opened, and John and his surveillance technician slipped in.

"You're late!" Duncan snapped.

The two men remained silent, waiting for Duncan to explode.

"Let me get this straight. You allowed two spoilt brats to scupper my operation?"

John took a deep breath. He wasn't used to working for anyone, but he had fallen into the money trap. Jasper paid well, but Duncan paid more, and if John played his cards right he knew he could have both.

"In our defence," he began, "we didn't expect the boys to visit their camp before school. Kate has strict rules—"

"I don't care about Kate's fucking rules," Duncan angrily interrupted. "You had to leave in a hurry."

"The night's gear was already packed."

"But you left in a hurry. What did you leave behind?"

"Nothing," John lied. He wasn't going to let on that he had lost his personal copy of Duncan's and Jasper's computer files or that he had returned to search for his SD card. He had ransacked Harry and Oliver's camp looking for the SD card, but the boys' stash of snacks had caught his eye. He had been hungry; he hadn't eaten for some time. He had foolishly pocketed the snacks.

"And you!" Duncan turned to the surveillance technician. "You allowed a pimply teenager to find your electronics."

The technician bowed his head and focused on his trainers. He had no intention of getting into a verbal battle with Duncan. After this pay-check he would leave.

It was John who came to his defence.

"To be fair, Duncan." His voice was calm and conciliatory. "That pimply teenager, as you refer to him, is exceptional. He has skills most hackers would die for. He found all our listening bugs, malware on their laptops, and the security breach on their WiFi. We had to use the kids' camp to get anywhere near the house."

"Excuses, excuses! You were both sloppy. I don't pay for sloppy. Jasper's men will be crawling all over the place tomorrow. Jasper won't mess about. Burn the fucking camp tonight. I don't want a trace of us being there. Got it?"

"Risky!" said John. "Jasper will have increased his security."

"I don't fucking care. Torch it!"

John glanced at the surveillance technician, whose head was tucked tightly into his chest, his clenched fists turning white. John couldn't see his face, but he had a good idea it would be glowing red.

"What's after the camp?" John asked, trying to divert Duncan's temper.

"We go after her."

"I don't think that's a good idea. Kate already has security, and Jasper will increase it."

"Your problem is you want to fuck her," Duncan snarled.

John smirked but he held his tongue. Yes, he did want to fuck Kate, but he wanted Jasper's money more.

"Kate is a different ball game," John said. "She's well liked. She has used her inheritance to help people. She's a silent partner in many businesses."

"What's the progress on this beach house?"

"Difficult to say. He hasn't enquired about property or land."

"You told me he would react to someone making offers on property using the Carmichael name," Duncan angrily retorted.

"He's playing things close to his chest. I'm not sure he's even told Kate."

"Well, find out. Text. Phone. Visit her in the gallery or bookshop. And take my computer wizard with you. He may prove to be useful."

Chapter Thirty-Six

Dawn was just breaking when Jasper and Malcolm finally extinguished the fire in the orchard. Harry and Oliver's camp was just a pile of ash.

"Who would set fire to a kids' camp?" said Malcolm to no one in particular.

Jasper just stared into space. He had a good idea who'd done this: Duncan, John or both. *Who's next*? he thought. *Kate*.

"What do you want us to do, boss?"

Bruce's gruff voice brought Jasper from his thoughts. He was a little surprised to see Bruce and his team.

"Kate phoned. The boys are upset," Bruce said, looking over what was left of the camp and shrubbery.

"This can wait. Find how they got in and repair it."

"If you have any more security, this place will be like Fort Knox," Bruce commented.

Jasper stared at Bruce. He was surprised that he knew there was a Fort Knox.

"I'm a James Bond fan." Bruce grinned and walked towards his team. "Pussy Galore," he said over his shoulder.

***

John had hung about, hoping for an opportunity to get into the house while Jasper and Malcolm were preoccupied. But Kate and the boys were sitting outside, Clare was in the kitchen, and then Bruce and his men had arrived.

John's luck had run out.

***

Kate stood with her arms around two red-eyed boys staring at the pile of ash that was once their camp.

She recalled the day two very proud boys had dragged her to look at their camp. Oliver had stuck his chest out and Harry had smiled. Oliver had stood at the camp entrance doing his dance and pointing, but Kate couldn't see inside.

"Look!" Harry had said, taking his mother's hand and pulling her towards the entrance.

"I'm not crawling in there."

"Just look inside."

Kate had reluctantly pushed her head inside. An earthy, cold, damp smell greeted her; she'd turned her nose up. The old carpet she had thrown out had found a new lease of life and was strewn with magazines, books, blankets and other bits and pieces.

"We had an idea someone was using our camp." Harry's voice was low and subdued.

"They were eating our food," Oliver added in the same sombre manner.

"It was our secret place." Harry gulped.

"Come on," Kate said. "Let's see what Clare has made for breakfast."

Oliver ran towards the house, leaving Harry holding his mother's hand.

Breakfast was a sad affair. No one offered any conversation. Jasper was particularly gloomy.

Oliver was happy when Kate said there would be no school, but Harry was downcast and sulked off to join Jasper in the office. Jasper was more than a little surprised when Harry slumped into one of the overstuffed white chairs. Jasper stared at his son, waiting for him to speak.

After a tense few seconds, Harry blurted, "I think I know why the camp was set on fire."

He wiggled off the chair, put his hand into his jeans pocket and pulled out an SD card. He dropped it on Jasper's desk.

"It's encrypted. It wasn't difficult to convert. You should read the files."

Kate stood in the office doorway, watching and listening.

"We built the camp in the old shrubbery so Mum couldn't extend the orchard." Harry turned and grinned at his mother. "We didn't do anything except talk. Olly made a food stash. Snacks, chocolates. He would make up stories, mainly about pirates. You know what he's like. If he was behind with his reading and he didn't want you to know"—Harry's eyes met his mother's—"I would help. Then Olly noticed that some chocolates were missing. I didn't believe him. I thought he was making it up so I wouldn't know how many he was eating. So we laid a trap. Someone *was* eating Olly's chocolate."

John has a weakness for chocolate, Jasper thought.

"Yesterday, when Olly didn't have a chocolate bar in his lunchbox, we ran down there to get one. All our stuff was strewn about. There was no chocolate. That's when I found the card. We were scared to tell you. I never thought someone would set fire to it."

Harry's head had dipped into his chest.

"Is that all?" asked Jasper, trying to hide his impatience with Harry. "Did you see anyone?"

"No! But you should ask Olly about the white van."

"What white van?"

"Olly swears it's the same van that's parked there every morning. But it's just a white van to me."

"Let me get this straight. A white van parked where?"

"On the pavement next to the field."

"Was it there when you came back from school?"

"No!"

Oliver came bounding in, pushing past Malcolm, Clare and Bruce, who had congregated in the open office doorway.

"What's up?" he said.

"We're talking about the white van," said Jasper, still trying to quell his impatience.

"The one parked down the road?" Oliver did a little jig. "Are you coming, Harry?"

"Oliver, keep still a moment and tell me about the white van." Kate gently held his shoulders and looked directly into his eyes.

"Harry doesn't believe me. It's the same van. There's red paint and a crack in the number plate. Can I go now?"

"Just one more question," said Kate in a calm voice. "Did you see anything else? Men?"

Oliver shook his head. Kate let go of his shoulders.

"Come on, Harry," Oliver cheerfully said.

"Tell them about the open doors."

Oliver stopped.

"Yeah. I remember. Two men were inside."

"He said they sat looking at a screen," Harry added.

"They were! I saw 'em," Oliver indignantly said. "You comin'?"

Bruce waited until the boys were out of earshot.

"Saw Duncan getting into a white van," he said.

Chapter Thirty-Seven

Kate opened the French doors to Jasper's office and nestled onto the couch, pulling her legs beneath her. Jasper's scowl softened.

"The boys okay?" he asked.

"I think they've almost forgotten about the fire."

"Probably the promise of a treehouse had something to do with it."

She smiled.

"Come here."

"I don't think that's a good idea."

"Mrs Carmichael, I would like you to read this," he said in a playful tone.

"Read it to me."

"For many years, I've paid for a secret private investigator." Jasper's tone was serious. "I trusted him with many secrets."

Kate jumped up and hurried to read the computer screen. Jasper eased her onto his lap.

"All these years, the bastard has kept a record."

"Blackmail!" Kate exclaimed. "This reads as if Duncan is working for Manning."

"Astute as ever, my love."

Manning is the face of an anonymous group of men that want revenge, Kate read on the screen.

"When I attended my last Freemasons', there were periods of silence, uncomfortable atmosphere. I had experienced the like when I was in the company of a group of criminals. It's a feeling you never forget."

"You never said."

"I think that these men have a score to settle with the Carmichael family."

"Jasper, not again!"

"My last meeting with John, he commented that selling investments and property wouldn't cover a diamond network, getting rid of Gypsy and Duncan, and a beach house."

Kate turned, her mouth inches from his.

"What does he mean, diamond network?"

"He's assuming I'm going back into diamonds. I asked him if I could restart the old network. Just as a precaution."

"Precaution for what? I don't like where this is going." She tried to lift herself, but Jasper's grip was firm. "We can manage. Gypsy's gone. We don't need a beach house. That leaves Duncan. We can outmanoeuvre him." Her words were impatiently rushed.

"Come closer. Let me nuzzle you."

"No nuzzling and no sex until we sort this."

"You're so fucking hot when you're angry. Look at you—eyes on fire, cheeks flushed. Are you wet?"

Before she could turn away, he claimed her mouth. She broke the kiss.

"Futile, my love. Feel the heat. I know you feel it. I feel it too."

***

Jasper was always the first to recover after sex.

"This isn't over," said Kate from the couch.

Jasper's eyes were fixed on the laptop screen. He hadn't heard her. Duncan had his full attention.

"Turn your mind to Duncan," he said.

"You know his cronies better than me," Kate said. Silence settled as they both considered the situation.

"Names would be useful," commented Kate.

"Not too sure who they are."

"Names of the Freemasons would be a start. I could look the families up. Find a connection to Grandfather Carmichael or Colin."

"I can't do that. It supposed to be secret."

"I already know that Manning's one." Jasper stared at Kate over the laptop lid.

"Names. Connections. Their grudge against Grandfather Carmichael's probably financial. Colin probably fucked a wife or two. I don't know." Kate shrugged her shoulders and opened the French doors.

"Don't go," Jasper said. "When were you going to tell me about Dan?"

Kate stopped in her tracks. She hadn't expected that. She'd had no idea that Jasper knew she'd been in contact with Dan.

"I went to school with—"

"I know," Jasper cut in. "I met him at the mayor's do, remember? You were laughing."

"Dan went to a private school, but he had no friends when he stayed here. He followed us around. He joined us at the airfield. That's where he met Michelle. He was besotted." Kate's face relaxed as she recalled those carefree days. "She led him on. Made out she wanted him." Kate paused and gazed out of the French doors. "It was A-level year. Dan was under pressure from his dad. Michelle had got into his head. He couldn't think straight. She was hot and cold towards him. One minute she was all over him, the next she insulted him. Dan has a gentle nature. He couldn't cope. One day, I came across him sitting on the bench opposite the Wells and Bury. I was a little put out. I've always considered that my thinking bench. He was crying. Michelle had insulted his manhood. So I sat beside him, put my arm around him, and he sobbed onto my shoulder." She paused. Her eyes filled as she stared at Jasper. "We met many times during that year. He would open up about his home life and what was expected of him. His father sounded a bit of a bully. And of course, he talked about Michelle." She took a deep breath. "He said he had me to thank for his straight As. I remember he kissed me and said 'I owe you Kate. Anything. Anything at all.'"

"I don't understand. What do you want from him?"

"As you know, Dan's never found love with Michelle."

Jasper's mind was whirling. Why was Dan spending so much time in Wellsbury? What was the attraction? He'd thought Dan was in London with Michelle. Who did Jasper know who was gay…?

Then the penny dropped. That barman who'd been at school with Kate had just opened a bistro.

"The barman…" Jasper was becoming more and more impatient, not letting Kate finish as he rapidly put two and two together. "It was Dan! He put money into the bistro. I wondered where he got the money from."

"Now the bit you won't like."

Jasper glared at her.

"There're discrepancies in the Carmichael Centre accounts. I can't put my finger on it. I'm rusty and I need more practice. And the lawyer and the new accountant are just too cocky."

"You're reading too much into their relationship. It's because I wasn't there."

"If we have a problem with the accounts, Dan will find it."

"What have you told him?" Jasper raised his voice.

"Just that I suspect we have a problem and that I'm too rusty to find it. There's no need to worry. The files he has are anonymous, just like the ones you gave me to check. Remember?"

Kate walked back to Jasper's desk and sat in the chair opposite.

"Dan does this sort of thing all the time. At the moment, he's still working in banking. All I've asked is for him to confirm the discrepancies."

"You're being vague."

Kate nodded. "I've taken precautions just in case Dan betrays me. Stop worrying! Concentrate on John and Duncan. Are they working together? Who's Duncan working for, and who's using the Carmichael name to buy property?"

"That's John."

"I have a feeling that John and Duncan are working together. Someone is helping themselves to Carmichael money."

"You don't know that."

"Let's see what Dan comes up with."

Chapter Thirty-Eight

John opened the passenger door of Duncan's Range Rover.

"You're late," Duncan snapped.

"I was checking Jasper's new security."

"And?"

"It's good. Too good. When I left it looked as if they were laying pressure sensors around the patio."

"So we get at Kate in the gallery."

"Hey, hold on. That's risky. There're too many people. I'll be seen."

"Do it when she parks at the back."

"She has security."

"Shoot the bastards. Stop finding problems. We haven't the time."

John didn't like Duncan's aggressive attitude. Targeting Kate was a mistake. She was well liked, and Jasper would seek revenge. Duncan had never seen the old Jasper; he had no idea what the man was capable of.

"At least let's follow her. Get an idea how easy it's going to be."

Duncan stared at the passers-by.

"We'll go today. Now."

***

With a nod to the two security men, Jasper strolled into the gallery. A wide grin covered his face as he watched his wife; she was totally oblivious to his presence and her surroundings except the painting she was staring at.

"I think we'll move this," she said in a calm, matter-of-fact manner. The two security men lifted the painting and waited for Kate to decide where it should go.

"Here!" She moved to a spot further along the wall. "It needs more light."

She turned slightly and caught sight of Jasper.

"This is an unexpected pleasure."

She walked towards him, smiling, and looped her arms around his neck, taking a moment to brush their lips.

"You can do better than that." He pulled her into a passionate kiss. "I've missed you," he murmured so only she could hear.

His fingers toyed with the band that held her hair back. She was smiling, her cheeks slightly flushed, her eyes glistening.

This is the Jasper I love, she thought.

"Lunch?" he said so the security guards could hear.

***

Duncan set a fast pace as he and John headed towards the empty units Jasper had earmarked for Kate's bookshop. He veered to the right along a dark alley leading to the stairs at the back of the units.

"What the fuck are we doing here? The only escape leads to a dead-end alley," John exclaimed, looking over the market square.

Duncan wasn't listening. He was finding John tiresome, with his perpetual negative attitude.

It was lunchtime and the market square eateries were busy. Duncan's gut was on fire, he had Kate in his sights.

***

A contented Jasper strolled through the Carmichael Centre, his arm around his wife's back. He had the love of his life walking beside him, and he wanted the world to know.

As they turned into the market square, out of the corner of his eye, he noticed that a red dot flicked across his hand. Jasper's gut churned. Kate was smiling as she turned her head to meet his gaze. The red dot jerked to the middle of her back. Without a second thought, Jasper pushed her to the ground.

He was in shock; his beloved had been shot. He lifted her into his arms, not noticing the blood trickling from her arm or the bump on her head.

People screamed and shouted, running for cover. Jasper momentarily lifted his eyes to the empty unit. He caught a glimpse of two men hurrying away.

Two security men appeared.

"Ambulance on the way!" one called.

"Two men on the roof. Empty unit," Jasper shouted at the security men.

A crowd had gathered and were intently watching Jasper. He had two hands tightly clenched around Kate's arm. Suddenly there was a screech of brakes. The crowd parted to let Bruce through.

The crowd's attention briefly left Jasper and focused on Bruce, who immediately took control of the situation and organised a search for the shooters. His attention turned to Kate; she was in shock and Jasper wasn't helping. Bruce calmly pulled a tie from the glovebox of his pickup.

"Let me," he calmly said.

Jasper seemed helpless as Bruce gazed into Kate's eyes and knotted the tie around her arm, just above the wound. Kate slowly calmed when Bruce slipped his work jacket under her head and wrapped her arm in his shirt.

"The paramedics are on their way." His fingers soothed her forehead. "I'll get the bastards, Kate."

"Don't go," she mumbled as her hand reached for him.

The ambulance screeched to a halt. Before the paramedics reached Kate, Bruce had lifted her into his arms.

"Go with her," he said to a white-faced Jasper. "She needs you."

The ambulance sped away with Jasper holding Kate's hand, clearly uncomfortable, while a paramedic stemmed the flow of blood.

Jasper stared at Kate, but she was a blur. He couldn't get the tenderness between Bruce and his wife from his mind.

***

"What the fuck?" John gasped as he tried to keep up with Duncan.

They were running out of the blind alley, and instead of heading towards the main carpark, Duncan had suddenly veered between the units towards the back of the shops and the George pub. He stopped by an old Ford Fiesta, smashed the driver's window and pulled wires from under the dash. The car started and John jumped in the passenger seat. Tyres squealed as Duncan floored the accelerator.

***

Bruce slipped into the hospital waiting room seat next to Jasper, who had his head in his hands.

"Watts' team is all over the place."

Jasper didn't move.

"Got a lead. They stole a car from the George. Old Fiesta. Dumped it on the waste ground by Kate's centre."

Jasper lifted his head. "Who the fuck did this?"

"Tweed jacket."

Jasper stood and kicked over a small table piled with magazines. At that moment, a doctor appeared and watched as Bruce righted the table.

"Your wife wants to go home," he said. "Something about the boys being worried."

The doctor waited for Jasper to say something but Jasper remained silent.

"Nasty egg on her forehead. The bullet passed straight through her arm."

Jasper kept his eyes fixed on the carpet.

"An Inspector Watts phoned. Said he'd like a word."

"Fuck Watts! Can I see her?" Jasper snapped.

"The nurse is cleaning her up. Someone will have to stay with her all night."

"I know the drill."

The doctor took a step back at Jasper's sharp, bitter voice. Kate appeared, arm in a sling. Their eyes met. She tried to smile, but in an instant, Jasper had her in his arms. His fingers lightly caressed the bump on her forehead. Her head settled on his shoulder as tears flowed, but her eyes found Bruce.

***

Jasper carried Kate into the living room and carefully laid her on the couch.

Harry and Oliver nervously watched and waited while Jasper and Clare made her comfortable.

219

Kate's eyes were open, and she smiled at the boys.

"You boys go outside while we get your mother out of these clothes," Clare ordered. Jasper knelt by Kate's side, gently stroking her hair.

"You know I've got to go," he murmured.

She smiled and nodded.

"They've stepped over my red line." His lips caressed hers. "And that's you. No more Mr Nice Guy." He put his finger over her lips. "They wanted to kill you to get at me. This has to stop." His mouth covered hers.

Her hand held onto his arm.

"Tell me."

"They dumped a car by the youth centre. Bruce is on it."

"Bruce?"

Jasper ignored the sudden concern in Kate's voice. "I'm thinking they're heading to the airfield."

"At the far end of the woods there's a narrow path that leads down the slope to the airfield. It's probably overgrown, so be careful."

Jasper stared at his wife. "How do you know?"

"Teenage years."

Jasper planted a soft kiss on her lips. She tried to smile as a tear trickled down her cheek. Jasper didn't know if it was for him or Bruce.

***

"I'm at the old airfield," Jasper whispered into his phone. "The tweed man is standing outside the far hangar. He's talking into his phone. Not too pleased."

"I'm on my way," said Bruce.

While Jasper waited he reflected on Kate's noticeable closeness to Bruce. He knew Bruce wanted Kate, and one move from her was all it would take. He had seen the glint in her eye whenever Bruce joined them. He resolved that he would be more attentive. After all, she was the key to his success.

Jasper was leaning against a tree when Bruce arrived.

"How's Kate?" asked Bruce as soon as he got out of the car.

"Lying on the couch with the boys watching over."

"Where's your car?"

"I had to convince myself that they could have walked from their abandoned car to here."

"You mad?!"

Bruce watched Jasper move his flashlight from side to side.

"What you looking for?"

"A path."

"There's no path here. It's all brambles and weeds."

"What's fucking wrong with you?" snapped Jasper.

"Nothing! It's you. You're acting strange."

Jasper stopped and stared at the weeds. His jealousy was showing. Kate had smiled at John, and she had reached for Bruce's arm. Was he losing her?

"What's this?" said Bruce, kicking weeds to one side.

They slipped and stumbled through weeds, brambles and tree roots before they reached the wire fence around the airfield.

"Well I never," said Bruce. "How did you know about this?"

"Kate."

Jasper stopped, opened his jacket and handed Bruce a pair of cutters. Bruce grinned and started to cut away a section of fence.

Jasper pulled his binoculars from round his neck and scanned the area.

"She spent her teenage years here."

Bruce noted that Jasper's voice had calmed.

"Got a plan?"

"Not yet."

They nestled into the undergrowth and waited.

***

Duncan and John sat on the floor of the hangar that Beth had used.

"The plane's been delayed," said Duncan.

"I don't like this. Jasper will have time to organise."

"Relax! What's he going to do? His mind will be on Kate. You saw how he fussed over her."

"You don't know him."

"He's pussy whipped. It's obvious."

John stood and pushed the hangar door open. He stared at the woods.

"He's not there," Duncan impatiently barked. "He's fretting over his wife."

"You never met the old Jasper. He went after anything or anyone if they hurt Kate."

"That's before he gave into soft, female ways. Relax. He'll be at the hospital, venting his anger at the staff."

John went outside, slid down the hangar door and sat on the floor, his eyes trained on the tree line. His SAS training had kicked in. Danger was lurking in those woods.

I know you're there, Carmichael. But where?

***

Jasper and Bruce crawled under the section of fence Bruce had cut away. They hadn't gone far when Jasper abruptly stopped. The night's stillness was pierced by the low hum of a small aircraft. They fell to the ground just as the dim runway lights came on.

The aircraft taxied towards the main gate, turned and stopped. Bruce edged forward. Jasper caught his arm and shook his head.

Jasper's gut churned. Something wasn't right. The plane had taxied away from the hangars, stopping in darkness.

Jasper trained his night vision binoculars onto the gatehouse. There were no guards.

Duncan and John were running towards the open aircraft door. A helping hand lifted them inside. The doors were still open when, from inside the plane, came the sound of two shots fired in quick succession.

"Holy shit," said Bruce. His words had hardly left his mouth when they heard two more shots.

***

Rupert Manning sat in his favourite armchair, smoking a cigar and sipping a large malt. He was feeling very pleased with himself. Duncan had reassured him that, by the end of the day, the Jasper problem would be solved.

His phone rang.

"Manning," he cockily said to the person on the other end.

"Don't use that fuckin' tone with me, you fuckin' incompetent fool."

"W-what do y-you mean?" Manning stuttered.

"Mean that fuckin' idiot shot Kate Carmichael."

"I, er, had no idea."

"Idea? Idea! You fuckin' dimwit! And you fuckin' want to run the fund. You couldn't organise a piss-up in a brewery."

"I'll sort it."

"Too fuckin' late. I've sorted it."

A shocked Manning opened and closed his mouth.

"Now, you fuckwit. You'll do exactly as I say. As soon as she's out of hospital, we visit Jasper."

"At his home?"

"Of course at his fuckin' home."

Manning heard the noise of a phone hitting a wall.

Chapter Thirty-Nine

Jasper carefully closed the kitchen door.

Malcolm stood in the shadows, waiting.

Bruce leaned on the work surface and rested his head in his shaking hands. The drive from the airfield had been a silent one. Neither wanted to talk about what they had just witnessed.

"Well?" said Malcolm, impatient for news.

Jasper walked with some urgency to the living room, leaving Bruce to fill Malcolm in. Clare sat watching Kate sleep.

"She hasn't murmured or moved since you left." Clare stood and pointed towards the door. Jasper nodded.

He eased the chair closer to his beloved and gently caressed her forehead. She moved and opened her eyes. She looked past him, but they were alone.

"What is it?" he quietly said.

"You're back," she mumbled, still half asleep.

"Are you in pain?"

She grimaced. "A little."

He searched the table for her painkillers, but she slipped back to sleep before he found them.

***

It was morning when Bruce entered the living room. He glanced over to Jasper, who appeared to be asleep.

Bruce leaned over Kate and stroked her forehead.

Jasper's eyes opened.

Kate's hand touched Bruce's face, and she smiled.

"You're safe," she murmured.

Bruce took her hand and kissed her palm. Their eyes danced. Bruce tucked her hand under her blanket.

"Don't go."

"I've got work. It's best if I leave. Jasper will be jealous. It's obvious how I feel about you."

"Tell me."

Harry and Oliver stopped in their tracks when they saw Bruce at their mother's side.

"Is she dead?" asked Oliver.

"No. Sleeping."

"How long have you been here?" There was an accusing tone to Harry's words.

"Just come to see how she is before I leave."

"You're leaving?" said a surprised Clare as she handed Jasper his morning coffee. Bruce and Jasper glanced at one another. Bruce wondered how long he had been awake.

"Stay for breakfast," continued Clare, who had turned her attention to Kate.

"Can't! Meeting the men."

"Did she speak?" asked Oliver.

"No, just opened her eyes." Bruce lied.

"Come on." Clare took Oliver's hand. "Let's get ready for school."

"We're not going," Harry said defiantly. "We're going to look after Mum."

"You're both going to school," Kate croaked, her eyes tightly closed. "End of it."

Clare tugged on Oliver's hand.

Harry glared at Jasper. "You don't love her. You always leave her when she needs you."

Kate opened her eyes. "Harry, stop. Your dad's been here all night." She held out her arm. "Come here. Both of you."

Harry ran to his mother, taking her hand. Tears trickled down his cheek. Oliver followed.

"I'm going to be fine. I need to rest. I need to know that my brave knights can carry on. Go to school. I want to know what you've both been up to." She gazed at Oliver. "No fighting."

Oliver leaned in to her and kissed her cheek. He grinned and ran towards the kitchen. Harry turned to follow, but Kate held on to him.

"I need you to be strong. Support Oliver. He will need you. Be there for him. Don't make me worry, Harry." Her thumb rubbed a tear from his cheek. Her eyes filled. "We have a special bond. Don't break it. Not over this. Jasper loves you, as do Clare and Malcolm."

"I love you," he murmured.

Kate stroked his cheek. "I know. Never forget that I love you very much. Have breakfast. Go to school like the brave son I know."

Harry smiled as he walked into the kitchen.

Kate hadn't realised that Jasper, Clare and Malcolm were intently listening to her.

"Now look what you've made me do," said Clare, wiping her eyes.

Kate smiled.

"I wouldn't mind a soft-boiled egg with soldiers," she said.

***

Kate was leaning on Jasper, slowly walking from the small office bathroom, when Watts appeared. He waited while Jasper made sure she was comfortable on the office couch before settling into the overstuffed chair opposite her.

"Thought you'd be at the airfield," Watts said to Jasper.

Jasper didn't answer.

"How're you feeling, Mrs Carmichael?"

"Headache, arm aches, but apart from that, fine."

"Bad do. My men can't find any leads. Whoever did this 'as just disappeared."

Watts waited for a comment from either Kate or Jasper, but none came.

"The thing is, eyewitnesses claim there were two of them. Stole a car, dumped it, then vanished."

The three exchanged glances as an unwelcomed silence drifted.

"There're reports that an aircraft landed."

"Just say what you've come to say," Jasper said impatiently. Watts' small talk was beginning to irritate him.

"Where were you last night?" Watts' voice had an edge.

"He was here, Inspector."

"Are you sure, Mrs Carmichael? He could 'ave nipped out while you slept."

"To do what?" Kate asked.

"The thing is, this whole episode has 'Carmichael' stamped all over it. I think Mrs Carmichael was accidently shot. The bullet was meant for you." He turned to face Jasper. "You knew the shooters. Probably from your past—or more likely, the criminal types you're in cahoots with."

Kate stomach flipped. She'd suspected Jasper was slipping back into his old ways. The inspector had just confirmed it.

"You knew the only way they could escape was by plane. You waited and killed them," snapped the inspector.

"Do you know how ridiculous that sounds?" Jasper retorted.

"I'll get a warrant and search that airfield. If there's bodies, I'll find them."

"He was here all night, Inspector," Kate cut in. "I didn't sleep much. When I opened my eyes, he was by my side."

"Mrs Carmichael, you'd lie to save him."

"That may be true. But last night he was here," Clare said, as she bustled into the office carrying a breakfast tray. "The coffee machine's a mess. Coffee all over the surface. Milk left out. Typical Jasper. And I wouldn't lie for 'im."

Watts stood and glared at Jasper. "All reading from the same hymn sheet."

"No hymn sheet," Clare said, placing the tray on Kate's lap. "Just truth."

Watts turned his attention to Clare, but she was busying herself with Kate's breakfast tray. He turned and quickly walked to his car.

Kate waited until she heard the police Mondeo drive away.

"What am I missing?" she asked, dipping her toasted soldier into a soft-boiled egg. Jasper ignored her.

"Jasper!"

"Duncan and John were at the airfield. An aircraft landed. I was suspicious. It stopped at the end of the runway lights. Duncan and John raced towards the plane's open door. A hand reached out and helped them in. Before the door closed, two shots were fired."

Kate breathed in deeply.

"Two more shots followed."

Chapter Forty

Jasper stopped typing. His troubled expression rested on his sleeping wife.

He hadn't left her since the shooting. She was healing, managing a short walk into the garden. She wanted to do more, but he wouldn't let her. Even though the doctors had referred to it as a minor wound, Jasper wasn't convinced. The bullet had gone straight through her right upper arm, her painting arm, and he was going to make sure it had all the healing time it needed.

His mind drifted to the day Kate was shot. The image of Duncan and John running towards the light aircraft and the subsequent shots were still fresh. The hit had been well organised, by a ruthless mastermind who would still have Kate in his sights.

The office door flew open. Harry and Oliver bustled in.

"She still sleeping?" Harry's voice was full of concern.

Oliver barged past him. "The kids at school say she won't recover."

"I've told you not to repeat that," scolded Harry.

"They say it was a hitman." Oliver was brimming over with school gossip.

"You shouldn't believe everything." Jasper was hoping Kate was asleep.

"They say you'll go after him." Oliver faced his dad.

"A taxi just dropped off two men," mentioned Harry, trying to divert Oliver's thoughts.

"Haven't seen them before," Oliver said.

Oliver turned and ran towards the door, nearly knocking over Malcolm.

"A Mr Manning and a Mr Michaels to see you." Malcolm stood to one side. Manning bustled in. "Sorry to hear about Kate." His voice was a little loud and empty.

Words, just words, thought Jasper.

"Don't think you know Michaels." Manning paused taking a moment to study Jasper. "He's interested in the trust."

Neither Manning nor Michaels waited for an invitation to sit; they lowered themselves into the chairs opposite Kate.

"I know a visit might appear unseemly, but life must go on," said Manning.

"What do you want?" Jasper said impatiently.

"Who did it? Do you know?" Michaels' voice was soft, barely above a whisper.

"Ask Watts," Jasper sharply replied.

"She's very pale." Manning's empty tone stirred Jasper's temper.

"What the fuck do you want?" Jasper looked towards the door. "Malcolm."

Malcolm stood just inside the door. Kate's eyes slowly opened.

"There's things we need to discuss," Manning said nervously, aware Jasper's temper was rising.

"Such as?"

"Well, there's Chester and the extensive Carmichael library."

"I've discussed the sale with Chester. He will be well provided for. The library will come here."

Michaels intensely staring at Kate made Jasper's gut somersault.

So, you're the evil mastermind, thought Jasper.

"Are you sure you know the full consequences of your actions?" said Manning, trying to get Jasper's attention.

"I'm just doing what Colin should have done years ago."

Jasper abruptly stopped talking as Michaels stood and stepped towards Kate. Jasper suddenly stood, readying himself to pounce on Michaels.

Michaels took a step back, the colour disappearing from his face. He had heard many a tale about the Carmichael temper but had never experienced it.

A loud gasp escaped from Manning when, without warning, Jasper's hands tightly clenched on Michaels' collar. Michaels swallowed hard as he stared into a pair of cold blue eyes intent on revenge.

Manning stepped towards the door.

A heavy fearful silence hung in the air.

"Jasper." A soft, calm voice broke the silence.

Harry, Oliver and Clare jostled into the office. Oliver's mouth opened and shut when he saw his dad's hold on Michaels. Stories about his dad's quick temper flashed through his mind.

"Jasper."

Malcolm moved to Jasper's side, taking Michaels by the arm.

Jasper kicked the coffee table over, his hand running through his thick salt-and-pepper hair. He flung the French doors open and filled his lungs with cold fresh air.

Kate slowly eased herself off the couch.

"Malcolm. Make sure Mr Manning and Michaels leave the premises and Wellsbury." She paused taking a moment to steady herself. "If they have a reservation at the hotel, cancel it."

"Who the fuck do you think you are?" snapped Michaels, finding his confidence now Jasper was no longer in the room.

The room stilled. Malcolm's grip tightened on Michaels' arm. Harry, Oliver and Clare turned their attention to Kate.

"Lady Carmichael. The woman you want dead." Kate's cold, matter-of-fact tone echoed through the still office.

Jasper stepped back into the office, just catching the word 'dead'. Kate suddenly felt hot. The room blurred, her legs buckled.

In two giant strides, Jasper gathered Kate into his arms before she hit the carpet. Kate's eyes flicked open. She tried to smile as Jasper held a glass of water to her lips. All eyes were on Kate, except Manning's and Michaels', who took the opportunity to slip out of the office and to their waiting taxi.

"She's not well, and she got up too quick," Clare said, trying to explain Kate's sudden condition.

"Have they gone?" Kate murmured.

Jasper nodded.

"You didn't mean it, did you?"

Jasper pulled a chair closer to Kate. "You know how I think about anyone who hurts you."

"That's not the way." Her hand found his.

Jasper's expression softened as he lifted her hand to his lips. His fingers caressed her hairline.

"Kate, darling, you're everything."

"Promise," she pleaded.

Jasper took a long moment. He dipped his head to focus on her hand. He wanted revenge. He wanted them to feel the pain.

"I promise they won't find the fast lane to the sea." His lips turned into a smile.

***

Embarrassment welled inside Harry as he witnessed his parents' private tender moment.

He silently slipped out of the office into the kitchen, joining his brother.

"He loves her," he said, picking a slice of toast from the rack.

"Of course he does. He just doesn't know it," commented Clare, stirring Kate's chicken soup.

"Did you see the faces of those men when Dad looked at 'em? They were scared sh—"

"Oliver Carmichael! Language!" bellowed Clare.

Oliver proudly grinned. His dad had some serious street cred.

"Not many dare cross Jasper Carmichael," added Malcolm, who had returned from seeing the unwelcome visitors into a taxi.

***

It was evening when Bruce strode into Jasper's office. He couldn't wait to see Kate, but she was sleeping. He wanted to touch her, but Jasper had an unwelcome look in his eye.

"She hasn't stirred since Clare's chicken soup," commented Jasper.

He didn't want Bruce anywhere near Kate, but he'd needed him and his men to follow Manning and Michaels.

Bruce turned to Jasper. "The two men in question left on the afternoon train. First class. Picked up at the station. Grey BMW. My men followed. This is the address." He handed Jasper a slip of paper. "There's a team in place. Just say the word."

"Kate doesn't want me to."

"It's got to end, Jasper," Bruce interrupted.

Chapter Forty-One

Gypsy had escaped Duncan and his team by the skin of his teeth. He had taken refuge in his secluded Spanish villa, only accessible by a steep, winding road that he rarely used, preferring his helicopter.

His mind flicked back to the last time he'd seen Kate. She wasn't a beauty like the women he attracted, but she was the type of woman you married. Reliable, loyal. She was a wife, mother; her love would be unconditional. She would never cheat on Jasper, but she was attracted to men like him—he had seen it in her eyes and the way she looked at her bodyguard, Bruce. He wondered if Jasper knew how lucky he was to have her.

He gazed at the drug- and alcohol-addled people surrounding his swimming pool. It would only take one to remove the bits of cloth that covered their sex for the orgy to begin.

He nodded at two young women hovering by him. They wanted him, and as far as he was concerned, they would do.

He wandered into his poolside bedroom and sat on the couch next to the glass coffee table. With a razor blade, he scooped the cocaine into a small pile. He turned his head and smiled at the two women, who were watching from the open door. At a wave of his hand, they eagerly joined him on the couch.

In turn they leaned forward and snorted the cocaine, then padded towards the waiting king-size bed, wiggling their hips and giggling as they dropped their tiny bikinis onto the tiled floor.

He dropped his swimming shorts and stepped towards the bed. His eyes feasted on their perfectly rounded young breasts and toned bodies.

Then his phone rang.

He stopped dead as he slowly moved his head in the direction of the sound.

"I told you not to fuckin' phone this number." His gruff, angry, loud voice made the women scoot to the other side of the bed. They watched intently as he sank onto the edge of the bed. His free hand tugged at his hair as he concentrated on the voice speaking in his ear.

"I'll get back to you," he said eventually.

Naked, he walked to the open door and vacantly stared. The loud music, raucous laughter and sexual acts that poured from the crowd floated over his head. His mind was filled with the news that Duncan was dead and he could return to England and resume his drug business. But the news that disturbed him was that they had shot Kate. It didn't matter to him that she was going to recover; his new associates had crossed a red line. Kate was off limits.

He had unfinished business with Jasper and his wife. Kate had unsettled his mind; her sparkling green eyes and smile had mesmerised him. Her upper-class, dismissive attitude had got under his skin. He had never wanted to taste a woman like he desired Kate.

He turned and smiled at the two beauties that were anxiously waiting. He leaned and rubbed his index finger in the remains of the cocaine on the coffee table, covering his teeth then his nostrils. His eyes roamed towards the women, but he didn't see them. Kate danced before his eyes.

***

An afternoon fucking did nothing to settle his mind. He opened the fridge door and lifted a jug of orange juice. No alcohol. He wanted a clear head.

He stood naked outside, staring at the mountains. He was alone. His staff had dispersed the drug-driven orgy and returned his pool to its pristine condition.

Carmichael could wait. He'd let him show his cards before he made a move.

What was more important was how to deal with his new associates: Mr Manning and Mr Michaels. They had organised the hit on Kate, and they would pay for crossing him.

It was only a verbal agreement, but they had shaken hands. They had one goal in common— the demise of Jasper Carmichael—and they needed a man like him to achieve it. He wouldn't fail like the others had. He hadn't asked questions; payment and getting the police to turn a blind eye to his drugs business was all he needed.

His phone bleeped a long text message. He cursed out loud when he read that Manning and Michaels had visited Kate at home. Their intention was clear: kill Kate to get at Jasper. Mr Manning and Mr Michaels had a lot to answer for.

His text message to his right-hand man was clear: *Follow and watch both men.*

Chapter Forty-Two

"Who was that?" asked Kate, lifting her gaze from her book. "You looked happy."

Jasper joined her on the couch and carefully placed her legs on his lap.

"Chester. He's over the moon with his apartment."

"I'm not surprised. Riverside, furnished."

Jasper began to massage her feet. He smiled when Kate closed her eyes and tilted her head back, reading forgotten.

"I would like you to meet Chester, but you're not up to a long car journey."

A contented silence drifted between two people who were perfectly happy with each other's company.

"Invite him here."

Jasper smiled at her soft, sleepy tone.

"We have plenty of room. Clare would love to impress him with her cooking."

She opened one eye. "Why are you smiling?"

"You're almost purring."

Kate opened both eyes, smiled and purred.

"Putty in your hands." She blew him a kiss.

Jasper reached for her uninjured left arm and gently eased her onto his lap. His lips brushed hers. A delightful sigh escaped her mouth.

"Kiss me," she murmured.

A comfortable silence drifted.

Kate nuzzled into the warmth of his shoulder; his hand rested on her head while he weighed up the possible dangers of going to London.

"You don't like the idea of Chester coming here."

"I think he's not up to the train journey."

"How old is he?"

"I've no idea. There's always been a butler called Chester."

His fingers toyed with the band that held her hair back as his eyes studied her soft features.

"We'll all go there, then."

"It could be dangerous."

She gazed into his eyes. "They won't try again. Surely!"

"Bruce already has a team watching Michaels' house," Jasper commented.

"Jasper!"

He ignored her tone.

"You're feeling better? I've missed my Kate." His lips lightly touched her forehead.

"Yes! It's Clare's chicken soup." Her voice had suddenly become light-hearted. "I was lucky the bullet went straight through. Missed all the vital bits."

"Kate! Don't make light of it. You were injured. I was worried."

"I didn't mean to worry you."

"I'll phone Bruce and then Chester."

Jasper flashed a reassuring smile before his mouth claimed hers.

***

It was a warm, sunny day when Jasper parked in his allocated parking bay in walking distance of Chester's riverside apartment. He eased his wife from the Range Rover passenger seat.

"Pain?" he asked.

"A little."

"Here, take these." He handed her two painkillers and a bottle of water.

Jasper held Kate's hand as they walked towards the riverside apartment. Harry walked the other side of his mother while Oliver skipped ahead.

"Morning, Lord Carmichael," said the doorman, opening the glass doors of the apartment block.

Oliver's mouth opened. He tugged his father's hand.

"Do you know 'im?"

Jasper smiled and rubbed Oliver's hair. The lift doors opened.

"I've never been in a lift before," said Oliver, hurrying inside.

The apartment block agent was waiting.

"Lord Carmichael. I hope everything is to your satisfaction. Mr Chester is quite taken with the apartment."

The boys raced towards the bi-fold doors and stared at the view.

"What river's this?" asked Oliver.

"Thames," said Harry.

"Wow!"

The agent nervously hovered while Kate and Jasper wandered ahead. She had never seen Lord Carmichael with this woman. He always had glamorous women hanging on his arm.

"Like it?" Jasper asked, slipping his arm around Kate's shoulder.

"Yes! It's wonderful." Smiling, she gazed into his eyes.

They joined the boys staring at the river.

"Can we go on a boat?" asked Oliver giving his dad the Carmichael smile.

"He can sail," added Harry.

"You 'ave a boat?"

"Yacht," corrected Jasper.

"Will you take us?"

"He's looking for a bigger one," Kate light-heartedly commented.

"Not before your beach house." Jasper's fingers stroked her face.

"Really?" returned Kate.

Jasper turned to the agent and in his business voice said. "Everything is fine. There's just one thing—Chester might want his own furnishings."

"Not a problem. We will cater for whatever he wants."

Jasper nodded.

The agent cleared her throat. "There's, er, something you should know. A tall, elderly lady asked to see the apartment. A slight accent, American or Canadian. We rang Chester. He said that was fine."

Alice, Jasper thought, hiding his surprise.

"I'll sort it with Chester."

***

Jasper parked outside the Carmichael residence.

"Why do you park wherever you want?" asked Harry.

"Probably because I'm Lord Carmichael. I own the apartments, and this is my house."

Chapter Forty-Three

Gypsy was tired of his Spanish villa. He wanted to be back in England.

He snatched his bleeping phone from his jeans pocket.

"Well?"

"Carmichael and the family just pulled up outside the Georgian house."

"Kate with him?"

"Yep!"

"How does she look?"

"Pale. Arm in a sling. He lifted her out of the passenger seat."

Gypsy sighed. The bullet had done more damage than he'd anticipated.

"His goons are outside Michaels' place. Photographing all the comings and goings."

Jasper's planning something, Gypsy thought. *Someone's going to pay.*

"He's serious about selling. Got chatting to the apartment agent. Chester's moving into the penthouse. The agent overheard them talking about a yacht and beach house."

"Just keep watching. Send me all of the photos," he snapped.

"Are you coming back?"

"Yes!"

Gypsy wandered into his office and opened his laptop. He had a lot to think about before he returned to England. What was Jasper up to? A yacht and a beach house?

***

Chester sat in the kitchen, writing on Carmichael-embossed paper. He had a lot to put right before he departed this world.

Was that a car? he thought. His hearing wasn't so good. No one should be parking outside, except Lord Carmichael. He hurried to a front window and was surprised to see Jasper and family standing on the pavement chatting and looking up at the house.

He ran his hands through his mop of silver-grey hair, fastened his waistcoat and opened the front door.

"This a lovely surprise," he said, holding his hand out towards Kate.

"Chester, my wife, Kate," said Jasper. "Harry and Oliver."

Kate was instantly mesmerised by this elderly man with piercing blue eyes and a mop of grey hair.

"Come in! Come in!" Chester loudly said, waving his arm. "I'll make tea."

Kate stopped and stared at the dark wood panelling that surrounded a high-ceilinged, open entrance and the stairs leading up to a gallery and bedrooms.

"Grandfather liked dark wood," commented Jasper, following her gaze.

"We haven't got a grandfather," said Harry.

"You're right. My grandfather, your great grandfather."

"What's a great grandfather?" asked Oliver, not keeping up with the conversation.

Jasper opened the living room door. The boys jumped onto one of the large brown leather chairs.

"What's that smell?" exclaimed Oliver, turning his nose.

"It's the same as the castle," Harry said in a disheartened manner. "It's just like that place. Cold and dark."

"I remember the cold." Oliver turned and met Harry's gaze. "We shared a bed."

They both grinned.

Chester bustled in carrying a tray of tea and biscuits.

"No cake, I'm afraid. I can pop to the shop?"

"No need," said Kate.

"Are you staying the night?"

The boys shot Kate a worried look.

"No. It's a flying visit," Jasper answered. "I wanted the boys and Kate to see the house before it's sold. And Kate needs to rest."

"Nasty business," commented Chester. "Have the police caught the culprit?"

"Not yet."

"Two men were seen heading to the airfield," Kate added.

"They escaped by plane?" Chester said in a surprised manner, trying to hide that he already knew.

"The police think Kate took a bullet for me."

Chester's gaze moved to Kate.

"My Carmichael temper has a lot to answer for. Manning and a chap named Michaels came to visit. I kicked them out. Do you know Michaels?"

"I don't recall the name," Chester lied.

"Pity! I was hoping for some leads. I thought it may be something to do with Grandfather Carmichael or Colin." Jasper was studying Chester's face, hoping for a flicker of emotion, but none came.

"Oliver, tell Chester where we've been," Kate said quickly, hoping to change the subject.

"We've seen your new home," said Oliver, helping himself to the chocolate biscuits.

"Oh?" Chester's expression fell.

"Kate has never seen any of my London properties," said Jasper. "Two birds with one stone, so to speak."

"You should have phoned. I'd have prepared a meal."

"No worries. The boys are looking forward to stopping at a McDonald's."

Harry and Oliver smiled at each other, and Kate shot Jasper a curious look.

"Are you keeping your London properties?" Chester asked as he sipped his tea.

"I'm selling everything Lord Carmichael and keeping everything Jasper Carmichael." Jasper's tone was crisp and to the point.

Again, Kate gave him a curious look.

"Dad's going to get a yacht so we can all go sailing," Oliver said through a mouthful of biscuit.

"Oliver, don't speak with your mouth full," snapped Kate.

Oliver grinned.

"You'll enjoy sailing." Chester's tone was flat, showing little interest.

"We're having a beach house too."

Chester's expression morphed into one of surprise. "You'll have to excuse me." He hurried out of the room.

"Oliver, do you think you could be quiet?" Kate held his head while she tried to wipe the chocolate from his mouth with her injured arm.

Oliver flashed her the Carmichael smile.

"Come!" Jasper held out his hand to Kate.

They walked through the entrance hall to two large, wooden, double doors. Jasper pushed them open.

"Ta-da! The Carmichael library."

He switched on the lights and watched Kate's wonder.

"It's massive. Look at these first editions." She turned and smiled at him.

"It's all yours. I would have sold it."

"You can't sell them. They're part of your history, inheritance. Think of Harry and Oliver."

"I don't want them," declared Oliver, squatting on a small footstool.

"Jasper Senior threatened to move the library to the castle," Jasper explained. "But he never did. Colin just wasn't interested."

Unnoticed, Chester joined them. Harry opened a cupboard jam-packed with hand-written journals.

"Can we take these?" he asked, turning to Jasper.

Jasper hesitated.

"I'll find a box," said Chester.

"I wonder if Grandma Alice or Granddad Colin will be in them," commented Harry.

Chester nearly tripped.

"How old would Grandfather Colin be?"

"No one really knows. For argument's sake, let's say he was sixteen when he joined up. You do the maths, Harry."

Harry was silent while he worked it out.

"He could still be alive. Do you remember him, Chester?"

"Harry, not so many questions," Kate interjected.

Chester slumped in a chair, dropping two empty holdalls. He was out of breath and his cheeks were flushed. Beads of sweat dripped off his forehead.

Kate wiped Chester's brow while Jasper fetched him a glass of water and Harry and Oliver stacked the journals into the holdalls.

"We should stay, Jasper," said a concerned Kate.

"No! No! I'll be fine. Just give me a minute." Chester was eager for them to leave.

***

Chester stood at the open front door, watching the Carmichael family leave. Jasper loaded the holdalls into the Range Rover boot while Kate checked two excited boys were securely strapped in. Chester had never understood the younger generation's attraction to McDonald's.

They had stayed longer than he would have liked. It was his own fault—he hadn't wanted to rush his writing—but it was important that Jasper had his old leather satchel.

Chapter Forty-Four

As Chester closed the front door, he heard the kitchen door creak.

"Have they gone? They were here a long time."

Chester inwardly cursed as Chanel perfume wafted towards him. There were traces of it in the downstairs bathroom. He suspected Kate had recognised Alice's signature perfume.

She slipped two arms around his thickening waist. He leaned back.

"I saw the car; they've been to the apartment." Her voice was just above a whisper. "Did you know they were coming?"

"Do you think I would have let them see me like this? I've always had short hair and been clean shaven."

"Leave London. Come with me. No one knows you in America."

"They went to their home."

"Who?" Alice raised her voice.

"I should have dealt with it all those years ago."

"Colin, what are you talking about?"

Colin Carmichael, aka Chester, moved towards the living room's fireside chair. His head slumped in his hands. His eyes focused on the carpet.

"There was no affection between us. It was a family marriage. My job was to produce male heirs. Only, they weren't mine. They had been fucking before we were married. Never dreamt she was fucking someone else." He paused. "Came home early. They were fucking like rabbits."

"So? You kicked her out," said Alice, guessing he was talking about his wife.

"Meredith took care of everything. I walked out, and I never saw her or the boys again."

"But there's Willis."

"He's not a Carmichael. He sneaks around frightened of his own shadow. He would never have come here if it wasn't for greed and some misguided idea that he would inherit the Carmichael fortune."

Colin's bitter tone shook Alice.

"Did Meredith know you were alive?"

"Yes! But he didn't know where I was hiding."

"I don't understand."

"Meredith knew that I wouldn't allow anyone but Jasper to inherit the Carmichael fortune. The only thing Meredith never got his hands on was my diamonds."

"Jasper has them."

Colin continued as if he hadn't heard her. "There was a group of them. Labelled me 'cuckold'. It was a Michaels who fucked her. He laughed in my face. I should have killed them. I hid and waited. I knew overconfidence would ruin them."

"Colin, you're not making sense."

"Their investments failed. To clear their debts, they sold everything at rock bottom prices. Of course, they didn't know it was me who was behind their financial downfall."

"Did Meredith know?"

"Your half-brother had no idea."

A heavy, thoughtful silence filled the living room.

"And now they're after Jasper," Alice said.

"It's obvious that Jasper's nothing without Kate. Kill Kate, and Jasper would suffer. Michaels went to their fucking house, for God's sake. He intended to kill her right before his eyes." Colin paused. "Jasper's business would collapse. To survive, he would go back to his old ways."

"You don't know that."

"It's only a matter of time before Lord Carmichael becomes the criminal Jasper Carmichael. It's Kate that stops him."

An uncomfortable silence drifted between the two old lovers.

"How come you ended up here?" Alice asked eventually.

"As long as I can remember, there's always been a butler called Chester running this house. It was winter. Snowing. Roads were blocked. I needed somewhere to shelter. I spent the night in this room. Had to make my own breakfast. There was no sign of Chester. He was dead in his bed."

"And?"

"I became him. Meredith rarely visited. Anyway, he had no idea what Chester looked like. Meredith Spencer would never look at what he considered to be an inferior being. And Jasper had never met Chester. So, you see, it was easy to become him."

"I don't know what to say."

"Say nothing. Go back to America."

"I can't. I promised Willis."

"Willis!" He scoffed. "His greed and hatred for Jasper led to an unfortunate association with a woman called Beth, who in turn betrayed a villain by the name of Gypsy."

"How do you know this?"

"I still have ties with certain people. Willis and that woman had an unfortunate accident."

"Colin! I feel like I don't even know you."

"No one does."

***

While Colin and Alice were talking, Kate and Jasper sat gazing at the darkening sky. Jasper was sipping a malt, and Kate sat between his legs, her back to his front.

"The boys asleep?" he said.

She nodded. "They really enjoyed today. Oliver keeps talking about boats. Harry's taken with the Carmichael journals. And of course, McDonald's."

He felt her body relax onto his chest. His lips nuzzled her neck.

"You do know that wasn't Chester?" said Jasper.

"I smelt Alice's perfume in the downstairs bathroom."

Jasper stopped nuzzling her neck.

"He had me fooled."

"I think it's fair to say he had everyone fooled."

"Except Alice."

"I can't remember what Colin looked like. People said he was dead. But there was no proof."

"He has a mop of grey hair and blue eyes."

"I'm taller than him."

"You have a mop of sexy salt-and-pepper hair and come-to-bed blue eyes." She grinned.

Jasper laughed and dropped his empty glass onto the studio floor. His lips returned to her neck, and his large hands cupped her breasts.

"I want to be inside you," he murmured between kisses.

"I need you inside me."

She tried to turn to face him.

"No. I want your arm to fully heal."

"We could try. I'll be careful."

"Kate! I know you and your 'don't keep me waiting'."

She giggled.

"You'll have to be satisfied with kissing and cuddling," he said.

"Well, don't stop. I need a lot of kissing and cuddling."

Happy laughter filled the dark studio.

Chapter Forty-Five

Colin sat alone in the kitchen of the Carmichael London residence, feeling that he was approaching the last chapter of his life.

He had never had a chance to say goodbye to Alice when she was shipped off to America behind his back. Alice was the only woman he had ever loved.

She had caught him unawares when she knocked on the front door. His failing heart had skipped a beat. A warm glow had slowly spread through him as his eyes captured her beauty. The same beauty he'd loved all those years ago.

She'd smiled, recognising his blue eyes, mop of hair and the Carmichael smile. She had waited till they were inside before wrapping her arms around him and kissing him. Oh, how those kisses brought back memories of their love affair!

She was full of pride at how their son had become an outstanding man with a wife and two boys. She had talked at length about his Carmichael Centre and the Carmichael brand. But Colin didn't let on that he already knew about his successful son. A son to be proud of. A Carmichael.

He had finally said goodbye to the love of his life. Alice had cried and kissed him long and hard, knowing this was the last time she would see him. He had watched her walk away. Only when she reached the street corner did she look back. Tears had trickled down his cheeks. He knew she was crying.

He had only had one more task to complete, and that was to protect Jasper from the mistakes he had made.

He regretted not spending more time with Jasper and his family. The stories he could have told those boys… But he would have put them in danger.

Kate had changed Jasper, but he was still a Carmichael. It was only a matter of time before the lure of power and diamonds replaced the love they shared.

His grandsons were also Carmichaels. Harry had his intelligence and Oliver his adventurous nature.

Jasper was lucky he had found love. Colin knew he should have run away with Alice, away from anything Carmichael. He could have had more children with Alice, but above all, Jasper would have been brought up as a true Carmichael.

Colin put these maudlin thoughts out of his mind and concentrated on the task at hand: revenge. He smiled as he slowly walked up the stairs to his bedroom.

He was pleased he had managed to slip his wartime satchel between the Carmichael journals Jasper had taken with him. It was important that Jasper had it before he passed. He grinned when he thought of Jasper opening it.

He took his time dressing. It was important he looked the part, just like he had during those secret wartime raids. He had fooled the Germans, and now he was going to fool six overconfident bastards.

He stared into the full-length mirror. His black suit fitted perfectly; the overcoat, gloves and hat waited in the hallway. He slowly walked down the stairs to the kitchen, where he hid his heart medication. The doctor had stressed that he should keep to the prescribed dosage, but tonight it didn't matter if he died of heart failure as long he completed his last job.

He struggled into his overcoat and slipped his wartime handgun into his overcoat pocket. He didn't have to check the gun, as he regularly cleaned it and practised shooting at a target he had rigged in the garden.

He closed the front door, secured his hat and slipped his hands into his gloves.

Michaels' house was two streets away, but Colin took his time going over his plan. It was simple: shoot all six men before they realised what was happening. With a bit of luck, they would all be sitting around a table drinking and talking. He had carried out such missions during the war and the years after, but he'd been much younger then and his heart had been fully functioning.

He stopped in the shadows and watched. It didn't take long to spot the men watching Michaels' house. He briefly wondered which was Jasper's man. But he couldn't digress; concentration was everything.

***

Zak Cohen had watched Chester leave the house. The lock on the kitchen door was easy to pick.

Word on the street was that Colin Carmichael was responsible for the robbery on Zak's recently opened jewellery outlet. Only Colin would have the brass to walk into the back and lift the box containing the quality loose diamonds. Colin would have easily recognised it; Zak had foolishly secured the box with the same silver strap used by his family to identify diamonds.

There was only one thief that would dare steal from a Cohen, and he was dead. Or was he?

Zak stood in the Carmichael library waiting for his raging mind to settle. He had to think clearly and behave in a controlled manner. In a blind rage, he had sacked his London staff, blaming their drunken tongues for the robbery. Colin would have found their watering hole. He would have plied them with drinks until he had the information he wanted. But deep down, Zak knew his own overconfidence was partly to blame. He had signed the consignment off without the security system being operational.

Zak began to methodically search the library.

*****

With a confident air that befitted his attire, Colin strolled up to Michaels' front door. The butler opened the door, looked Colin up and down and waved him in. As the door closed, Colin turned and hit the butler across his head with his gun. He fell like a sack of potatoes.

Colin stood perfectly still, then moved to the room where the loud conversation was coming from. He slowly opened the door. It was the library. No one looked up. Why should they? He looked just like them.

Colin didn't hesitate; his only goal was to kill these men. He aimed at each in turn and pulled the trigger. He left Michaels till last. He dropped his hat on the table and grinned as fear spread across Michaels' face. No words, just a clean shot in the head.

Colin picked up his hat and placed it on his head, pulling the brim so it shaded his face, and walked towards the river where he had intended to throw his gun. But his chest felt tight, his heart was thumping, and he was short of breath. He dropped the gun in the first bin he came across, hoping it would be emptied sometime in the early hours.

He slowly walked back to the place he referred to as home. Each step became heavier than the last, and his vision was blurring. He was sweating.

He closed the front door behind him and leaned against it, trying to regain his breath. One, two, three, four, five steps. He slowly sank onto the cold tiled floor. He couldn't breathe. His fingers pulled at his collar and tie; it was useless, but he had to try. Sharp pain in his chest, then another. The darkness was beckoning, his life flashed before him, his eyes were shutting, he was falling into the darkness, with newborn baby Jasper in his arms.

***

Zak froze when the front door opened and closed followed by a loud thud. He waited and listened before he peeked out of the library door. A body lay face down on the hall floor. Zak moved to check if the man was still alive when the sound of the kitchen door creaking echoed.

Zak slipped back into the library, leaving the door slightly ajar. A tall figure stopped just inside the hallway and stared at the body. After a long moment, the figure turned and left the same way he had entered.

Zak waited for silence to fill the house, then struggled to roll the body onto its back. Cold blue eyes flicked open. Zak cried in shock and fell onto his backside. He backed away from the body, shaking his head. He could feel his heart thumping as if it was trying to get out of his chest.

The body moaned while Zak leaned against the hallway wall, gathering his thoughts.

Chapter Forty-Six

Jasper slipped out of bed, taking care not to wake Kate. He had arranged an early morning call with a South American. Jasper was wary of any involvement with South Americans, but for his diamond network to be successful he needed access to the South American diamond dealers.

Half an hour later, Jasper was in the kitchen, pondering on his conversation with the South American. His lack of interest in the diamond network bothered Jasper. Suddenly, the kitchen door opened and Bruce walked in.

"What's happened?" asked Jasper, pouring Bruce a coffee.

"This is too sensitive to be said over the phone," Bruce uttered, his voice tight as he pulled up a stool. "Are we alone?"

Jasper nodded and waited while Bruce swigged his coffee.

"Bruce!" Kate said as she strolled towards the kettle, not caring that her flimsy night-robe left nothing to the imagination.

A shocked Jasper pulled her towards himself for an early morning kiss, trying to hide his surprise and wondering how long she had been downstairs.

"Bruce has something important to tell us."

"It was just after nine when we first saw the figure," Bruce began, his eyes on Kate. "Dressed in black. Hat pulled over his eyes. He went straight in Michaels' house. You can't see the meeting room from the road. We thought we heard six faint shots."

Bruce had Jasper's complete attention.

"And the figure?"

"Walked calmly towards the river." Bruce stopped and stared into Jasper's expectant eyes. "I followed. The figure briefly staggered and changed direction. The gun was dropped in a bin."

"You didn't touch it," interrupted Jasper.

Bruce shook his head. "But I got a good look at it. Looked like an Enfield."

Kate moved to Jasper's side, her hand was resting on his shoulder, but her eyes were talking to Bruce.

"The figure continued staggering towards—"

"He went into my house." Jasper interrupted.

Bruce nodded.

"The strange thing was, no lights came on. I went round back. The kitchen door was unlocked. I carefully walked into the hall. He was lying face down. I'm sorry, Jasper."

Jasper stood and walked into the early dawn air.

"Are you sure?" asked Kate, moving closer to Bruce so her leg brushed against his. Her two hands were wrapped around her tea, her glistening eyes danced. He could clearly see the curves of her body through her robe. Desire stirred.

"Who else lives in that house but Chester?" he stuttered. He pushed his stool away from her.

"Was he dead?"

"I assume so. I didn't hang about. Kate, stop!"

"Touch me. I need—"

The kitchen door opened. Clare stopped and stared at the two.

"Malcolm's with Jasper," Clare said, filling the kettle.

"Did you touch the body?" Kate asked Bruce matter-of-factly.

Bruce shook his head.

***

Hundreds of miles away, Gypsy was listening to a similar story.

"This guy walked in and shot the lot of them. The place is crawling with police."

"So! Michaels' secret group is dead." Gypsy's thoughts drifted down the phone. "And my deal along with them. Where's Jasper?"

"Wellsbury. He stopped for diesel and McDonald's."

Gypsy was silent for some time, locked in his thoughts.

"What do you want me to do?"

"Disappear," Gypsy said. "We'll wait till the heat dies down."

"What about the drugs?"

"Continue with the old arrangement."

Gypsy put the phone down and stared at the morning sun.

***

Jasper didn't have to wait too long for the law to arrive. Watts came knocking at the door just after lunch.

"What do you want?" Jasper snapped.

"That's no way to greet an officer of the law," Watts replied, slumping into one of the overstuffed chairs in Jasper's office. "Rang the office. Amanda said you were here. I didn't believe the gossip. You're working from home to look after Kate." Watts grinned.

"Say your piece and get the fuck out." Jasper moved his new reading glasses into his hair.

"It's that butler. Chester. Found dead." Watts studied Jasper's face, waiting for a hint of emotion.

None came.

"I'll deal with it." Jasper lifted the phone from the cradle.

"No, you won't. He's the main suspect in a shooting."

"Chester?!"

"Six shots. One bullet in each head. Execution style."

"Chester's an old man."

"We have witnesses that saw him staggering to the house after the shooting."

Jasper's stomach churned. *Colin,* he thought.

"You haven't asked about the victims."

"I probably don't know them. Don't have many friends in London."

"You know Michaels and Manning. They visited, remember?"

"I kicked them out."

"Why?"

"I'll tell you why." Jasper stood from his desk, his hands leaning on the surface. He glared at Watts. "Michaels was menacingly walking towards Kate. Kate had just been shot. Remember?"

"You thought they meant her harm."

"I was taking no chances."

For a long moment, an uneasy silence hung between the two men.

"You were in London yesterday, at the house. What did you and Chester talk about?"

"Careful, Inspector." There was meaning in Jasper's voice.

"All seems a bit odd. You saw Chester yesterday. Six men were shot and Chester's a suspect."

Before Jasper could react, Watts walked out of the door.

Chapter Forty-Seven

Kate needed a distraction. The little voice at the back of her mind was telling her Jasper was hiding something. She feared it was diamonds.

She went to check on Harry, who was in the library sorting the Carmichael journals. The journals were scattered over a long wooden table. At the far end was an old leather satchel with the government crest.

Clutching the satchel, Kate hurried to the kitchen, where Jasper was talking to Bruce, Clare and Malcolm. She met his eyes and pushed the satchel into his chest.

As soon as Jasper saw the government crest, he knew it belonged to Colin. He emptied the contents of the satchel onto the table. He gave birth, marriage, death certificates, a wallet, various bank accounts and the deeds to a beach house a cursory glance. The last envelope was sealed with the Carmichael wax emblem.

He broke the seal and handed the sheets of paper inside to Kate.

"This is unusual paper," she commented, running her fingers admiringly over the pages.

"Dates back to grandfather's day. There's a supply in the London house."

Kate leafed through the pages. "There's no date on any of the pages, and there's different writing on each page, as if he's added to them over time."

"Kate!" Jasper said, in his 'get on with it' tone. She looked up and smiled.

***

Jasper,

It pleased my fading eyes to meet your family. I never dreamt I'd have grandchildren.

Harry has my intelligence, or should I say the Carmichael intelligence. But you must keep him away from the diamond curse.

Oliver has my spirit of adventure. Let him be free. That's the only way he'll be happy.

You and Kate have a presence, the type that when you walk into a crowded room people stop and stare. If Kate was of mind, you'd have influence and power.

I'm sending my personal papers to you. They mustn't fall into the wrong hands.

When Oliver mentioned boats and beach houses I nearly fainted. You own a beach house. I believe you've already seen it. I have spies everywhere. It's in your name so no one would link it to me. No one ever found me there. It was falling down when I bought it. One of those arty types had it built. I imagine Kate will love it, and you will bring it back to its former self.

I'm not a good man. I need the thrill of stealing diamonds, and the riches they bring. I'm still at it. I've never found redemption, but I never found a Kate.

Alice and I are two of a kind. All we wanted was money and a good life.

I loved her. She was stunningly beautiful, and still is. She's on her way back to America. I believe Kate recognised her perfume.

You and Kate are blessed. Two wonderful boys, and a deep love.

Whatever life throws at the two of you, trust in love and loyalty to weather the storm.
Colin.

***

Being here on my own, alone, my memories come to life, as if they happened only yesterday.

***

Alice.
I should have run away with Alice. God knows we discussed it many times.
It all started when two ruthless men driven by greed and the lust for power had a falling out.
I first met Meredith Spencer when he was a young lawyer. He wanted nothing but power and wealth. His way to the top was simple: marry into an established law firm. And that's what he did. His wife introduced him to the top legal minds of the day and to their rich clients. That's how he met my father, the first Lord Carmichael. They were cast from the same greed-and-power mould. They became great friends and business partners, until they had a falling out. Meredith was no longer privy to Jasper's dubious and sometimes corrupt business deals. Jasper made a fortune and Meredith was furious. But Jasper had one big weakness: young women.
Enter Alice, Meredith's half-sister, the Spencers' dirty secret. Same mother but different fathers. Meredith never thought of her as a Spencer. When she arrived at his door, she was destitute. To save herself, she agreed to Meredith's cunning plan: bed Jasper, read his papers and report back to Meredith.

Jasper and Meredith considered women to be inferior. Consequently, Jasper was careless with confidential papers.

She's a female version of Meredith. Cunning and ruthless.

I hated my father. I blamed him for my mother's death. I abhorred the idea of an old man fucking the young, beautiful Alice. He was a brute.

It's true I fucked her on her wedding day. And I kept on fucking her. She was like a drug I couldn't get enough of.

Jasper was so full of himself he didn't even notice she was pregnant.

Meredith organised everything: Jasper's trip to America when you were due, doctors, orphanage.

It breaks my heart now. They wouldn't let Alice hold her son. I wanted to hold her, but Meredith wouldn't allow it. I had a job to do. The doctor wrapped our son in layers of blankets and handed him to me. I can still hear her howling cries as I walked away.

I was crying.

I never drove to the orphanage.

I was the leader of a criminal gang. We were on the fringes of crime, but my diamond robberies made them good money and satisfied my need for danger. A by-product from my wartime activities.

The whore and a wet nurse were waiting. She was the one that saved you. I watched as she cradled you in her arms, her eyes full of love.

I now regret what I did.

***

Jasper.

I named you Jasper to spite my father. Only the firstborn of the firstborn were called Jasper. I was the youngest, so they called me Colin, but I'm a Jasper. My brothers didn't deserve the name Carmichael.

My old heart aches for what I did to my Jasper. I regret that I left him with criminals. I regret that I never gave him the attention he so badly needed. I close my eyes and I see his blue eyes looking at me, begging for a smile, a touch, but to my shame I ignored him. I fucked that whore instead.

I have some comfort though, in so much as I saved him from prison.

I sent him to Wellsbury. I knew Wellsbury well. The airfield was just a field until the ministry used it. An ideal place for diamonds to enter and leave the country. Wellsbury was a place that time had forgotten, ripe for my son to make his own way and fortune.

The Isaacs lived in my house, they were family, and I knew they would keep an eye on my Jasper. And if he got in trouble, they would tell me.

One of my good deeds was rescuing the Isaacs from the Germans. I learnt a lot from Jacob, a master diamond expert. Hannah loved me as if I was the son the Germans shot. She gave me the love I didn't know I needed.

The last time I saw my son, he thought I was in prison. Everyone thought I was in prison, but my father had a lot of influence. Many rich and powerful people had fallen into his trap, and they owed him. I would disappear, and when the time was right, I would reappear.

You could never do that today.

***

The family I forgot.

I have another family hidden in the back of my mind. Thinking about them gives me pain. I treated them appallingly.

We married out of family duty. I fucked her, but the children she bore weren't mine. I'm the biggest cuckold that ever lived.

I unexpectedly returned home one day. They were fucking like rabbits. IN MY BED. I kicked him out and slapped her around.

Meredith decided that they should leave the country for America. He organised their passage to America and a place for them to live.

I couldn't care less. I wanted rid of them.

Meredith was more concerned about a scandal that would ruin the Carmichaels. And let's not forget, he had an invested interest in the Carmichael brand.

I couldn't care less about my family or the Carmichael brand.

I was Colin Carmichael, rich diamond thief, and while I was basking in my fame, my wife was being fucked by a Michaels. Her children were Michaelses and not Carmichaels.

They humiliated me. I was full of myself. I strutted around like a peacock.

Michaels was fucking her before we married. I often wondered why her boys never resembled me.

They're all dead except for Willis. Jasper's half-brother. A weasel of a man, no backbone. A typical Michaels.

Has big ideas, does Willis. Thinks he's heir to the Carmichael fortune, and if Meredith was alive, he would want him to inherit.

Over my dead body.

No Michaels will have Carmichael money.

***

Michaels.

Michaels and his clique of followers made my life hell. I should have dealt with it back then. But I didn't.

He wants revenge for a Carmichael banishing his relatives to America. My contacts tell me he has his eyes on Jasper. He's behind Manning getting control over the trust fund. Jasper's going to lose a lot of money.

I shall have to do something about Michaels and his merry band of followers.

I know where he lives.

I know when they all meet.

This is the last straw. There's been an attempt on Kate's life. She's the glue that holds Jasper and the boys together.

I shall have to act.

My heart permitting, I shall give destiny a helping hand. I shall have my revenge against Michaels and his weak band of followers. And Jasper and Kate will have their destiny.

Execution style is an audacious plan. One I'm familiar with, but I was younger then and my heart was healthy.

***

Diamonds.

I can't leave them alone.

The thrill. The adrenaline rush.

I have a small collection here. In my wartime satchel, along with important papers.

I've always been a diamond thief. I've never stopped.

I let people believe that Colin's diamonds were in the box I gave Jasper.

My diamond hoard is at the beach house.

Zak Cohen is opening a shop not far from me. I sat in the coffee shop opposite, watching. Memorising his staff. It didn't take me long to find their drinking hole.

Zak's a typical Cohen—has no idea how to get the best out of people. Long hours, poor pay; too much to drink and they were spilling the details of Zak's open day delivery of jewellery and diamonds.

I wandered around to the back of the shop. Luck was with me; the diamonds were being unloaded. Always a good sign when luck is on your side.

I didn't hesitate. I recognised the box with the diamonds in. I walked through the back doors, nodded at the men, picked up the box.

Candy from a baby.

I wonder where Zak got these diamonds from. Their quality is outstanding. Worth a lot of money.

They're in the satchel.

***

Destiny.

I'm not a believer in destiny. But as I sit reflecting on my past, I realise that I may have been wrong.

I've always believed people make their own destiny. I made mine. Yet as I look back, I can see how I thwarted destiny.

I believe Spencer and Carmichael blood were meant to mix. Their children would go on to do good things. Use their good fortune to help those not so fortunate. Even hold seats of power.

I'm beginning to sound like my father.

I should have made a life with Alice. A generation of Spencer and Carmichael blood mixed. The power blood mix.

I shouldn't have deserted my son.

I shouldn't have let the Michaelses humiliate me.

My son having children with a Spencer was destiny. Even though Kate only has a trace of

Spencer blood, she is a Spencer. Her features resemble the Spencers'. Thankfully, she hasn't their greed or ruthlessness but she has their inner strength and determination. She has good business sense.

I'm convinced their destiny is to do good. Kate is already using Meredith's money to help those that are not so well off.

However, I fear that destiny will be thwarted once again.

This time, it will be diamonds.

***

"It's blank." Kate's voice was full of emotion. "The last page. It's blank."

She dropped the pages on the kitchen surface. She glanced over to Jasper, who was staring at the large leather wallet.

Their eyes met.

"You're not a Spencer." His hand stretched to touch her face. "You're kind, caring, loving. Spencers aren't like that. They're greedy. Manipulative. I could never fall in love with a Spencer."

He stood and pulled her into a kiss.

Chapter Forty-Eight

Jasper picked up the leather wallet.

"Jasper, leave it. Don't look inside," Kate pleaded.

"Don't be concerned."

Jasper smiled as he pulled out several small, sealed paper bags. The contents of one bag spilled onto the work surface. There was a long moment of silence as they all were mesmerised by the sparkling gems.

"Kate, these are our destiny."

"You don't believe that. We don't need money… I was at a low point when I talked about a beach house."

But Jasper wasn't listening. He was transfixed.

Kate turned and ran to her studio, slamming the door.

"She's closed the door," said Clare, holding a cup of tea.

"Leave her," said Jasper.

"What you going to do with 'em, boss?" There was a tinge of concern in Bruce's voice.

"Nothing," Jasper lied. His mind was whirling with the possibility of Lord Carmichael, master diamond dealer.

"Bury 'em. Kate's right. They're nothing but trouble." Malcolm's chilling voice made Jasper lift his gaze. He was surprised to see Malcolm's worried expression.

The sound of the Evoque engine drifted into the kitchen.

"I'll go after 'er," said Bruce, dying to escape the heavy atmosphere that had descended on the kitchen. But deep down, he wanted to be with Kate. To hold her and kiss her. He was more than disappointed when Jasper said he was going to her.

"She'll be going to the river. Give me a lift," said Jasper, collecting two coats off the pegs.

"The boys will be worried. You should pick 'em up," said Clare.

Jasper stopped. "This is something Kate and I have to solve. It's been hanging over us for far too long."

"What do I tell 'em?"

"Tell them we love them very much, but we have to talk."

"But you've taken coats."

"It's going to take a long time."

***

Bruce jealously watched Jasper walking towards Kate. Jasper hadn't said a word since leaving the house. *As if he's planning something,* Bruce thought. His gut was telling him it wouldn't be good for Kate.

Jasper took his time approaching Kate. She sat on her thinking bench, staring at the river. He would have to be careful what he said and how he said it. She would need careful coaxing to accept Colin's diamonds. He expected her to resist his seductive technique.

"Go away," she said firmly.

"This is going to be sorted, once and for all." His voice was almost a whisper. He lowered himself next to her so their shoulders rubbed.

"I can't look at you."

Jasper stayed calm, focusing on his wife's irregular breathing. Tension was building. He took a deep breath.

"You know you're the world to me."

Only a partial lie, he thought.

"It doesn't feel like it." Her voice quivered as she tried to quell her emotions. Jasper stretched his arm along the back of the bench, careful not to touch her.

"We may need extra funds when I've sold everything Lord Carmichael," he said in a flat tone, trying to nip the rising tension in the bud.

"We will manage. And don't forget, I have money." She turned her head so she could read Jasper's expression.

"Harry might not go to that school," he said in the same tone, trying to gauge Kate's mood. He was banking that mentioning Harry would change her train of thought.

"I'm not sure he wants to go. I was thinking we should spend a day there. Let him get a flavour of the place. Instead of filling in forms and going for interviews, I've asked for an appointment."

Jasper swallowed his smile. He'd skilfully deflected Kate's thoughts.

He sat silently, waiting for signs she was relaxing.

"I want to kiss you." His voice was low and full of emotion. Her reply surprised him.

"I want you to kiss me."

His arm moved to her shoulder, pulling her into him. Her body stiffened. He held back. Kate was still resisting.

"Do you love me?" he said hesitantly into her ear.

"You know I do."

"Well, talk to me."

An uneasy silence lingered.

"I'm caught," Kate said.

Jasper turned to study her face.

"I can't live without you."

Jasper relaxed.

"I don't want you to return to your criminal ways. You're legit at the moment. I want it to stay that way. I don't want the police breathing down our necks. You've been stabbed and I've been shot by people out to get you. Will it never stop?"

"You can't make a judgement on Beth's obsession to get even with me." He paused, letting his words hang. "My criminal associates would never order a hit on you. We have a code, you know that. Michaels and co were not criminals. They had no code. You are under my protection. You know that."

"What about Gypsy?"

"He would never hurt you. I'm a different kettle of fish."

"You're so glib."

"I know the people I deal with. We have a mutual respect. We don't betray or double-cross. Colin made that mistake. Things may have been different if he hadn't double-crossed Anton. And we all paid the price."

An uncomfortable silence settled.

"I can't leave it alone, Kate. It's part of who I am. Colin was a master diamond thief, and I'm a master diamond dealer, fence—call it what you like. You have to face that."

"In some ways you are so like Colin. You set up a secret network of safe houses. You have cars stashed around the place. Colin was very apt at disappearing and reappearing. And you're both masters of disguise."

"Okay." Jasper hesitated, carefully choosing his words. "Let's consider this. My old network is intact, but it needs money to start up."

"Money we haven't got."

"I could move funds. And you could pay Harry's fees."

"Oh, for goodness' sake! We're not going on the merry-go-round of ifs. We could do this or we could do that. Just fucking kiss me before I leave."

Kate's sharp tone shook Jasper. He quickly realised he had used the wrong tact.

He swiftly lifted her onto his lap. His mouth crashed onto hers, swallowing her doubts and fears as he caressed her tongue.

Kate was more than a little breathless when she rested her head on his shoulder. "That was some kiss."

"It was meant to be. I'm not going to lose you over this."

"Suggest a way forward then."

"Let's start again." Jasper's tone was surprisingly conciliatory. "We both agree that we can't live without each other."

Kate nodded.

"So, it follows that we have to find a way to live together."

"I could turn a blind eye," Kate said.

Jasper shook his head. "I need you in my bed. To love me when I'm slipping into despair. To advise me. And to be on my side."

"You're a contradiction. Sometimes I feel I don't know you."

"Yes, you do! I'm the same man that you fell in love with all those years ago. I'm the man you were loyal to. I'm the man that gives you mind-blowing orgasms."

She couldn't help but smile. "I'm the woman that set you on the path to redemption."

"You're the woman that taught me how to love."

He turned his head, their lips brushed.

"Kiss me," she murmured.

"Tell me what you want."

Kate closed her eyes as she considered her options. Did she want Jasper to be unhappy? No. Could she live with an unhappy Jasper? No. Had she changed him? Yes. He was no longer the bastard that used her for rough sex. Was he faithful? She didn't know. Their sex life had changed. Did he give her mind-blowing orgasms? Yes.

"Kate…"

"Above all, I want you, Jasper. I want us to grow old together. I want you to keep loving me. Be faithful. You can have your diamonds. But don't involve me in the details. I don't need names, places, or anything like that."

Kate's soft, soothing voice calmed Jasper's pounding heart. He sighed. He had got her for as long as he wanted.

"Don't deceive me," she said. "Don't lie. Just the need-to-know will suffice."

Jasper's large hands cupped her face. "I want to love you," he whispered between kisses. "I want to make love to you. Now. You choose: the back of the Evoque, the grass by the bench, or that small stretch of sand by the river."

She giggled. This was her Jasper. The one she fell in love with. Her fingers stoked his hairline.

"By the river."

He laid their coats on the sand. Their eyes danced their special love dance. Her fingers flicked the buttons of her blouse, exposing her white lace bra. His fingers circled her hard nipples while her hands struggled with his belt.

"Kate, let me."

Their naked bodies were on fire. Her legs wrapped around his waist, his mouth nipped her and sucked her breasts. Delightful sighs escaped her mouth.

"Don't make me wait," she uttered.

He smiled.

"I love you," she murmured.

"I know."

His mouth swallowed her cries as unimaginably intense sensations began to flow. She threaded her hands through his hair, urging him to move. Her orgasm was building.

"Now, Jasper!" she murmured.

The pain in her shoulder was forgotten when they climaxed together.

They lay in silence, waiting for their breathing to calm.

***

They were blissfully unaware of the man whispering into a phone nearby.

"Well?" a voice barked into his ear.

"He's fucking her by the river. Both naked as the day they were born. They must've 'ad an argument. Make-up sex."

Gypsy didn't care that they were fucking. Since he'd been at his villa, he'd had more than his fair share of fucking. He was bored with young women only too eager to be fucked. His cock was satisfied, but his mind needed to be stimulated. Jasper Carmichael would provide that stimulation.

"Police?"

"No sign. His man left ages ago."

"I don't like this," Gypsy growled. "Six dead. His butler dead and he's fucking his wife. He's up to summat."

"I'll carry on watching, then."

***

"We ought to move before we're seen." Kate reached for her blouse.

Jasper smiled and pulled her back onto his chest.

"Just another moment." His fingers circled her back. "We'll do the beach house up. To your exacting requirements," Jasper whispered into her ear. "Harry will decide if he wants to go to that school. I'll have my diamond fix," he said, before she could object. "Just a little dabble. Enough to satisfy." *And buy me a new yacht.*

Chapter Forty-Nine

Jasper pushed his new reading glasses into his hair. He couldn't concentrate; Kate plagued his thoughts. Even though they had made love, she hadn't given herself to him like she normally did. He feared he might be losing her trust or her affections, or both.

Bruce appeared in his mind. She'd be with him on the school run. She always had a glow when she returned.

An unfamiliar voice interrupted his thoughts.

"Clare said come straight through."

Jasper's keen eyes watched Dan, the accountant, walk to his desk. Dan dropped a USB stick onto a pile of papers.

"Kate has nothing to be worried about. You're not being fiddled." There was a tinge of bitterness in Dan's voice.

"That'll put her mind at rest. Thank you," Jasper said calmly.

"I didn't do it for you."

"I know."

Jasper opened a side drawer in his desk and pressed a newly installed button. He'd been concerned at the lack of a way to record his office conversations, but hadn't wanted to involve his IT team. The fewer people who knew about his secret recording, the better.

"You know?"

"Kate and I don't have secrets."

Dan stepped towards the French doors that overlooked Kate's studio.

"She'll be back soon," Jasper told him.

"Christ knows what she sees in you. I suppose you've corrupted her free thinking."

Jasper rubbed the back of his neck as he felt his muscles twitch. He thought of Kate. She wouldn't be pleased if he argued with Dan. So he let an uncomfortable silence drift.

"Looking back, I should have made a move on Kate. But we were going to different universities," Dan remarked as he gazed towards Kate's studio.

"I believe at the time you had eyes for Michelle."

Dan turned and glared at Jasper. "She likes me and I like her."

"Thinking of dumping your new beau?" Jasper's sarcastic tone riled Dan.

"I could have fucked her."

"But you didn't, and now it's too late."

"I could take her from you."

Jasper laughed. "Many have tried and failed."

***

Kate walked through the kitchen door with Bruce at her shoulder.

"Is that Dan's car?" she asked cheerfully.

Clare caught her arm and put a finger across her lips. She pointed to a recording device that Jasper had switched on from his desk.

"Listen."

She handed Kate a pair of headphones.

***

"You think you're so fucking clever. She was shot because of you."

Jasper felt his temper stir. Why couldn't people leave them alone?

"Her life will be in constant danger while she's with you. There were two hitmen, according to the police. Your fucking airfield was used."

"Watts has a big mouth." There was more than a hint of bitterness in Jasper's voice. "The thing is, Dan, not many people know that you can get to that rooftop from the alleyway. I think that the shooters had inside information."

Dan began to fidget uncomfortably.

Jasper had never told John about the alleyway. So someone must have told Duncan. This *someone* probably moved in the same circles as him.

"You don't get it, do you Dan? Whoever gave the shooters that information is responsible for Kate being shot. It was Kate they wanted. They knew she would be visiting the market square on that day. What they didn't expect was that I'd be with her. And yes! She *was* shot because of me." Jasper stood. "She's my rock. But you know that. Take away the rock, and the tower comes tumbling down."

Dan had turned a beetroot red.

"I haven't found the bastard. But when I do…"

"Dan! This is a pleasant surprise." Kate bustled into the office, giving Dan a hug.

"The files are clean, Kate," Dan said nervously, his eyes fixed on Jasper.

She smiled and moved towards Jasper. He slipped his arm around her waist as she planted a soft kiss on his cheek and slipped the USB stick into her jeans pocket.

Angry jealousy soared through Dan as he watched Kate kiss Jasper.

"Have you time for tea, Dan?"

"No thanks, Kate. Anyway, I prefer coffee."

"That's no problem. Jasper prefers coffee."

But Dan wasn't listening; he was hurrying towards the office doors. By the time Kate caught up with him, he was already driving away.

When she returned to the office, Jasper was pacing.

"Before you vent your temper, just listen," Kate began in her no-nonsense voice. "My gut told me the accounts were doctored, but I couldn't find where or by whom. Before I gave Dan copies of the files, I had a word with your IT whizz-kid. He suggested that I mark my USB and he loaded a programme—don't ask me what sort. When activated, it deletes everything." She lifted the USB from her pocket. "This isn't my USB."

Jasper raised his scowling eyebrows.

"There's no scratch." She pointed to the side of the USB. "Dan's copied my files and kept the original for himself."

Kate disappeared and returned with her laptop. The file she opened was labelled 'Dan'. Jasper watched as she searched for the file 'Untitled'.

"I don't know how this works, but the whizz-kid somehow embedded a virus into the files. He's a real genius."

"So whoever has those files has the virus," Jasper muttered.

"All I have to do is click on this icon and the files are destroyed."

Without any hesitation Kate clicked on the icon.

"You never told me," Jasper said, placing his hand on her shoulder.

"At the time you were struggling. Best not to worry you."

He closed the laptop and lifted her from the couch. It was only a short walk to her studio and the chaise longue.

***

Later that day, Jasper sat in the Range Rover watching Kate waiting by the school gates. She was putting on a brave face, but he knew she was hurting. She had trusted her old friend and he had betrayed her.

Jasper's heart had wept when her tears had flowed. He had supported her hips when her movements spiralled out of control. He had watched her heartache build into a climax. He had wrapped her in his arms when she collapsed onto his chest, tears still flowing.

Jasper hoped he could repair the hurt that Dan had inflicted. He wondered if she would ever find it in her to forgive her old friend.

Jasper guessed that Dan was in cahoots with Michaels. But Michaels was dead. He pondered on the possibility that Dan would pass information onto Gypsy and Watts.

As far as Jasper was concerned, whoever Dan was dealing with would pay.

Oliver came skipping along the school drive, his satchel dragging behind him, cap around the wrong way. He knew that would annoy Kate, as would his tie halfway around his neck and the undone top button of his shirt. Oliver loved teasing his mother. He waved and flashed the Carmichael smile.

Harry reminded Jasper of himself, always perfectly turned out. Satchel over his shoulder, cap tipped slightly back, his tie straight. He smiled when he saw Kate.

***

Jasper pulled into the Riverside Café carpark. Kate raised her eyebrows. The Range Rover had barely stopped when the boys flung the rear doors open and raced towards the café.

He took her hand. "I thought you would enjoy a change of scenery." His voice was light, trying to put her at ease.

"Jasper, about this morning…"

His fingers pulled the band from her hair. "I'm your best friend, your lover, your husband. You needed me. It hurt me to watch you in so much pain. I felt helpless."

She turned to face him, her green eyes brimming over with love. "I love you," she whispered. His hand cupped her cheek, and she leaned into it. "No one will hurt me again. I'll toughen up. Promise."

Jasper knew his wife. She would never toughen up. She was too trusting and loving.

Their loving eyes danced, his finger gently traced her hairline.

"You're my happiness, my life, my beloved."

Jasper kissed his wife. At that moment, she was everything to him.

Chapter Fifty

Sunday was Harry and Oliver's special day, when they had Kate all to themselves.

They grinned at each other as they watched her painting. She was healing and more like her old self.

Jasper opened the bi-fold doors to the studio and, catlike, walked behind Kate to slip his arms around her waist and nuzzle her neck. A smile crept across her face as she briefly stopped painting. She relaxed into his embrace, tilting her head. He smiled and kissed her neck.

The old Kate, his Kate, was back.

Jasper turned and winked at the boys, who were grinning like Cheshire cats.

Clare opened the internal glass door to the studio. Before she could speak, three men—Watts and two strangers—pushed her aside. Kate's body stiffened.

"Who the fuck are you? How dare you barge in here?" Kate angrily said, glaring at the intruders.

Jasper caught her by the waist, pulling her into his grasp. The boys leapt to her side.

"Clare, show the visitors into the living room." Jasper's words were unusually calm.

"This will do, Carmichael," said the tallest of the three.

Watts, who had stood silently behind the newcomers, pushed between the two men.

"These men are from the Met. Lewis and Jones. Come to give an update on the shooting."

Before Kate could answer, Jasper said, in his 'don't mess with me' voice, "This is our home. No one tells me where to greet people." He took a long moment to glare at Lewis and Jones. "You will go into the living room. Clare will bring refreshments."

He released Kate. Two frightened boys tightly gripped her hands.

Jasper was concerned when Kate took the boys outside. He watched her kneel and put her arms around them. Oliver's head slumped onto her shoulder, and if Jasper wasn't mistaken, both boys were crying.

He turned and glared at the three men.

"Let's cut the crap. You're not from the Met. You've upset my wife, and my boys are crying."

"I apologise for barging in," said Lewis. "We were out of order. In my defence, I have been influenced by gossip. You and your family are not what I was led to believe."

Jasper glared.

"There's no progress on the shooting, but we're hopeful that this will change when we get a warrant to search the airfield. Whoever shot at Kate made their way there."

"You appear confident."

"We are," interrupted Jones.

Lewis whipped his head around, glaring at Jones.

"There's something else," Lewis continued. "What do you know about Chester?"

"He's the butler at the London house."

"He's a little more than a butler." Lewis paused, trying to gauge Jasper's reaction. "A man dressed in black walked into Michaels' house and shot six men. He then calmly walked out. Not many men are capable of doing that. A hit squad, maybe, but one man without backup?" He raised his eyebrows in disbelief. "Chester was seen staggering to your house. A body was found lying on the floor." He handed Jasper a photo of a dead man. "Recognise him?"

"No."

Lewis was surprised at Jasper's curt reply. "That's Chester."

"No, it isn't."

Lewis tried a different tact. "Michaels and Manning paid you a visit."

"I kicked them out."

Lewis raised his eyebrows.

"They were threatening Kate," Jasper said.

"You must hate Manning for taking over the fund."

"Dislike, not hate. But every cloud has a silver lining. My life had taken different path."

"Come off it, Carmichael. You're going to lose money."

"Short term, but long term I'll make money."

Lewis raised his eyebrows again.

"Think about it. My time won't be split between two businesses. I'll be able to concentrate on the Wellsbury business."

"Tell me about your London visit."

"Not much to tell. Kate needed a change of scenery. She had never seen the London house or my properties. The boys had never been to London. Two birds with one stone."

"You visited Chester's new home."

"No different to how I treat any of my employees."

"How was Chester?"

"Just the same. He wasn't expecting us. So he was a little untidy, a bit flustered."

"You weren't suspicious?"

"About what? He wasn't expecting me. I like to feel that my staff can relax and be themselves when I'm not about."

"Was anyone else there?"

"Not to my knowledge."

"What do you know about the robbery at Zak's London outlet?"

"Nothing. I didn't even know Zak had a London outlet."

"I'm working on the theory that there's a common denominator that links these crimes. Kate's shooting, six men being shot and robbery at Zak's."

"I'm not following," said Jasper.

An awkward silence filled the living room.

"My gut tells me you're in this up to your neck, Carmichael."

"Are you saying I had Kate shot? Don't be ridiculous."

"My gut tells me Chester was an imposter. And you knew. This imposter robbed Zak's diamonds and shot six men. The question is, who was this person that killed with a wartime gun and stole only diamonds?"

"You tell me."

"Colin Carmichael."

The name dropped like a bomb. But Jasper remained impassive.

Chapter Fifty-One

When Colin Carmichael opened his eyes, he was in a strange bed. Attached to his right arm was a bleeping monitor. Fluids were dripping into his hand through a cannula.

I'm alive, he thought.

He was in hospital. He closed his eyes and tried to think back. Jasper came into his mind. He remembered finishing his letter and slipping his satchel into one of the holdalls. He remembered the pains in his chest. The image of men slumped over a table. The fear in Michaels' eyes when he pulled the trigger. Cold tiles and Zak Cohen's shocked face when their eyes met.

A smug grin crept across his face.

"Mr Chester!" cried a female voice. "The doctor's on his way."

Colin tried to move, but he was too weak. He turned his eyes to the ward doorway. Zak Cohen stood with one of his cronies, talking to the doctor.

Colin heard the doctor's stern voice—"Not yet—he needs rest. Probably tomorrow."—before he slipped back to sleep.

It was dark when he opened his eyes again. The dull pain in his chest had gone. He buzzed for the nurse.

"The doctor's very pleased. You've responded well to treatment." Her soft calm voice comforted him as he sipped water. "Your visitors have just left. Very concerned, they are."

Colin offered a smile. *Like hell*, he thought, as he closed his eyes and feigned sleep.

When the grey of dawn filled the hospital ward, Colin slowly moved his feet onto the cold floor. He waited a long moment, expecting the pain to return. The cannula had been removed, and so had the monitor.

He carefully stood, keeping his hand on the bed as he tried unsteady steps. He sat back on the bed, tired and weak, but then Zak Cohen flashed into his mind. He wanted revenge. He wanted his diamonds.

Colin opened the locker beside the bed and was surprised to find his clothes.

Fifteen minutes later, Colin Carmichael, with the help of a stick, was following the hospital's yellow painted footsteps to the way out.

A cold blast of air hit him with the opening of the automatic doors. The chill revived him as he slowly walked away from the hospital. His getaway was uppermost in his mind; he needed a car. All of a sudden, beads of sweat formed on his forehead. He lost his footing and fell to his knees. On the tarmac before his eyes was a key fob.

That's lucky, he thought. *A good sign*.

He slowly eased himself up and pressed the fob. A Nissan Micra answered the call.

Colin didn't care who owned the car. His mind was on escape. He helped himself to the sweets that were on the passenger seat and the bottle of water stuffed in the door bin.

The sun was high in the sky when Colin stopped the Nissan by the veranda that ran the full length of his beach house.

He struggled climbing the three steps that lead to the veranda. He clung to the wooden rail and gazed at the old studio. Jasper flashed into his mind. *It's all yours,* he thought. *Whatever you find.*

His chest pained him when he tried to breathe. The warm wooden veranda floor welcomed him. He closed his eyes and listened to the sea crashing against the rocks.

The tide's in, he thought.

Chapter Fifty-Two

Jasper sat with Kate at the coffee shop opposite her gallery. She was having a break from gallery paperwork. He leaned over, kissing her cheek.

"Have you heard from Lewis?" she asked between sips of tea.

"They are refusing to let me in the London house. Ongoing inquiry."

Kate and Jasper were unaware that Zak had returned from London, or that he stood listening to their conversation from his shop doorway.

"Did they say anything about the body?"

Zak's ears pricked.

"No." Jasper took a swig of her tea pulling a face. "I don't know how you can drink this stuff." He coughed. "I've got to wait until they've finished."

A young waitress placed a coffee in front of Jasper. He smiled and mouthed, 'Thank you.'

"Do you have any idea how big the library is?" said Kate, changing the subject. She'd had enough of dead bodies, Colin Carmichael and diamonds.

Jasper raised his eyebrows in confusion.

"I think we should build a new library," Kate said, in her matter-of-fact way.

Jasper choked on his coffee.

"It's like this," Kate began, ignoring Jasper's coughing. "We have Carmichael books, Spencer books and Isaacs books."

"Kate!"

"I'm thinking an extension to the Isaacs'. Probably not from the library, but we could extend into the garden or into that field at the back where you were keen on a helipad."

"Kate!" There was displeasure in his voice.

She turned and smiled.

"Any ideas?" she asked.

"Don't give me that look."

"What look?" She couldn't contain her laughter.

"You're incorrigible," he said and began to laugh.

Zak turned and walked away, thinking, *He's going to take her to the gallery and fuck the living daylights out of her*. He didn't hear Jasper mention a visit to the beach house.

***

The next day, when they arrived at the beach house, they were surprised to see a Nissan Micra parked outside.

"What the…!" Jasper shouted.

Jasper sprinted towards the veranda, stopping dead when he saw a body. His gut told him it was Colin. Jasper fell to his knees and cried. Kate rested a comforting hand on his shoulders. Tears were dripping onto Colin's dead body. She kissed Jasper's hair before leaving him to say goodbye to the father he'd never truly known, but had always been there when needed.

Kate walked back towards the Range Rover, quietly talking into her phone. "Bruce. Meet us at Carmichael Castle. Come in the pickup with tools. Bring a trusted man."

Bruce didn't ask questions. He didn't need to. Kate's serious, grave voice spoke volumes.

Kate manoeuvred the Range Rover as close to the veranda as she could. With the car rug tucked under her arm, she walked to Jasper and placed a gentle hand on his shoulder. No words passed between them as they rolled Colin into the rug and then into the rear footwell of the Range Rover.

Jasper didn't comment when Kate got into the driving seat and joined the motorway towards Carmichael Castle.

When they arrived, Bruce and Malcolm were waiting at the entrance to the castle.

"Jasper, where's the mausoleum?" Kate quietly asked.

Jasper pointed to an overgrown track on the left.

Bruce and Malcolm followed Kate and Jasper along it. The mausoleum was at the end of the track, hidden behind a small coppice and an overgrown shrubbery. A vacant-looking Jasper walked towards the mausoleum's iron doors. He angrily tugged at the padlock and cursed.

Kate, Bruce and Malcolm anxiously watched Jasper walk towards a protruding pillar. His large hands moved slowly over each stone until one moved. He gently eased the stone just enough for his hand to reach inside.

Bruce reached into his tool bag, pulling out an oil spray and hammer. Jasper handed him the rusty key from the pillar, and with considerable persuasion, the key finally nestled into the lock and turned.

Hinges that hadn't moved for years creaked. Doors groaned as Bruce, Malcolm and Jasper pushed them open.

With the light from their mobile phones, they gingerly walked down the cold, wet, slippery steps that led to the resting place of Jasper's ancestors. Stale, earthy air drifted up their nostrils as Jasper shone the torchlight onto stone crypts.

"We can dig a grave, boss," Bruce whispered, as if frightened he might wake the dead.

"No. Colin should be here with the other cruel bastards."

Kate gripped his arm. "At the back here. There must be room."

"Here!" said Jasper.

The three men pushed and slid the stone lid to the side of the tomb. Thankfully, it was empty.

It took all the strength of the three men to manhandle Colin's body into its final resting place.

Kate held tight to Jasper, her soft voice piercing the thick, cold atmosphere. "We should say something."

The contents of her stomach churned, and a cold shiver meandered down her spine as the stone lid was pushed into place.

Jasper put a reassuring arm around her. "Here lies Colin Carmichael, the last son of Jasper Carmichael. Father of Jasper, the son he gave away on the day he left his mother's womb."

"Stop! He loved you. He just didn't know how to say it." Kate's voice echoed through the deathly silent mausoleum.

Bruce and Malcolm took a step back.

"He didn't know how to love Jasper," Jasper said. "No one ever loved him except his mother. When she died, so did love. Colin became like the rest of the Carmichaels—only he didn't crave power, but diamonds."

"He should be buried with diamonds," Kate thoughtfully added.

They silently walked from the mausoleum. Jasper locked the iron doors and returned the key to its hiding place.

"Malcolm, you drive Kate home." Jasper turned to Kate. "Clare and the boys will be worried. Bruce and I will dispose of the Nissan Micra."

"Jasper, give yourself time to—"

Jasper cut over her. "Time to what? Grieve? Colin was—"

"Stop! Think! He was there when you needed him."

"I needed him to take me out of that hellhole he left me in." Jasper walked to the pickup and Bruce followed.

There was an uneasy silence between Jasper and Bruce as they drove back to the beach house. Bruce disapproved of how Jasper had treated Kate, and he didn't care if Jasper knew it.

"I'll make it up to her," Jasper muttered as they stopped next to the Nissan Micra.

"You don't appreciate her."

"I know, but things will change. When I've tidied up."

Bruce didn't ask what that meant.

"Let's have a look around," said Jasper, walking to the beach house.

"What we looking for?"

"Colin said his diamond hoard was here."

"You believe him?"

"Why should he lie?"

Jasper found no diamonds in the beach house, and to make sure the police didn't either, he threw a match into a stack of old, dry, wooden furniture.

The light was fading when Jasper and Bruce turned their attention to the old tumble-down studio.

"Kate would like that," said Bruce, nodding towards the view.

Jasper didn't give the view a second glance. His mind was on Colin's diamond hoard.

"There might not be any diamonds," said Bruce.

"Oh, there is! My gut tells me."

Jasper was hiding his doubts. Maybe there were no diamonds—but why would Colin lie?

Jasper pulled the studio door open and looked inside. The weather had taken its toll. Torchlight reflected on very thick cobwebs that covered the small desk, table and chairs, the easels and brushes that were strewn across the floor.

"A good gust of wind will finish this place off," commented Bruce as he casually pushed furniture out of his way.

"I've got to be sure there's no diamonds. If the law searches this place and find diamonds, they'll put me inside."

Jasper righted a rickety chair that lay next to the desk crammed against the back wall.

He ran his fingers along the desktop.

"This reminds me of my desk. Only smaller," Jasper commented.

He pulled the front drawer open and ran his fingers inside, feeling for a small lever.

The side of the desk sprang open. A canvas bag fell.

Bruce looked on as Jasper reached inside the bag and pulled out a handful of diamonds. "Fuck me!" he exclaimed.

***

Bruce waited at the back of the old Victorian building for Jasper. He was late, half an hour late. *Not like Jasper,* he thought.

Jasper had cut the Nissan's engine and coasted onto the derelict land by Kate's youth centre. He'd emptied the contents of the glovebox and soaked them in petrol. Flames filled the inside of the Nissan as he jogged away.

Bruce was taken by surprise when the passenger door sprang open and Jasper leapt in.

"You're late."

"I found this in the glovebox."

Bruce stared at the ID card.

"She's a nurse! Colin stole a fuckin' nurse's car."

"I'll put it right."

Bruce turned towards Jasper. "How?!"

"Envelope stuffed full of cash. Through her letter box."

Bruce started the Range Rover. "You're no fuckin' Robin Hood, Jasper."

"I know," he said, securing the canvas bag between his feet in the footwell.

Chapter Fifty-Three

Jasper walked onto the patio, stretching his back and moving his stiff body from side to side. He had been staring at his laptop screen far too long.

It had been a disappointing morning. His Zoom conference call with the team that were guiding him through the minefield of the Carmichael trust fund had resulted in disagreements.

And then he had lost his temper when a diamond supplier had refused to join his diamond network.

He wished Kate was with him, but he didn't want her to know the details of his diamond dealing. So, he'd persuaded her to let Bruce accompany her to the burnt-out beach house. On reflection, she hadn't needed much persuading.

She'd looked lovely. Her hair lay on her shoulders, her eyes sparkled and her cheeks were flushed. She was happy, but not for him. For the man who had helped her into his pickup.

Jasper wandered into the kitchen, loosening his tie. He sat opposite Clare, who was busy rolling out pastry. She took one look at him, poured a coffee and slid it towards him. Jasper Carmichael looked as if he had the world upon his shoulders.

"Business troubles?" She had heard Jasper shouting.

Jasper stared into the brown liquid as if it could answer all his problems. "I wanted to go with her," he lied.

"Bruce won't let anything happen to Kate."

"He's just called. She walked into the sea."

Jasper's worried tone made Clare stop rolling the pastry. "She wouldn't do that. She wouldn't leave you and the boys."

Jasper sipped his coffee. "I thought she was healing after Dan's betrayal."

"Kate's too sensitive. You know that."

"She leaned into me. I felt the tension leaving her. And then Lewis barged into the studio."

"She just needs time."

Jasper met Clare's gaze. "Diamonds have come between us."

"Kate's your destiny, not diamonds. Kate's your diamond. You don't need those shiny pieces of carbon. You have Kate."

Clare's words whirled in Jasper's mind. He lifted a diamond from his waistcoat pocket.

Clare gulped.

"This is from Isaacs' collection. When I'm struggling, I hold it and think of her." His eyes fixed on the diamond. "Her strength is always with me."

Clare refilled his coffee mug and resumed rolling her pastry.

"I stalked her. Even before I met her, I wanted her. I had beauties falling at my feet. But I wanted her."

"You love her."

"I didn't know what love was until Kate."

"She's your destiny."

"Bruce is bringing her back."

"Talk to her."

"I don't deserve her. She quells the darkness that lies deep inside me." Jasper bowed his head and laced his fingers around the back of his neck.

Clare had been waiting to get a few things off her chest, and she wasn't going to miss the opportunity.

"Do you want to go back to the Jasper that came to Wellsbury?" She stared at his bowed head. "The arrogant bastard that treated everyone like pieces of shit?".

Jasper lifted his eyes. He had never heard Clare like this.

"The Jasper that played cat and mouse with the police and the London gangs?" She paused. "God knows what she saw in you." Clare sat on a stool. "'aven't you noticed what you're doing to her?"

Jasper went to speak, but Clare waved her finger. She was on a roll and she was going to have her say.

"How many times has she left the house to be alone? She's in turmoil with what diamonds are doing to you, her and the boys. They are a curse."

"I need her."

"Need to fuck her like the others."

"I don't fuck her. I haven't touched another woman since Kate. I love her. I adore her."

An awkward, tense silence hovered. Clare suspected Jasper was lying. Tales of him with women on his arm at London parties had reached her.

"The way I see it, you can't live without Kate." She paused. "Accept Kate's the only diamond you need. You don't need the money. Get your adrenaline rush somewhere else."

"You forget my reputation."

"I'll say this and then I'm finished. Fuck your reputation. Walk away from all that shit that surrounds the Carmichaels. Make your own dynasty."

At that moment the kitchen door opened and in walked Kate. She smiled. Her cheeks were a delightful pink, and her green eyes sparkled.

He's fucked her, Jasper thought.

He rushed towards her, cupping her cheeks.

"Don't you dare do that again." His tone was firm but his sparkling blue eyes glowed with love.

His lips brushed hers as he pulled her into him.

"I'll come to London," she said into his shoulder. "I'll be by your side when you confront the fund men. I'll know if Dan's involved."

Jasper stretched his arms, resting his hands on her shoulders so he could look into her eyes.

She shrugged. "I know Dan's methods. I was the one that taught him. He won't have changed. He hasn't the imagination. The only difference is I'm out of practice."

"Kate!"

"You'll have to support me when I meet those grey suits that are interfering with my inheritance."

"Why didn't you say?"

"There was always something more important."

"Not this time."

Jasper couldn't hide his relief. Kate was his.

***

Bruce stood in the kitchen doorway, watching Kate give herself to the man that didn't deserve her.

It was all too much for him. He walked away. He couldn't watch Kate sacrifice happiness and love to Jasper Carmichael.

They'd been walking towards the sea when, out of the blue, Kate had begun talking about her marriage.

She felt like the little boy who put his finger in the dam hoping to stop the water. Whatever she did, it couldn't stop the inevitable. There was a time when she and the boys had meant everything to Jasper. But the seed of the Carmichael curse was growing.

She couldn't take the boys away from him. They loved and needed him.

Bruce had asked if she needed Jasper, but she didn't answer. Her silence and her eyes told him everything he needed to know. She wanted him and he wanted her.

But how could he tell her that the thought of Jasper inside her made him angry? How could he tell her that Jasper lied to her? How could he tell her about Joanne and the other women Jasper had on his arm, and that ultimately Jasper would hurt her?

His silence and anger had upset her. She had run from him and into the sea. He had run after her, looped his strong arms around her waist and lifted her into his arms.

"Take me," she had murmured. "Before I give myself to him."

Their lips joined as he carried her to the trees that lined the gully.

The journey back to Wellsbury had been difficult.

"Kate, leave him. You don't need him. He'll hurt you."

"I know. But it would break Harry's and Oliver's hearts."

He had lifted her from the passenger seat.

"I love you, Kate."

She had looked into his eyes and smiled. "Tell me you understand."

He didn't answer.

Chapter Fifty-Four

It was spitting with rain when Jasper bought a coffee from his favourite street vendor. He was deep in thought. Clare's little lecture bothered him. He *was* a selfish bastard as far as Kate was concerned.

Zak stood in his shop doorway, waiting. As soon as Jasper had bought his coffee, Zak sidled up to him.

"Jasper! A word."

Jasper continued sipping his coffee as if he hadn't heard Zak.

Zak was a little put out at being ignored.

"I accept you haven't got my stolen diamonds," he lied. "Word on the street says it was Colin. Nonsense—Colin's dead." He paused, waiting for a reaction. "I need diamonds." Zak couldn't hide the desperation in his voice. "No questions. No calls, emails, texts. Burner used once."

Jasper remained silent, irritating Zak even more. And then Zak played his last card.

"The thing is, those stolen diamonds belonged to a client. I was just the go-between."

That caught Jasper's attention.

"Dangerous game, Zak."

Zak sighed. At last, a reaction.

Jasper could smell his sweat. *Zak's unusually nervous,* he thought. And then that little voice in the back of his mind that had guided through his darkest days woke and repeated '*Trap*'.

"He's turning the screws," Zak continued, his eyes focused on Jasper.

First mistake, being a go-between. And now you owe, Jasper thought.

"If I could lay my hands on some diamonds, the heat would be off."

"Do I know the client?"

"No, but you know the collector. He's sitting over there."

Jasper had already seen Gypsy and Dan sitting in the coffee shop opposite Kate's gallery.

He casually laid his hand on his satchel while he dropped his empty coffee cup in the recycling.

"Have you got cash?"

Zak could only just hear Jasper's low voice as they walked towards his jewellery store.

Out of the corner of his eye, Jasper saw Gypsy and Dan snigger. His little voice shouted '*Trap*'.

Two minutes later, Jasper was looking around Zak's small, one-person office. No windows, just room for a desk and two chairs. This office was only a slight improvement on his last office in the old school.

Zak moved his chair to one side and fiddled with the dial on his safe.

"You can 'ave the lot if you 'ave diamonds," said Zak, pulling the safe door open.

Jasper's eyes widened as bundles of notes fell onto the dusty floor.

"Dealing in money, Zak?" Jasper commented as he pulled a small jiffy bag from his satchel. "Nothing you can't handle."

Zak's eyes widened when sparkling gems fell onto his blotter.

"How much?"

"Do you 'ave more?"

"Depends."

Zak smirked as his chubby fingers greedily touched each stone before lifting his magnifying glass from his desk drawer.

"These are old," he remarked as he eyed the gems. He waited for Jasper to make a slip, but Jasper was too astute to fall into Zak's clumsy trap.

"Do we have a deal?" asked Jasper, mesmerised by the cash in Zak's safe, his mind already planning how to launder such a large amount.

"My client will need more, same quality."

That's no problem, thought Jasper. "How many?"

"Depends on the quality," Zak replied.

"Don't try it on with me, Zak," Jasper snapped, collecting the diamonds.

Zak eyes narrowed and he leaned into his safe, lifting bundles of notes. "Ten grand in each bundle. I'll 'ave everything you've got."

"Have you got more?"

"Don't concern yourself about cash."

Jasper stood, and without a flicker of emotion, he coldly said, "The wood that overlooks the airfield. Tonight. Bring the money."

"Time?"

"When it's safe. Just don't bring company."

"What about Kate?" Zak said as Jasper left, but got no answer.

He reached into his bottom desk drawer and lifted his bottle of malt. He didn't bother with a glass. He needed all the help the amber liquid would give him to betray Carmichael.

***

The rain had become more persistent by the time Zak snuck out the back of his shop and headed towards The George.

He didn't see who was following him, but he knew a tail was there and The George was an ideal place to give them the slip. The George was busier than usual with people sheltering from the rain. Zak easily blended with the crowd that surrounded the bar and slowly moved towards the back door and the alley beyond.

With his cap pulled over his eyes and the collar of his raincoat turned up, he briskly walked to his old home in the Victorian school, his safe place where he hid money, clothes and his car.

Only the brave would dare venture down the rat-infested passageway that led to his old office. He retched at the stale, urine-laden stench that oozed into his nostrils, wondering how he'd managed to live in such a place. But it was an excellent hideaway for his money. He slowly removed bricks from the wall and pulled out bin liner after bin liner full of twenty-pound notes.

The rain was relentless; he was wet through. He was gasping for breath when he shut the boot of his old car. He hadn't time to regain his breath, so he just threw his old raincoat onto the back seat and set off for the wood above the airfield. He had to be there waiting for Jasper, along with Watts and Gypsy.

His burner phone buzzed. Jasper was running late. He was going to be there before him to set the trap.

Zak's headlights and wipers struggled in the heavy rain, but he barely noticed. His mind was full of revenge. He was about to be instrumental in bringing about the downfall of Jasper Carmichael.

***

When Jasper left Zak, he went in search of Kate. He needed her special treatment to quell his stirring demons.

He found her in the bookshop office, head bent over paperwork. He took a long moment to admire his wife. Her hair was down, her glasses pushed wisps of hair from her eyes. Just gazing at her calmed him, but he needed to be inside her, like he had all those years ago before he went on a mission.

He slowly walked towards her and lifted her hair.

"Come." His voice was low and full of want.

"This is unexpected," she said as a slow smile crept across her face.

The bookshop bathroom was small, but needs must. He lifted her onto the narrow counter.

She closed her eyes and thought of Bruce.

***

"You never refuse my sexual demands," he murmured.

He leaned into her, their foreheads touching as they calmed after sex.

She smiled.

Something's wrong, he thought, but he hadn't time to dwell on it.

Chapter Fifty-Five

Zak was calling Jasper all the names he could think of. He sat in the police Land Rover with Watts, Gypsy and Dan.

"He's not coming," said Zak, checking his watch. "He'd be here by now."

"And you know because?" said an angry Dan, who hated being cold and wet. Gypsy had forced him to be there when the cuffs went on Jasper.

"Jasper doesn't do late. He doesn't like to be away from Kate too long."

"Fuck!" Dan shouted.

"Take your turn. We'd all like to fuck her." Gypsy laughed.

"Keep your minds on the job," Watts impatiently said.

***

Jasper was running late; he shouldn't have fucked Kate. He hurried towards his office, but loud sobs caught his attention.

He glanced into the living room. Oliver was on Kate's lap, crying.

"I don't understand!" sobbed Oliver.

"The kids at school tease him about Grandfather Colin's diamonds," offered Harry, reading Jasper's surprised face. "He told them he didn't need grandfather's diamonds, he has his own. They laughed. Oliver doesn't like being laughed at."

"They say I'm like him. But I don't steal diamonds." Oliver's voice was quivering.

Jasper put a comforting hand on his shoulder.

"It is true that Grandfather Colin was a master diamond thief," Jasper said sympathetically.

"But I don't steal diamonds. I have my own." Oliver's red, puffy eyes glared at Jasper. "They're jealous cos they haven't got one."

Kate's hand stroked Oliver's head while she kissed his hair. She gave Jasper a half smile.

Jasper couldn't bear to look at her. He turned and walked away. How could he look at her? The old Jasper had surfaced. He was going to trade diamonds for money. Money he would have to launder. His plan was risky but he had the advantage—he was familiar with the wood and the airfield.

***

"What are you doing?" Kate's voice had an impatient edge as she glanced to the floor to see what she had trod on. She bent and picked up the remains of a mobile phone, and dropped them into her shirt pocket.

Jasper abruptly turned from the studio bi-fold doors looking at Kate in the doorway. He had no recollection of walking into her studio. He had no idea how long he'd been there, staring at the rain hitting the glass. He couldn't remember texting Zak.

One word. *Abort.*

He had intended to be in his office, organising diamonds and finalising his plan. But his mind was muddled with thoughts of Kate.

Kate was his diamond. He didn't need those glittering gems.

Oliver, in his childish way, thought of Kate as his diamond.

Kate said she needed him. He made her happy. But could he believe her?

What more did he want? He had the unconditional love of a woman. Or did he?

He had two healthy boys. His wealth had given him an enviable lifestyle.

Kate had pleaded with him to give diamonds up and become legit. And with her guidance, he had ignored his criminal instincts.

The police and the gangs had lost interest in him. Until now.

People wanted revenge for what his grandfather and father had done. He was going to repay them the only way he knew, and all the promises he had made to Kate would be broken.

His heart skipped a beat. Through his tear-filled eyes, she looked lovely as usual. Her long hair was free, his oversized white shirt open to her cleavage, her feet bare.

With urgent, decisive steps, he moved towards her. His large hands cupped her cheeks as he claimed her mouth. She was taken by surprise. Losing her footing, she stumbled backwards. He caught her and walked her backwards into the hallway, his mouth never leaving hers.

"Jasper," she gasped as her back met the hall wall.

"Don't leave me. Don't leave me," he said between kisses.

A delightful sigh escaped her mouth.

His teeth nipped her bottom lip. His hand cupped her bottom, pulling her into him.

A loud cough broke the spell. It was Bruce.

"Boss! I've just seen Gypsy, Watts and Dan getting into the police Land Rover."

Bruce couldn't take his eyes off Kate.

"The rain's getting worse. The river's over its banks. It won't be long before roads are flooded."

***

The rain was relentless when Zak Cohen checked that his money was secure in its secret place.

Jasper hadn't shown. Zak should have trusted his last text: *Abort.*

Zak shivered in his wet clothes. There wasn't a part of his body that wasn't dripping wet. He needed dry clothes.

Through water-covered eyes he could see the flickering lights of The George. The road was a river of fast-flowing water. He stood and tried to gauge the depth of the water. He convinced himself it was below his knees.

He took a couple of steps into the water. *No problem,* he thought.

Three steps.

Four steps.

Five steps.

Six. His foot slipped into a hole, he lost his footing and fell onto his back. The water covered his head. He gulped and spluttered, trying to regain his breath. He panicked, frantically moving his arms and legs but to no avail. He was at the mercy of the water.

The end came when a tree branch bobbed in front of him. He tried to push it away, but it pushed him under.

His last thought was of Jasper, and how he should have trusted his message, *Abort.*

Chapter Fifty-Six

Kate didn't look up when the studio door opened. She just assumed it was Jasper.

"I want to go to the bookshop. Goodness knows what damage the rain's caused," she said, watching Oliver puddle jump on the lawn.

She waved to him. After yesterday's tears her son was happy, grinning from ear to ear. He lifted his hand and froze. Dan was staring directly at him. Oliver sprinted to the bi-fold doors, thumping on the glass.

A cold shiver trailed down Kate's spine as she opened the doors.

Oliver rushed past her, side-stepping Dan, shouting, "Dad! Dad!"

Gypsy and Watts tried to grab him, but Oliver was too nimble.

Dan stood at Kate's shoulder, far too close for her liking. She turned to face him. He took a step closer, pinning her to the glass.

"It's just a matter of time till you're mine." He rested his palms on the glass either side of Kate's head. His sickly voice made her stomach churn.

A large hand gripped Dan's neck, and in one swift move he was on the floor, coughing and spluttering. Gypsy's dark eyes rested on Kate.

"Where's your husband?"

"Here!" Jasper barged past the intruders and wrapped his arms around Kate.

"We have a warrant," said Watts, waving a piece of paper.

The atmosphere was caustic. Jasper refused to sit. His fists were tightly clenched, his cold, blue eyes fixed on Dan.

Oliver, who had followed his dad, suddenly raced to Watts and snatched the warrant from his hand. Watts' and Gypsy's grasping hands were too slow to catch him.

Gypsy loudly cursed. In temper, he turned to Jasper. "Know this, Carmichael. When you're behind bars, I'll be fucking your wife."

Jasper's clenched fists turned white.

"Old warrant, Inspector," said Kate as she glanced over the paper that Oliver had given her.

"Fucking leave." Anger exploded from Jasper's mouth.

"Zak's dead." Dan's words fell like a stone through tense atmosphere.

Surprised expressions covered both Kate and Jasper's faces.

"He was found early this morning. Face down in flood water," the inspector said in his calm, official tone. "It looks as if he was trying to get to The George. Any ideas, Carmichael? He was your friend."

"Zak wasn't a friend."

"You were in his office. Yesterday. What did you talk about?"

"Diamonds. Zak's stolen ones."

"You 'ave 'em," Gypsy growled.

"No! I've told you before. I knew nothing about Zak's London venture."

Inspector Watts casually dropped a small polythene bag on the coffee table.

"Found this phone in Zak's pocket. Know anything about it?"

"No!"

"Last message: '*Abort*'."

Jasper's expression remained impassive.

"I'm interested to find the person who sent it."
Watts took a deep breath, his eyes fixed on Jasper.
"Zak was going to turn you in, Carmichael. Double-
cross you, just like your old man did his partner."

The atmosphere thickened.

"He told us about his plan. Diamonds for cash.
True to your heritage, you couldn't resist." Watts
paused, waiting for Jasper's impassive expression
to flinch. "We were waiting. The wood above the
airfield. But you never showed."

Silence.

"Where were you last night?"

"Here!"

"And everyone will verify that, I suppose," Dan
sarcastically said, turning his eyes towards Kate,
who stood silently with Oliver standing between
her legs.

"Nothing to say, Mrs Carmichael?" asked Watts.

"Nothing, Inspector. Jasper was here all night."

Oliver nodded.

"You don't appear concerned about Zak," the
inspector continued.

"Zak's a Cohen. I'm a Carmichael. The two
don't mix."

"Funny that. His family said more or less the
same thing."

"Zak was a bastard. Shunned by his family. We
had that in common."

"Zak's safe was empty. What do you know
about that?" added the inspector, trying to keep the
questions on track.

"Nothing."

"But you were in his office."

"Yes."

"What about Harry?" snipped Dan.

"You leave Harry out of this," snapped Kate.

"What's this?" Gypsy was more than a little perplexed.

"Zak was training Harry to be a diamond thief," Dan gloated.

"That's not true," retorted Kate.

"When did this happen?" Gypsy fidgeted.

"Saturdays. Sonny Jim there"—Dan nodded towards Oliver—"went to football, and Harry went to Zak's."

Gypsy suddenly felt uncomfortable as he realised that Harry must have been in Zak's shop when he'd visited.

"Zak said he was a natural. Fast learner is our Harry."

"Shut up with your lies." Kate eased Oliver from between her legs.

Jasper moved, putting a restraining hand on her shoulder.

"We're getting nowhere." Inspector Watts stood, frustrated with Dan's pointless intervention. He inwardly cursed. He only had himself to blame. He should have waited for Lewis and Jones, but Dan's glib tongue had persuaded him otherwise. "This conversation isn't over."

***

For the second day in a row, Kate was consoling one of her boys. On this occasion it was Harry, who was devastated at Zak's death. Tears flowed and too many questions were asked that Kate couldn't give a satisfactory answer to. There was a side to Zak that Harry had never seen, and she wasn't going to shatter her son's vision of his friend and the bond they shared.

Chapter Fifty-Seven

Inspector Watts sat in The George, staring into his empty pint glass, mulling over the facts that led up to Zak's death. Watts considered that it might be his ill-conceived revenge plan that was responsible.

The text message on his burner phone had been opened at six o'clock, giving Zak more than enough time to cancel.

Two things bothered him.

Why did Jasper cancel? Maybe he'd had second thoughts. Maybe he'd realised he would lose Kate.

And why did Zak continue with the plan after the text message?

Watts wasn't interested in side issues like Colin Carmichael shooting Michaels and Manning, heart attacks, hospitals, burnt-out Nissans. He wanted Jasper Carmichael behind bars, and he'd just lost the best chance he'd ever had.

His musing was abruptly interrupted when a pint of beer was pushed in front of him. He looked up into the cold eyes of Gypsy, who was squeezing into the seat next to him.

"It's not a good idea to be seen talking to me," Watts said so only Gypsy could hear him.

"Where's Zak's car?"

Watts hesitated for a moment. He didn't want to tell Gypsy too much.

"We can't find it."

"Have you looked?"

"Of course we've bloody looked."

"The money must be in the car."

"My men are busy with the floods."

"Fuck the floods. Find the car."

Watts resented Gypsy interfering with his investigation.

"Don't play games with me," Gypsy growled. "I know too much. A word in the right ear, and you can say goodbye to your pension."

Watts reddened.

"Concentrate on Carmichael. He knows all Zak's hiding places."

"I can't…"

"Just fuckin' do it. He's walking around the centre."

Gypsy pushed the table to one side, spilling beer onto Watts' lap.

***

Jasper had left Kate and the boys armed with mops and buckets in the gallery. She had hardly spoken to him. Her silence was cutting him in two.

He wandered about the centre as if in a dream, trying to concentrate on the flood damage, but it was useless. He had been so close to having the cash that would have solved his problems.

He recalled the late-night conversation with Kate. She had unexpectedly marched into his office and slammed the burner phone on his desk. He was speechless when she'd said 'Abort'.

She'd been angry.

"I can explain."

"You fucked me with every intention of deceiving me."

"No! Yes!"

She'd opened the door to leave. He had leapt up, slammed the door shut and pinned her against it, his palms flat either side of her head.

"I couldn't fucking do it. My heart was breaking. Satan was stirring the darkness that lies deep inside. The old Jasper surfaced. The cash would have financed a diamond network. I could have travelled the world dealing in diamonds. And then I remembered the last time I left you." He had paused, looking into her cold eyes. He had never seen Kate like this. She was more than angry. "My demons were stretching the love that bonds us together. You'd just given your love to me, and I had returned it. I never want that bond to be broken."

Jasper's thoughts were broken by Oliver tugging his hand.

"Dad! Dad! Come quick."

Jasper followed Oliver to the gallery, where he found Kate in a venomous exchange with Dan.

Jasper paid no attention to Dan; he was solely concerned with Kate. Her hair was down, cheeks red, eyes bulging, hand running through her hair.

"Stop this!" Harry's voice was a worried cry.

Jasper stepped towards Dan. Without a word of warning, he grabbed him by the collar and dragged him outside.

"If you ever upset my wife again, I'll finish you."

Dan looked into vicious blue eyes.

"You don't frighten me, Carmichael," he defiantly replied.

Jasper's hands gripped his neck. Dan went red and coughed.

"Jasper, stop!" Kate yelled from the gallery door.

"Sleep with one eye open." Jasper's voice and words had an unmistakeable meaning.

He released his grip, and Dan fell onto the wet floor.

"This isn't over, Carmichael."

Jasper moved towards Dan, but Kate caught his arm.

"Not now."

Jasper pulled her into his shoulder and kissed her hair.

"I love you," he whispered so only she could hear. "Don't ever forget that."

Jasper looked down into two pairs of very worried eyes. He smiled at his sons.

"She's safe with me."

Kate held her hand out, and Harry and Oliver wrapped their arms around their mother and father.

"Dan deceived me," she said, not listening to Jasper.

"He wants you."

Jasper stroked her hair, but the word 'deceive' made his stomach nervously churn. Dan wasn't the only one who was prepared to deceive Kate. He was no better.

Chapter Fifty-Eight

Jasper ran his hand through his hair. Kate was in silent mode and he couldn't bear it. He stood at her studio door, watching her study her laptop screen.

"I want to talk," he said.

"I don't."

Jasper closed the laptop, grabbed her hand and pulled her into the garden.

"I want to talk about other things besides Dan," he said as they walked towards the orchard.

"So do I."

"You first."

"I would like to move from Isaacs' House," she blurted.

They stopped and their eyes met.

"Why?"

"It's not big enough now we have inherited three libraries."

"No!"

"That's it."

"My turn. I want to make it up to you."

Kate's temper stirred. She went to speak but he put his forefinger over her lips.

"My people have found a beach house. It's not far from Colin's beach house. I suggest we go tomorrow to look at it."

For what seemed like an age, Kate was silent, letting Jasper hang.

"How big is it?" she said eventually. Her voice was calm.

"Big enough for all of us."

"What about London?" she asked.

"Next week some time."

"What about the libraries?"

"I'm toying with the idea of a new unit in the centre."

He noticed her stiff shoulders relax and her lips twitch into a smile.

"It would have to be big. Two or three floors."

"Whatever you want."

Her displeasure with Jasper melted as a smile filled her face.

A warm glow passed through him as their lips met.

***

It was mid-afternoon when Jasper met Inspector Watts outside Zak's jewellery shop.

"Your fingerprints are all over the place," announced an impatient Watts.

"But not on the safe or any diamonds."

"Carmichael!" bellowed a gruff voice.

An angry Gypsy was striding towards them. He wasn't paying attention to the men repairing the flood damage around the open manholes. Flood water had filled the shopping centre's drainage and sewage system. Without thinking, the raging Gypsy kicked the safety fence surrounding the manhole to one side, his evil eyes fixed on Jasper. The toe of his large shoe caught the edge of the open manhole. He stumbled, losing his balance.

There was a loud crack as his head hit the hard ground.

Karma, thought Jasper as he stared at the dead man known as Gypsy. *One to go.*

"You!" said Watts accusingly. "If you hadn't been here."

"You asked me to meet you," said Jasper, turning his head so Watts couldn't see his smile.

***

The meeting with Watts had finished unexpectedly early. Jasper had time on his hands. Time he could use talking to Old Man Hill about closing his garage. It had been a thorn in his side since Kate had become a silent partner.

Jasper parked at the rear of the garage, anticipating that Old Man Hill would be alone, closing up. To his surprise, loud voices were coming from inside the garage workshop. Jasper hid between the cars that littered the workshop awaiting repair, and listened. Mr Hill was at the back, arguing with Dan.

"We can't buy individual parts. The whole unit has to be replaced. I've got to wait for the parts," Mr Hill shouted. "We should replace all four to be on the safe side. The car's a death trap."

"I need it tonight."

"Use one from outside."

"I wouldn't be seen dead driving one of those."

"They're a sight safer than yours."

Dan started to pace.

"I need the fucking car." In temper, he kicked at the black bin liner Mr Hill had been collecting empty boxes in. The boxes were once again littering the floor. "I didn't leave it here, so you must have moved it."

"There's a world of difference between moving the car slowly than tearing down the motorway."

"I'm taking the car. It'll be fixed in London."

"It won't get to London. I don't know how it made it here."

"Where's the fucking keys?"

The two men walked towards Mr Hill's small office.

"I'll not let that car leave until you've signed."

Through the grimy office window, Jasper could just see Dan leaning over the desk.

"Fuck you, old man," he said.

Chapter Fifty-Nine

Kate began to feel excited as the Range Rover negotiated the tarmac road that lead to the clifftop beach house. Jasper parked in front of the three-car garage. He held her hand as they slowly walked to the house.

It was love at first sight for Kate.

The open-plan living space was fully furnished, along with a fully equipped, state-of-the-art kitchen. Jasper opened the bi-fold doors and looped his arm around her waist as they stood on the terrace, marvelling at the sea views. Jasper turned and pointed towards the corner of the terrace.

"That's the only bedroom at the front of the house," said Jasper. "I thought it would make an excellent studio. Or I could build a state-of-the-art studio. The choice is yours."

The remaining three bedrooms were at the back. They all were en suite with bi-fold doors that opened onto an immaculate lawn.

"This is the master," Jasper said, showing her in. "We'll change the furniture. We're not making love in that four-poster."

Kate giggled.

Tucked away in the far corner of the grounds was a cottage.

"Ideal for Clare and Malcolm. There's even a spare room for Bruce."

Jasper stared at Kate, hoping for a flicker of emotion when he mentioned Bruce, but none came.

Kate stood on her tiptoes and kissed his cheek. He smiled.

"We don't have to decide straightaway, but I've put a returnable deposit down."

"Jasper!"

It was his turn to kiss her.

"There's no swimming pool. I know you're not a fan of swimming pools, but we could extend the back and have a small indoor one."

"No swimming pool."

They had lunch at an upmarket yacht club. Kate suddenly realised that was why Jasper had insisted she wore a dress.

"You look stunning, Lady Carmichael," he had whispered in her ear in his husky, sexy voice. She was sure she had blushed.

The club staff and some of the clientele knew Jasper. A smile hid Kate's unease as she wondered how long he had been visiting the club.

Jasper guided her to the terrace that overlooked the expensive, neatly moored yachts. Jasper ordered sushi, but Kate wouldn't contemplate anything that wasn't cooked.

"When are you going to tell me how much?"

He smiled. "All in good time."

"You seem to be well known."

"Being the new chairman has many perks, one of which is his own private room." He grinned. "Let me show you around and introduce you to the staff."

"Chairman!"

He introduced her to all the staff as Lady Carmichael before showing her his private suite.

"You have some explaining to do," she said as he locked the door.

"Later."

She sighed as the zip to her dress slipped down her spine while his lips caressed her neck.

"Jasper!"

"Shh! I'm going to worship you as you deserve."

His soft lips slowly trailed across her body as her bra fell onto the carpet. He feasted on her breasts while his fingers slipped inside her panties. He gently moved her to the bed. Delightful moans escaped her mouth as his tongue caressed her soft curves. With haste, he removed his clothes.

Their legs entwined as they kissed. Her fingers laced through his hair.

"Don't make me wait," she uttered.

He deftly slipped inside her warm, inviting place. Ripples of pleasure spread through him when she gasped.

***

Kate lay across Jasper's chest.

"Don't ever stop loving me," she sleepily mumbled. "I'd die if you did."

A voice at the back of Jasper's mind whispered, '*You're a bastard, Carmichael.*'

He moved her atop of himself, his mouth devouring hers. His hands were splayed on her back, holding her, when her phone rang. Jasper reached to the bedside table and answered.

"Put her on." Clare's loud, curt voice echoed.

"I would like you to know how much I appreciate what you do for us," he said.

"I don't do it for you. I do it for her."

Kate lifted the phone from Jasper's hand.

"The boys okay?"

"Upset cos you 'aven't returned."

"I'll send pictures of the beach house. You'll like it. You and Malcolm have a cottage. Three-car garage for Malcolm."

"I don't like you being alone with him for so long."

"Jasper's chairman of the yacht club."

"That was quick. He can't be trusted. He's a Carmichael."

Kate's face twitched. *Where's this coming from?* she thought.

"Don't forget to print the pictures for the boys."

"Inspector Watts rang, wants to see the both of you. He's coming tomorrow after the school run."

Jasper had intently watched Kate's frown while she listened to Clare. He could see doubt in Kate's eyes. Doubt he'd thought he had eliminated.

He couldn't meet Kate's gaze. He had briefly made his beloved so happy, but his intentions were not honourable. He was on a mission, a diamond mission, and all the pieces were falling into place. Between Colin's hoard, the diamonds from the London house and Jacob Isaacs' collection, he had enough to establish a diamond network. He had set up his safe houses, but he couldn't make a move until he had use of his London house and control of the Carmichael trust fund.

The back of Jasper's neck twitched. He turned. Kate was studying him. A forced smile crept across his face.

"Jasper, what's wrong?"

"Nothing," he lied.

Chapter Sixty

Inspector Watts watched Kate stop at the school dropping-off point. She walked with the boys to the school gates and stood a while as they went inside.

Her hair moved with the gentle breeze; she had a contented look about her. Gypsy would have called it the 'well fucked' look.

Watts couldn't help but wonder what she saw in Carmichael. She deserved better. Gossip had it that their marriage had rocked more than once.

However, Jasper was no longer in the sights of the authorities; his business was legit, thanks to Kate. Watts couldn't prove Jasper was involved with the robbery at Zak's London outlet or his mysterious drowning.

But his gut told him different. *Leopards don't change their spots.*

***

"Go on through. They're waiting in Jasper's office," Clare said when Inspector Watts walked into the kitchen.

Kate sat with her legs curled underneath her, chatting to Jasper who sat at his desk, his specs resting on the end of his nose. Watts thought his legs would give way when she smiled at him. Clare bustled in carrying fresh pots of tea and coffee. Jasper gave the inspector a 'take your eyes off my wife' look.

"I'm a messenger," began a nervous Watts. "You can go to the London house and do whatever you want. I believe you're selling it. The police have finished, even though they haven't identified the body. They found no evidence linking the dead body in your house to the shooting of six men." He sipped his coffee and looked directly at Jasper, waiting for a comment. But none came. "I'm afraid you might be upset by this, Mrs Carmichael. Your friend Dan was in a fatal car accident."

Kate placed her tea on the coffee table.

"His car was in Hill's Garage. Needed new parts. There was a delay with a delivery. Dan wouldn't wait. Mr Hill made him sign a paper stating that he took the car knowing that there were safety issues. Don't know how the paper would stand in a court of law." He paused. "Dan ran into the back of a lorry. Killed instantly. Of course, until the car has been examined, we don't know if the worn parts were responsible for the crash."

A lone tear trickled down Kate's cheek.

"Were Michelle and the boys with him?"

"No, they were in London. His latest man-friend was with him though."

"The barman?" interjected Jasper.

"No! Gypsy's right-hand man."

Jasper raised his eyebrows.

"The trust fund will be contacting you, Jasper," continued the inspector. "Without Dan meddling in your accounts, it seems you can do whatever you want. I believe the same applies to your inheritance, Mrs Carmichael."

"Dan?!"

"I was also surprised. It seems that Dan had his fingers in many pies."

"How's Mr Hill?"

"A bit cut up apparently. Garage closed today. Two of his mechanics were in The George speculating that they would be out of a job."

"You're well informed, Inspector," remarked Jasper.

"Have to be with anything that concerns you."

"That's a little unfair," said Kate.

"My spies tell me you were both looking at a beach house. Lunch at that posh yacht club. Not only that, Lord Carmichael is the new chairman."

"I don't think that's any concern of yours," Jasper retorted.

"How can you afford beach houses and yachts?"

"Who said anything about yachts?" Kate interjected.

"Inspector," Jasper began, "some time ago, as Lord Carmichael, I heard about a yacht club that needed some tender loving care. It's no secret that I have a weakness for yachts. One thing led to another and I agreed to take over the chairmanship. I'd put it out of my mind until Kate mentioned a beach house."

"You own a beach house. Well, the land."

"I'm having it surveyed. It seems that the land isn't suitable for development. I'm not an expert, but each year the sea erodes a little more of the beach. Climate change and all that."

"So, you thought you'd buy your wife a beach house." Sarcasm oozed from the inspector's voice.

"I can buy my wife what I fucking like."

"Touchy, aren't we?"

"Inspector, let's get something straight," Kate said in an irritated manner. "Yesterday we spent quality time together viewing a beach house, visiting a yacht club, having a lovely lunch."

"You've missed out the time you spent in his private suite."

Kate went a delightful pink.

"That, Inspector, is private and no one's business but ours."

***

Inspector Watts had inadvertently given Jasper the news he was hoping for: Jasper was free to take control of the trust fund and live in the Carmichael London house, a house he planned to be his headquarters for his diamond network. But before he could do anything in London, he had to re-open his network, and that meant a trip to the Caymans. And that meant leaving Kate.

The grey of the morning light was just dawning when Jasper left for London. He had stayed in his office all night, using the preparations for London as an excuse not to sleep with Kate.

She was his weakness. A night of love making would weaken his resolve to leave her.

***

Kate's nerves were on edge when she opened the door to Jasper's office. The room was empty. He had left for London without saying goodbye.

Her heart began to thump, and a lump formed in her throat, making it difficult for her to swallow. She opened the desk's secret compartment. The diamonds were gone.

She regretted telling him that she didn't want to know about his diamond dealing. But nonetheless, he should have told her he was leaving. Somehow, doing it this way, it seemed final, but maybe she was overthinking his departure.

She slumped into his desk chair and cried.

***

Kate had lost count of how many times she had phoned, texted and emailed Jasper with no answer.

She told no one that Jasper had left without telling her. She just slipped into the role of running the Carmichael Centre and caring for the boys, until two weeks later, when a registered envelope post-marked 'London' was waiting for her after a day dealing with the problems of the Carmichael Centre.

Clare, Malcolm and Bruce were sitting around the kitchen table with worried expressions.

"The boys?" Kate asked as she stared at the large envelope.

"In their rooms doing homework," answered Clare.

Kate's hand shook as she ran a knife along the sealed flap. She eased the papers from the envelope. Her eyes began to fill. Clare was up in a flash and wrapped her arms around her. Malcolm and Bruce exchanged worried glances as they read '*Divorce*'.

Kate turned her head into Clare's shoulder and sobbed.

***

While his wife was crying, Jasper Carmichael sat on a plane heading for the Caymans. He had instructed his solicitor to send divorce papers to Kate two weeks after his arrival in London. Consequently, he hadn't had to think of her. If he had, he wouldn't have been on a plane.

He opened his attaché case, lifted out his black book and ticked the names that had agreed to meet him. He turned the page and highlighted the properties he was interested in buying. The next page contained bullet points of instructions to his bank: accounts and shell companies in various names that had to be opened. Finally, he highlighted the super yachts that were for sale.

He closed his book and congratulated himself for being so well prepared. He closed his eyes and drifted into an uneasy sleep.

He was arguing with Kate about diamonds. She couldn't understand why, after all their hard work to make Jasper Carmichael a respectable businessman, he was going to put it all at risk for diamonds.

He tried to explain how he craved the adrenaline rush of power, of control, to be the best Carmichael.

Then they were making love. He was on top of her, her blonde hair was free, she was smiling, he kissed her, her hands were in his hair, her legs wrapped around his waist, he heard her sighs as he entered her soft, warm, welcoming place. The taste of her was still on his lips.

"Kate," he murmured.

A hand gently rocked his shoulder.

"Mr Carmichael, are you alright?" A steward's gentle voice woke him.

He opened his eyes and took the offered glass of water. But the thoughts of Kate still danced before him. He would miss her support, her love and her control over his demons. But surely he would find another Kate.

Chapter Sixty-One

Kate hadn't the luxury of time to heal the deep emotional wounds Jasper had inflicted. She had two devastated boys that needed her love and support and there were people who relied on her for their livelihood—she had to be strong.

Her first concern was the boys. Oliver was the most demanding of her time; he couldn't sleep unless Kate cuddled him. He couldn't understand why she and Jasper hadn't had make-up sex—after all, that's what mummies and daddies did when they argued.

Harry tried to put on a brave face, saying he didn't want to worry his mother. But when Kate was occupied with Oliver, he cried on Clare's shoulder.

Kate didn't cry on anyone's shoulder. She knew Clare, Bruce and Malcolm were silently supporting her.

Clare made sure Kate had at least one meal a day. Malcolm kept Isaacs' House running, and Bruce looked after the Carmichael Centre. But no matter what they did, they could only watch helplessly as Kate slipped slowly into the abyss of despair.

Kate was oblivious to the deterioration in her physical and mental health. If she was fortunate enough to sleep, she would wake in a cold sweat with images of Jasper kissing her, holding her, loving her. If only he had said goodbye. If only he had explained, she would have understood.

She relentlessly pushed herself, putting her wealth, practicality, common sense and love to their best use. She didn't question how Jasper had settled the running battle with her lawyers about the Spencer inheritance. She just accepted the money.

She had read the divorce papers over and over. There were papers giving her the Carmichael Centre, Isaacs' House, the Carmichael library, but there was no cash settlement.

Her young lawyer didn't understand why she had accepted all that Jasper had offered. She had smiled when he had shouted, '*Screw him!*'

But her lawyer didn't know Jasper like Kate did. She knew he intended to return into her life—how else would he quell his demons? If she didn't cut the umbilical cord that tied them together, he would emotionally destroy her again, and she couldn't let that happen.

When she received the deed to Colin's burnt-out beach house, she knew Jasper's return was imminent.

Bruce had been with her when she read the deed to the beach house.

"What is it?" he said.

She waved the papers in front of him.

"The deed to the beach house. It's in my name. You know what that means."

He stepped towards her and wrapped his arms around her.

"I can't do this anymore." There was desperation in her voice. "He's wearing me down. He knows how to manipulate me. He won't sign any papers. He won't talk to me."

Bruce lifted her chin.

"Do you want him?"

"Here? Now? No! But when he turns on his charm… I fold like a house of cards."

"He wants to use you."

"He'll use the boys against me. And then there's sex."

"I'll give you all the sex you need."

"I have needs, and I need a lot of…"

His soft lips found hers. Her hand reached for his hair.

***

Jasper sat alone having a late breakfast on the deck of his newly acquired super yacht. Breakfast was the time he read his private investigator's reports on Kate. He opened his laptop and stared at her photograph. Her head was turned towards the camera. Her blonde hair was down and her eyes were on fire. That was his Kate, the Kate he loved and missed.

He flicked through the photographs his surveillance team had sent, stopping and studying the one of her sitting on her favourite bench overlooking the river. Her head was in her hands and he was sure she was crying.

He tried to recall how many times he had hurt her, how many times he had reassured her he would only dabble in diamonds. He'd thought he could have both, her and a diamond network, but when his father had died, leaving Jasper more diamonds, he'd realised he couldn't deceive Kate any longer.

It had been two years since he had left her. In that time, he had set up a diamond network, from suppliers of uncut to sellers of cut diamonds. He'd laundered millions of dollars. Women wanted him, but he didn't want them.

He thought of the things Kate had done to get him out of her system, but he knew changing the name of the shopping centre to the Spencer Centre, converting shopping units into smaller offices and Zak's old jewellery shop into the Spencer Library wouldn't work. They were soulmates, they couldn't live without one another, yet the very love that bonded them together was slowly destroying him. That's what he had convinced himself of.

He flicked on to a picture of her and Bruce. He was lifting her out of his pickup, she was smiling, his hands on her waist.

He's fucking her, Jasper thought. *Kate needs a man that can satisfy her.* Jealousy filled his body.

It was time they talked face to face about divorce and the boys. His fingers touched the laptop screen, slowly moving over her smiling face. He missed her. If only he could see her alone, maybe meet somewhere isolated…

That was when Colin's beach house flashed into his mind.

Chapter Sixty-Two

Kate and her slimmed-down team of employees had finally moved into the new office block. It was only two storeys, reception on the ground floor. The first floor had an open-plan main office with individual offices for the law, accounts and IT departments. She had her own office at the back where she could work in relative silence.

She stood by her office window, watching old and new faces settling in. Amanda hadn't hesitated when Kate asked her to stay on. Jasper's computer whizz-kid was ironing out teething problems with the new computer system. Her new, young legal team looked uncomfortable in each other's company, but she was sure that would change.

She turned and gazed at the new Spencer Library that Bruce and his team were working on. She had overheard two young women in the office referring to Bruce as hot. They were speculating what he was like in bed—apparently he'd had many lovers.

She smiled. *If only they knew*.

He was no longer that rough bear of a man who had moved her out of the flower shop. He was still big and strong, but somehow the roughness had softened. He had taken to wearing a beard. She didn't like beards, but it suited Bruce. It was well trimmed, along with his hair, which was just the right length as far as she was concerned. He always wore tight-fitting T-shirts that showed off his muscular chest to best effect. She smiled at his loose jeans that hid his manhood.

"I think I deserve an ice cream," shouted a happy Oliver as he walked through the open-plan office. "I can't remember the last time I was really naughty."

Amanda and the office staff grinned.

Oliver stood in the doorway of his mother's office, cap pushed back on his head, tie pulled away from his neck, top shirt button open, grinning.

Kate smiled at her son. She was happy for him; he had finally left behind the trauma of Jasper leaving.

"We persuaded Clare and Malcolm to drop us off," added Harry, who had joined them. He was immaculately dressed—*just like his father*, thought Kate.

"We never have downtime," said Oliver, sitting on a chair and swinging his legs.

"What do you suggest?"

Oliver jumped up. "We could go to the café. You could have a tea, and we could have chocolate ice cream."

"You do need a break, and we need quality time with you," said a thoughtful Harry. "It's been too long."

They both flashed her the Carmichael smile. The smile that had pulled on her heart strings all those years ago.

"You go," said Amanda. "We'll finish off here."

Kate closed her laptop and collected the papers off her desk.

"Yes!" shouted Oliver, punching the air as he ran down the open-plan office, while Harry stayed behind to help his mother.

***

The boys were out of the car before Kate had switched off the engine. Together, they pushed through the café door.

"Two chocolate ice creams and a tea, please!" shouted Oliver.

Neither of the boys paid any attention to the stranger who sat in the corner next to the counter, staring at his phone.

"I think Mother should have food." Harry's quiet voice made the stranger look up.

"She didn't say she was hungry."

"A toasted teacake as well, please," said Harry.

The café door opened. The stranger looked towards it and froze. He didn't believe his eyes. He'd spent the day looking for her, at the bookshop, the gallery—he'd even watched Bruce and his team working on the new Spencer Library.

Kate slipped onto a chair next to the door. She lowered the zip on her jacket, revealing a white blouse. He was startled by the change in her. Those sparkling green eyes were cold and dead. Her hair, once blonde with flecks of grey, was grey with flecks of blonde.

"Inside?" asked Molly, the café owner who'd known Kate for years, as she placed Kate's tea and teacake on the table.

"She feels the cold," answered Oliver, tucking into his ice cream.

"We could go outside, if you like," offered Kate.

Kate's soft, calm voice brought tears to the stranger's eyes.

"No!" Harry's voice was unusually loud.

Molly pulled up a chair. "I've been meaning to ring Amanda for an appointment. I know how busy you are."

"I'm not that busy." Kate smiled, shivering as she glanced towards the counter.

"Kate, are you alright? You look as if you've seen a ghost."

Blue, piercing eyes were staring at her. She shook her head.

"Only, I was thinking of a new café," Molly continued. "But it's the cost. There's talk of a marina being built."

Kate raised her eyebrows.

"You know, on the coast."

"That's miles away."

"Riverside properties are being snapped up. Private mooring and all that."

"Have you got a business plan?"

"I will have."

Kate smiled. "Talk to Bruce and then we'll have a meeting."

Molly stood. "You really need downtime, Kate. Forget him."

Kate's stomach was somersaulting. He was staring at her. He might have had a beard, long hair, black-rimmed glasses and an off-the-peg jacket, but his disguise didn't fool Kate.

"She's ace at cuddling," grinned Oliver, lovingly gazing into his mother's eyes, shaking his head as she tried to wipe the ice cream from his face. "Come on, Harry. Let's go stone skimming."

Kate and the stranger were alone. Their eyes met. He opened his jacket and his fingers tapped his waistcoat pocket. Kate's diamond pocket.

"I could do with a new painting. I've sold the last one." Molly shouted from the kitchen.

She appeared at the kitchen doorway drying her hands on a towel.

"When was the last time you had me time? Leave the kids with Clare. Paint. Walk. Relax. You need a man, Kate. How long has it been?"

Kate smiled. No one knew about Bruce, the man in her life.

"I'm still married."

Kate had signed the divorce papers. She didn't understand why Jasper hadn't.

"Don't give me that. He doesn't care about being married to you."

Kate walked to the counter with her empty cup. She brushed passed Jasper; he caught her hand.

"Saturday," he whispered.

***

Kate was lying in Bruce's arms when she mentioned in her calm, casual manner that she had seen Jasper. His body stiffened when she said she was meeting him at the beach house. They argued, she insisted that she had to meet him to settle the divorce. And then she kissed him, in that irresistible Kate way.

"Love me," she murmured.

***

Bruce had arrived at the beach house before either Kate or Jasper and settled behind the trees that overlooked it. He watched a clean-shaven Jasper race up the gully. Jasper stopped, his blue eyes searching for her.

Kate was late.

Jasper impatiently ran his hand through his long hair. The sound of an approaching diesel engine grew louder. Nervous, Jasper ran towards the car. He didn't wait for her to switch off the engine; he pulled open the driving door and lifted her from the seat.

His hands cupped her face as he gazed into her green eyes and stepped back. Her eyes were cold.

"What's wrong?" he nervously said. This wasn't the Kate he knew.

"We have to talk."

"Talk! I don't want to fucking talk. You're my wife." Jasper's temper stirred.

"Estranged."

"You're still my wife."

"Sign the papers."

"That's why you're here."

"What did you expect?"

"Expect?!"

Jasper began to pace, trying to control his surging temper, his hand pulling on his hair. This was not what he had expected. He'd thought she would be happy to see him. They would kiss, and then he would fuck her.

"I'm not signing any fucking papers. So you can forget that." Jasper was angry; he wanted to hurt her. "Satisfy you, does he?" Jasper snarked.

Kate reddened and her eyes flared as her temper stirred.

"Touchy subject, Kate! He must mean a lot to you."

"Divorce me!" she yelled.

"No! Not now. I know you want him. How does it feel to break your marriage vows?"

"And I suppose you haven't?"

"Need to know only, Kate."

He stepped close to her. She could feel his breath on her face.

He crashed his mouth into hers, but she didn't respond. He pushed her away. She lost her footing and fell.

Jasper's temper flared. His blue eyes were on fire. His hands loosened his belt.

Bruce moved from his hiding place, ready to pounce.

Kate tried to stand, but Jasper pushed her onto her back.

"You know what happens when you defy me. You need a fucking you won't forget."

"Boss!" shouted a voice from the gully. "The cops know you're here."

Jasper stepped back and angrily glared at Kate.

"I will fuck you."

He turned and jogged down the gully.

Bruce ran to a shaking, crying Kate. He lifted her into his arms.

"You're here," she whispered.

"Always."

Chapter Sixty-Three

The staff had long since gone home; Kate was alone in her office, working. She had no inclination to go home. Clare and Malcolm were away, and the boys had just started boarding school.

Bruce was having a night out with his team. He hadn't wanted to leave her, but she'd insisted. She had her security to protect her.

The sound of the lift doors opening broke Kate's concentration. She looked through the dark main office to see two men marching towards her office. Her heart stopped.

They were not her security.

She knew who they worked for.

Their intention was obvious.

She closed her laptop and stood when they entered her office.

"Mrs Carmichael!"

She nodded and followed them. It was futile to resist.

Jasper always got his way.

***

Bruce left the pub early. He wasn't enjoying the beer and banter; he wanted to be with Kate. He stopped outside Kate's office as the black Range Rover pulled away. He instinctively knew something was wrong. His heart skipped a beat as he ran into the dark office, shouting her name.

Her office was in darkness. Her laptop was on her desk along with her phone.

He ran back to his pickup. *Beach house*, he thought.

***

The Range Rover had stopped at her beach house. Kate was expecting Jasper.

"This way," said the driver.

She followed him through the gully to the beach, where a man was pushing a small dinghy into the sea.

"In you go," the driver instructed.

"Where's Jasper?"

"You'll see."

***

Bruce skidded to a halt. He jumped out of his pickup and raced towards the sea just as the outline of the dinghy disappeared.

"Kate! Kate!" he repeated.

Bruce turned at the sound of footsteps. A right hook to the chin, and the would-be assailant was flat on his back. Bruce gripped him by his collar and glared into a pair of frightened eyes.

"You're a dead man," the assailant defiantly said.

Bruce's grip tightened around his neck. "Where are they taking her?"

The man grinned. "Fuck you."

Bruce yelled, lifted the man above his shoulders and threw him onto the ground. Before the man could recover, he was face to face with Bruce. Bruce yelled again and head-butted him. Blood was pouring from his nose.

"Don't fucking mess with me," Bruce angrily said.

The man staggered to his feet just as another right hook met his cheek. He lay on the ground. Bruce gripped his collar.

"Where are they taking her?"

"Y-yacht."

"The rest!"

Another blow.

"For Christ's sake! Fucking stop. I'll tell you. Jasper's in a bad way. I'm waiting for the doctor."

"Why does he want Kate?"

"Nurse him. When he's better, he'll release her."

"You're lying."

"That's all I know."

***

Kate's heart was in her mouth as the dinghy bounced from wave to wave. The driver was talking into his phone as the outline of a yacht came into view. He manoeuvred the dinghy alongside a rope ladder dangling on the side of the yacht.

"Up you go," said the driver.

She clung to the ladder with the driver breathing down her neck. When she got to the top, Kate gripped the offered hand of a man dressed in a white coat.

"Mrs Carmichael! I'm a doctor. Your husband has been badly injured. There was an explosion on his yacht. I've done all I can. He insists on you nursing him."

"Should he be in hospital?" Kate nervously asked.

"Yes! But Jasper insists it's out of the question. I've left all the medical supplies you need." He stood by the ladder that Kate had just climbed. "Good luck."

"This way," said the driver before Kate could ask more questions.

As she turned to follow, she stumbled on a gun lying on the deck. Without a second thought, she scooped the gun into her hand and into her jacket pocket, where it was easily concealed. She wondered if the doctor had dropped it. The driver stared at her before turning to the stairs leading further into the yacht.

"Come on!" he impatiently shouted.

Jasper was in the master suite, lying on a king-size bed. Kate gasped at the cuts on his pale face and the dark rings under his eyes.

"Kate," he murmured.

She pulled up a chair and held his hand.

"Kiss me," Jasper mumbled.

She gently brushed their lips as her hand caressed his forehead. He struggled to open his eyes.

The driver stood by the door watching and listening.

Kate pulled the sheet from Jasper's body. Tears fell at the sight of a blood-stained pad surrounded by dark blue bruises.

"Kate…"

"Shh. Let me heal you."

She turned to the driver. "Help me put him on his side."

"The doctor said…"

"Fuck the doctor. I want to see his back."

She filled a basin with warm water from the bathroom and carefully cleaned the cuts on Jasper's back. With a pair of tweezers, she carefully removed pieces of debris.

The driver lifted Jasper while Kate changed the blood-stained sheet.

Jasper began to moan.

"Nearly finished, my love." Her lips brushed his forehead.

She gently removed the blood-soaked pad that covered the wound in his side.

"Kate!" Jasper yelled as she poured antiseptic into the open wound. It needed stitches, but the doctor had only left sterilised wound closures.

"I need you over here," she said, thinking the driver was still in the room.

The engine burst into life and the yacht moved.

"He's busy," said a gruff-voiced man.

"Hold the wound together."

"It's bleeding."

"Just fucking do it."

When the wound was closed, a large bandage was tightly wrapped around Jasper's waist.

Kate lowered herself into the chair by Jasper's bed and tried to relax when she heard the cabin door close and the lock turn. She tried to gather her thoughts, but voices drifting through the broken skylight caught her attention.

"He was a mess. Some big guy roughed him up."

"They know we 'ave her," said the driver. "Did you tie up the loose ends?"

"Here's the money you gave 'em."

"As soon as Jasper can move his money, we go."

"What about her? We should honour the family."

"We'll have to see. No mistakes like uncle."

Bruce knows I'm here, Kate thought.

***

Days and nights merged as Kate nursed Jasper. The driver brought her food, and soup for Jasper.

But sleeping in a chair next to his bed was taking its toll.

The sun was just rising when Kate climbed onto the deck. The cool morning air filled her lungs and refreshed her face. Bruce occupied her thoughts. He would be worried. In her heart, she knew she wouldn't see him again. She closed her eyes and he was walking towards her, grinning. He wrapped his strong arms around her; she felt safe and secure.

"What the fuck do you think you're doing?"

The driver's angry voice pierced the still morning air.

Kate didn't answer. It would be a waste of energy. She turned towards the stairs.

Jasper sat on the edge of the bed. The driver was busy organising pillows so he could sit up.

Gruff Voice appeared with a bed table and a laptop.

Kate looked into Jasper's cold blue eyes. Eyes she didn't recognise.

"Don't do that again."

Jasper's voice was full of a meaning that frightened Kate. She shivered. Was this the Jasper she had loved? Was this the Jasper that she had given herself to? The man that had referred to her as his beloved? The father of her two boys?

Gruff Voice handed her the laptop.

"I need to work, Kate. My hands hurt too much." Jasper's voice had suddenly become conciliatory.

"It might be a good idea to leave work for a day or two," Kate nervously replied.

"Kate! Just sit next to me and do as I ask. You know my password."

Kate typed '*My beloved*' and a photo of her looking into the camera, smiling, filled the screen.

Jasper's hand touched her thigh. "I'll always love you, Kate. But not the way you want and deserve."

He pointed to a file named 'Network'.

"They think that you're conciliating my money. Find out who these two jokers are." Jasper whispered.

"What's he saying?" Gruff Voice moved towards the bed.

"Do you think I could have a cup of tea? Jasper doesn't want anything," Kate said in her best aristocratic voice.

"Her ladyship wants fucking tea!" Gruff yelled.

Kate felt Jasper's hand squeeze her thigh.

"That's my Kate," he whispered.

Jasper watched as she clicked on the faces that were members of his diamond network.

"They were all on the yacht when it exploded. So, who are these two jokers?"

Jasper raised his eyebrows when Kate opened the file named 'Colin's Gang'.

The family that interested her were the Wilsons. Jasper had murdered Max in the indoor swimming pool at the mansion. As far as Jasper was concerned, he'd deserved it after roughing up Kate. The remaining brothers, Charlie and Matt, had died in a drunken car crash.

"Why?" Jasper asked, pointing to the file on the Wilsons.

"You said you don't know them. They're not part of your current network. So, I'll look into the past. The Wilsons have a grudge. It seems Charlie Wilson had two sons."

Jasper followed Kate's gaze to the two men that were standing in the doorway.

"Sorted his fucking money yet?" asked Gruff Voice.

"Not yet. But I'm nearly finished," Kate answered.

***

"Kate!" Jasper whispered.

She had fallen asleep with her head resting on his bed. She slowly opened one eye.

"Get me a gun."

Chapter Sixty-Four

Kate staggered onto the firm sand of the beach. She was coughing and spluttering. Her eyes focused on every step as her feet emerged from the cold sea.

Without warning, her legs gave way and she collapsed. Her eyes turned towards the setting sun, and she slept.

***

Kate couldn't breathe. Her eyes abruptly opened, only to be covered by water.

She panicked as another wave covered her.

The sea was claiming her.

She tried to stand but she was too weak; the cold sea had penetrated every part of her.

She didn't want to die. People she loved danced before her. Bruce, Harry, Oliver, Clare and Malcolm merged in her mind.

She thought she heard her name.

"Kate! Kate!"

She turned her head towards the faint orange glow of the rising sun and crawled.

"Kate! Kate!" Followed by the splashing of feet.

She was dreaming.

Suddenly, the water no longer covered her. Warm lips touched her forehead and then each eye. She was wrapped in strong, warm arms.

Water was being tipped over her face.

"Kate, open your eyes. It's me. Drink."
She felt an open bottle held to her lips.
"Drink. You're safe."
She opened her eyes. He was smiling.
"I thought I'd lost you."
She stretched her hand to touch his face.
"Bruce!" Her voice was barely above a whisper, but the love in her eyes said all he needed to know.
He leaned so his lips could touch hers.
It wasn't a dream.
He had saved her.
"I'll take you to the hospital."
"No! No one must know where I've been."
"Kate! You need medical help."
"Take me home."

***

Clare was sobbing, and tears fell from the unemotional Malcolm's eyes when Bruce lifted Kate from his pickup.
Kate tried to open her eyes and smile, but tears trickled down her cheeks.
And then the darkness fell.

***

Strong arms held her. She was lying in warm water. Lips caressed her neck. She was safe.
"You're enjoying that too much." Clare's curt voice echoed as she dropped towels onto the bathroom stool. "I don't know why you had to get into the bath."
"She was cold and shivering."
"She needs something warm inside her."
Bruce felt Kate's hand grip his thigh as the bathroom door closed and a sly grin crept across her face.

***

While Kate and Bruce lay in a bath of warm water, Clare had arranged three small tables in Kate's bedroom so they could eat with her.

Kate pushed her chicken soup to one side and started to sob.

"I never thought he'd be cruel to me."

Bruce was by her side in a flash. He cradled her head on his shoulder.

"No one must know where I've been. Not even the boys. He'll come after us." Kate looked at Malcom. "Make sure everything is locked."

"I'll stay with her," said Bruce.

***

It was mid-afternoon when Kate wandered into the kitchen, where her three trusted friends were having afternoon tea.

Bruce leapt from his stool, wrapping his arms around her and kissing her hair while Clare flicked the kettle on.

Kate smiled at Clare when she pushed a pot of tea towards her.

"Have you told the boys?" Kate asked anxiously.

"All they know is that you've had the flu. But Harry has seen this article."

'The last of the notorious Carmichael family feared dead. Jasper Carmichael's super yacht mysteriously exploded. Dead bodies were seen floating in the water.'

Kate stared at her tea, not daring to look at her friends.

"He's not dead. But badly injured," She blurted. "He'd arranged a meeting with his diamond associates. They turned on him. Beat him up. Then the yacht exploded. I think that was Jasper's backup plan." She paused to refill her teacup. "Jasper had a second yacht. That's the one I was on. When he got to his yacht, those men were on board. He didn't know who they were."

"They were the men that abducted you?" asked Bruce.

Kate nodded.

"A doctor had left medical supplies. He left when Jasper became difficult. I suspect he's dead, along with the man that waited for him." She paused. "I found a small gun on the deck. Probably the doctor's."

"Who has the gun now?" asked a concerned Malcolm.

"I gave it to Jasper."

"Who were the men?" asked Malcolm.

"Charlie Wilson's sons."

"Where are they now?"

"Bottom of the sea."

Clare gasped.

"He did it?" asked Bruce.

Kate nodded as tears trickled down her cheeks.

Bruce lifted her onto his lap and she nestled into his shoulder.

"Jasper asked me to get a gun. I'm not proud of what I did."

"You did what you had to," said Clare.

"I distracted Gruff Voice while Jasper shot the driver. That's what I called them. Before Gruff Voice could react, Jasper shot him." She paused. "Cold blood. Without a second thought."

A heavy silence filled the kitchen.

"I thought Jasper was going to shoot me. But he said he couldn't. He loved me too much."

She felt Bruce's body stiffen.

"You've nothing to worry about," she whispered so only he could hear.

"Before Jasper put me in the dinghy, he told me to keep my mouth shut. I'd seen what he's capable of. His last words to me were that he couldn't love me the way I wanted and deserved."

"He put you in a dinghy," repeated Bruce.

"I climbed down the ladder. He waited while I started the outboard and moved towards the shore."

"Where's the dinghy?"

"I don't know. It capsized and I had to swim."

Another heavy silence filled the kitchen.

"You see why it's important that this stays between us. Jasper keeps his word."

Epilogue

Five years later

Mason Clark, aka Jasper Carmichael, confidently strode into Kate's Wellsbury gallery. He had read many favourable articles on her emotional Sunset and Sunrise series. Kate had always painted her emotions, and he wanted to see for himself the path they had taken since he had he left her.

One journalist had described her paintings as, *'showing the artist's own journey from darkness into light.'* Another had written, *'With the forthcoming sale of her Sunset and Sunrise series, Kate Carmichael has put her dark days with Carmichael to rest.'*

Gossip and his private investigator had confirmed: she had truly moved out of his darkness and into the light with a new man, Bruce. He couldn't believe she had found love with Bruce.

Kate leaned against the wall at the far end of her gallery, taking a breather from the crowds that milled around, admiring her paintings. The Sunset and Sunrise series of paintings had helped her heal after Jasper had left her on the beach, but the man that was striding towards her carrying two glasses of wine, smiling, was the one who had lovingly put her shattered heart back together.

She recalled how they had rekindled their love. It was while she was painting the Sunset and Sunrise series. She hadn't wanted to return to the beach house and the tumble-down studio that held so many unhappy memories, but he had insisted and he was so happy. How could she say no?

He had held his hand over her eyes as he guided her towards the sound of the sea. He had slowly removed his hand, and she had gasped. There were no signs of the old tumble-down studio. In its place was a new purpose-built wooden studio he had lovingly built for her.

It was open plan, the bed at one end of the room next to the bathroom, the kitchen and her studio at the other. Bi-fold doors lead from her studio onto a veranda that commanded stunning sea views. Comfortable chairs were scattered in front of the inglenook fireplace.

Bruce had stood nervously watching her. The studio filled her with joy, as he did. She couldn't imagine life without him. She had stood on tiptoes and looped her arms around his neck and planted a soft kiss on his lips. She felt his strong arms pull her into him as he took control. His firm kiss was full of intention, an intention that she desired. He'd lifted her with ease and gently laid her on the bed.

"I'm not him," he had whispered as she slowly removed her clothes.

"Shh. Don't make me wait."

***

"He's here, Kate," said a slightly nervous Bruce, handing her a glass of wine.

"I know. Mason Clark."

When Kate had read the guest-list, the name Mason Clark had leapt out. Her stomach had flipped as she realised Jasper had returned.

Bruce gazed at her ring finger, and his gold rope wedding ring that she now wore.

"Don't look like that. I love you. You make me happy," she whispered, placing a reassuring hand on Bruce's arm.

Kate watched Mason Clark work the room with his young wife clinging to his arm. He had finally agreed to divorced Kate when he'd learned he was about to become a father again. His dark hair was now a shining silver, as was his beard that disguised his Carmichael features. Rimless spectacles hid his piercing blue eyes.

He was immaculately dressed in his designer clothes. His fingers rested in the pocket of his waistcoat, touching her diamond. He looked as if he owned the place as his eyes scanned the room, looking for her.

Their eyes finally locked, and his fingers left his pocket. Kate smiled. After all this time, he still needed reassurance that she was there.

She wondered why she had put up with Jasper for so many years. Was it the fear that he would take the boys from her? Or the mind-blowing orgasms?

He had declared his love over and over, only to destroy it with his addiction to diamonds and his criminal ways. She had loved him more than she cared to admit; she had given herself to him over and over. She had stood by him when things got tough. But he wasn't to be her destiny. This man was.

She tightened her grip on Bruce's arm and looked into his kind, loving eyes.

"Take me to the studio."

"What about all these people?"

"I don't need these people. I need you inside me."

Bruce raised his eyebrows, more than a little surprised. She had never used those words before.

"Him and his wife are walking over."

Too late. She cursed out loud.

"Mrs Carmichael, I assume." Jasper's voice had a southern American twang. "Let me introduce myself." He grasped her hand. Kate stepped back into Bruce. "Mason Clark, and this is my wife, Lucinda."

"Pleased to meet you," Kate uttered in her business tone as she tried to control the unexpected surge of emotion.

Jasper's keen eyes watched for tell-tale signs that he still affected her. He glanced down at her ring finger as unexpected feelings of regret and jealousy spread through him. He hadn't paid much attention when she had returned the Carmichael wedding ring. But he hadn't expected the Carmichael heirloom to be replaced by an expensive gold rope ring that reminded him of their legs entwined. He inwardly cursed as an image flashed across his mind of a satisfied Kate lying naked on Bruce's chest, their legs entwined. He considered Bruce an uneducated oaf incapable of arousing a sexual woman like Kate.

Jasper had always considered himself to be an exceptional lover, until he had made love to Kate. She had taken his skill to another level. The sensations of their intense climaxes would remain with him forever. Out of all the women he had fucked, none compared to Kate. Making love to her stirred so many emotions. She was soft, warm, wet, welcoming, all rolled into one. She was home.

He jealously wondered if her delightful sighs and 'Don't make me wait', led Bruce to her special place. The place where she'd turned his darkness into light.

Lucinda's proud southern drawl brought him from his musing. "Mason's bought two of your paintings."

He flinched when she put her arm through his.

"Powerful emotions in those paintings, Kate. May I call you Kate? You must have been going through a difficult time."

Jasper had quickly regained his confident composure and was staring deeply into Kate's eyes, trying to convey a hidden meaning that only she would understand. But her eyes were vacant and showed no understanding. He cringed when Bruce placed both hands on her hips, and she looked up lovingly into his eyes.

"Honey! We must leave or we'll miss our flight," said Lucinda, unaware of Jasper's eye play.

At that moment, Lewis and his police team bustled into the gallery.

"What's he fucking want?" Bruce mumbled so only Kate could hear.

"It's been an absolute pleasure, Mrs Carmichael." Jasper took advantage of Kate's distraction to confidently reach for her hand. His soft lips grazed her hand as he looked up into her cold, vacant eyes.

"Get the fuck out of here. And don't come back," she quietly said through gritted teeth.

Jasper stopped in his tracks. He couldn't believe his ears; his Kate would never talk to him in such a hateful tone.

"Mrs Bruce," Lewis sarcastically shouted as he strode towards her. "You may have changed your name, but you're still Mrs Carmichael—or should I say Lady Carmichael?"

If only they knew, Jasper thought. Did they think he would give Kate up? She would always be his.

Suddenly, Kate and Jasper had become the centre of attention. Jasper let go of her hand as his eyes settled on Lewis. His stomach churned in an unpleasant way, even though Lewis's bluster didn't fool him. Jasper had friends in high places and they were prepared to give him time to settle some affairs and visit the gallery. All for a handful of diamonds. Lewis must have been beside himself, not being able to arrest him.

His mind was on Kate. His private investigator had failed to mention she had taken Bruce's name. He felt as if he'd been punched in his gut. She was a Carmichael, and she would always be a Carmichael, he thought. In a daze, he watched her greet Lewis with her fixed business smile and cold eyes.

"Lewis!" she said as she started to walk towards her business counter.

Jasper hadn't noticed that Bruce had left Kate's side. He had taken the only diamond he cared about away from him; he sought revenge. Bruce was busying himself instructing the staff Kate had employed for the day. What did she see in that oaf?

In a daze, Jasper Carmichael walked past Lewis's police. Lucinda was chatting to him about missing their flight, but he wasn't listening and he couldn't care less. His mind was filled with Kate. She had changed; he had never seen that vacant look in her eyes. He couldn't believe she had stopped loving him. Because deep down, he hadn't stopped loving her. She was his beloved, his diamond, his rock. She gave him strength to carry on; she was his hope and that would never change. The possibility that Kate would find love with someone else had never occurred to him.

Suddenly the image of Kate struggling down a swaying ladder to the bobbing dinghy flashed into his mind. He'd known she was crying. She hadn't stopped since leaving the Scottish inlet.

If it hadn't been for her, he would have died from his injuries or those two Wilsons would have shot him.

But he didn't care what she had sacrificed. It didn't change anything. He would still lie and deceive her, but he couldn't kill her.

His phone was ringing.

"Answer your fucking phone, Mason!" shouted Lucinda.

They were in their bedroom, packing. How he had got there, he had no idea.

"Yes!" he snapped into the phone.

It was his private investigator.

"According to the marriage records, she married him the day after your divorce was finalised. At a place called Gretna Green," the investigator lied. He'd had enough of Jasper's temper; he wanted him off his back.

Jasper ended the call and threw his phone across the room.

"You're fucking mine!" he yelled.

"What's that, honey?"

He stared at Lucinda and knew he could kill her without thinking twice.

***

Kate's heart felt heavy as she watched the man she had trusted and had given her unconditional love to walk away.

Jasper Carmichael would always have a special place in her heart. But she'd never imagined he would be so cruel to her, destroying her love and breaking her heart.

She had fallen into the abyss of despair; she hadn't wanted to live. And if it wasn't for the man striding towards her, grinning and shaking the gallery keys, she would never have loved again.

Her beaming smile filled her face, her loving eyes glistened, a warm glow flowed through her when their eyes met. He made her happy. He loved her, and she loved him.

Bruce looped his strong arm around her waist and lifted her into a passionate kiss. Her legs circled his waist as her hands cupped his head. His mouth was warm and soft. She needed him. Her fingers frantically moved through his hair.

"I love you, Kate."

"I need you."

Their tongues danced as he carried her into the gallery's small bathroom. He eased the dress from her shoulders and lifted her onto the counter.

His fingers lightly trailed her spine, igniting every nerve in her body. His mouth consumed each breast in turn. A delightful sigh escaped her mouth.

"Don't make me wait, my love," she said. "Don't make me wait."

Author Profile

I'm in what I refer to as my twilight years. After spending many years in the industrial and academic worlds, I now have time to concentrate on my lifelong dream of writing.

When I'm not writing, I'm in the garden, my passion being roses, which always inspire me with their colourful blooms and fragrance. Visits to the beach are also a source of inspiration, along with people watching.

Jasper's Diamond is the second book in the Jasper Carmichael series. Jasper and Kate are old friends, and they continue to keep me company.

For updates from Frances Parker-Smith follow her on Twitter @fparkersmith or visit her website francesparkersmith.wordpress.com

To contact Frances Parker-Smith, please email francesparkersmith@icloud.com

***

What Did You Think of *Jasper's Diamond?*

A big thank you for purchasing this book. It means a lot that you chose this book specifically from such a wide range on offer. I do hope you enjoyed it.

Book reviews are incredibly important for an author. All feedback helps them improve their writing for future projects and for developing this edition. If you are able to spare a few minutes to post a review on Amazon, that would be much appreciated.

Publisher Information

Rowanvale Books provides publishing services to independent authors, writers and poets all over the globe. We deliver a personal, honest and efficient service that allows authors to see their work published, while remaining in control of the process and retaining their creativity. By making publishing services available to authors in a cost-effective and ethical way, we at Rowanvale Books hope to ensure that the local, national and international community benefits from a steady stream of good quality literature.

For more information about us, our authors or our publications, please get in touch.

www.rowanvalebooks.com
info@rowanvalebooks.com